C000246678

MARTHA

WALKER ZUPP

First Montag Press E-Book and Paperback Original Edition December 2019

Montag Press
ISBN: 978-1-940233-65-9
Design © 2019 Rick Febré

Montag Press Team:
Project Editor – Charlie Franco
Managing Director – Charlie Franco

A Montag Press Book
www.montagpress.com
Montag Press
1066 47th Ave. Unit #9
Oakland CA 94601 USA

Montag Press, the burning book with the hatchet cover, the skewed word mark and the portrayal of the long-suffering fireman mascot are trademarks of Montag Press.

Printed & Digitally Originated in the United States of America
10 9 8 7 6 5 4 3 2 1

The author wishes to thank those at Montag Press, George Green, Zoë Lambert, Charlie Gere, Mike Narouei, Luke Gallagher, James Bone and The Storey

For Sue and Michael Ponsford.

WALKER ZUPP

MARTHA

MONTAG

Facts

In 2082 an unidentified object crashed fifty-five miles east of New Zealand in the Pacific Ocean. The object, long rumoured to have contained dormant bacteria, was subsequently shipped to an undisclosed location by the multinational bank and financial service provider I.T.C.B. Holdings plc. Why I.T.C.B. would want to hire a pharmacologist to study an extra-terrestrial object, and to lay claim to an extra-terrestrial object in the first place, no one can say.

Harmon

"Florin!"

The Utton Police Academy graduates shut-the-fuck-up.

"Let's talk about Florin for a moment."

Police Commissioner Eric J. McKinley's a thin bastard, thin bastards being the *in*-thing at the moment—as reported by E.T. News (*England Today*: Sondra Mïk reported on the commodification of bulimia in the Scotia Belt modelling industry re: the pervading use of *Orlistat*: a weight loss drug designed to lower calorie intake) at 8:12 p.m. last night—and so he's merely a coat-hangar for medals, his second wife Elektra McKinley née Melatonin-Caruthers in all likelihood using him as such. Her collection of vintage Atticus Manville Frocks® have all slipped Eric's emaciated frame in the vain and soul-destroying search for space. And he's got cancer. That might also have something to do with it.

Below him the graduates sit like the un-massacred-but-soon-to-be shell-shocked critters on any beach. In the back row, newly commissioned Const. Harmon Chikenyyt scribbles in a diary. He's taking notes. If anyone else in the Class Of 2089 did this they would suffer an immediate psychiatric evaluation. Most of them just want easy access to drugs and men/women.

Commissioner McKinley clears his throat. "Of all the Scotia Belt (Hereafter abbreviated as S.B.) correctional facilities, none faced greater peril than Florin. Thirty officers stationed there. *One* survived the riot and its subsequent destruction. I have the pleasure of addressing that person, Detective

Chief Superintendent Anya Egelblöm, today – can you see her? She's sitting behind me." And yea. Everyone can see the crumply white woman besotted by grey-gold dreadlocks sitting in a Lucky Mark IV Travel Device (I mean, there's not a single propagandist for the word, "wheelchair…") on the further side of McKinley. The type of wheelchair reserved for the top 1.3% of academics, media tycoons who like to boil their eggs at 35°C, and Austrian mercenaries who would drink and kill, *in that order.*

Pan down from the stage and push through the new officers—clean-shaven chins, clenched hair-buns—all the way to the back row where newly commissioned Constable Tara Blimmen, doomed also by the businesswoman bun, is staring at Harmon's diary. "You getting this down?"

"Shut up," he says.

"He needs to know if you can see her."

"*Shut up.*"

"Wheelchair lady's not amused."

E. J. McKinley deflects some pretty deafening silence with an equally deafening silence. Egelblöm rolls her eyes. The other members of the Grand Poobah Police Council or whatever fan makeupped faces, gripping pamphlets demonstrative of name and rank and nothing else. McKinley finishes up, sweating.

"So, yes, Florin was pretty bad."

He peers back at Egelblöm who dangles a frugal nod. Then he turns back, and finishes.

"Yea, just, play the music…"

The S.B. National Anthem, "Fuirich Air Falbh Bho Dhaoine Le Cnapan Mòra," ("Stay Away From People With Big Lumps") muffles around the auditorium as the graduates file out of the building. Commissioner Eric J. McKinley—who's always been a bit of a rebel—holds his left breast, recalling a time when he was a musician on the road. Well, not "on the road," but certainly next to a road.

◊

Several years prior: E. J. McKinley drops an ice cube in his glass and picks up his guitar. It's a pretty quiet bar, especially on Tuesdays like this. You'd think being on the border there'd be a few Hydrogen Drivers, but nope. Just locals—and the landlord/resident-Frenchman Michel Deikan.

E. J. leans over to the microphone.

"They call me McKinley…I write songs."

He gargles some water. Then he strums his guitar, and sings.

> There once was two British boys
> Who grew up on the border
> One of 'em was short and stout
> But taller than the other
> Opposites they were but
> Good friends they remained
> Until the referendum
> Put all of us to shame

He smiles and shakes his guitar.

"Come on everybody! Help me with the chorus!"

> There's nothing like a British sun
> When there's not two lands but one
> Give us something sovereign but profane
> I'll always see a British sun
> But I gots to blank the folks that won
> The day the bloody country went insane

Michel Deikan leans on the Rascal's Piss pump. He squints at Californian diplomat and ethnologist Theodore Olpio, who three years prior published his *Monograph on Black Supremacy* (Maple Books, 2086) wherein Olpio, himself a shameless Caucasian, identified only two races: "Black," and, "Other Scum," (O.S.) and argued that the Black race was superior to O.S. and within it the African held the highest place. Although the book was unnoticed when first published in Canada by Ontario mayor-cum-loony Elijah "Fig" Newton, it shot to the top of the bestseller list a year later, read widely ergo ironically (i.e. as far as T. Olpio was concerned) by O.S.s and very little by Black people, like, *anywhere*, so now all these years later T. Olpio's rolling a cigarette next to his pint. The Frenchman prods him with a curious finger.

"Hey…"

Olpio pulls his head up and says, "What?"

"Qu'est-ce que tu penses?"

"Of what?"

"Putain, de guitar hero là-bas."

"He sucks."

"Oui…" The angry landlord watches our hero (for now, sort of) trundling into half time, and pouring water over his head.

"Thank you everyone! I hope you're enjoying it," catching his breath, "we're gonna take a break now, but we'll be back in fifteen minutes—" He bangs the microphone, staining the dark room with that unusually offensive feedback. He walks offstage towards the bar.

M. Deikan clears his throat. "Eric, mon homme."

"Don't sound so surprised," Eric complains, "we talked before I went up."

"Qu'est-ce que je t'ai dit avant ton set?"

"Fuckwit, don't play any uni—"

"Correct. J'ai dit fuckwit, ne joue pas de chansons union-ists. Pour l'amour de Dieu.'" Deikan continues, "oulez-vous une émeute dans cet endroit?"

"Oh yea, Mike," the guitarist adds, sarcastically, "these four people are gonna tear this pub a new asshole, I'm *really* scared."

M. Deikan folds his arms. "Je te paye. Le moins que vous puissiez faire est de faire ce que je dis—" He snatches T. Olpio's empty glass. "Plus jamais."

"All right," McKinley caves, "I'll play something else next time."

"Non," Michel replies, "plus jamais tu ne chanteras dans ce pub."

Eric slams him knuckles on the bar, blinking. "Oh come on man! This is my fuckin income!"

"Eh bien, maintenant vouz savez ce qui se passé quand vous baisez avec la direction."

"But I'm not fuckin with you!"

"Je vais vous dire ce que vous pouvez faire, Eric, vous pou-vez me payer avec de l'argent réel—"

McKinley's eyes widen.

"Pour une bière. Peut-être alors, peut-être, je vais envisage de vous garder sur."

"Oh for—All right!" Eric interrupts himself, "shit…get us a Rascal's Piss."

Michel, rigid with conquest and grimacing, grabs a glass from below and starts pumping.

"Ils tournent si vite."

Olpio sniggers and lights a cigarette. "Got any bottles…?"

M. Deikan pushes a sorry pint of Rascal's Piss towards the future commissioner of police, takes his money, and drops it in the cash register. He peers at the ethnologist and says, "Le seul que nons avons est Mai Ling."

"I'll have one of those," Olpio says, fingering his change.

Mike the frog de-fridges the beer in question and flings it on bar. He takes the man's money and shuts the cash register. McKinley sips his pint, observing his fellow patron's unopened bottle. "Hope you got good teeth," he says.

"Kid's got a point," optics flicking between bottle and frog, "can you open it?"

"Kid?" McKinley frowns as Michel comes over, "I'm nineteen—"

"Yea whatever," Olpio adds.

Michel assaults the bottle with an opener on his many-keyed landlord's key-chain.

"Chose stupide." Olpio squints at the landlord. "What's wrong with you?"

"Ce n'est pas attraper la lèvre—!"

The besmirched ethnologist grips the bottle, and smashes it over M. Deikan's head. He falls on the ground. Olpio jumps over and loots the cash register, stuffing notes in his pockets and pouring loose change into a pint glass. He runs out the door, screaming, "R. I. P. niggaahhh!"

Eric, who's been standing way back with the other four customers throughout this process, peers over the bar. "Hey Mike…"

M. Deikan holds his bloodied head. He turns over, and gapes at E. J., who in turn stares attentively at the ostensibly damaged homosexual. He asks a stupid question. "Are you all right?"

"Pourquoi êtes-vous debout là?"

"Mike," naïevly apologetic, "I'm sorry."

"Jésus, homme."

◊

Eric's got a basic flat. A kitchenette and living room with a table and chair (note the singular), a toilet, and he can't afford toilet paper so he spends a lot of time in public toilets. It's either that or his only towel, a face cloth that sways from his sink, the soaping dips of which are filled with Vatiquinone™ capsules: a small molecule drug used for the treatment of noise-induced hearing loss and metabolic disorders. Sitting up in bed this grey-maroon morning with a funny fearful feeling in his gut, the type experienced when there is crucially almost no money left. I.e. you're still able to buy stuff like bubblegum, (re)assuring any person they're not totally broke even if—this pattering the back of tiny minds—cumulative gum purchase will in due course leave a person with absolutely no money. But the trick works for a time, and each time he does it Eric feels better about his situation. The cigarette lighter clicks, and Eric inhales. Gum. Cigarettes. Same thing. The phone rings. He groans. The weight of the I-hate-people-but-need-money state of mind is too much, and so he's like, "Fuck off…" The phone begrudges his airspace again, and he slides out of bed to answer it.

"Eve, it's too early—"

"Eve?" Robyn answers, softly.

"Who's this?"

"It's me."

"Robyn?"

"Yea."

"Oh," he says, dragging on his cigarette, "hey, what's up?"

"Uh…I don't know how to tell you this."

Eric nods, and stares at the ceiling bored. "You could try saying one word after another…"

There's a faint giggle from Robyn, but it's not much good. Social maneuvering will be required.

"Are you all right?" Eric asks.

"Um, no...I'm not."

"I'm sorry to hear that. What's up?"

"...Mark died yesterday."

"You're joking," followed by a kind of silent puff, "oh god, I'm sorry Robyn. Shit."

"Yea, I thought I should tell you."

"Jesus, Robyn, that's terrible, oh...oh man. What, where's, what happened?"

"He just uh, sorry," she pauses for a moment, "he got hit by a car."

"Oh Robyn, that's terrible. I'm so sorry."

Robyn adds postscript. "You remember Andrei?"

"Yea," Eric exhales aggressively, "I remember Andrei."

"I bumped into him at the hospital and he was just like, 'Wow, two siblings widowed in the same family, way to go.'"

"Oh God, look—"

"I couldn't look at him after that."

"Robyn, don't, don't listen to that type of garbage, I mean—"

"He's such a cunt."

"Yea, Robyn, you gotta understand that Andrei is a, he's a cunt, uh...he's a really unhappy man. That's why he says stuff like that, okay?"

"He's crazy."

"Yea, it's just, it doesn't actually have anything to do with you, j—Remember that," he stubs out his cigarette on the wall, "Robyn?"

"It didn't sound like that."

"Jesus Robyn, um...god, okay. Let's forget all that, all right?

Let's forget all that. What do you wanna do?"

He trudges into his kitchenette, and perches himself on the countertop, punctuating, "Robyn?"

"I need to sort everything out."

"Yea."

"Could you, uh…could you take Ebba for a few days?"

"Uh, I don't think that's a good idea."

"She's your niece."

"I know but, this, here isn't a good place for a kid, you know?"

"I just need to be alone for a few days."

"Robyn, don't do that. That's what men do; and you're not a man, that's just, you're better than that."

"What's that supposed to mean?"

"Oh Christ, um, never mind, it doesn't matter."

"I'll put her on the train tomorrow morning, so just be there."

"Yea, I'll be there."

"I swear to god, Eric——"

"I'll be there, I'll be there."

"Okay, I'll, I'll talk to you later."

"All right, bye now."

"Bye."

"Bye…"

He drops the telecommunications device, and switches the exhaust fan on. The next day is sunny and windy. The trains are on time.

◊

McKinley walks up and down the platform half-listening to, much like those constabulary pamphlets he'll be forced to confront in forty years, the announcements concerning arrival and departure, flagrantly unassailable and repetitive like an alcoholic.

"Rhythm, rhythm," Eric improvises, "oh lord, me got rhythm—"

> I got so much rhythm
> I don't know what to do with it
> I head up to the shop and all
> I gotta do remember it

He shakes his head, telling himself, "That's terrible."

The train approaches the platform. He realizes he can't even throw himself in front of it. After all that would be the ultimate familial middle finger to the mourning Robyn, and not to mention (nay more importantly) would be responsible for a subsequent fear of public transport on Ebba's innocent part in all this. The fact that her Uncle, not suicidal so much as chronically apathetic, threw himself in front of her ScotRail train because he couldn't be bothered with his own existence or worse - hers. He sighs a bromide, peering up and down the platform to see if his niece is getting off. "God, she must be what, nine?" he says to himself while a dozen emotionally ugly people get off the train, "ten?" Suddenly, there she is, with her coyote brown suitcase.

Eric flips his lid. "Oh shit," he gallops over to her, "EBBA!"

The young woman observes this insane man running towards her, and says, "Uncle Eric?"

"Yea that's me, Jesus, how are you?"

"I'm fine," she replies, "how are you?"

"I'm good, just—PHEW! Outta shape," he grips her suitcase, "let's get out of here."

They sit next to each other on the bus home. Her suitcase fills his lap. She watches semi-detached house after semi-detached house jog by like dejected cattle. Her Uncle finally breaks the silence.

"Your dad was a…a good m—"

"My dad was an asshole," she confirms.

"Y-yea," Eric replies, "he was actually."

"You don't have to agree with me…"

Eric is confused. He looks at her boobs, and asks how old she is.

"Sixteen," she replies, sharply, "why am I here?"

"Ask your mum, but do it at some later date," he says.

The bus jerks over a bump. It starts to rain. The driver chuckles; at the weather or his own vocational weariness it is hard to tell. A tall Lebanese woman with a child's rucksack chews gum in the disabled seat. Next to her is a gym-attired Englishman humming a shit tune. Ebba assesses the situation.

"Jesus," she looks out the window, "what *is* this place?"

"The border," her uncle coughs, "do you have a boyfriend?"

"I don't like boys."

"…Girlfriend?"

"No," she says, "I'm sick of women."

Eric yawns, "Good girl."

Later that night, after all the dropping off and/or moving in one does on a required weekend off in an unknown house—hopefully in some quiet border-town quarter filled with pub stereophonics up and down the streets, chippy aromas and Cullen skink looping with burnt Lorne sausage and Arbroath smokies, stovies, clooties, mince and tatties and cock-a-leekie soup—E. J. drags his niece along to The Shifty Faust for a gig, which he finishes around 8:34 p.m. He pours, as is tradition, the half-empty glass of water over his head, and buggers off.

As he's shoving his red guitar back in its too-small case, the next act—slightly-less-renowned-than-E. J. McKinley guitarist Falupa Jiggy—sets herself up. Eric waves at her, advising, "Hey, uh, the microphone's pretty temperamental tonight."

She plucks her E-string. "Got another cable?"

"No," he replies, "that's what I mean. There's no cable so be careful with it. It's just a pain in the ass."

Falupa tunes her D-string. "Uh huh…"

Eric takes his case to the bar and sits with Ebba. She sips her soda water, and asks if her uncle does this every night. "I try to," Eric says as he waves down the Polish landlord Stev Karp, "Stev, you got any lager?"

Karp's eyelids sag. "Co myślisz?"

"Right, a pint of, pint of lager then." Karp slugs to the other end of the bar and grabs a pint glass from above. "But yea," Eric continues, "it's not always the case. There're only so many places you can play," watching his niece nod indifferently, "Did you like it?"

"What…you?"

"Yea."

"You were good. I thought your songs were pretty."

"Oh, thanks," Eric smiles, and his lager is delivered. S. Karp goes on to illustrate his state of being by taking the required amount of money and dropping it in the cash register. McKinley sips the ice-cold beverage, and snoops at his niece from the corners of his bashful, woebegone eyes. "Do you write songs? Or poetry?" he asks.

"I'm not so sure…"

"Eh. Do what you like."

"Are you happy? Doing this?"

"I'm not rich but, yea…I'm doing okay."

"How do you, like—?"

"What?"

"How do you not forget about everything if this is like, your life? How do you remember reality?"

"Oh," Eric says, "you're talking about my wife."

"W—No, I'm not—"

"Yea you are," he replies, half in the room. He listens to Falupa Jiggy's concentrated strumming, maffling to himself, "I heard that – where did I hear that?"

"Uncle Eric?"

"That's good, uh – yea," turning back to Ebba, "how do I remember reality? Good question," he sighs, "I probably dedicate each song I write to Celine in one way or another. I still miss her, if that's what you mean."

"No," she says, "it's just like, my mum's on another planet—"

"This may seem an insensitive thing to say," Eric begins, "but do you think it might have something to do with your Father?"

"Well, yea, but when you talk to her it's like she's not in the room."

Eric's eyes address the beer matts below him. "Your mum's, uh – she's a little sick, I think," he sips his beer, "but I'm not surprised when you live with someone like that. Like your Dad," he looks at Ebba, curiously, "did he ever hurt you?"

"No."

"Not like either of us could do anything about it now, I mean, me and your Dad, not you and your Dad—Stev," he leans over the bar, "you got my money?"

Karp clicks his tongue, and raises his eyebrows. "Daj mi minutę."

"Thank yoooo," Eric coos as the landlord disappears. Then he stares into his glass, and says, softly, "You manage."

◊

Later, the future commissioner is sleeping on his couch. Ebba sleeps in his bed. She has bad dreams. Not nightmares, but bad dreams. Boring dreams where you recognize where you are and who you're with but at the same time it's inconsequential, and insignificantly dangerous. For example, your father has a baffled look on his face. You keep missing the train. There is a storm. At the same time though, a not-quite-right determinant in all of it. Your father's face seems to be every other face you've ever seen. The train's totally silent pulling through, like a film without the sound. And a gaggle of greyness—the storm—crawls over the dirt, like there's been a roadwork paint spillage, the man responsible running for help in a wage-addled frenzy of vocational shame.

Ebba sweats awake. She sits on the edge, and scratches her forehead. She gets up and goes in the living room in a desperate childish juncture where she flops her brunetting mane to one side.

She gets as far as the coffee table before Eric shines his torch. He falls off the couch and screams and she screams. But everything's okay: It's just her, and it's just him. Ebba spits out, "What the fuck?"

"I'm sorry! I thought you were a burglar or something!"

"W—Why are you wearing a bra?" she stammers.

"I,' Eric looks down, and yes, a bra, a yellow bra, "Ah yes, I can explain."

"Are you drunk? Where did you get—?"

"No, I'm fine, I just, I may have a little bit of a weird habit, okay? It's just – this is Celine's."

Ebba puts her hands over her mouth. "Oh my God...

you're wearing your dead wife's bra?"

Her uncle explodes: "AND YOU WERE SPERM IN YOUR DEAD FATHER'S BALLS AT ONE POINT HOW FUCKING WEIRD IS THAT?"

He rubs his eyes. Then he mumbles and hyperventilates for a bit. "I just uh, sorry, I'm sorry," he folds his arms, and leans forward, "I don't have anyone. It just makes me feel better."

Ebba covers her eyes.

Her uncle starts blowing his nose. "I can't breathe," he looks at Ebba, "what are y—don't cry, honey." Ebba folds her arms, saying, "I'm sorry…" She snivels in the dark. Eric turns a lamp on, and walks over to her. "Don't be sorry it's all right."

"I'm sorry."

"No, no, sshhh – it's all right. Have a hug from a guy in a bra," and they share a giggle amongst the tears, "you're okay, honey. You wanna watch some TV with me?"

Ebba nods and says, "P. P. O'Leary should be on this time."

Eric picks up the remote, asking, "What channel?"

"Two-fifty," she says.

Eric gives her the remote and says, "Here, take control, you drive."

◊

Back at Harmon's graduation, Tara laughs at Commissioner Eric J. McKinley's speech.

"Fuckwit."

Harmon clears his throat and asks after his colleague: "Tara."

"What?"

"Are you going to the graduation party?" he asks.

"What do you think?"

"Do you think it's worth it?"

"Probably not," she replies, "but I heard last year they had these, like, little gift bags and you get a key chain, or whatever. More importantly."

Harmon flinches at the notion of a key chain, "I think I'll pass."

He and his fellow graduate are suddenly submerged in a constabulary soup. There are deliberations everywhere. Tongues and teeth are flapping and clacking. Tara winks at a graduate called Fenway Ilyich. Then she smiles at his friend Yuri Polk. She turns to Harmon. "You're coming to the pub."

"Am I?"

"Me and Yuri," she explains, "later on. Pub. Group of us."

"I don't know," he moans.

"Jesus Christ," she complains, "loosen up."

"I don't want to screw up everything on the first night."

"No, but this is, like, your last chance to get pissed and not have to worry about tomorrow."

"No, but that's the point," Harmon says, "that's what I'm worrying about."

Tara scoffs. "Yea, and the day after that."

"Who was that you winked at?" Harmon asks.

Tara can't figure out if Const. Chikenyyt's a jealous 7 on a scale of 1 to 10, or if he's on the autistic spectrum, the spectrum making itself known in the annals of the prospective make-out session on a viridescent leather couch adjacent to your mobile, which for personal reasons will be switched off for the next hour or so. Either that, or Harmon Really Cannot Wait To Go Out Policing—He's already asking you who you're winking at, for Christ's sakes.

Tara smiles. "Shit you are good. Motherfucker can't even see my, hey," she pokes Yuri's shoulder, "Yuri, you see this shit?

Motherfucker can't even see my face."

Harmon feels the sweat running from his armpits, "That's the idea."

"Cunt's awake," Tara says.

As per sub-cultured initiations with reference to constabulary institutions, all these bright, young faces, a few of them at least, march quietly down streets and back alleys boasting 24-hour dental practices into The Cock and Bull, which for lack of a better phrase is a "filthy dive". Some individuals, Utton mayor Balthazar Khaskheli IV notwithstanding, may argue that such descriptions of local drinking establishments are inaccurate, nay obscene. But they miss the point. To be able to be obscene is precisely why people go to pubs—Not to mention certain Police Academy graduates who attend The Cock and Bull the night before they're shipped off to their respective districts around the S.B. During these nights graduates invariably consume either *Meprobamate*: a carbamate with hypnotic, sedative and muscle relaxant properties, or *Azaperone*: a neuroleptic drug with sedative and antiemetic effects used primarily in veterinary medicine—They drink beer too.

Some stay here in Utton City Centre. But most are redirected to Fergnan, Blukleim and Florin, which lay on the border with England in the so-called Wastelands. This is where all the quiet people are sent. People like Harmon. So naturally the twenty four police graduates sat currently in The Cock and Bull grasping glasses full of Rascal's Piss and the occasional G&T are betting on one Const. Harmon Chikenyyt getting exiled to Florin with the rest of the burn-outs and/or people who aren't actually burn-outs but individuals who read for recreation.

"Harmon," Fenway Ilyich waves his pint at the daydreaming constable, "HARMON."

Chikenyyt flinches. "Hmm?"

"What are you drinking?"

Meanwhile, under the table, Tara slides her hand in Fenway's crotch, and says, "Harmon doesn't drink."

"But he's a copper," Fenway says, gasping for air, "we're all coppers now. And all coppers have a drink." He gulps his pint.

Tara looks at Harmon like she'd rather be touching his glands. "Harmon's teetotal," she says.

"Jesus," Fenway says whilst flipping his erection under his beltline, "more for me and Yuri then."

Yuri Polk sneers and follows Ilyich to the bar. Harmon looks at Tara. He excretes that significant I-don't-want-to-be-here rush of warm air, the stuff of legends.

"Thank you for that."

"You could beat him up any day," she replies, sharply.

"Apart from this one," Harmon adds, "and tomorrow, and the day after that."

Tara folds her arms over the table. She nods in that inexhaustibly feminine way, that when it happens at the right time (usually a bad one) is just about the most wonderful thing in the world with reference to fortification, especially in a pub or restaurant with food and drink rattling past. All the machinery well oiled, ready for the journey.

"How's your soda water?"

Harmon shrugs. "Tastes like soda water."

"It was free," she adds, "it better taste like soda water."

She beams, and Harmon chortles into his highball. Yuri and Fenway return with three pints of Rascal's Piss.

"Best beer in the S.B.," Ilyich plants himself, lifting his pint, "and that's saying something. Cheers."

They all clack their glasses together, drink, and look around the room. Harmon stares just above his own lap, at the edge of the table. A lot of these graduates will die in their first year. Fenway glides his hand up Tara's inner thigh. She stands up.

"I gotta use the toilet."

Ilyich smiles and says, "Rascal's Piss at work."

She leaves the men at the table. Fenway stares into his pint for a minute until, in a moment of bullish aptitude, he casts his eyes over Harmon, and says, "Bets are on you getting sent to Florin. On the border."

Harmon cogitates on this. "Yea…"

"…"

"…"

Fenway stares at him. "You don't talk much, do you Harmon?"

The teetotaller shrugs.

Yuri flicks his eyes between the two graduates. He slips a series of cards on the table. But Ilyich isn't done here. *No. He's not quite ready for the requisite game of Barbu or Kaiser, All Fours, Oh Hell, Sheepshead, Hokm, Rook, Solitaire, War—He might be ready for War, not that it would involve the attrition-particulars of repetition or even real cards for that matter—No,* Fenway thinks. He scratches his neck, adding, "When I was a lad growing up in Blukleim there was a quiet kid there. She never talked around me. Every time I saw her in the hallway or something she'd look away or play with her phone or pretend to look at another boy when she was actually thinking about me. And that last bit fits in because for some weird reason I wasn't scoring too well with the ladies. I should be doing better than this, I thought. There was a reason, though…" Harmon runs his hand across the forearm.

"It turns out," Ilyich continues, "that girl was telling all her friends I was bent. 'Don't touch him,' she was saying, 'he takes it up the arse'," he sips his pint, "but life goes on, and a few weeks later she was in the hospital. She wasn't too well. Doctor said she'd been hit by a bus, or something. The girl's Mother—she was a nurse—didn't see the girl too much but still, nothing ever got past her. She knew what happened, so, 'No,' she said, 'It was that Ilyich boy who broke my girl's jaw.'"

Harmon readjusts his beltline. He's sweating. "You reckon they'll send you to Blukleim?"

Ilyich turns red. "They won't do that. That shithole?" turning to Yuri playing cards by himself, "you ever been to Blukleim?"

"Nope," laying a joker on the table.

"Well if you ever get the chance," Fenway says, "don't."

Tara walks back to the table. She shoves the men over, and sits down. "Anything interesting happen?"

Ilyich clears a blockage in his nose. "Same shit. New day," he looks at Harmon, "they got sunlight in Florin, Harmon?"

"Probably," Chikenyyt replies.

"Because I heard they sold it to the Russians so they could build a community centre." He laughs and drinks his beer. No one else does. "Tara," he adds, "are we fucking tonight or what?" which is of course a total act of male compensation wrought by one of those awful Summer jobs your parents made you do when you were young. Those early explorations into the pursuit of happiness with reference to the many hours of impending adult life put in, and pleasure (that is, money) taken out.

Fenway Ilyich was the best junior mechanic in the S.B. "The Fiveway Fixer," "Fiveway Fenway," "Fenway the Fixer," "[...] that kid with the bowl haircut who works at Papa Chubb's," or the ever-popular "Son of Chubb," quick to word of mouth, inaccurate as weather reports...

◊

Mister Chubb owns and runs Papa Chubb's Garage in the Wastelands, five ways out from Utton, with a semi-detached shack housing a fish-cooking apparatus and a collection of Anti-Semitic pornography. Every morning he has black coffee and a cigarette. He'd rather not. But he always does, and sits in his shack performing masturbatory actions until forcing himself to engage the Presbyterian-but-not-really part of his sizeable brain, and looks online for the cheapest parts. They're never cheap. But he buys them anyway. Any other garage would do the same. And that's what he is. The same.

Fenway fiddles under a car in the garage. Papa Chubb gapes through the office door at his summer student, examining the license plate. He gulps his coffee, and joins the relative sunlight in dissatisfaction. "Did we book that in?"

Ilyich wheels out from under the car. "Book what in?"

"This car," joining his junior mechanic, "I don't remember—"

"Oh this, it's a personal favour," Fenway explains, "I know the guy."

"I ain't payin' you to do personal favours."

"So don't pay me for this one."

"Goddamn right," Chubb confirms, "Jesus. We got six cars in today. Inspection week."

"It's fine," Ilyich wipes the oil off his cheek, "we'll get through them all."

Mister Chubb strangles his tie and says, "Thanks for the confidence padre." He walks back into his office.

Ilyich wheels back under the car. "Prick…"

In Chubb's air-conditioned cave (and yes, he does keep the door open) a water dispenser lounges in the corner. There are new paper cups. Chubb pulls one out. He fills it. Then he quaffs down an aspirin: the Acetylsalicylic acid inhibiting platelet aggregation and discouraging arterial and/or venous thrombosis. He dials Loma's (a.k.a. his ex-girlfriend's) number, and answers an unasked question.

"Loma?" he coughs, "um…look…I'm sorry about what happened last night. I think I was tired…tightly strung."

"You threw your dinner at me," Loma says on the other end.

"Yea I did, didn't I?" He sits down, swirling his cup. "I think there's something there but I can't – every time I think about you I get angry."

"What? At me?"

"No," he clarifies, "myself," then a laugh as delicate as glass, "maybe that's just how it is."

"So that's it?"

"Well, I don't see anything moving forward. I don't think I should be around other people – do you?"

"I really…I really don't want to end it like this."

"Yea, well, it's gotta," he clears his throat, "bye…" He hangs up, and hears boots clicking, outside, across the workshop floor. There's also the yapping of cheap leather bought second-hand from a Japanese vendor of Chinese extraction named Hakaru Wang in April.

Fenway rolls out from under the chassis. The customer, Patrik Brücke, lifts his right hand and wiggles his digits.

"How's my baby," he says as Ilyich stands up, lending a greasy handshake, "how you doin'?"

"I'm good Mister Brücke," the mechanic replies, "just finishing up."

"That's nice," Patrik does a kind of sexual moan, "how much?"

"Don't worry about—"

"Come on Fenny. Have a little backbone. Actually, I got one for you," the leatherman mimes holding a snake-like object, "extracted it this morning," and Fenway illustrates that perplexed grin that always follows a poor joke, "just kiddin'." Brücke turns to his darker purpose. "How old are you?"

"Seventeen."

"Seventeen? Shit. You look older than that. Girls throw themselves at you,"

Fenway nods a negative.

"Boys?"

It's another negative. The junior mechanic explains that he doesn't get much, nay any.

"Pretty sad, Fenny," his customer notes, "I was fuckin this guy last night. Incredible. They say it's an art form. Some universities say that now. What university you go to?"

"L.E.S."

"England? Political Science and Economics? Damn. Rather you than me. Though I didn't go to university. Not smart enough. Had to hedge my bets somewhere else," he thinks about his prospects, "anyway, I'll tell you, and I mean this – you want anything, just give me a shout."

"Thanks," Ilyich says, "but I'm okay."

"Come on," he pokes Fenway's shoulder, "nothing?" He runs his tongue under his upper lip like a pink razor. He unzips his trousers and pulls his dick out. "What about this? You want *this*?"

Ilyich frowns. "No."

Brücke is quiet. Then he puts his dick away, and zips up. "That's fair," he says, "every man to his own." He laughs.

"Hey buddy," Mister Chubb says as he hangs out of his office, "no one wants to see that," he points outside, "not in here." Brücke stares at Mister Chubb. Then he tugs his lapels, and struts out.

"That's your mate?" Chubb judges as he walks over to his summer student, "you can do better than that, kid."

"That's how he is," Fenway replies.

"It ain't right."

"You got a problem with gay people?"

"Kid," Chubb shakes his head, "people like him say they're gay to get sympathy, get away with stuff. They make real gay people look bad. And that ain't right is it?"

Fenway shrugs. This is followed by the unmistakable Chubbish slurping of coffee. "So who the hell are you?" Chubb asks.

Brücke returns with a gun. "How about this?" he says, clearly unhinged, "how about this old man?"

Mister Chubb throws his cup in the bin. He studies the man. "You're joking."

"I ain't jokin'," Patrik spasms, "get over there."

"Where?"

"Over there, by the toolbox – g-go on," pointing his gun at him.

Mister Chubb strolls towards the toolbox.

"I hope you know what you're doing," Chubb says.

"You ever been held up before?"

"You ever killed anyone before?"

"Nah, not yet." Brücke jogs in place.

Chubb looks at his captor. "If you're gonna kill me, just do—" BANG, the back of his head flies off. Blood goes everywhere.

The body tumbles over the toolbox. Fenway grips the car in shock. "Oh shit," he covers his mouth, "oh shit!"

Patrik screams something indescribable. He laughs and looks at Ilyich. "Y-You want a job?"

"Don't kill me," Ilyich pleads, quietly.

"Nah, it's nothing like that," Patrik breathes heavily for a moment, "it's just like Mullein said."

Some years have passed since Mister Chubb was murdered at the eponymous garage. It marked the end of an engineering dynasty, and the beginning of the blood-soaked and quite nasty career of one Zachary Mullein, who, as always (Derpoloxin dosage permitting) plants himself in others.

◊

One Sergeant Copernicus Kapoor, erstwhile member of the Fergnan Football Fan Disposal Unit (F.F.D.U.), plummets a cube of bio-engineered cannabis in front of four new Florin Police Station recruits: Constables Sheek Erasmus, Varsity Nertúny, Garthman Lewbâdak, and Harmon Chikenyyt. It lands on the table, situated in one of the dodgier brief-rooms next to the women's toilets, with an arrogant thud. Kapoor hangs his arms by his sides.

"That's what it's like when I drop my trousers," there's a moment of prolonged silence, "you interested Chikenyyt?"

Harmon stares at Kapoor's groin for no other reason than the fact that he just mentioned it.

"No sir—"

"I'm talking about the cannabis, constable," he corrects.

"Oh, yes, sir."

"Don't be," he corrects, again, "it's illegal."

Harmon is *very* confused.

Kapoor plants his hands on the table. He leans forward as Sheek, Varsity and Garthman lean back—Apart from Harmon. He just pulls out his diary and begins the junior notes that lose credence after the first week. The sergeant's peepers rake from book to weed.

"This is Derpoloxin Hashish. Shortened to Derpash when it found a market on the street. After which it got shortened to D.E.R.P.," he bends over to the block and sniffs it, "it's one of the," he coughs, "shit, one of the most powerful hallucinogenics on the planet. It used to be restricted to government use but luckily for us and Harmon, I'm being ironic here, this is no longer the case."

Harmon puts his pen down. "But can—"

"Please tell me you got that," Kapoor pleads.

"Yea, but cannabis isn't a hallucinogenic."

"Well THAT'S where you're WRONG—"

Harmon's superior pulls down one of those rolled-up charts near the projector (the 90° angle where the wall meets the ceiling). On the chart is a digital reproduction of a photograph of renowned pharmacologist-cum-lecturer Doctor Norvin "Wristy" Tubaniña, taken when he was an unusually well-read postgrad at the Instituto De Peculiaridades in Nicaragua. After academia, Tubaniña was hired by his Father, Doctor Alberto C. Tubaniña who operated a euthanasia clinic called, "Salida," in the far north of the S.B. Ironically, it was granted its first practicing license when Alberto C. died. His son subsequently took over and branded the new legal clinic Boundaries®. (He would stay there until the Americans picked him up, as pharmacologists with high IQs often are, "picked up," by radical capitalist nation-states.) There Boundaries® (re)opened under new management and made over £1,000,000,000 profit (net) in the first quarter, after which business died down substantially. This confused the accountants: How and why death became a fad equivalent to the punk-rock super-group *Let Dogs Run* or rimless spectacles was a mystery as far as the Boundaries® finance department was concerned.

On the other hand, perhaps it was, like the ridiculous

availability of rimless spectacles or L.D.R. MP3 downloads, because people didn't have to wait anymore. Death was at their disposal, whenever they wished. And so, in an act of shameless commodity, supply and demand notwithstanding, it was a case of the public not really needing it. Well, some of them did. But on the whole Boundaries® acquired an extensive list of, "clients," because those, "clients," thought killing themselves was the new in-thing. In the pursuit of popularity, therefore, their lives were lost, much like the early Chinese explorer Jia Dan travelling to the edges of his world at a time when no one else would dare, only remarkably less impressive...

◊

In the Boundaries'® waiting room a new, "client," called Ben Calm coughs and sniffs. This air conditioning is not helping his cold. A redheaded nurse (not crucially, but a redhead nonetheless) struts into the waiting room. She rests her hands on a pouch hanging from her belt. The pouch is full of *Sodium phosphate*: a saline laxative that increases fluid in the small intestine thirty minutes after consumption for up to six hours, and *Polycarbophil calcium*: a stool stabilizer and synthetic polymer of plyacrylic acid hybridized from divinyl glycol and calcium.

She smiles, "Hello, Mister Calm."

"Hi," Ben replies.

"Would you like to follow me, please?"

Calm asks if he could have a wheelchair.

"Oh," the nurse replies, noticing his left leg, which is significantly bigger than his right, "of course. I'll have to make a note of it for your record though."

"That's fine," he says, after which he stares at the ground.

The nurse snaps her fingers and a small male nurse called

Lewsham Mankiewicz appears in a doorway with a wheelchair. "There you go," the redhead adds as she scrolls through her tablet, "for the sake and improvement of our records, what is your disability?"

"It's my penis," Ben replies.

The other nurse, Mankiewicz, says, "What about it?"

"It drags," Calm explains, comically. The redhead types away, adding, ironically, "I know it's a drag, but what exactly is the problem?"

"No," the, "client," says, "you don't understand. It literally drags."

"Heh," she types slowly, "can you not walk then?"

"Not that well, no." She smiles and points at the wheelchair. He swings his rear into it.

"Christ." Ben reaches down to his left foot and tucks the tip of his penis under his sweatpants. "Bit chilly."

Lewsham Mankiewicz sighs, and pushes him to the Holy Room.

The only thing, "clients," complained about in that wholesome first quarter was the Holy Room. They didn't go in for the parsonical bullshit, you know, the whole, "Are you terribly sure you want to end your life there's so much to live for," conversation. One, "client," a substantial shareholder in I.T.C.B. Holdings plc (InternationalT-CorpBank)—(By the alias of Hickman *Beca*, so-called because of his use of *Becaplermin*: a drug used for the treatment of diabetic skin ulcers encouraging the proliferation of cells involved in wound repair.)—didn't even know what a priest was. Not that that stopped him from dressing like one for his last week because he thought black tops and little white cubes just above your thyroid cartilage were the in-thing, along with rimless spectacles, thin bastards and anything to do with the punk-rock super-group *Let Dogs Run*, I imagine. It's sufficed to say, then, that Mister Beca died with a phlegmatic grin on his face. As such, Ben Calm is wheeled into the Holy Room.

"This is Father Din," the redhead says, pointing at the priest in that way that assumes the pointee is legally blind, "he's going to have a little chat with you."

Father Din is sat at desk. His hands are folded over his belly. "Thank you, nurse," he says.

"No," she replies in a rehearsed kind of way, "thank you." The redhead and Lewsham exit.

B. Calm folds his arms, exhibiting a strong palisade of body language. "There's nothing you can say that'll change my mind."

"Are you terribly sure you want to end your life?" Din asks, "there's so much to live for."

"Give me an example," his guest replies.

"Shit," Din is totally bewildered, "you're the first person to ask that. Uh, let's see…getting laid. That's something to live for."

"Did you even look at my file?"

"I'll be honest with you," Din apologizes, "I didn't. I usually improvise these things. But I'll level with you – why do you want to do yourself in?"

Calm points at his crotch. "Do you know how big my penis is?"

Din's eyes flick to and from the picture of Jesus Christ on the wall.

"This is still the meeting right?"

"Yes."

"Oh right then, uh, no, I don't."

"Forty-two inches."

Din blushes, remarking, "You're a bad muthafucka."

"No," Ben complains, "I'm not."

"Sorry?"

"I've had one erection my whole life," he explains, "and it almost killed me because it takes so much blood my brain gets starved of oxygen, so I basically have a stroke. But trust me, sex is the least of my worries. I'm a lecturer in quantum physics."

Din shrugs.

"I can't teach without people staring at my dick. I can't even walk to lectures anymore because it drags along the ground. I have to take Rettermol to dull the pain."

"Have you tried," the priest mimes an article of clothing, "wearing it like a scarf?"

"Oh yea," Ben goes into sarcastic academic mode, "because no one would look at a guy addicted to Rettermol and think, 'That scarf is totally not his dick.'"

"Hey, I'm just throwing ideas out there."

"Can I go?" He looks back through the frosted glass.

Father Din sighs, and leans back in his chair. "I used to sing in the youth choir at church, you know, the one's that get shipped around choral festivals. I was the only decent tenor. So every Sunday, my vicar, who also happened to be the choirmaster, he'd just…you know…listen and smile. And when the other children went home he'd make me stay, and I'd give him a blowjob. Not a great blowjob by any means, because, well, I could never fit it in my mouth. But as good as I gave," he takes a pen and draws circles in his diary, "Ben…I can call you Ben?"

"Yea."

"I just need to know, and this is something you can do for me, uh – what's it like?"

"What's what like?"

"Having a," Din clears his throat, "big one. What's it like? Do you feel powerful? Do you like sticking it in holes and seeing how far it can go? Do you find solace in that, well, we could agree you find no solace for a start, yes?"

Calm nods to an extent.

"…but has it pleased you? Did it ever yield pleasure, giving way to torment, for both parties?"

Ben thinks for a moment. "I really fancied this girl who lived on my street," he begins, "so I had a dream about her. Seemed innocent enough. We were gearing up to go on vacation. She stood there in a green top, wearing sunglasses. And all of a sudden, it was like she was the most attractive person in the world and I realised, like, it was my duty to make love to this woman. Nothing would, or could transcend that experience. Nothing. I thought about it all, you know, having her in bed. But the more vivid that idea got, in the dream, that is, the more she looked like my uncle. The green shirt, the sunglasses – all of a sudden there's this middle-aged man and here I am thinking about getting it on with him, or her, or whatever. I felt terrible. Like I wanted to die," he looks at the priest, "and that was it."

◊

Dr Norvin Tubaniña stands at the podium. He's ready to address the Boundaries® clientele in a sort of tearoom. The platform is characteristic of self-help seminars attended by ex-Hydrogen drivers and single fathers, and the room itself is the calling card of any medical establishment that excels at a kind of dummy comfort. The clientele today consists of ten individuals, B. Calm included, sitting on infantile plastic chairs, like visiting parents keen to comment on a teacher's claim that their offspring are servants of Lucifer, if not Lucifer himself.

Tern-Love Posem, another, "client," has this ridiculous

grin on his face, as if at any second, a prostitute will appear in the doorway and take away from him his immortal virginity. Then there's Clarmi Jhan, who, of all the people to fancy at a time like this, fancies her executioner: The Chief Needler Doctor Norvin Tubaniña himself, who says, "For the sake and improvement of our corporation, the rules of Boundaries must be adhered to at all times. The first rule of Boundaries is there is to be no use of the following words: 'executioner,' 'hangman,' 'headsman,' or," he turns briefly to a junior needler, "my favourite," and turns back, *"firing squad"*. There are no big concrete walls with holes in them, or anything like that. We're merely helpers. But come to think of it, so are the soldiers in a firing squad really."

He raises his finger academically.

"De lo contrario," he continues, "we know your names. We know your histories, your reasons for being here. Our database has your complete chemical and biological makeup reducido a unos y ceros. You may think this to be a dehumanizing process, but it's merely a precaution, in the same way that a firing squad or a needle is a precaution. You need not concern yourself with such base concepts. Indeed, what matters here is la real-idad última, that of death. La muerte es limpia. La muerte es Buena. Pero la muerte, de manera crucial, es débil. Es por eso que todos aquí esocogieron la muerte. La muerte no te eligió. Eso es imposible."

Falupa Jiggy—ex-guitarist and avid medical reader—rais-es her hand, having considered for three seconds the notion that, "Death is clean. Death is good. But death, crucially, is weak. That's why everyone here chose death. Death did not choose you. That's impossible." Tubaniña stares at her hand suspiciously, adding, "Yes?"

"Surely," Jiggy asks, "this concept of death as a negative-positive, that is, a weak force determined by the element of human choice, is totally contradictory to the work of the euthanasia scholar M. L. Wolkan, a woman whose work you claim forms the bedrock for Boundaries' policies and procedures?"

"What you find in M. L. Wolkan's work," Tubaniña replies, "is medical fabulism. Fabulism does not constitute procedure. What we do at Boundaries is inspired by or built upon Wolkan's work – it is not indicative of it."

"Yes," she says, "but critically the philosophy of death you've outlined is skewed. You'll be hard-pressed to find any customer enrolled in any euthanasia institution who hasn't been chosen by death in some way. It's clearly the other way around. It's us who are weak. And it is death that is strong or overbearing. Death targets at will, a will we are incapable of understanding. Why else, *how else* could we succumb to such a force?"

"I think you're being ideologically insensitive—"

"You for example," Falupa turns to Ben Calm, "why are you here?"

Ben rubs his temples, and explains, "My penis is forty-two inches long."

Posem says, immediately, "You a bad muthafucka."

"NO, I'm not, I'm not a bad mother fucker, it's – it's that I can't live a normal life. Therefore, I hate my own abnormal life. I suppose death has chosen me in that sense."

Falupa gestures, like she's just discovered fire. "Evidence," she claims, "the dick did not choose death. Death chose the dick."

"That's quite enough, Miss Jiggy—"

"I'm just being pragmatic," she interrupts, again, "to suggest what you have is worse than anything I've said because it's emotionally insensitive, emotionally bankrupt—"

"THAT IS QUITE ENOUGH MISS JIGGY!"

Ben Calm holds his head in his hands, imagining a place bereft of flustered pharmacologists.

"I'm, uh," Tubaniña clears his throat, "I apologize for my outburst," he trails his eyes over the room, like an optic slug, "for your last week I suggest a positive contemplation of your choice. It's your life. Es tu vida. As for you, Miss Jiggy, I look forward to," a junior needler grabs his arm, and he relaxes, "…I look forward to answering any sensitive questions you have. For the sake and improvement of today, have a good day…"

Doctor Tubaniña was pretty popular with customers in that blissful first quarter. He played rugby for the Locher team, and caroused at the Boundaries® bar on Thursday nights. An infectious conversationalist fluent in Russian and French, he entertained, "clients," with all the confidence of a Prestonian shampoo salesman, periodically popping *Pregabalin* capsules: an anticonvulsant drug used for neuropathic pain, epilepsy and orthodox anxiety disorder.

It was like he didn't do that much needling, or any needling at all. It was as though, having legitimized his father's business, all that heavy lifting had been passed to junior needlers and nurses like Lewsham Mankiewicz. That, however, is a tenuous analysis. That's the thing, or what you can never trust, about workaholics, melancholicos and presidents: They make it look so damn easy. Except it's not. And with that in mind, there's one place Doctor Tubaniña never goes; what the staff call the, "last chance saloon": The Deferral Suite. If you feel like you can't go through with killing yourself for whatever bizarre reason, and bear in mind you're paying these people by the hour, you can always defer. At first, "defer," seems like the wrong word. It's not like you're going to get needled next week, or the week after that. When you, "defer," that's it. You're out. And it actually makes perfect sense. All you're doing is postponing death until death, which is natural death and probably what you were trying to avoid in the first place: old age, arthritis, adult nappies, dementia, and tubes in your gut so you can shit properly.

The junior needlers think the whole deferment idea is a sick joke.

Tubaniña just thinks it's a joke: a valid, tick-all-the-boxes, worth-a-little-giggle-on-an-afternoon joke.

Later Ben finds himself in The Deferral Suite. On the other side of the dental-white room is Nurse Lewsham Mankiewicz. The, "client," taps his right foot in twenty-five degree thuds. He looks at Lewsham. "Can I ask you something?"

"What's up?"

"Are you here," Ben asks, "to make sure I don't kill myself?"

"Hey! You're pretty smart. That's absolutely correct."

"Oh," he thinks before he continues, "would you lose your license?"

"Yep…you're not thinking?"

"No, I'm just interested that's all—"

"Oh, cool."

"Yea."

"Mmm-hmm," Lewsham mumbles, nodding. He leans back on the wall, examining the door that leads to the needling room. He looks back at Ben. "Can I ask you something?" The, "client," forms an unstudied smile as the nurse tacks on, "so – you got a big penis?"

"Well done."

"You ever thought about doing porn?"

"I have a PhD in quantum information."

"Yea, but," Lewsham un-phased, "did you ever think about

doing porn?"

"I say again, I have a PhD in quantum information."

"You reckon people who make porn are dumb?"

"I don't," Calm clarifies, "but I think people go into porn for two reasons. Either they enjoy sex, or they've simply run out of options. And since neither of those applies to me, I think I'll stick with data compression, entanglement concentration and noiseless channels."

"You feel sorry for them?"

"Who?"

"The porn people, the ones with only two choices?"

"Yes."

Lewsham broods and sucks his teeth. "But, like, you can't be the only man with a forty-two inch penis."

"Feels like it."

"No, but you don't know that either."

"Okay," Ben adjusts his butt, "w—is this where you get a bonus or something if you get me to defer?"

"Hell no," Lewsham answers, "I'm just trying to understand your reasoning."

"You're being a jackass," the, "client," posits.

"I'm just being pragmatic," the nurse says, "let's assume you're the only person in the world with a forty-two inch penis, which you say you are. Totally unique. Almost like you're the last of your species. And you're just gonna kill yourself like that? Just seems like a cop-out to me. What about your research?"

"It's a job."

"What about your colleagues? Do you not think you affect people, that they need you?"

"What do you mean?"

"I mean, like, if you don't turn up to work one day because

you're sick, do you not think the day's any different for your colleagues as a result of you not being there?"

"They won't have a dick to stare at."

"Is that it? How do you know they look at it?"

Ben narrows his eyes. "I know."

"So you're just gonna leave this planet?"

Ben leans back in his wheelchair, nodding. He breathes for a moment. Then he coughs. Lewsham asks if he's all right.

"What?"

"I said, are you all right?"

"Yea I am, I was just, thinking…"

"Thinking? What about?"

"Doesn't matter what."

"I'd bet my left nut it does. What are you on thinking about?"

"I was thinking about my mum, alright?"

"See," Lewsham says, "that there's a classic."

"Fuck you."

The door opens. A junior needler cloaked in a Cal Poly Camona-coloured body suit waddles over. "Mister Calm," she waves at Ben, "would you like to come this way please?"

Lewsham's eyes track the academic rolling out, and finally meet the junior needler's. She smirks, and shuts the door behind her. Ben finds himself in a small sunlit room, like a slightly less menacing dentist's office. There are potted plants of the Mongolian variety: the Bindweed, the Saltwort on the windowsill notwithstanding, and everyone's decked out in picnic attire: jeans, blouses, cravats, Cuban shirts and the occasional pair of leather trousers, which aren't particularly summery but in terms of the overall description of the aforementioned season they will have to do.

Doctor Tubaniña stands in the middle with his arms in the air. A junior needler meticulously gloves each hand. The latex snaps against his brown flesh. "Oh, we must be almost finished," Tubaniña announces, "Mister Calm is here," the junior needlers and nurses clap, "I hope you don't mind our attire."

"No, it's fine."

"It's casual Thursday," he explains, "every Thursday is casual Thursday. Miss Jiggy was just here. She had a few things to say about it, but not anymore, as you can imagine," an air of dolefulness fills every face in the room, "are you squeamish?"

Ben clears his throat. "Not really."

"Good. Mister Posem refrained from telling us about his distinct fear of needles. He practically had a seizure when I gave him his injection. We got through it though AAACCHHOO! Excuse me," he sniffs, "there's always the pill option."

"Whatever's easiest for you," Ben says.

Tubaniña cocks his head. "Señor Calm," he smiles, "you really are the last one, aren't you?"

A junior needler wheels a trolley over to Doctor Tubaniña. On top, there are three injection vials and three needles: 1. *Thiopental*: a barbiturate administered for the induction of complete anaesthesia; 2. *Pancuronium*: a neuromuscular blocking agent; 3. *Potassium Chloride*: an often-crystalline powder used in fertilizers and explosives, but utilized here to induce cardiac arrest.

The first two needles are sucked up, and jabbed in. The last takes a little longer. Well, it certainly feels longer, considering the, "Wristy," commentary: "Did you know, Mister Calm, that my father was the Chief Needler before me?"

Ben stares at the third and final needle, and says, "Didn't you open last year?"

"We got our *license* last year," he resolves, "daddy's little venture has always been here, albeit in a supra-legal capacity," he jabs the needle into the vial, "much like death, an entity is admired if and only if it has passed through that which is transcendent, and yet totally legal…"

A clear liquid fills the chamber. He holds it upside down, like a baby. "Looks harmless, doesn't it?"

"Yea."

"Te sentirás un poco pinchazo. You'll feel a little prick." He rubs alcohol on the, "client's," arm. "Then you'll feel very sleepy, like you haven't slept in years."

The needle pierces the skin.

"It's okay."

A few seconds pass. Then he drags the needle out.

"Hold that there."

Ben presses a piece of cotton on his arm.

Tubaniña plops the needle on the trolley. "You're a trooper," he wipes his hands on a disinfectant napkin, "now…just relax…" He observes a junior needler picking at her nails under her latex gloves. He returns his gaze to the, "client," smiling, not at, but with B. Calm's slowly, undeniably slumping head. The grin evaporates in a dull flash of empiricism. "It's weird, isn't it?"

Ben's eyelids droop. "What?"

"Everything," Tubaniña says.

The academic slumps forward.

"Catch him!"

The junior needlers flop him back. One of them checks his pulse, confirming, "He's dead." Doctor Tubaniña nods. "I need a drink."

Upon entering the Deferral Suite, Lewsham is just standing there. Tubaniña puts his hands in his pockets, and says, "I told you." Then he looks around the room, like he's lost his car keys. "Fuck it."

◊

Back in the Florin Police Station, Copernicus Kapoor points at the digital reproduction of the postgrad photograph of one Nicaraguan pharmacologist Doctor Norvin "Wristy" Tubaniña.

"You know who this is?"

Harmon is speaking for the other recruits when he says, "No."

"Used to be employed by the United States government. Drug research. Torture. Before that he ran a euthanasia clinic in this country, but let's talk science for a moment," Kapoor composes his mind, gathering pieces and information locked away in clearly labelled colour-coded files in his head, "Derpoloxin, or D.E.R.P., is a result of bioengineering on Wristy's behalf. So firstly tetrahydrocannabinol is the psychoactive substance in marijuana, and diethylamide is used in the production of lysergic acid diethylamide, otherwise known as L.S.D.," sniffing his armpits, "the chemical equation for D.E.R.P., however, is $C_{41}H_{55}N_3O_3$ if any of you want to write it down for reference..."

Harmon writes it down for reference. The last thing he wrote down for reference was a factoid uttered by Garthman Lewbâdak forty-three minutes ago in the locker rooms: It concerned COAnàb a.k.a. Coimhearsnachd ola agus nàbaidhean ("community of oil and neighbours"), a cartel formed after the first Border Skirmish (2065) by the leading chemical companies in the newly formed S.B., which included C.B.T.G., Fairsmit and Lubban Inc. It became the largest cartel in the S.B., controlling two hundred firms in fifty-three countries, in addition to eight hundred and fifty six cartel agreements with organizations such as Solar Blue (Nicaragua), J.B.J. (Japan), and The

Allman Brothers Company (Malaysia). Lewbâdak mentioned the saturation of *Cannabis Indica* on the market as a production-necessity of more popular by-products, such as natural oils for shampoo manufacture, and fibre used in faux-Panama hats bought by American tourists in Florida.

"The production of Derpoloxin is, more or less, a mystery," Kapoor continues, "or you could go down Wristy's route, which is, as he says, 'It's all in the wrist.'"

Harmon stops his scribbling. "What's the point?"

"Interrogation," his superior answers disinterestedly, "militarily speaking, you offer the prisoner a joint—"

"What if they don't want a joint?"

"People always want a joint, Harmon. Besides, D.E.R.P. does its work in one puff. Originally, they were lacing joints, but then Tubaniña got so adept at his bioengineering that he was able to instil the properties of Dicanine ergo Derponine ergo Derpoloxin into the plant itself. The hallucinogenic became part of *Cannabis Indica's* biological makeup and so," he points at the block, "it's all in the wrist."

D.C.S. Anya Egelblöm enters the room in an act of disabled providence. Her wheelchair squeaks through, her body jilting forward when she stops to address them. Sergeant Kapoor and the newly mind-fucked recruits stand up. They salute her.

She coughs apologetically. "At ease," she says. She examines, briefly, each recruit. She stares at Harmon, saying, "You have a nice face constable."

Harmon looks at Kapoor, who gets pissed off because he's looking at him instead of Egelblöm. "Chikenyyt, ma'am," the recruit labels himself.

"Chikenyyt," she mutters with an alarming smile, "plucky little thing, aren't you?"

Kapoor strokes the block of D.E.R.P., stating further, "They've all been briefed about tonight ma'am."

"Thank you, sergeant," she says, "have they tested a sample?"

Kapoor's a bit unsure about this. "Is that wise?"

"If they want to know what it is they're dealing with," she looks at Harmon, "because I'm sure they do, give them a hit. Just a little one. And that's an order."

"It's just weed, right?" Sheek Erasmus makes public, "I mean, I never smoked at the academy—"

"Yea," Kapoor mumbles to himself, "and everyone loves COAnàb…"

"I smoked before that," Sheek makes clear, "not at the academy. Before I was at the academy, you know? And the weed I smoked then is like this stuff, right? It's just weed, yea?"

"No, constable," Egelblöm shakes her head, "it is not, 'just weed'," her wheelchair swivels ninety degrees, "but you're about to find out, aren't you?"

Kapoor rolls a few baby blunts, like, baby blunts. Even a softy like Tubaniña could take one of these. Kapoor shares them out, but Harmon declines. "I'm fine thanks."

Erasmus grips the blunt and lights it. "You sure?" he splutters, "this is good shit."

"I'm all right," Harmon interrupts.

Kapoor dabs a nod of approval. Meanwhile, Lewbâdak, Erasmus and Nertúny get spaced. The first to fall is, obviously, Erasmus, who wouldn't know a cannabinoid if it danced naked in front of him exposing its medicinal properties. He starts to go through that bullshit rookie stage, that is, the dire maintenance of some sort of groovy, freeloading spirit. It's a kind of liar's paradox: a sign hung around his neck may say, "I'm sober," while a sign posted to the floppy back of his bullet-proof vest may say, alternatively, "I'm really high," and so the two factoids coexist in contradiction. "You ain't gonna party sergeant?" Q.E.D.

"I've done quite enough," Kapoor declares, "had to drag myself out of it a few times."

"It's mellow," Erasmus teases, "like an otter."

The sergeant asks if he's a seasoned smoker, which Erasmus gawks at as if he was asked if he's ever had sex with children. "No, man, only at school," he argues, maintaining a goofy smile, "are you playing music?"

Kapoor chuckles, like he just showed up from the Ionian School.

"No, seriously, man," Erasmus asks, "are you playing music?"

"There's no music, constable. You're imagining it."

This pisses Erasmus off. "Yea there is," he insists, "it's Schnipple My Dipple by Let Dogs Run."

"You talk a tremendous amount of bollocks," Kapoor says.

"Schipple My Dipple? You never heard it? Let Dogs Run? Kind of punky?"

Kapoor says, "No."

"Well, listen now, it's playing, turn it up—"

"It's not," Kapoor hopes to clear up, "there's no music playing."

"You're a liar and a charlatan!"

The sergeant sighs. "Oh boy…"

One of the most culturally enmeshed uses of cannabis is on the Indian subcontinent where high-caste Hindus are allowed *Bhang*, a chewable cannabinoid, at religious ceremonies; monk-like individuals, *Sadhus*, use Bhang to focus their thoughts on the seraphic, and to tolerate their often foodless fasting. In turn, Keralan fishermen smoke *Ganja*, that is, compressed female flower heads, to diminish fatigue, which is generally looked down upon by the middle classes…

◊

Suddenly, Harmon, now covered from head to toe in riot gear, says, "What was that?" He's holding a Colt AR-15 assault rifle. Elsewhere, Egelblöm leads Lewbâdak, Erasmus and Nertúny along with twenty other officers into a raid tank, which is a large, rectangular vehicle used in drug busts and other tasty activities by the S.B. Police Force.

Sergeant Kapoor stares at Harmon, replying, "What was what?"

"That," the recruit says, "it was like a whole bunch of time just lapsed."

"It did."

"What do you mean?"

"That's how time works," Kapoor chortles, "you daft?"

"No, it's different," Harmon shakes his head, his helmet bobbling, "what have we been doing since the briefing?"

"We need to get in the raid tank like pronto."

"I want answers!"

"Jesus Christ, all right," the sergeant caves, "hop up front with me and we'll talk," they both climb in, shut the bulkhead, crouch past the twenty-three officers sat along the sides and Egelblöm attired in full authoritarian regalia, and settle into the cockpit, "besides," Kapoor adds, "you're gonna see some cool shit from here."

He shuts the cockpit door. "You kids blacked out," he presses a big red button, which has **START** written, boldly, on top, "buckle up." Harmon buckles up, and changes the subject, "Is this diesel?"

"Oh, so now the engine's got your attention? Can't blame you."

"Aren't these things illegal?"

"Yep. Hold on to your helmet." He rams his foot in the accelerator, and the raid tank shoots out the depository gates, careering up a gravel road and tanking off into the wastelands.

◊

Two drug dealers, Zachary Mullein and Ropo Adeyemi, sit counting money on chairs made out of blocks of D.E.R.P., which, with reference to this particular flat, is what Adeyemi's gone for in terms of domestic aesthetic, thanks, it must be said, to one kebab-shop owner Jean-Marc "Hijira" Maalouf operating in London. Accompanying their money-counting is the beautiful-but-a-wee-bit-highfalutin music of Ulysses Lachnér: erstwhile Presbyterian leader, composer and reader of molecular pathology in England, who on return to Scotland became a radical member of the Scottish Federal Assembly (S.F.A.), a supporter of Ainsley Cromwell's, *"Ourselves, Alone,"* movement, an ex-member of the S.F.A., and subsequent leader of the Presbyterian-but-not-really Belt Guild; instrumental in the recognition of the S.B. as one legitimate and independent nation-state. Lachnér served as its Viceroy-General for four and a half years until his death from pneumonia in 2068. He also composed a bit of music on the side—Mullein tries to ignore this offender of the saxophone quartet persuasion by saying, "When's the Alchemist coming?"

Adeyemi's eyebrows go up. "Who?"

"The Alchemist, you know?"

"What in the goddamn hell are you talking about?"

"I need her to tell me if I'm dogging or not."

Adeyemi rolls his eyes. "You're not dogging, mate."

"I don't much want to put it to the test either."

"Yea," Adeyemi snorts, "how's this," he cocks his Walther P-22 and points it at Mullein's groin, "how about I put things to the test?"

Mullein laughs, like he's cool with having a loaded weapon pointed at his dick.

"Or you could ask the police," Adeyemi suggests, "yea, that's it. Get them in here right now—"

The back of the raid tank smashes through the apartment wall. Zach and Ropo scamper with a few rolls of money as concrete and plaster flies everywhere. The bulkhead opens, and the back of the raid tank flops on the ground. Police flood out, Egelblöm trailing behind. "They're not alone," she shouts, "there should be twelve of them!" Guns go off. The house is immediately saturated with the screams of hookers. Garthman Lewbâdak leans around the corner to fire back, but a bullet rips through his helmet. Blood paints Constable Eli Reggol, who kicks the dead recruit over, saying, quickly, "Should've read the papers." He unloads several rounds into the guilty doorway opposite. A hallway or two over, at the bottom of the staircase, Mullein cocks his AMT Hardballer handgun. He runs upstairs into the master bedroom where he's faced with two terrified pink-haired fish-netted hookers. He shoots both in the head and wipes the handle with a cloth. He places the gun next to a lifeless hand. Then he jumps out the window. Downstairs, Adeyemi shoots Varsity Nertúny in the shoulder, and reloads his Walther P-22. "Motherfucker runs off on me," he mutters to himself, looking up at the ceiling, "I bet you're hiding up there." Nertúny appears from around the corner with a dagger aimed at Adeyemi's chest, but the dealer launches his palm into the constable's jaw and shatters it. Nertúny falls flat on his face. Adeyemi shoots him in the back. Kapoor removes the Nigerian's head with a shotgun blast, and turns, fleetingly, to Egelblöm. He gives her a thumbs-up, a gesture she promptly returns. On the roof, Mullein slides down the cheap panelling onto the ground. He throws a roll of money in the neighbour's backyard, and runs out to the wastelands. The dark swallows him alive.

Downstairs, Kapoor struts with the arrogance of a bonobo, periodically scratching his crotch. "Reggol," he orders, "make sure upstairs is neat."

"Erasmus," Reggol says to the recruit, "with me." The latter tracks the weathered cop upstairs.

Kapoor hastily turns to Harmon, asking if he's all right. Harmon examines the cheap décor. He can see the screws holding the chairs together, edging out of their sockets from wear-and-tear. It's an easy fix, but everyone's too doped up to care about mending furniture. Either that, or they're too busy considering four-dimensionalism and whether or not anything truly exists (temporally, that is) at any one time during its existence. For example, a rimless bottlenecked cartridge plunks in Harmon's forehead, killing him instantly.

On that note, almost exactly the same thing happened to the Nicaraguan President Emelda Villaverde who led the Fundamentalist Opposition from 2028-2037 when it defeated the Liberals, and she succeeded Antonio Bardabadas as President. Villaverde was a woman of great integrity, but inflexible. She lacked Bardabadas' ability to understand or rather sympathize with Nicaraguan-Albanian aspirations, or working-class demands, which, as a result, filled her period of office with intensifications of financial strife and increased ethnic unrest. In particular, anarchy was extrapolated from the growing Albanian population, culminating in the bloody Matagulpa Strike of 2037 during which, on the way to address protestors storming microchip mills in surrounding areas like La Garita and Solingalpa, one Tiberius Q. Tubaniña shot Villaverde in the head.

The oddest element of this whole event occurred prior to the shooting when Emelda, exiting the National Assembly in Managua, stood for a brief time in the sunlight, and said, to herself, softly, "Veré claramente después de esto, creo…" immediately after which her forehead was blown off.

Belgium/London

1:32 p.m., Croix-Michel, Belgium.

Yanis Van Hoof is running through a field of sunflowers outside of Liège because a group of far right protestors crashed the registry office where he was trying to marry his long-term boyfriend Emiel Petit, who performs acoustic Thato Nikosi covers at the on-campus Muchos Frijoles at Université de Liège.

But now, legs hotfoot through stalks, petals, ligules, filaments, anthers, sepals, receptacles, scales, peduncles, ovules, styles, stigmas, phyllaries, stamens and pistils.

Inside, there are corollas and ovaries of ray and disk flowers. Pulling out, away from that we see the photosynthesized heft of green bracts dragging flowers down. Below, feet sling in dirt, an average molecule of which may be illustrated thus: $C_{349}H_{401}N_{26}O_{173}S$ or we can go totally empirical and say that a weak Humic acid forms the majority of dirt with Carboxylic, Phenolix, Alcoholic, Quinonic, Ketone and Methoxl groupings. Saccharides also, hexapeptides of proteinaceous material (bits of H_2O) and aromatic carbon: hydrocarbon, single/double bonded carbon atom rings dancing in miniature microscopic voids of matter.

11:51 a.m., en route to Croix-Michel.

Yanis is sat in his kitchen, watching television. There are reports of protests near the registration office. He adjusts his watch, sucks his teeth and tightens his tie. His fiancée enters the room, fiddling with his cufflinks. Duck quacks penetrate the open window, providing a sort of Gaia-type reassurance, the type found in the exterior seating of Muchos Frijoles, scattered with inexpensive wooden chairs and ashtrays. Emiel puts his hand on his fiancé's shoulder. "Es-tu prêt?" Yanis grinds his teeth. He looks down at his shirt. It's not quite white; a grey scale string wrapped around him. It's tight. He's already started to sweat. "Oui."

"Nous serons en sécurité à la fête."

Yanis looks at his fiancé. "*Allons*-nous?"

Emiel does one of those quick nostril bursts. "Oui, allons-y. N'aies pas peur."

Yanis stands up, frightened, obviously—Can you criticize someone for being scared? It's more of a case of highlighting how said fear isn't necessary. And this isn't a telling-off so much as an in-context alert, a scaring-back-to-reality via reassurance, anti-fear, then apathy, courage-cum-lethargy and coasting. The TV is turned off.

Outside, the car doors open, and they both step in. Emiel drives while Yanis pivots his thumbs. They leave Rue de Chera through Cortil. Then they drive on to N689 and join the N30, then the N62 at Beaufays. The windows go up, and Emiel looks at Yanis. "Hey, vous voulez de la musique?"

"Non."

"Nous avons besoin de musique. Se détendre."

"Comment puis-je me détendre quand les gens veulent nous tuer?" Yanis complains.

Emiel leans over the steering wheel. The sun fills his face. "C'est une belle journée."

Yanis cuts his eyes. "Tu es fou."

Emiel tells him to shut up. The radio is turned on and tuned to a channel playing *Original Israeli* by Harari, an Israeli rapper based in London. Oh, that rugged post-Neoreggae sound. A minor, B flat, G flat—Then, poetry.

> I'm going hard on this Hanukkah
> You light a candle nigga
> Call my ugly ass a cracker
> I concur so pull the trigger

As a rapper, Harari is infinitely subtle with half beats scattered and continual movement. There are no clean prophets in Hip-Hop. Only *dirty* prophets.

Right now, Yanis is trying to figure out what type of prophet his aunt is: The Archbishop of Mechelen-Brussels Her Eminence Dominique Van Hoof. She doesn't pump out Hip-Hop albums. She leads this far right anti-L.G.B.T.Q.+ movement across the country, the majority of the anger being south of Brussels and closer to Luxembourg. And she doesn't lead in a Lieutenant-General-Sir-Thomas-Picton-type-of-way; rather she's more of an Air Chief Marshall Sir Pranav Witherspoon.

Assuming there are no clean prophets, because by nature of being a prophet there's something worth prophesying ergo something worth complaining about, is Auntie Dominique a bona-fide dirty old prophet? There's another type we haven't covered. The false prophet. The liar. He or she who chooses easy passage, easy because complaining, *real* complaining is bloody difficult. (Just ask any member of the opposition in the U.K.)

> Let the self-hate be profligate
> Anti-Semitism disseminate—NAH!
> I'm jokin', when I talk
> The rabbi chokin

She's a false prophet then, Yanis thinks.

"Yanis."

But tell that to her followers. She's got representatives from the three most important human factions: radicals, statesmen and women.

"Yanis…"

> Truth hurts
> Me flirts
> Pussy squirts

She's probably a repressed lesbian.

"Yanis!" Emiel slaps his fiancé's thigh as a police car overtakes them.

"Quelle?"

"Réveillez-vous, nous sommes ici," Emiel says as Yanis rubs his eyes, "d'accord?"

Yanis mumbles, "Tante Dominique?"

Emiel looks ahead, replying, assuringly, "Baise-la."

The registry office is in an old converted farmhouse with an added two stories. It looks more like an embassy; especially given that Gendarmerie surround the building. The Belgian Gendarmerie were abolished in 2001, but reinstated in 2079 after a series of Buddhist terrorist attacks involving napalm. In addition to those shitty police vans with the tiny wheels, the officers wear scallop caps and blue shirts. They tuck their trouser legs in their boots—to their right is another group of fully armoured Gendarmerie with batons in back-slings and HK416 assault rifles.

Inside, Chief Registrar Lina Noël waiting for her first appointment: Emiel and Yanis. She watches the Gendarmerie and the forty-four protesters through the window. The protestors carry no signs, only themselves. They are, in effect, the most dangerous kind of protester. By showing up somewhere, Noël thinks, you've already made a statement. The addition of a physical footnote like a placard adds nothing to one's ideological table, whereby all the legs have been infringed by a new piece of anti-leg legislation that you totally don't agree with, and so then you feel the need to not only show up to the respective anti-anti-leg legislation demonstration, but also to bring a placard outlining your position, Noël concludes.

The protesters spit and laugh. Two women are playing chess under a tree. The tall one forfeits when they see Emiel and Yanis roll up. One Gendarmerie officer addresses his men. "Agréable et facile…" Gay marriage has been legal for years. Then the, "far right," woke up. There'd be heterosexual couples getting married, and there they'd be, calling them fag enablers. It happens in cycles. People get too comfy, or they think they do. The most horrible things carried out by humans can be blamed on one, that's all it takes, one semi-intelligent individual, who for some reason forgets how good their life actually is, and so they start looking for reasons for their unhappiness, which are usually imagined and/or purely paranoiac. And so the Gendarmerie seal together, forming a wall between crowd and car. Cups of coffee are launched. The two fiancées scuttle inside as the crowd attacks the Gendarmerie. Batons are laid into skulls. Bodies are crushed against the building.

"Pousser!"

Legs are kicked.

Stomachs are punched.

"Putain de fascists!"

Eyes are poked.

Inspecteur Laurent Goossens, the oldest Gendarmerie there, reckons he hasn't seen anything like this since 2079. He fires his rifle at the sky, but that just pisses the protestors off.

Yanis and Emiel give each other nervous periodic glances in Lina's office. She stubs out her Ölümsüz cigarette, and stands up from her desk. "Excusez moi." She leaves the room, and stands outside. She looks at her colleague, down the hall, standing in front of the double-locked entrance. "Marcel," she asserts, "éloigne-toi de la porte." Marcel smiles. The door blows open. Several bullets go into Marcel's chest and he pops. Lina Noël screams with her patrons as protestors fill the corridor, their feet squeaking across the clean white tile.

In the office the two fiancées spring up. Yanis examines the available exits. *That door might go through to another office,* he thinks. *Maybe outside.* Emiel examines the available weapons. He considers using Noël's desktop computer keyboard as a bat, or maybe his chair as a battering ram. Yanis starts to run but his fiancé grabs his arm. "Où vas-tu?"

"Je ne veux pas mourir!"

"Restez avec moi!"

Yanis shakes his head. "N-non, courir!"

In the corridor, those two chess players pull Lina's hair—If you get an angry person and map their brains with an M.R.I. scan, you'll find that the putamen and insular cortex are lit up like Harrods. Now give that angry person a photo of a loved one, and you'll see how nothing changes. The M.R.I. is the same. And if you get an erection or your nipples get hard during the M.R.I., don't worry. It's okay. The putamen controls movement too. But dig this, your frontal cortex, the judgement and critical thinking bit, does jack-diddle when you're in love. But if you hate someone or something, lesbians or daytime television, for example, your frontal cortex is alive and well. Therefore, hate is not an expeditious reaction. On the contrary, there's a great deal of mentation and coherence

of thought. But try telling that to someone who's had a gun
barrel shoved down their throat.

Three bullet wounds snap across Noël's chest and she falls
over dead, squeaking like bare feet across the tile. Office work-
ers are running for the hills. There's a small fire in the corner.
Someone aims a barrel in Emiel's direction. They pull the trigger. Outside, Yanis sprints through the forest; twig snap, leaf
up, branch down, shrub stare, weed lick, chest up and down,
puff out, suck in and subsequent lung pain. He runs out of the
wood and into a sunflower field.

The shade stops.

There's a tree in the middle, and Van Hoof, suddenly, feels
an emotion that doesn't exist.

◊

King George VII monuments himself in the music room
at Buckingham palace. It's raining outside. The King is an
accomplished pianist; accomplished inasmuch as he can play.
The pervasive structuring of notes and scales fills his head con-
stantly. That type of expression gets locked in. The King can
play a song halfway through, have a long, a very long, weekend in Berkshire, fly back home and pick up where he left off
with an ease envied by amateur architects and gigolos. Music
validates that spooky filler of existence, invariably confirming
that any interpretation is greater than that which is interpreted,
that is to say, music makes music: the whistler gets it right after
lunch; the singer in the shower nails it halfway through; those
awful childrens' violin recitals end up becoming things of pro-
found beauty.

The monarchy, even, has a way of singing. In the beginning, the institution is grown to represent something tactile.

Then it becomes like a dog whistle: silent, but sharp. Ideas are left to fend on their own. Monarchies are literally far out.

Maurice Parent O.B.E. and Master Of The Household To The Sovereign Currently Staring Out A Window, enters the music room. His shoes clomp across the floor, and are punctuated by the attention-grabbing cough of a guy who knows his ass from his elbow.

The King turns, greeting, "Maurice," he smiles like he hasn't seen sunlight in three thousand eight hundred and forty-two years, "how can I help you?"

"Phone call, sire."

George hates phone calls: bearers of great and bad fucking news, and so, as you can imagine, then, The King unaccountably hates adult life.

"What type of phone call?" the King asks, wisely.

Maurice, trying desperately not to use a term of endearment concerning custard, says, "His Majesty Nicolas, sire."

"Oh Nicky," he takes the phone, "thank you, Maurice." The master makes to leave, and George waves at him, motioning for him to stay.

The King returns to his window, beginning, "Hallo Nick. Es regnet hier. Was ist mit dort? Ich habe heute keine Verpflichtungen. Ich bin in meinem Lieblingszimmer…ja…spannende Tage."

There's a pause. George's face lowers. "Du hörst dich müde an. Was ist da los?"

Over by the couch, Maurice picks at his cuticles. He listens to The King's replies.

"Ja?" He puts his left hand in his pocket. "Nein, der nicht gut ist. Sie sollten es nennen, was es ist…das sollten Sie tun. Gesunder Menshenverstand, Nicky."

His seventy-six year old back muscles begin to tense beneath the gabardine jacket. "Ja, ich weiß dass ich nicht verhe-iratet bin. Ich bin mir dessen bewusst." He clears his throat. "Nein, ich bin nicht böse auf dich – w-was singen sie?" Maurice Parent is fluent in German and tuned in.

The King starts speaking in English. "This isn't my fault Nicky. Yes, yes you can. I know you speak English. Don't lie to me," he turns red, "but you know how to say, 'fuck,' I—" George ends the call. The final sounds of an angry Belgian echo around the room. Flecks of rain collide with the window. Maurice walks over to The King to retrieve the phone. The Royal runs his hand through his ginger beard. He says to Maurice, sombrely, "I need to be alone."

"Yes," he nods, "sire." He leaves the King by the window and shuts the door behind him.

George sinks forward. Tears run down his face onto the carpet. He lifts his hands up and splats them on the window.

"Let me out," he whispers, "God, let me out."

Parent patrols His Majesty's Kitchen. The TV is blaring E.T. News. There are scenes of demonstrations in Belgium with agitators singing, "Le roi Anglais a sucé une bite!"

Parent picks up the remote and changes the channel to C.C.B. News. He tosses it back on the table, and turns to face the Chef de Cuisine, Sous Chef, Pâtissier, Chef de Partie, Sauc-ier, Poissonier, Entremetier, Rotisseur, Gard Manger, Commis, Expediter and fry cook, who gradually cease yelling, preparing, baking, grilling, tasting, fishing, dicing, roasting, cooling, plat-ing, waiting and frying. Parent points at the television. "From now on," he orders, dryly, "the TV stays on this channel. Is that understood?"

There's an awkward murmur of affirmation. Maurice ex-its, brushing his crotch free of dust and other fine powders. As such, there are certain people who are tasked with holding everything together. They dot civilization like dairy-milk buttons. Maurice is one of them.

In Belgium, a chopper of the CH-47 Chinook variety lands in the grassy bit in Parc de Bruxelles. It's been sectioned off. The Van Hoof people picket the perimeter. They throw one-liners and Molotov cocktails. The Belgian State Security Service or *Veiligheid van de Staat* (V.S.S.E.) surrounds the helicopter opposite the Belgian Federal Parliament building. The building itself is currently undergoing refurbishment, overseen by the Bureau of Architecture, Research and Design, making it impossible to drive any sort of official car through, hence the helicopter.

The hatch opens and the ladder drops. The Prime Minister Clement Verlinden and the Minister of Defence Yana Verhoven get out. They are beetled over the lawn by the V.S.S.E., and cross Rue de la Loi. They enter the Parliament's courtyard. Civil servants stand like lollypop men in the parliamentary lobby. Verlinden looks over Verhoven's shoulder addressing a series of advisors. Then he looks at Yana and says, "Nous irons bien, allons-y." As they climb the refurbished marble stairs to the cabinet room, Clement is confronted by Minister of the Interior Jayden Geert de Lambrechts. "Er is nog een aanval geweest in Namen."

"Laten we erover praten," Verlinden says, soberly.

"En al de koffie is weg."

"Actually," Verlinden replies, "from now on, English, I want everything in English. We don't know who's listening," he puts his arm around Jayden, "as for the coffee, we'll have to manage without it."

Upon entering the cabinet room, they are faced with total cacophony. Robbe Peeters, Secretary of State for Asylum and Migration, jams his middle finger in Ines Dupont-Desmet, the

Minister of Finance and Fiscal Fraud's chest, ranting about how all of this is actually a ploy by Her Eminence Van Hoof to let in a whole bunch of, "*Nègre de sable*". Dupont-Desmet discards that comment with the flap of one withered hand, arguing instead that Van Hoof has several dodgy bank accounts in Belgium and Switzerland, and how this basically constitutes a breach in national coffer security and, look, I'm not even gonna bother explaining what Ines thinks. Find someone who can explain economics to me, and I'll meet them halfway with a unicorn.

Anouk Van de Velde, the Minister of the Middle Class and Self-Employed, tries to ignore current issues altogether. She snivels up to Daan Coppens, Minister of Budget, complaining that the country needs to subsidise the building of basements in highly populated areas, which should, in theory, raise house prices. Why she wants to do this, I have no idea. Maxim Cools, Minister of Pensions, sees where this conversation is going and interjects, appropriately, "Mais voulons-nous être une nation d'acheteurs, ou de vendeurs?"

Mauro Baert, Secretary of State for Equal Rights and Poverty, is talking about his toe fungus, which as any sexually frustrated podiatrist will tell you, can be decimated with lasers, but on your own borrowed time and money. Baert complains that Belgian Healthcare doesn't cover optical amplification i.e. lasers. Then again, there's no reason why you should trust anything said by a man who wears an ushanka indoors.

Verlinden and Verhoven, who are actually married, sit down and settle the cabinet. Verlinden peels apart a Euro-politik smile, from temple to temple. This sprout can grin. "English, please," he says, rather seriously, "we're faced with a crisis on our hands. This, uh, movement has gained momentum with the likes of which we've never seen before. We need to stamp it out, simply, and what I want from you…"

"Warum müssen wir auf Englisch sprechen?" Minister of Foreign Affairs Océane Bosmans interrupts.

"Because we might be under surveillance," Verlinden repeats as before.

Minister of Energy Anke Janssen laughs, interrupting, "Al deze renovatie is naar Clement's hoofd gegaan!"

Verlinder raises his fist and slams the table three times. The room becomes silent. Yana Verhoven rubs her temples, imagining herself in a field not unlike the one we left Yanis in.

"Things have gone mad here," Verlinder states, leaning over the table, "and we must be prepared to accept how mad things really are. If we can't do that, there will be civil war," the cabinet turns white(er), "and I have no interest in going down in history as the greatest tyrant since Emmanuel Macron. An ideological border has been formed, it stretches…"

"…from Tournai…"

◊

In 2014, Belgium nominated its first poet laureate, Lucie Janssens. The current poet laureate, however, is Muhammad Albronda, author of *Caicos Butterflies* (2072) and *Two Poems In Abun* (2086). He lives in Tournai in a totally bare apartment. He wakes up with bits of dream falling out of his ears. He gets up quick, pen to paper. It won't be good, but something like it. He drinks coffee, and eats a bowl of muesli. Opening his shutters, he sees people packing their cars and leaving town. They're verbally abused by passers-bys dressed in wife-beaters.

Coffee and injustice go well together, he thinks. There's nothing like an artist getting pissed off with a cup of coffee in their hand. He looks at the piece of paper and picks up his pen. Scribbling once more, he wipes the sweat off his forehead and pulls his fingers through his goatee. He finishes the lines, which read:

> Two girls pack up their things
> Lay them flat like fishes.
> Two girls pack up their things
> Call no men with badges.

Good poets do not deter.

"…to Liège…" Parc de la Boverie fills up with L.G.B.T.Q.+ refugees. There are many rows of tents and boats full of suitcases, dogs, same-sex couples with children, transvestites and pangenders that cross the canal, landing in the park. But they're not arriving. They're running from something. With this in mind, in Tournai, Muhammad starts writing the second stanza:

> Blood is on my bored hands
> My fingers touch each breast.

In the park, transgender women defecate in cans, lesbians urinate under trees, and gay men bathe in the canal if they can avoid being bottled by the people protesting their arrival on the other side. Threesomes of bisexual teenagers, without a care in the world, touch each other, laughing under the summer moon, cracking cans of lager open. A cross-dresser clips her nails.

Yanis Van Hoof, completely naked, reads the *Communist Manifesto* in his one-man tent. Book on cock, he rubs his cheeks and smells his palms. Beads of sweat roll down his olive skin. He breathes and his belly goes up and down. Muhammad keeps scribbling in Tournai, into the night.

> Blood is on my hetero hands
> Do nothing, Muhammad.

Tomorrow, the refugees will pack up and march north to Tongeren, or, *Aduatuca Tungrorum*, as it was known under Roman ownership. The oldest city in Europe; you can see it in the buildings. The structures are commonplace, like sulphur.

It's May, Yanis thinks. May the month, and yearly position. If there's a May there'll be a June. And if there's a June there'll be a July. And in the words of the early 20th Century philosopher-cum-dairy product Slavoj Zizek, "And so on, and so on..."

"...to Bastogne..."

Bastogne becomes the two-way city. The L.G.B.T.Q.+ community rides out through Marvie and flood into Luxembourg. What Van Hoof supporters there are in Luxembourg drive past the former group and settle in Harzy, Benonchamp and Mageret. Each side throws insults at the other. There are acts of public obscenity. Two old queens go for it on top of their mint green Fiat. The roof buckles under their sagging buttocks. Muhammad Albronda re-drafts his poem in Tournai, adding things, like:

> I lost you like a mind
> Left by men with clenched fists.

The Van Hoofite demonstrations take the form of uninspired miming involving food and other household items. One of these is the all-time No. 1: The Hotdog In The Bagel Hole. The face behind it is indicative of an aseptic odium chilled below sea level like Martian H_2O, bereft of the Albrondan songs of self-flagellation.

> I lost you like my mind
> Broken by slit Belgian wrists…

In Brussels, Océane Bosmans folds her arms. "Und Luxembourg? Where do they stand?"

As she does this, Muhammad Albronda reads the final stanza to himself.

> How far this raw reaches?
> Luxembourg, through East?
> "Tomorrow, do again?"
> I asked the downcast priest.
> She laughed, and wiped her hands:
> "That I do. That is the least."

"Luxembourg is sane," Verlinder clarifies, "they agree with our policies, views. There's a clear border, ideological and physical, between Luxembourg and the extreme south. There's nothing to worry about, I would argue, as I'm sure Yana would. But Luxembourg is not Belgium. And neither is Van Hoof, although she'd like to think it. But she is dangerous. And as far as her support is concerned, it's growing at a frightening pace," he looks at Yana, and then his cabinet, "we need to play it safe."

Albronda completes his poem. He puts his pen behind his ear. A dead Ölümsüz cigarette sits like Emiel's corpse in that registry office. Albronda sees history in his cigarette: a shape of time, and question marks grammar-clung like paint mucking downwards to nothing.

Dirty floors aren't funny. They're terrible, normal things covered in histories. It's like you're stepping on the faces of David Starkey and François Furet: old, dead men, who said,

"This is the truth of the matter. This is what happened. And after that, this happened."

Cigarette butts tell stories. In those stories, people smoke. Albronda types up the poem. He deletes words and plunders his thesaurus. He indents three sentences. It's finished. He emails it, in protest, to the office of His Majesty Nicolas, King of The Belgians. After he does this, Albronda lights another Ölümsüz, humming three notes to himself: C, B and A. He turns to look out of his window.

◊

In London, simultaneously, let's push into Houghton Street, WD3A 9AF.

The London Schools of Political Science and Economics (L.E.S.).

Push into Meak House.

Push through the concrete, brick and steel into the Zilber-schlag Theatre, where someone is giving a speech. "And that is the model of resilience and patience, which must be maintained should there ever be conflict in Europe…"

The speaker's podium is preceded by six rows, the sixth of which supports the well-fed backsides of pseudo-Marxists with thin beards who stare at the ceiling, hoping their collective collectivism collapses the dull white roof on the guest speaker.

"The Great Britain we know today was thrust into the wastelands in a vote of independence from the European Union. But we have learnt, evolved and become something new, as all countries must in the Madame Tussauds exhibit that is world history…"

The fifth row is full of neo-Blairites who get annoyed at the pseudo-Marxists behind them who grunt contracted assertions like, "AHEMsocialismworks…"

The fourth row Holists observe their own sandal-clad feet on the emblazoned wood panelling, which was probably supplied by the third row's ancestors: The Northern Green Belt offenders: students from Leeds, Preston, the great shipping city of Whitehaven with pairs of limbs crossed in arrogance, the crossing indicative of Scottish chieftain rather than Eton toff, however.

"But of course we have I.T.C.B. You see, the honey pot before you has many fingers being dipped in and out of it on any given day. So if we were to have a nuclear conflict, that dipping would end. Demand would cease, followed immediately by supply. And bear in mind that that is our legacy as a species. It is regressive and destructive to consign one's legacy to the arms of the skeleton in one's closet…"

The second row can be reduced to a series of place-names: Wiltshire. Somerset. Reading. Working. Crawley.

One Julian Gamby-Dixon Esq will visit High St Kensington after this lecture to purchase the same shoes worn by the guest speaker. Gamby-Dixon fingers will circumnavigate the expensive threading. He'll touch the throat line above the welt and heel. He'll examine the anal guise of the eyelets and think to himself, "I am this shoe." And so it is by grace of credit, through coin-inventory, that people like Gamby-Dixon can remember their fucking names.

"If war is the only option then let it be contained and finite. Don't involve the world community. Don't involve your neighbours. Unless of course they're the ones you're fighting for whatever valid reason. Because it must to be valid. But there is nothing valid about the destruction of a species by that species. Show me someone who argues the opposite, and I'll show you a liar…"

The first row of the Zilberschlag Theatre seats Reactionary advisers Sami Toller-Wallace and Faisal Reddy, along with
three reporters, one of whom is from L.E.S.'s student union
newspaper, *The Platypus*, so not really a reporter so much as a
propagandist, which knocks it down to two reporters. There
are, in addition, three lecturers in politics: Professor Elise Ee-
ikenboom (a Belgian), Professor Octavio Winthrop, and Dr
Jack Hearst. There is also a man with a moustache. Be wary of
men with facial hair—Or not.

The guest speaker is none other than Foreign Secretary
The Rt. Hon Conall Tuckey MP: "It is the job of our generation to preserve this human contract, this sapiens doctrine,
this logically empathetic way of life." His reedy voice stabs the
air-conditioned atmosphere. It bends the glass coddling the
galleries.

"And British diplomacy will be on the front line of this philosophy," he finishes, "thank you very much." His eyes lower to
Reddy and Toller-Wallace in a "how-did-I-do?" kind of way.

Faisal puts his thumbs up.

Sami flares her nostrils. It would be good to explain why
a British civil servant just spoke on the topic of Europe, Sami
thinks, but she doesn't work at I.T.C.B. Holdings plc. Tuckey
sticks his tongue out as he descends the stairs leading to the podium. He looks up at the gallery, and then at Sami, who leans
in to say, "There's gonna be a civil war in Belgium." Tuckey
bears an ultra-careful smile, the type seen when the Father of
the Bride is informed that his wife is banging the Groom in
the toilets.

"Oh yea?" Tuckey mumbles.

"Far right movement," Sami adds, "almost a party."

"Are they nationalists?"

"They're religious conservatives."

"Sam," Tuckey condescends, "I'm a religious conservative."

The Foreign Secretary may think he has this contract with long-established Protestant ideas and values with an unparalleled antagonism towards change or innovation, but he does do a hell of a lot of Christmas shopping, and plays squash in the newly added gymnasium at Harrods.

"No," Sami interjects, "but—"

"Let's, uh," Tuckey sees Professor Eikenboom rubbing her face as though she's heard the news herself, "let's talk at home, yea?"

The Foreign Secretary walks away with his advisors.

The guy with the moustache is talking to Dr Hearst, stroking it throughout the conversation.

The Foreign Secretary exits Meak House onto Aldwych road. Toller-Wallace and Reddy flank him. They turn right on to Kingsway Road, and go down to the Holborn tube station. Tuckey plugs in his ear-buds. He scrolls through the music on his phone, and settles on Hip-Hop. Dickeater, to be precise; his album, *You Lost Me At Punani* (Harari Records™, 2079), to be even more precise.

Dickeater is an openly, nay aggressively, gay Hip-Hop artist and intellectual currently signed to Harari Records™. Tuckey likes to play that seminal Dickeater track *Bucket Boy*, titled with reference to the passive partner in anal intercourse, in times of political stress. He steps on the Piccadilly line at Holborn, and presses play. The acid-jazz drumming excites him, as does the peculiar chord sequence of D major, F minor, A major and G minor. Dickeater starts rapping:

> I suck mo dick than a motherfucka
> Got ya sista in da trunk
> But I'll never fuck her

The Foreign Secretary gets off at Green Park, and hops on the Jubilee line.

> I make sure my boyfriends
> Are taller than me
> Cuz I don't want no kneepads
> Like Fernanda Li

Tuckey laughs.

> She got dat reactionary pussy
> Man you catch me in da club
> Gay crackers don't push me
> Whip out my dick face-fuck
> That face twice with my boy
> Kân-Tâpe eatin chicken-fried rice

Kân-Tâpe's a Thai rapper and frequent collaborator with Dickeater, hence the cameo and ironic ethnic slur. Consider also the didactic nature of the lyrics, the rhyme scheme composed in the hedonistic, Utton-based headquarters of Harari Records™…

◊

It's raining. P.P. O'Leary alias Toklo Aakulu, son of Greenlandic Resettlement leader H.B. Aakulu and Kalaallit Liberal Tajaq Kleist, who was both feared and respected by the S.B. government for her insistence on prerequisite land taxes to be paid prior to their resettling, insofar that her people would not be considered hypocrites by the indigenous population when it came to public services such as health care, fire brigades and food banks on the blinking cusp of town, is leering in a kitchen shop window. O'Leary considers for a moment why he came to this place. Not the kitchen shop, but Utton in general. The rich Uttonistic district stands behind him. There are restaurants full of couples sitting at tables not talking to each other. The waiters and waitresses slime the tables, their eyeballs scanning for empty plates, pocket-sized tips and dirty napkins. The self-titled O'Leary peers back at the kitchen shop display. He doesn't need any of this shit. But you always have to act like you're doing something, or going somewhere, when you're alone on the street. And you've lost your comfy television-presenting job. And all you can do is postulate yourself through an evening of visual retail therapy, alone.

"Paul?" O'Leary jerks his nut and says, "Call me Toklo," to no one in particular.

"I scared you, man," British Culture Secretary Piers Meak says, "how are you?"

"It's uh, *Piers*, isn't it?"

"Yea, man, how are you?" shaking O'Leary's hand and smiling, "need some pans?"

"What? Oh yea, no. I was just, you know…"

Piers chuckles, noting, "What do I know?"

"Looking," P.P. mumbles.

"Fair," Meak nods, "where you headed?"

"I was just, uh, going for a walk."

"You live 'round here?"

"Yea."

"Course you do, don't you?" grinning again and running his right palm through his wet hair, "what are you doing these days? You still doing Sky-Watcher?"

"That?" O'Leary almost vomits, "no, that's all done now," staring briefly at a bread knife in the window, the 25 cm X97.5 Anti-Flour Bread Knife with an old-lavender handle. "Sorry," he points to nowhere, "I'll let you go, I gotta get back home."

"Hold up man," the cabinet minister says, "you all right?"

"What?"

"Are you okay? You look exhausted," he puts his hands in his pockets, staring up P. P. O'Leary's emaciated nostrils, "you good, amigo?"

"Yea, I just remembered, uh, I didn't clean up after dinner so I should probably—"

"Can I ask you something," Piers clears his throat, "you like hip-hop?"

◊

Harari Records™ is a block or two from that kitchen shop. Tonight, a party's being thrown for Big Riddim, whose debut album *Insult me, suck Bullet*© went platinum in seven minutes. Harari Records™ is pretty cock-a-hoop about this, as you can imagine, along with the album's producer Piers Meak.

The elevator up is made of mirrors. There are infinite O'Learys and infinite Meaks. The latter turns to the former to address this sorcery de décor. "Do you know what infinity multiplied by zero is?" O' Leary looks at the man, sadly.

"Zero?"

"No, man," Piers informs, "it's zero."

"That's what I just—"

"Infinity times zero is zero," nodding as though he's just won a regional mathematics competition, "fucked up, innit?"

The two men reach the fourteenth alias tippity-top floor,

and walk into the offices of Harari Records™: Meak's entrance is applauded by various accountants, secretaries and investors, and some rappers, I guess—But mostly I.T.C.B. Holdings plc- or COAnàb-related individuals, like Carlos Apple-Tennyson.

Meak leans over to P. P. O'Leary, and says, "Yabani's a *big* fan of yours."

"Who's that?"

"Big Riddim."

"Meaning?"

"No," the culture secretary shakes his head, *"Big Riddim's a big a fan of yours."*

"Oh," O'Leary raises his eyebrows, "that's a person."

"It's his party—Yabani—!" He hugs Big Riddim. The young artist spits fiyah.

> Gotta say hello
> To my white Negro

The producer shrugs, modestly. "You should be proud of yourself," he congratulates, downing his champagne, "the album's sound my ni—" the room goes silent as Piers makes a fatal mistake, "nihhhhhhh," Big Riddim's face depicts many levels of thunder, "nihhhhhhh," P. P. O'Leary covers his mouth, awaiting the inevitable doom, *"nigggg,"* Piers is *literally* turning red, "NIGGegligee is not where it used to be."

There's a terrible silence.

Big Riddim starts laughing. Everything returns to normal. "Come on, man," he says, acting as if nothing remotely racially insensitive just happened, "I got the words, you got the music; you put that shit together in a blender," Riddim does a blender impression, "and boom! Masterpiece." For the next few minutes they talk about stuff for which P. P. O'Leary has absolutely no frame of reference, like that time when Dickeater came into the studio with a loaded elephant gun. Or that time when Big Riddim's pants fell down during a take. Or that time when Yachel Harari himself entered the recording studio with a live crocodile named Fernanda.

Riddim suddenly recognizes P. P. O'Leary. "Mate," he pushes Piers Meak out of the way, gaping at the unemployed television personality, "you know P. P. O'Leary...?"

"He is, as they say," Piers tacks on smugly, "my plus-one."

Big Riddim grins like the O'Leary's Biggest Fan he is, screaming, "MATE, YOU ARE OUT THERE!"

The rapper shakes P.P. O'Leary's hand for five minutes straight, inviting him, subsequently, for a D.E.R.P. spliff.

Having now congregated in a parakeet-blue room, P.P. O'Leary is sat, quite rightly, in a furry prune-coloured throne. Big Riddim, Dickeater and Kân-Tâpe sit together on an L-shaped red couch opposite. O'Leary says, "So," as Kân-Tâpe takes a serious hit of D.E.R.P., gawking at the guest of honour, "how do you know me?"

Big Riddim beams. "You're a legend."

"Fucking unit, mate."

"Boss man."

"All I watched when I was growing up," Riddim explains, "was Sky-Watcher."

"Me too, man," Dickeater adds, "when I was at school we'd all be like, 'Yo P. P. O'Leary said some heavy shit last night,' like some meaningful shit, you know what I'm saying?"

"Damn straight," Kân-Tâpe splutters, "when I was growing up all my family spoke was Thai so the only way I could learn English was on TV and that was you man," another pensive suck on his spliff, "come home, watch Sky-Watcher – you were, like, my teacher."

Big Riddim sees this as an opportune moment to quote his album.

> You're hedging bets heavy-set
> Watching too much on the TV set
> The planets: Jupiter, Mars, aligning near me
> Bitch I fly clean like P. P. O'Leary

He laughs, affixing, "Legit, like, half the album is about you, man." The others giggle and do their little handshakes, and P. P. O'Leary just sits in his throne like the King that dropped the plum duff.

"Hey, Mister O'Leary," Kân-Tâpe asks, "you ever rap?"

Big Riddim stops laughing, saying, "Man, what the fuck?"

"You can't be askin' that shit," Dickeater agrees.

"What if you were in Mister O'Leary's house," Big Riddim posits, "and all of a sudden he start askin' you if you do TV and shit? That'd be equally offensive, ain't that right P.?"

O'Leary is terrified. "I'm not offended. It's okay."

"Nah nah nah," Big Riddim shakes his head, "but seriously, P., this chinky bitch come into your home, would you start prying if he do television and shit?"

"...Uh..." the ex-host turns white, somehow, "no, no I wouldn't."

"What you do then?" Big Riddim asks, decisively, as a flash of anger rips across his space-cadetting eyes.

O'Leary stumbles over his words. "I'd, I'd, well I'd...um, I'd respect him, and he'd respect me."

"Damn straight," Dickeater confirms, pointing at Kân-Tâpe, "that's because Mister O'Leary's a real nigga. He's been around for *years* and he's studied some crazy-ass bullshit and, therefore, he don't fuck with your broke Thai ass."

"Whatchu mean," Kân-Tâpe objects, "my album made like twice as much as yours!"

"Nigga, get out of here, *Udon Thani Grab 8 Punani* made two quid."

"Only reason your album's lucrative you sucked that nigga's dick—"

Dickeater pulls a gun out of his beltline.

He points it at Kân-Tâpe, yelling, "What the fuck you just say?"

P.P. O'Leary hides in the corner while Dickeater demands an apology from his colleague. "I'm counting to three,' he shouts, cocking the gun and aiming at Kân-Tâpe's crotch, "ONE," Kân-Tâpe hides behind a pillow, "TWO," O'Leary stands up and starts rapping:

> Don't fuck with me bitch
> I'll kill your ugly ass
> Cuz I got some money
> Something. Oh—*shit*…

Big Riddim stares at his guest, saying "Yo, P., you okay?" Tears run down O'Leary's face.

> Don't fucking kill me
> I'm unemployed, I've lost everything
> I'm a fucking loser who can't
> Bear to be an ethnic minority
> So I changed my name to P. P.
> O'Leary. I miss my friends
> And family. My wife divorced me
> Because she found somebody else

More fun to be with so how do
You think that makes me feel?
Fuck it, oh god I don't know
What I'm doing anymore.
All of it has gone to pot. Shit.

P.P. goes quiet and sits back on his throne. Kân-Tâpe, having passed out from that hit of D.E.R.P., is sprawled out on the red couch. Dickeater returns the gun to his beltline. He falls back onto the couch, next to Kân-Tâpe's feet. Big Riddim sits, briefly, on the red arm. He gets up and walks over to some speakers. He plugs an aux cable into his phone, tapping the screen. A song with a soft melody starts; then a thickening by cello, an underpinning superseded by a heavy bassline, but not too heavy, like how the sky isn't too blue. There's an occasional fluttering of chords, a parting of musical seas and minor Martian canals.

"Yea," Big Riddim nods, smiling, "that's it."

Dickeater mumbles, *"Harari, bitch."*

Kân-Tâpe is comatose.

P.P. O'Leary is, for the record, still very depressed.

◊

In Number 10 Downing Street, Conall Tuckey waves goodbye to Faisal and Sami. He almost immediately bumps into the Education Secretary Ivor Seaby.

"All right, Conall?" Seaby says.

"El Greco here?" Tuckey asks.

"Haven't seen him," Seaby says, "he'll be busy after the meeting I can tell you that."

The two ministers climb the stairs. Tuckey trips, noting,

"Whip's always busy."

"How long you reckon today?" Seaby asks. "If it's about the next election…"

"Which it is—"

"Two hours," Tuckey estimates, "at least."

"Last election was a cock-up."

"Brooke-Valentine and her lot."

"If I've learnt anything from staring at bee vee and her Pinkos," Seaby meditates, "it's that we're in dire need of seats."

"And eyeliner."

"Yea," Seaby snorts, "that too…"

Reactionary Party Chairman Joram Falack sits at the far end of the cabinet room. He doesn't look up as people arrive. His peepers are tucked in a dossier. Something tasty: a thick steak of a brief, collected, compiled, numbered, sent via courier, received and examined by an arse sat upon itself.

Joram reads a lot. He's never had a girlfriend. He actually, actively, refuses to have partners. Not in a nasty way. He vetoes relationships because he has a lot of work to do. Feels he'd never be able to put the time required aside (Note, *"aside"*.). Feels he'd be doing any partner wrong by having a partner in the first place. He's a human memorandum—In the evenings, he microwaves oats and honey for his supper and stands in his Bond Street flat garden, alone. Then he looks up. "Joram…" And up. "Falack…" He imagines the girls he knew at boarding school naked. "JORAM," the Party Chairman looks at the Home Secretary Katie Ropple-Christiansen. "You awake, Joram?"

"Yes," Falack replies, "always."

"Sorry, I know you hate this, but do you have a pen?"

"Yes," the chairman asserts, "my pen."

"A spare pen, I mean."

Joram excavates his jacket pocket, commentating, "You'll find the English language," handing her the pen, "serves you well if you—"

"Yea," Katie interrupts, "thanks."

Falack simmers back to his dossier. The day before, it's an average night in Soho.

◊

Filip Wronski and Santiago Paredes are two bouncers both averaging 7 ft. who work at Bucket's Club on Greek Street. It's 1:32 a.m. They got there at 6:46 p.m., and set up the barriers. The lights went up. The music came on. *Tampon Anthem* by Elizabethan Underworld.

BOOM-BOOM-BOOM-BA-DUMBOOM
BOOM-BOOM-BOOM-BA-DUMBOOM

Or something to that effect. And considering there are only twenty-five customers, all of whom have work tomorrow, it will probably be a 3:30 a.m. finish. Bucket's Club is owned and run by transvestite Thelonious Rothstein, who also manages the bar. Drinks are mixed as feet squish and shuffle on the bar floor. Flutes clink. Tumblers gong. Brandy sniffers are lifted, and shot glasses thud on the counter.

Rothstein discards the excess absinthe, pushes the customer's Sazerac towards them, and leans over the bar, saying, "That's thirty-five pounds."

The tallest of four women gives him a hundred pound note, and the bar owner raises his eyebrows. The till opens, regardless, and change is given. The four women migrate towards the end of the bar. They lean, and watch people dancing. The shortest woman, known professionally as Miss 89, has headphones on. She doesn't hear the lightest of bass-drops from *Tampon Anthem*, which, yes, is still playing. And the fact that *Tampon Anthem* is still playing is indicative of a trick of the trade: play a track list of forty songs for the first half of night. Then play the same track list *backwards*, followed by a few chill-out songs. Fin.

Contrastingly, Miss 89's headphones are blasting *Rabat* (Shugga Tunes™, 2037) by Teddy Akonawe, which is often credited to Thato Nikosi because the original 2029 16 rpm LP *Tenors and Moroccan Trombones* recording was reissued in 2037—2037 was at the peak of the Nikosi craze and labels wanted to make a fast buck by using his name. Nikosi plays tenor saxophone on *Rabat*, but he didn't write it; neither did the other people on the album: Kungawo Powell II, Zwane Bailey, and Maluleke "Yellow Man" Virtue. That all said, there's this dirty baritone saxophone at the beginning and a tenor trombone that slides over it, subsequently. It would plant the seed that would become Nikosi's *Meditations On Candiru Fish* [Harari Records™, 2067], which is more spiritual than all our little church books put together.

"Hey…" an inebriated voice says.

Miss 89 casts her eyes over a drunken guy standing in front of her talking. He stares at her boobs, adding, "Why are you wearing headphones?"

"I need my music," Miss 89 says in a flat Dutch accent.

"You French? Come on," the man replies, "I want to paint you."

He takes her hand and they strut to the unisex toilets, decked in red lights. Smoke is everywhere. Asses are shaken. Spit is spat. Thighs are jiggled and various glands battle cardio-vascular aptitude. Zwane Bailey's piano solo starts as they enter the unisex toilets. They find a cubicle, and in they go. She performs a dental hygiene check-up on the man with her tongue. He gets an erection faster than, say, P.P. O'Leary would. Those five G&Ts aren't helping, either. She gets his cock out and gives him a handjob with her left hand.

Bailey lets Nikosi swing in.

She yanks harder and harder. She starts tensing her right arm: The subclavian vein pumps blood down the arm, through the cephalic, basilic, median cubital and median antebrachial veins.

Trombones and saxophones wrap up. Nikosi, Yellow Man and Powell whistle terminus.

"Ik ga je naar huis sturen," she says as she steps away, targeting his nose. She folds her right arm back, forms a fist, and extends it at 74 km/h into his face—The bone clicks. His head slaps the wall and he slumps onto the toilet, dead, with blood running down his face onto his bare penis. The woman scrolls through her music library and settles on *Jet-Black Bean* by L.D.R., which is featured on The Lambing Men Soundtrack (Shugga Tunes™, 2085). It is, for the first-time listener, punk rock prescribed at the perfect tonnage.

She looks at her date and enquires, coolly, "Ben je ongesteld?" She hits play.

Filip Wronski and Santiago Paredes are fired the next day. Those four women become regulars on the circuit, mapping the area. No club is untouched. But most of their time is spent in Club 1001, just up the road from Bucket's Club. The days get butchered there.

◊

The next day, in the cabinet room, Prime Minister Fernanda Li appears above Joram Falack's dossier. She smells like orange juice. She doesn't appear out of thin air; instead she is pushed into the room by the rest of the cabinet. Then a guy in blue overalls, who, to be fair, does appear out of thin air, says they all have to leave because the cabinet room is due for refurbishment. Joram Falack has reached the conclusion that one does not simply, "finish," refurbishing political buildings like parliaments or congresses, because to do that would undermine the whole point of governing institutions: that they, like the national bodies they govern, must always be in a state of becoming, Joram thinks.

"Why wasn't I told about this?" the Prime Minister says, "do we have another room?"

"The robing room!" the First Secretary of State Naomi Dietrich yells, accidentally, "y-yes, why not? The robing room's doable."

The Chancellor of the Exchequer Seren Vogt, replies, "It's not though, is it?"

"I think the robing room's fine," Conall Tuckey adds, "I mean, it'll do for now until the bloody painting gets—"

"Varnishing, mate," the man in blue overalls says.

"What?"

"VAR-NI-SHING."

"For Christ's sakes," Ropple-Christiansen complains, "let's do the Royal gallery."

"Sounds suitable," Defence Secretary Nooda Shakra concurs.

"Suitable? Yes," International Trade Minister Rebecca Lipscombe disagrees, "Appropriate? No. I suggest the Lords Chamber. Safe pick I'd say. Less chance of interruption."

"If you're worried about interruption," Justice Secretary Grace Blackstock replies, "we can tell people to shut up. I mean, we are the fucking government."

The Baroness Imogen Muffet of Devon, the Leader of the Lords, shakes her head in disgust. "I really don't see the need for such language, I mean, really."

"Jesus Christ."

"Besides," the Baroness affixes, "they're fixing a leak in the roof, so we can't go in there anyway."

The Health Secretary Barnaby Pale suggests the lobby, and everyone, including the guy in blue overalls, says, "No."

Ivor Seaby perks up. "Who said, 'Jesus Christ'?"

Transport Secretary Lauren Blanton-Criddle looks at him. "What about Jesus Christ?"

"Someone said it a minute ago."

"I think I did," Grace Blackstock answers.

"Now there was a man," Ivor notes, "who knew where to hold meetings."

"Hey," Piers Meak begins, "so Jesus is standing talking to his followers, and he's like, 'If there're any rapists here, can they stand up?' So this guy stands up, and Jesus says, 'So tell me, why do you rape?' And the guy looks at him and says, 'Well, I don't, but I hate to see you standing there all by yourself.'"

"Wait," Barnaby Pale concentrates, "so, is he standing up to begin with?"

Baroness Muffet shivers. "Who?"

"Look," Nooda Shakra interjects, "that's not relevant."

Environment Secretary Sienna Bloodworth offers the option of sitting outside, only to be shot down by the Work and Pensions Secretary, Jasmine Chalker, who sniffles interminably.

"I'm not," Sienna replies.

Piers Meak interrupts with, "A Reactionary, a Pinko and a Scotsman—"

"Will you shut the fuck up?" Blackstock turns red.

Communities and Local Govt. Minister Molly Rayburn interrupts them, saying, "The members' lobby, the bit with the Churchill arch?"

"No anterooms," Chalker posits, sniffling, "please."

Meanwhile, Northern Ireland Secretary Bobby Glass mumbles to the Welsh Secretary Rhys Driscoll, "Did you know that badgers are the state animal of Wisconsin?"

"Do we have animals?" Rhys asks, "national animals?"

"Well, I've never seen a lamented alpaca," Glass looks at Driscoll's feet, "or a lamented Reactionary."

International Development Minister Willow Patel, says, finally, "The hall, what's the name of—Stephen's, St. Stephen's?"

"Out of the question," Joram Falack says, "I'm not having any of that."

Seren Vogt scrunches up her brow. "What do you mean you're 'not having any of that'?"

"I mean it's not *suitable*," Joram clarifies.

The Business, Energy and Industrial Strategy Minister Trevor Mannings says that they should build a new room altogether!

Willow Patel, somehow, latches onto this, asking, "Do we need planning permission if we want to add on to Westminster Palace, like, say you want to build a fuckin big-ass moat—"

The Chief Party Whip, Sander "El Greco" Papadimitriou, steps up to the current challenge facing the Reactionary Government. "Right," he shouts over them all, "I'm fed up with this. Number twelve. Let's go." El Greco is referring, here, to the residence of the Chief Party Whip, situated two doors down from No. 10 Downing Street. So, a decent bit of street-cred, but not nearly as cool as No. 10.

Ropple-Christiansen slips Falack's pen in her pocket.

"I'm sorry," Bobby Glass says to someone on the phone,

"we're moving. I can't meet you."

"Let's call it off," Seren Vogt is doing the same, "I – no, I can't do tomorrow."

"Yea," Piers Meak, also, is on the phone, "pepperoni. To be honest, mate, just go for it with the toppings, but no pineapple or anchovies – you know how I hate those."

Papers are sifted. Zippers are yanked up. Everyone's brief-case is bollocked off to El Greco's ephemeral territory.

Meanwhile, in No. 10, the man in blue overalls rolls up his sleeves in silence. A tattoo in Dutch appears.

GEBOREN OM BELASTING TE BETALEN!

He plucks a tiny knife from his boot-sole, and inserts it into the wallpaper. It hits the primer and the undercoat. The blade is dragged out, after which he pulls out a wireless microphone from behind the tongue of his right boot and feeds it into the slit. He pushes the microphone up through the wallpaper. There are riddles of nicks, and separations. He seals it up, and paints over the evidence. The room is being received loud and clear somewhere. And no, he doesn't have a moustache.

Adjacent, so to speak, in Number Twelve's living room, there is chequered upholstery and faux-Persian rugging linked together with the stink of hegemony. Fernanda Li examines the seating plan: El Greco and Driscoll are in the kitchen doorway. Seaby, Mannings and Pale cross their legs on the couch, the first staring at Baroness Muffet sitting on what Ulysses Lachnér would call a "poof". Blackstock is watching Ropple-Christiansen play with lampshade frills at the window. Rayburn lounges in an armchair, precipitating jealousy from ministers on each arm: Chalker sniffling on the left, outstaring Bloodworth's calves on the right. Patel balances his ass on a glass table. Blanton-Criddle scrutinizes the ass-balancing from the book cabinet, which is full of titles like *The Jewish Problem* (Winthrop, 2084), *Drilling For Oil For Dummies* (Keighley-Jarvis, 2045), *I'm No Fascist! A History Of British Constabularies* (Zilber-schlag, 2065) and *The Films of Pet'ka Dvorak* (Meak, 2082). Bob-by Glass, leaning on the atrocious orange wallpaper is reading the titles, nodding his head as though he authored each one. Lipscombe studies the wallpaper from the spine of the couch. Falack and Shakra stand in the corner on their phones, that is to say, they are clearly standing together. Tuckey, Vogt and Dietrich stand next to Fernanda Li, who chairs the meeting in front. There's an unhealthy flushing sound. Meak exits the bathroom, fanning the air. He joins El Greco and Driscoll in the kitchen doorway.

"Right," Li begins, opening her brief, "I'd like to call this cabinet meeting to order; the purpose of the meeting being, of course, the need for a significant majority in the next election, which as far as we can see will be in 2091. So what I need from all of you is support," El Greco folds his arms, sneering, "and ideas to flatten the Opposition and anything else that comes our way. So yea…ideas?"

Everyone looks at the faux-Persian rugs. Ropple-Christian-sen stares out of the window at a duck. Seaby looks at Tuckey, mouthing, "Go on…" but Tuckey's not gay when he's on duty.

"Well," Grace Blackstock finally sighs, 'I think we missed out on the L.G.B.T. vote."

"L.G.B.T.Q. plus," Seaby corrects.

"Yea," Blackstock says, "whatever."

"Brooke-Valentine's cats did a good job with that Gay Pay campaign," Meak adds, "got a lot of votes with that." The

U.K. has an L.G.B.T.Q.+ population sitting somewhere between 10.5 and 15 per cent, but bear in mind that these are spooky numbers, that is, no one really knows how many. For the sake of suggestion, 12 per cent of the U.K. population (80,000,000) is 9,600,000; of this 9,600,000, 20% (1,920,000) earn over £300,000 a year. In turn, that's a pretty wealthy ergo powerful gay lobby. But you'd be wrong to think they all voted Reactionary, Meak understands. In a 2089 L.G.B.T.Q.+ election poll, 23% said they'd vote Reactionary (2,208,000), which, compared with the 46% who said they'd vote Pinko, isn't great. Therefore, having examined this fairly rubbish situation, it's crucial then that the Reactionary Party does something, "faggy," for the 2091 election, as Meak understands it.

Glass is unconvinced. "Did they though?"

"Do you see the Pinkos struggling with a majority of two in the Commons?" Meak asks, "cuz I sure don't."

"I think," Lipscombe starts, "before we start praising the Opposition we should pick out what they did wrong."

"No," Meak disagrees, "but in terms of their campaign it was brilliant."

"That's not the point."

"What else could the point possibly be?"

"Thank you," the Prime Minister interrupts, "yes, that's enough, please." She nods at El Greco, who nods back. Piers Meak has been noted.

"Sticking with the gay theme," Ropple-Christiansen chimes in, "I think we all agree it's something we should exploit. That's the wrong word for what I mean to say, but you all get the point."

Tuckey licks his lips, Rayburn clucking, "I think Gay Pay was the death-throes to be honest. What else can you do apart from that?"

"Think of something," Seren answers.

"Logically, let's say," Blackstock explains, "the Pinko campaign was all about diving in, empathy, that type of stuff. Therefore, we should do the opposite."

"You mean," Ropple-Christiansen understands, "we should almost set an example of gayness?"

"Exactly," Blackstock concurs, "if we want to win those votes, we need to be entrenched in it ourselves."

"It's a simple case of representation," Dietrich says.

"If it's so simple," Meak grumbles, "then why haven't we cracked it?"

Tuckey looks at Seaby.

Joram slides away his phone. He lifts his bright head. "What about Belgium?"

Wood creaks and fibre stretches as the entire cabinet turn to face Joram and Nooda in the corner. "If I may," Joram enquires, "have the floor for a few moments, Prime Minister?"

"Of course," she says.

Joram smiles. He puts his hands in his pockets and paces the room, like an unpopular teacher entrusted with the after-you-leave-high-school speech. "Naturally," he asserts, "some of you will have seen the news. The upheaval in Belgium is quite extraordinary. Basically what's happened is a split has occurred between the north and the south. Bobby, you'll appreciate this," Glass sniggers, "the north is still governed by Clement Verlinden. We met him last year at that aid drive in Chelsea, didn't we, Willow?"

"Married chap," Patel tacks on, "bit wet."

"He and his party," Falack continues, "still control the north, but following a far right resurgence in the south led by the Archbishop of Mechelen-Brussels, and a general takeover of civil offices, et cetera, it would appear that they might have a civil war on their hands."

Seren Vogt laughs, smiling at Katie by the window. Trevor Manning puts his hand up. He's not sure why. "I hate to be devil's advocate," Manning says, "but does Belgium have any oil reserves of its own?"

"No," Tuckey burps, "they import everything."

"Then what's the cause of the split?" Manning asks.

Falack stops. "What do you mean?"

"I'm sorry," Trevor confesses, "but you can't expect me to believe a country's splitting down the middle because of a few differences in opinion," a chilly silence spreads through El Greco's gaudy living room, "I mean, come on – if there's no oil involved the chances of civil war are basically nil. What's more why should we be interested?"

"What's your point, Joram?" Li intervenes.

"My point, Prime Minister," the party chairman replies, "is that if we were to intervene in Belgium in the name of the L.G.B.T.Q.+ community; there are literally refugee camps full of lesbian, transgender, gay, queer, all sorts of people along the border; if we intervened for their sake, the support we'd get here, in the U.K., would be indispensable."

"Define intervene," Dietrich interjects.

"Define landslide," Falack shoots back.

"None of this was in the manifesto," the chancellor explains, "if we chuck our policies, that's gonna send a message."

Joram looks at her and says, "It's cheaper than abolishing tuition fees."

"So we'll only win the next election if we invade Belgium," Tuckey summarizes, "great."

"Worst-case scenario," Falack promises, "not an invasion, so much as an occupational hazard."

"Christ," Dietrich complains, "that's the same bloody

thing."

"Worst-case," Falack says, again, "worst-case scenario, but it's fine because we'll never get to that point."

"Everyone out," Li orders, "except Joram and Sander."

Piers Meak calls a number on his phone as he briskly exits the room, saying, "Does Super Kebab take card...?"

Cushions are fluffed and feet are shuffled over the various rugs. Willow leaves two beautiful butt-prints on the glass table. Nooda goes to leave, and Joram says, "Can Nooda stay? She's my rock. It's her idea as much as mine." Li studies the Defence Secretary, and ushers her toward the couch. Faisal Reddy and Sami Toller-Wallace enter the room. The latter puts her phone away, apologizing, "Sorry we're late."

"How was L.E.S.?" Li coughs.

"Boring," Toller-Wallace assures.

"Advisors on loan," the Prime Minister says, licking her eyes over the party chairman, "always tell the truth, Joram. Fun fact."

Joram sniffs.

"Now," she goes on, "tell Sami and Faisal what you just told me."

Falack's a bit irritated because he's now relayed the same story three times, that is, he's already told Sami and Faisal. But he tells Sami and Faisal, again, and everyone nods, but you can't help but notice how this is all a bit Malka Zilberschlag. Zilberschlag (2002-2073) taught in the L.E.S. Maths Dept., and her backyard had a little shed. You'd open the door and it'd lead to another door. Open that door, and it led to a tiny dark space. No windows, lights, nothing. Eight ft. long, four ft. wide, seven ft. high. This is where Malka went if problems needed solving. She'd lie on her back and do sums in the dark. But it's not just like that with Maths; it's applicable to many areas, and the most important decisions are made in small rooms with few people. What's more, the dark doesn't have to be real. It can be metaphorical, racial, diplomatic, or political. Dark is everywhere. Dark is good. And for all we know, Professor Zilberschlag may have just been secretive about her mental contrivances.

There are no mistakes. Proclivities collide.

◊

Detective Chief Inspector Gazsi Pasternak looks over the dead body like paperwork. He licks his front teeth, commenting, "Homicide?"

"Well," the Coroner pulling at his latex glove, "duh."

Pasternak blinks, and takes out a tissue. He blows his nose. The coroner walks around to the other side. He highlights the cadaver's facial damage with his pinky. "No finger prints. Only a palm print, so, a print from the hypothenar eminence: one of those two fleshy bits on the palm. And the print isn't British."

"Nothing is," Pasternak comments, wryly.

"Nationless, in fact," the coroner says, smiling, "no record of any passport. The perpetrator might as well not exist."

"That's impossible." The coroner concurs, going on, "That's not to say it never existed, though. Merely that it's been removed – on purpose."

"By a government?"

"Quite possibly," the coroner posits, "yes. And looking at the aim of the palm-strike, the skill, if you will, the killer's well trained," he counts the boxes of latex gloves on his desk, "I think you're dealing with a mercenary. Someone who's been trained at a military academy, like Norwich or Sandhurst. Somewhere like that."

"Is it a hit?"

The coroner shakes his head in total confidence, explaining, "Hit's are clean," he studies the dip in facial structure, purpled and swollen, "this was recreational."

"Why?" the detective asks, perplexed, "for what?"

"For fun," the coroner leans against the table behind him, "I've seen a lot of things in this room, but I've never seen a mercenary kill for fun," he pulls off his gloves and throws them in the bin, "they'll kill for money, obviously; they'll kill if there's something preventing them from getting their money – but not fun. There's no fun in that job," he looks at the body, "you need to nick these people, Gaz."

Pasternak asks if there's more than one.

"Certainly," he says, "if they're not here now, they will be soon. And if they all kill for fun like this one did, you better watch out, because they will not hesitate. They don't care."

◊

Every week, El Greco sends out a notice to Reactionary MPs outlining, in order of importance, upcoming parliamentary business. Three-line whips are the most important items on any whip notice. They're usually reserved for the second readings of Bills. But right now, Li thinks, it's a good idea to make every piece of parliamentary business concerning the oncoming Belgium Bill a three-line whip because they have a majority of two. And she'll be damned if the Reactionaries get even more dichotomized.

El Greco exits the living room and, in his office, joins the other Reactionary whips: Faith Midgley, Nur Coombs and Erin Jernigan, all of them right, honourable members of parliament. Apart from Baron Quentin of Berkeley, the whip for the House of Lords. He's just Quentin Squibb (*Esq* in his younger days…). "O-kay," El Greco rallies, "the circular is going out next week. Everything's three-line, all right?"

"Everything?" Coombs asks.

"All of it," El Greco clarifies, "Belgium Bill's green lit. Faith," he snaps his fingers, "list."

Midgley produces five printed lists. Sander grips them, saying, "We got more homophobes in this party than a Dumfries local—that doesn't leave this office by the way—so I've compiled constituencies close to each other. Make it easier to whip your MPs. Faith, you got Salisbury, South Swindon, South West Wiltshire, Chippenham and Devizes, yea?" Faith folds the list, and puts it in her pocket. "Nur, my dear, you've got Barking, Battersea, Beckham, Bermondsey and Old Southwark, Brent Central, Chelsea and Fulham, Jesus – Ealing North and Finchley and Golders Green. Can you handle that?"

"I'll manage," Coombs notes, writing the names into her phone.

"Dinner tonight, yea?" El Greco clarifies.

"Yep."

"Ok-ay…"

Squibb, subsequently, looks at Erin Jernigan like WTF.

"Erin," the Chief Whip continues, "you're Bassetlaw, Boston and Skegness, Coventry South, Gainsborough, High Peak, Kettering, Loughborough and Wyre Forest. Don't get lost."

"I'll remember those," Jernigan asserts.

"And uh," El Greco flings a grimace at Baron Squibb, "Quentin, is it?" the whip for the House of Lords stares at him, "you're Irish."

"British, as far as I'm concerned," Squibb replies, "nonetheless, whoop de fuckin doo."

"If you could just do Belfast West, Belfast East, Belfast

South and Belfast North in that order, that'd be grand," El Greco nods, "Jake's a bloody nightmare."

Squibb squints at the list, asking, "You want us to black book them?" A black book is a whip's lover, rapist, wife and priest compressed into one entity. For example, if there's a married MP who makes love to a veteran Romanian gigolo every Tuesday at 2:38 p.m. in the Euston Station Travelodge, it is advised that the whip write it in their black book. You never know when you'll need it. And not necessarily, "need," as in, "need-to-damage," rather, "need," as in, "help," sometimes. Many an MP's *'ath 'hath* been saved by the black book; collection, identification and protection; but occasionally, by all means, blackmail the bastard or bitch.

"Send letters, texts," El Greco lists off, "but if you call them, don't call the MP. I want wives, husbands and partners because they'll relay the orders and that's better for us," he looks at Nur, softly, "so you all carry on with that. We meet back here in a fortnight."

"Phone numbers?" Jernigan remembers, "you want to bug them?"

"I'm working on it," the Chief Whip adds, "got a meeting this afternoon. Numbers in tow." He laughs and his whips laugh. Then he tells them to stop laughing.

◊

Later, D.C.I. Gazsi Pasternak sips his filter coffee in Kafés kai Malakíes, the address of which is 20-22 Tavistock St, London VC6F 2PH, just in case you're recently divorced, mildly asthmatic, a Liverpool F.C. supporter, and in need of some damn good Greek coffee.

"You read Plato?" Pasternak asks El Greco, sitting opposite, "one day, Plato's just teaching in the academy and a student asks him, 'Hey, what's the point in you teaching us all these theories? What's to be gained from them?' And Plato's stood there. It's hot and he's balding. The sun's burning his head. And he turns to one of his slaves and says, 'Give this young man an obol,' that's a Greek coin, 'so he can feel like he's gained something from me. Once you've done that, expel him.'"

"Mmm," El Greco mumbles, nibbling his couscous, "that's interesting."

"No," Pasternak declares, "but it's true, though – so are you talking to me because you want advice, or because you want something? Because if it's the second one, I'll leave right now."

"I think you miss the point of the story."

"No," Pasternak slurps a good dose of coffee, "no – I'm London Met. I'm not MI6, well, let's be honest, MI5, this is domestic, isn't it?"

"What do you vote for?" El Greco mutters as he signals for the bill.

"I vote Pinko."

"Not who," the Chief Whip explicates, "WHAT do you vote for? Do you vote for change, stability, foreign," coughing suggestively, "intervention?"

"I'm not gonna bug a third of London for you."

El Greco sighs. "That's a real shame, Gazsi; a real shame," then a change in tone, like channel surfing, "but if you can't do the job, then I'll find someone who can."

"That doesn't make me feel any better."

The Chief Whip stands up, replying, "It's not supposed to," before flinging an au revoir and exiting the café.

Zach

Our house is redder than a pomegranate subject to vivisection.

You drag your feet up the driveway. You think all your possessions can fit in your rucksack, but now there's all manner of things in front of you. Things you never knew you had: a wife and kid, and house. Enough for most—for you, it's hard to say. It's hard for you to talk. I look at your feet, and your ankles and your calves, and your thighs and your crotch and your stomach, both arms slink up your sides; and your chest, and your nipple-silhouettes. Your collarbones are showing. They mistreated you—And your neck and your chin suck themselves in. Your nose is crooked and your eyes are sad.

We eat early. Jan plays with his cabbage. Flesh is yanked and sliced. Incisors tear sinew – knives and forks, the polite consumption of water. You point at your glass and say, "Helps with my head."

"What's wrong with your head?"

"It's cloudy," you say, "it needs time to readjust." You sigh and look at me when you do it. Well, you always used to do that, but it was less retrograde. Your brain is scratching the inside of your skull, trying to get some sort of messages out to our little world of solar-panelled neighbourhoods. Grass brown as dough. But there's only the tiny thud of two eyelids. You lick your upper lip, and the glass of water touches the table at 10°, working downwards: 9°, 8°, 7°, 6°, 5°, 4°, 3°, 2°, 1°, progressing to one perfect naught; the glorious nil. The water sways from side to side, like your eyes on Jan and me. That chilly paternal staring: an examination of little fingers on proportionate hands.

When we go to bed there's no hanky-panky whatsoever. Usually by the time I brush my teeth your hands are all over me. When you're on leave, they are.

There's a man on our street called Carlos Apple-Tennyson. He smells like burning plastic. I see him every morning when I go to work, extending his house. The grey-cream concrete he scrapes off his spatula, watching me sometimes when he does it. But I shrug and turn away. It's dead weird being studied. I might invite him over for dinner tomorrow night.

Carlos.

I'll cross my legs at the table because I'll want him in me. Cold showers. Fingers on wet flesh and warm towels. No wound is left unlicked; the television on in the background and the smell of burning plastic. "Zach," I say, exiting the shower with a towel wrapped around me, "you there?"

"What?" you mumble in another room.

"I'm off soon," I say.

"…"

"I'll be back around six," I add, "do you want anything?"

You appear without a shirt and say, "You got a job?"

"It got pretty boring, me, just sitting around."

"Where's Jan?"

"At school."

"He there now?"

"Yea, I've been letting him walk there by himself. It's just down the road."

You squint at me. "Is that *safe*?"

"He's been doing it for about a year."

"Take that towel off."

I take it off, and you lurch forward. You put your hands on my hips, and shave the water off my skin with the edge of your palms. It runs down my thighs and ankles onto the red carpet, frightened.

It is 9:34 a.m. and I am at work. Secluded on the far right corner as I walk in, guarded by Human Resources director Stourton Bigglesworth, are four cabinets full of work permits. I look at them when nothing matches on the computer. I didn't know we employed so many people. New faces. Non-descript faces. They examine me examining them. Innsbruck Latard appears in the doorway, the coffee mug straining his wrist.

"Tara," he says.

"What?"

"You got a few minutes?"

"Not really, I'm gonna be honest with you."

"It won't take long."

I look at him and say, "Is this about the aliens again…?"

◊

Zebedee's Garden Centre (Z.G.C.) is a glass building visited by single mothers during the day, and summer-student-cum-night-watchman Innsbruck Latard at night. He shines his torch on plants and ferns, looking for burglars. His torch, at best, is erroneous and unsteady. In two months, opportunism prevailing, he'll quit and start work at an office, maybe. Work his way up the ranks. This is a decision made with money, location and the abundance, or so he thinks, of easily persuaded women in mind. Latard sits on a lawn chair. Snapdragons and petunias surround his feet. He drags his torch across aloe vera, anthuriums, carnations, coxcombs, gardenias and poinsettias. Turning off his torch, he looks up at the stars. His breath drifts towards the Milky Way, and vanishes like all those Croats,

Serbs, Romanians, Slovaks and Germans launched into space by the Malaysian Allman Brothers Company's ill-fated space program, headquartered in Kronstadt; endorsed by COAnàb and the dank nothingness of space, under which Latard ponders the possibility of a comfy office existence. Not for one nanosecond does he bear in mind the possibility of displacement, or disappointment. He hears something by the Queen Anne's lace. There are feet there, feet of an unknown variety. He shines his torch, and hears a body fall to the ground.

"Hey, get up! Come on!"

No reply.

"Dude, it's over. Get up!"

Outside, a breeze picks up. The ground starts to shake, and a sharp, high-pitched note pierces Innsbruck Latard's ears. He covers one, trying to aim his torch. The intruder, realizing the ever-expanding size of the spanner thrown in the works, jumps up in defence mode: "This isn't me, man!"

"What?"

"That ain't—" the burglar is baffled and terrified. "That fucking noise!" He cups his ears, running over to the inexperienced watchman, who says, "Don't move!"

"I'm not moving, man!" The noise becomes unbearable as a blinding Byzantium-coloured light illuminates the garden centre. "What the fuck is that!?" the burglar proclaims.

Suddenly, there is the purest of silences. The light dims. Latard's view of the Milky Way is blocked by a huge black rod, which settles in front of the garden centre's doors. He waves his torch, saying, "We're closed!" after which a sharp extremity shoots through the doors, retracting, and leaving a gaping hole. "I said we're closed goddamnit!"

The doors burst open and a group of eight crab-like creatures enter Z.G.C. Their eyes oscillate on short stalks as their six legs toss the cheap gravel about, snapping at the night with chubby claws. They file past the aloe vera and form an arcing, protractor-like line around Innsbruck and the intruder. Every claw, now, thuds onto the gravel. The Alpha crab, or what Innsbruck assumes to be the leader, extracts a pink triangle on a stick from its back pocket.

It is, as it turns out, a translating device, held up subsequently to multiple drooling jaws. The same sharp note fills the room, but, this time, it's cut short by a warbling voice: "Can you understand me-me?"

Innsbruck and the intruder stare at the crabs.

"A nod," the crab warbles, "will suffice-fice."

The two men nod.

"Excellent," the crab declares, "we are Complacency, but you may call me Scott. We have travelled six billion lactatés from our planet of Njooftpub to be with you tonight. Many lunar cycles ago, our female parent visited the Z.G.C. and placed great sentimental value upon said visit, making it her dying wish to be returned to the aforementioned entity. No more than two lunar cycles ago, the female parent in question died of internal haemorrhaging, and was subsequently cremated by my third brother Anthony-thony—"

The crab on the far left waves his claw. *Friendly*, Latard

thinks.

"We wish," Scott goes on, "to spread her ashes over your gardenias-ias."

The intruder pulls a gun, saying, "I don't know if this is a joke or something, but I'm gonna fuckin kill some," he looks at the crab who just waved, "I'll kill Anthony!"

Anthony whimpers, turning to his siblings for reassurance.

The crab on the far right, alternatively, lifts a short metallic rod in its claw, which immediately emits a green arc of electricity that absorbs the intruder in a mist of shrieking, the resultant flaming skeleton snapping over the carnations.

"Jesus Christ!" Latard says.

"Jesus Christ is not here," Scott explains, "I am-am…"

The skeleton continues to smoulder, the smell of burnt flesh filling the garden centre. "The proposition remains. Let it be said that none of us are what you would term, 'big fans,' of our female parent. Each span of our life is short. We seek closure of this chapter in order to regain control of our lives. Complacency seeks liberty. Liberty seeks Complacency-cy."

Innsbruck, having exhausted all surprise in his neuronal populations, stares at Complacency. Abigail's claws are scarred. Anthony is missing a leg. Scott's eyes, having apparently been beaten senseless, are milky-white. The siblings shrink away, gurgling honestly. Innsbruck, acknowledging the death of an abusive parent, sighs.

"I get it. Do what you gotta do."

"You are correct-ect," Scott says, wiggling his eyestalks.

Anthony extracts a pyramid-like urn from his back pocket. Once again with the back pocket, Latard thinks. Anthony pops the top, and the others gather around him. Raising it above his eyes, he empties the scarlet ashes over the gardenias. They twinkle like the ocean. The ash settles, and a thin pink stem starts to grow. It shoots up over the white flowers and sprouts a bulbous red blossom. It sways organically, transfixing Latard whose pale-blue summer-student peepers gape deep into the cardinal flower: a new species, part Complacency, part gardenia. And, like, in a state of botanical euphoria, he reaches out his left hand to merely, for one jiffy-sliver, glimpse a feel of this gorgeous—

An arc of green electricity squirts out if Abigail's rod and obliterates the maternal blossom. Ash is thrown into the air.

Scott lifts his translator, warbling, "Sanctimony," he posits, "is the lowest form of parenting-ting."

Complacency starts the long scuttle back to their spaceship. Anthony swivels, briefly, to look at Innsbruck, after which he crabs into the warm Byzantium light. The airlock squeaks. The ground shakes. Latard hides under the anthuriums as bursts of gas fill the garden centre. And the massive black rod propels itself into the night sky, vanishing, once and for now at least, for all.

Latard peers through the anthuriums at the Milky Way. He smiles. Maybe, one day, Latard thinks, this story will get him laid. But he'll have to tell it just right to some speculative woman in some speculative office's kitchenette – because otherwise, who would believe him?

◊

"I say again," my eyes feel hard, "is this about the *aliens*?"

Innsbruck turns red and says, *"No,"* defensively, "I mean if you wanted it to be, it could, well, no…it's not."

"Okay," I say, "let me just, click this thing, and move it there, okay."

My colleague continues to stare at me blankly.

"Well?" I say.

"Come with me into the kitchen," he says, "I'll get you some coffee."

"I don't want coffee."

"Come on," he teases, pulling away, "Come on…please."

We leave the room and walk across the office. Cubicles' keyboards are clicking. Soda is being sucked. There are sniffs and lips popping. People are asleep on their desks. Now we're in the kitchen. He slams his mug on the countertop, refilling it, offering to do the same for me. Then he comes at me like a forklift and kisses my forehead. I push him back. The man is confused.

"What are you doing?" he says.

"What am I doing?" I reply, "what are you doing?"

"It's what you want, isn't it?"

"How would you know what I want?"

"Well," he deciphers, "you've been sending me signals."

"What signals?"

"It's hard to explain to a woman."

I stare at him and recommend, "Try."

"Well—"

"And stop saying, 'well'."

"Okay—"

"And don't replace, 'well,' with, 'okay'." Those are two of Innsbruck's favourite words.

"You," he says almost burping, "were checking me out."

"When," I ask delicately, "was I checking you out?"

"Like a month ago."

"A month ago?"

"Yea, and I thought—"

"Innsbruck, you're," I pat his chest, "you're wrong, man…"

I walk out.

There are a group of workmen in white overalls chipping the blue paint off of the walls. Another one swirls the new pigment. White foundation is rolled on in due course, coating the workmen's shirts. Tiny ladders retch under brushes. That thin bubbling sound is eked out in each stroke of hue. There are blue chips on the carpet, and they grin, on their ladders, over the cubicles. It's all work.

Going home involves a supine dose of traffic politics. The heated seats are sweaty, and the rubber is quick. I park the car parallel to the house. The neighbours are lit like diodes, and the sky shuts up. I walk inside and shut the door. Jan is sat watching TV. Cartoons, honking and bonking. "Hey dude," I sit next to him on the couch, "you okay?"

"Yep."

"Where's your dad?" He shrugs, and I look at the television. "What are you watching?"

"TV," he says.

I take off my jacket. I scrunch his thick hair. There's a moose on the TV with a trombone. I ask again where his dad is.

"He's in the shower."

"Yea? Where was he when you got home?"

"He's been in the shower for ages."

"How long have you been home?" He doesn't answer, studying the trombone-playing moose on the TV. "Hey, forget the moose, show me your watch," his wrists are dirty, "where was the hand before, when you got home?"

"It was over here."

"It's been an hour?"

"I guess so."

"Okay…"

I jog over to the bathroom and knock on the door. "Zach?"
I can hear the shower pummeling the tile. I open the door and
you're sat in the shower. You're covered in shampoo. Your
chest hair is straight and you're holding your knees. "Hey," I
turn off the tap. "What are you doing?"

"I was trying to wash the dirt off," you say.

I pull you out. "What dirt?"

"The dirt from outside, you know?"

"Yea," I wrap you in a towel, and sit with you on the floor,
"how'd that go?"

"Didn't work."

"No?"

"It's uh," you crane your neck towards me, "it's hard being
a policeman." You blink in the mist, and your skin drips. The
bathmat squelches beneath me.

"I know that," I say.

"I don't want to be alone."

"Okay."

"I want to be with you."

"Okay."

"I want to be with you."

I wipe some shampoo from your nostril and say, "You are."

Then you sniff, saying "No, but it won't always be like
that…"

I look at the bags under your eyes, "…people die, but now
I want to be here, now, can I do that?"

I hold your face. "You are here," I brush your cheek with
my thumb, "let's watch some TV."

"I'm all wet."

"It doesn't matter."

I take you to the couch and you sit with Jan. "Talk to your
dad," I say. In the kitchen, I turn the kettle on. *A cliché, I know,*

but I don't give a fuck.

You tweak your eyelashes and look at Jan, "Hey man."

The towel tugs beneath your thighs. The sofa pillows are crushed, the never-ending fate of feathers. There is a bending of cushions and socks on feet.

The kettle clicks.

Mammalian copulation is triggered by hormones and influenced by pheromones. Contrastingly, human copulation is learned, ostensibly recreational and therefore largely voluntary. Slugs have a three-hour courting period where pheromone-laced slime is secreted. That's the problem for us humans: an abundance of fucking and no one has a clue what it means. Slugs have it easy. They reproduce and get on with their sluggy night, assaulting, I assume, any lettuce in sight. Humans, on the other hand, feel the need to prescribe meaning to their reproductive process. And we do, but it's usually trite and simplistic.

We have a shower together. Parts are shaved, and fingers work their way into the backsides.

Land slugs use aerial pheromones.

Muscles are pinched, and feet cross one another. Our spines crack forward and fluid falls from between legs.

The slime of *Helix aspersa* is high in glycoproteins. It is known to stimulate elastin, collagen and dermal components that repair the effects of photoaging.

Humming is stifled in the mist. Towels are patted. We share the wet-hair feeling, strung along an inarticulate sense of stolen time.

◊

Doctor Euripides Byrony's practice is in Utton Central, opposite Brian Cuomo's underperforming music shop Ciconia's Nombre. The shop is named after Gustav Ciconia (2035/2038-2088), a Belgian composer of canons, motets and secular pieces along with two musicological critques: *Opulentos Musica* (2068) and *Mea Musica Est Terribilis* (2073). Although it's difficult to say when he was born exactly, and whether he was an ecumenical bitch or a chorister, which are basically the same thing, the former critique is less bullshitty.

Jan has a cold and it isn't going away. Byrony's waiting room has lots of ferns and a table with magazines in the middle. To the left of this by forty-five degrees is Miss Emery *"not-Anemone"* Antoinette, the secretary. Perched in a glass box, she ruminates on her pink laptop. She is, as anyone who frequents Doctor Byrony's office will tell you, an amateur rapper:

> The colours, they represent numbers
> A five is a red, and a nine is another
> That's how the stock market works
> You make a thing a word, make a 4 to 1 bet
> Now your world is being reversed
> Plus you're seeing colours
> Personally they hurt me and those
> Broke-ass motherfuckers in Fergnan
> Who aren't credit-worthy

Doctor Byrony appears in that standard-issue white coat. "Shall we see the young sir now," he says as I get up, brushing my trousers, "best if mum stays here." I sit back down. They disappear into his office.

I pull my chair closer to the door and listen. Papers are rustled and a stethoscope is slammed on the table. "Now," Doctor

Byrony begins, "take those trousers off so I can see your juicy cock—Just kidding! Take your shirt off."

I'm not sure if seven year olds get paedophilia jokes, but hey-ho.

"Mmm hmm," more rustling, "right arm up. Mmm hmm… say, 'ahhh'," I hear the sound of a dry mouth, "come on, where's my, 'ahhh'?"

"AHHHHH."

"Good boy."

It sounds like an oxygen tank is being dragged. Pressurised gas is inhaled. Byrony respires. (Well, I hope it's Byrony respiring.)

"All doctors, hey," he chuckles, "all doctors drink."

No reply.

"Do you know how oxygen cures a hangover?"

"No."

"Well let me tell you my boy! When you drink vodka like I do, preferably straight and from my left boot, the ethanol inherent in the vodka encourages the production of nitric oxide synthase, which creates capase-three enzymes and subsequent cell apoptosis, which in our profession is called, 'programmed cell destruction'. Sounds like a cartoon, doesn't it?"

"Not really."

"Anyway," Byrony takes another hit, "you basically starve your brain of oxygen, so it makes perfect sense then to suck in some oxygen, then, doesn't it?"

"Yep."

"Santa Maria," Byrony confides, "I wish I could talk to my wife about these things. I feel safe with you, Sian."

"Jan."

"I don't know why I'm telling you this; I like talking to you about these things."

There is a period of silence.

"I want you," he says, "to take this prescription to you mum. Miss Antoinette will sort you out with your medication."

"Thank-you-Doc-tor-By-ro-ny."

I try to look normal when they come out. Doctor Byrony runs his hand over his bald head. He stares at Miss Antoinette's breasts, jiggling from her flow:

> Vernacular, this oh double dee
> Old language never changes
> Rearranging estranges
> That's why I make it dangerous
> With these characters
> And base-line parameters
> I was born to be a barrister
> But the El en ay tee
> That really fucked up my canister
> I was no longer a character
> So I couldn't be a barrister

Byrony calls another patient over. It's an older woman with nystagmus. They leave, and the door locks.

I look at Miss Antoinette. She fills out a form and stares at my son. "He'll be a handsome man, Missus Mullein," she stops writing, "it is *Missus*, still, isn't it?"

◊

We leave Jan at home and walk outside. The Saturday afternoon tumbles away. Your hands are in your pockets. I link arms with you. We're almost in step with one another. The deep sighs of joggers are dulled by passing cars. "How do you feel?" I ask. "Better," you reply.

There are some kids on bicycles at the end of the road. They don't have any helmets. They call each other names as they roll in circles. I look back at you. "Do you think you'll ever be like you were?"

"I don't remember what I was like."

"Why not?"

"Guess he's dead, that guy." You wave at them, and they slow down. They call you a paedo and you shout back, "HEY!"

They freeze. You disconnect from me and flop your wallet open. The kids' eyes widen. You reach a few notes out, saying, "Take it."

"That's a hundred quid!" one kid says.

"Fucking hell," the other says.

They move closer and take the money.

You stand back. "Buy some helmets," you say as they look at each other, "there's a place in town that sells helmets. I want the change on my porch before six. You understand?"

"Yes mister."

"I know your dads," you go on, "and they know me. And I want my change. Is that fair?"

"Yea."

"All right," you start to walk back to me, but then you turn around and shout, "WHAT ARE YOU TWO STARING AT?" They shoot off on their bikes, a nervous laughter sprinkled on top, "SIX O'CLOCK!" you say, again.

◊

It is early morning and the window stings my eyes and skin. My right arm surrounds a chalk outline, a man-space. I dangle my legs over the side of the bed and rub my eyes. I get up and look into Jan's room. He's sleeping. He's okay. The parietal lobe prunes all sensory information: touch, smell and sight. It becomes integrated through proprioception and mechanoreception so you can feel everything. It's also the most active part of the brain when you're sleep-deprived.

I go to the kitchen. You're sat at the dining table, deconstructing one of Jan's many toy cars. This is a police car. Tiny screws are twirled and plastic wheels on paper-thin axels. The whole chassis drops. The car becomes a bunch of coloured bits. "Zach?" I mumble.

"…Hey," you reply, organizing the pieces.

I walk over and hang my arms around your neck. "Why you up?"

You separate the axels from the other bits. "Couldn't sleep."

I rest my forehead on the back of your head. "No?" Toy manufacturers use a variety of plastics such as Polyolefins like polyethylene and polypropylene, P.V.C., and Acrylonitrile butadiene styrene, which is prone to flaking. "What are you doing?" I ask.

"See if I can fix it," you try to put the vacuum-formed shell back together, "one wrong move and the axels fall out of place." The chassis and the shell click into place. You rest the car on the table. The screws are dropped back into their respective shafts and tightened. I smell your beige jumper.

"Jan doesn't play with them anymore," I say.

"With what?" you mutter back.

"Toys."

"There's nothing worse than that," you flip it over, wheeling it back and forth, "spooky."

"You remember," I ask, "the tenants before we moved in?"

"I think so."

"They said there was a ghost in the house."

"Yea?"

"Didn't like children."

"Jan's okay," you say.

"He's got flu, Zach—"

"The toy thing bothers me," you frown, "it's weird."

"It's normal," I say, "you just replace them with something else. Important things."

"When he gets older."

"Yea," I slither off and ignite the kettle, "it's Sunday." I run the tap over last night's dishes. "Church day."

You creak back in your chair and look at me. "You going to church?"

I nod and you start laughing.

"You still got faith?"

I scratch my breast and say, "Just about."

Religion has the same effect on the brain as music, water, sex, food and recreational drugs. The nucleus accumbens or NAc is located in the basal forebrain. As part of your reward system, it releases dopamine when provoked by rewarding stimuli. This results in an incentive salience, or wanting. Addiction rears its ass here—So, you didn't come to church with me, but we did fuck when I got back.

Harmon

Harmon—unaccustomed to *The Binning Men* or *The Kings of Brick*, the operetta by Oliviér Snell and I. K. Burst (alias Snell & Burst) first performed in 2089 at the Burch Theatre and concerning the Mayor of Luton and his family, and two Romanian bin men who find themselves jointly reigning as Mayor despite their egalitarian principles; the performance itself containing a lively dance based upon the Nicaraguan Palo de Mayo, traditionally accompanied by a maypole—hears the aforementioned operetta play for several moments, before he drifts off again into oblivion. He wakes up in the Florin Police Station interrogation room. He can feel the sweat rolling down his face. Egelblöm's wheelchair squeaks forward. Sergeant Kapoor looks on with the intensity of a gas station attendant. Harmon shakes his head. "What's going on?"

Kapoor squints, saying, "What do you mean what's going on?"

"What do you mean," Harmon replies, "what do you mean what's going on? The bust? What happened?"

The now-bearded Doctor Fenway Ilyich F.M.E. (Force Medical Examiner) slides between the two policemen. "Can you two stop, please?"—*This is no graduate*, Harmon thinks. *He's wearing a lab coat.*

"What's he doing here?" Harmon asks, unconvinced. Kapoor and Egelblöm turn to Doctor Ilyich as if he just mentioned in passing that he was gay.

"You can't trust him," Chikenyyt goes on fanatically, "he was crap at the academy; he'll be crap in the field!"

"Doctor Ilyich," Egelblöm explains, "graduated top of his

class from the L.E.S. Medical School – not the academy."

Fenway expels a tiny giggle. Then he shines a torch in Harmon's eyes, suggesting, "I don't think he remembers anything."

"That's impossible," Egelblöm exerts.

"Harmon," the doctor interjects, "you said we went to the academy together. Prove it."

"Fenway," Egelblöm objects.

"No," he goes on, "answer the question, Harmon. Tell me something only I would know."

The sweaty graduate studies the room. He searches for nonconformities, contradistinctions and dissimilitudes, but he can't find a single one. It's a carbon copy of the one in his dream. Was that a dream? What's going on? "Okay," he looks around at the others, "you told me about a girl who bullied you at school, so you broke her jaw."

"Well," Ilyich puffs, "that isn't true."

"Fine," the graduate says, "you prove it now."

"I don't have to prove anything."

Harmon slams the table "What's with the double standards!?"

"Stop it," Egelblöm shouts, "both of you!" She turns to her deputy. "Kapoor – a word in private."

The two superiors leave the interrogation room and gather in that one-way mirror observation gallery. There's a table full of recording equipment used on a drug-trafficking case months ago, a mug with two-finger's-worth of coffee and a portrait of Scottish Field Marshal and subsequent Defence Minister (2065-2078) Nadezhda Bettelheim-Loganach with each cheek beset by a three inch Hebrew curl. Sergeant Copernicus Kapoor sweats in the near dark. Egelblöm holds up three fingers, un-ironically. "Observe these fingers, sergeant."

"Yes, ma'am."

"One," she begins, "you told me their hallucinogenic paths wouldn't get confused by other hallucinogenic paths, which given that drooling thing through the glass is clearly not the case." She drops her index finger, leaving two. "Two: You told me that if our dogger picked up the scent of Mullein it would be impossible for him to lose it, which, I'll say again, given that drooling thing through the glass is clearly not the case." She drops another, leaving her middle finger. "Three: You assured me that memory loss would not occur. You said that Harmon would have ninety-nine per cent recall of everything he'd encountered, and able, therefore, to report back like any able-minded agent," she makes a very disappointed sound, like an unhappy nasal emptying, "either you were lying to me, or this is a substantial fuck up."

"I agree," Kapoor begins, "what—"

"With the lying or the fuck up?" Egelblöm asserts, "I don't think you understand the heft of the situation, sergeant."

Kapoor sniffs. "What do you want to do…?"

Egelblöm peers through the one-way glass. The dogger appears to be lost, irretrievable perhaps, like all of those COAnàb satellites blasted off from Kronstadt. These satellites were patented by one Professor Jefferson Tanaka of Tanaka Labs and Associates®, posted parallel to the L25 in Locher (SC4 8IK, P.O. Box 873); opposite the tree that very faintly resembles Ulysses Lachnér. Egelblöm pivots her wheelchair to face the window. "Give him some food in the mess hall. Also," she looks at Kapoor, suspiciously, "because I know you're freaked out by this too—"

"The bust," he adds.

"Yes, the bust. It hasn't happened yet," she says, "how could he possibly have experienced it?"

"More importantly," the sergeant offers, "the tip off – you

don't by any chance think we've been tipped off anonymously and subconsciously by our own agent?"

Egelblöm emits an errant sigh, as if Doctor Norvin Tubaniña himself has informed her that she could walk this whole time, and that it was merely a sense of vocational duty that kept her in that Lucky Mark IV Travel Device.

"I don't think we understand the potential of this drug," Egelblöm meditates, "but I suggest further exploitation, even if we're not sure what we're exploiting," she sighs, "derp, derp, derp; it is a funny word."

Kapoor humours her. "Derp!"

"It's not funny when you say it," his superior scolds.

Humour of the Egelblöm persuasion is hard to come by, it being humour cultivated from no sense of humour. This is, by comparison, also practiced by Pope Leo XXIV who has among other things overseen the dissolution of Catholic trade unions and the reformation of the Catholic Church into a quasi-Marxist doctrine of authoritarianism, materialism and the proletarian capacity for utter destruction, wrapped together rather loosely by the infallibly-Latin motto, "De omnibus dubitandum." The humour, or the lack thereof, consistently and/or crucially takes the form of the following joke, oft told by Leo at official dinners and Catholic banquets throughout Europe...

After negotiating all forms of rain and sleet, Kilkenny-born Father Dermot Heaney rolls up to a monastery seeking shelter, after which he's treated to the best fish and chips he's ever had. After dinner, Heaney trots round back to thank the chefs, who are two monks. Brother Rob and Brother Jason.

"I wanted to thank you for dinner," Heaney says, "Very good. But out of curiosity, who cooked what?"

"Well," Brother Rob concedes, "I'm the fish friar."

"Then you," Heaney deduces, "must be——"

"Yes," Brother Jason answers, "I'm afraid I'm the chip monk."

The total failure of the joke lies in Leo's inability to see through his own anecdotal veil; to feel any sense of humility whatsoever in the aside, probably directed towards the 1st Earl of Whatever, or Lady Oh What A Big Hat I've Got. Leo, much like D.C.S. Egelblöm, has an immense capacity for cumulative shame…

◊

Anya Egelblöm considered her fishmongering work—especially then, at the age of twenty-one—a real detriment to her attempts at iconoclastic contrarianism. So she quits the fishmongers on a Monday in November. This pisses off the fishermen because it's a Monday and they've barely started the week, and if someone's got the will power to quit on a Monday then *how in the halibut* are they gonna muster the joie de vivre to get through the week themselves?

Later on, she walks by the Lachlan harbour, on the East coast; the mouth to the Minister's sea. Everyone fishes here. She kneels down and scratches her ankle, watching all the Napier green- and pale chestnut-coloured trawlers trudging back through the harbour. She tosses her fishmongering keys overboard and considers joining the police – that is, after her cycling career takes off.

The next morning, she gets up and oils her bicycle's chains. She checks the gear cable housing. She's a little paranoid about the slightly warped fork holding the front wheel, but as per every other morning she inspects it and finds nothing wrong.

Bugger. Bugger. Bugger.

She's either partially blind or not blind at all; so not blind, in fact, that a fork-inspecting job in Turkis™ is totally deserved. She zippity-zips her jersey, locks the "bulkhead" to her magnolia-coloured basement flat and goes for a ride. After reaching the top of the hill, she begins her descent. The wind skims her face, her legs and up her nose and armpits. "I'm unemployed!" she shouts into the air, after which a misogynistic stick flicks itself in her front spokes. She careers off the road into one of those walls that divide the farmland. "Ah fuck—!" She thumps in thistles and her bike lands on top of her. She grips the top tube in rage and flings the bike off her body. Breathing angrily, she hears a dog barking nearby. Brushing the grass and thistles off her bicycle shorts, she whispers, "Christ..." thinking about her account with I.T.C.B. Holdings plc. She performs a few of those mini-calculations needed when your income ceases. Your savings are all that's left. Then questions like, "Can I afford to go to the bakery this week with the money I have?" which usually stipulate answers like, "No."

That dog is getting closer. An old farmer pokes his head over the wall. "Are you all right?" It's farmer Piotr le Manche, he of the Le Manche Farming Dynasty, suffering from dementia. "Anya? Is that you again?"

Anya smiles and says, "Yea..."

"You all right?" he shouts back.

"Got a stick stuck," she explains.

"I too had a stick stuck once," he replies. "Weeks, I had it. Couldn't walk," the immensity of the sun backlights his balding head, "where'd you get it stuck?"

Anya starts to laugh. "In my spokes."

"You want the usual coffee and moral support? I'll meet you at the bottom of the hill. Don't worry about pissing off the neighbors. I own the land."

"I know," Anya assures, "you sai—"

"What?"

"Never mind…"

Later, they're both inside le Manche's farmhouse. Old China cups and saucers jangle over counters topped with *Zofenopril*: a drug that reduces high blood pressure; *Psedoephedrine*: an alpha- and beta-adrenergic agonist used in the treatment of urinary incontinence and rhinitis, and *Lobeglitazone*: an anti-diabetic medication shown to reduce blood sugar levels and improve liver function.

The doughy sound of an old farmer mumbling Scottish folk-tunes; an attempt to de-green domesticated tomatoes, or the malnourished parsley waving goodbye at le Manche trilling into the next room. His labrador, Copernicus, sits under the window. He's as black as the inside of a goat, and he watches le Manche offer a biscuit to his guest.

"If that's where we're at," she says.

Piotr pries open the biscuit tin. "Not easy being sixty-five."

"Piotr," she corrects, "you're seventy."

The farmer's eyes bulge. "Fuck off. I'm not seventy."

"My birthday card's on the window."

And so it is. It has pictures of tomatoes on it.

"Shit," he mumbles, picking up the card, "you're right. Fuck," then he grabs two biscuits and drops them on table, "sorry, Laura."

"Anya."

"Shit, sorry."

"It's okay."

"Anya – that's a pretty name," she lends a modest beam, "hmmff…look at that smile." He drinks his coffee and munches on a softened biscuit. He puts his veiny hands on the table. "Reckon I'll have to kill Copernicus pretty soon. Two shells, back of the head," he jabs a finger in his grey hair and pulls the imaginary trigger, "old dog."

"How old is he?"

"I don't know. Dog years," he leans in, secretly, "back legs gave out the other day, like he was paralyzed. He was in the uh, in the green you know?"

"The field?"

Piotr puts his hands together, smiling, "The field. Back legs gave out, like he was paralyzed," he sips his coffee, "no dog ever had it so good. Ain't that right Copernicus?" He gives Copernicus a few head-scratches. The dog's eyes squint with each stroke. "Good boy…"

"I quit my job yesterday," Anya says.

"Well done," Piotr returns, sitting back in his chair, "what you got in mind?"

"I'll take it easy for a bit."

"You take it easy for as long as you like," he goes on, "and if someone tells you to stop taking it easy, tell them they can go bugger themselves."

"Thanks Piotr."

"No problem, Olsa. Is that right?"

"Doesn't matter."

"Maybe that man will call you." Anya raises an eyebrow, returning, "What man?"

"He's seen you riding up and down my hill. Asked me if I knew you. So I said yes. Gave him your number."

"Who's the man?"

"Now isn't that the question?"

He drinks his coffee. Then everything is crystal clear. "Oh, shit," he says, "I shouldn't have done that, should I?"

"No, you're all right," she assures, "I just don't get who'd be interested in me, out here."

"I'm interested in you," Piotr says, resting his hands on the table, "I am…"

But then everything's like mud again. He's trapped in his head, staring out at suppositions grown out of once-tilled earth. Anya connects with the dorsal part of his right hand. She thinks about the mystery man, although she's actually thinking about Copernicus.

Later, in her flat, she launches her bike against the wall. Then she gives the possibly-torqued-although-in-all-probability-not-torqued-at-all fork a good hard stare. Cuz in her mind it's not only fucked, but also unfuckable; what available money there is lending itself to imperishable goods, electricity and gas.

She walks over to the sink and fills herself a glass of water. Then the phone rings, and she answers it. "Yea? What? You've been watching me ride?" An unsure smirk fills her face. "Oh I gotta find out, do I?" She starts getting irritated. "If you're really from Team Argonaut I'm gonna have to see you in person. I'll be here tomorrow. So if you want to pop in and shatter my dreams you're welcome." She slams the phone down, and peels her top off. "Prick," she grabs her boobs and shakes them, "Y'all just want these titties!" Marching to the bathroom, she adds, "Asshole," to herself and slams the door shut.

The next day, begrudgingly/excitedly, Anya Egelblöm sits in her kitchen across from Desmond Horatio-Mungo Bhatia O.B.E., eating her words by the spoonful. Sir Desmond, known by the Argonaut Team and colleagues variously as Mondo-Mungo, Dezzy, Dizzy, Batman, The Chronic, and Desmond The Pleasant Dwarf, recently celebrated second place overall in the Tour de France. But (this being the "Mondo" bit) next year, he wants to come first. He turns down a cup of coffee, asking instead for water. This is cool as far as Anya is concerned because it's free, but she is in fact unaware of the great danger in which she just placed him. Danger of Relapse: a

D.O.R. situation. Batman has only recently (say, three months prior) been released from rehab for caffeine-addiction, the ward itself overseen by Dutchman Upstart De Kook, Knight of the Copper Order, former composer and companion of Sicilian Viceroy Bianca McSalvadoré, who in truly unforeseen and tragic circumstances was admitted to the very same ward in this chilly month of March. Egelblöm eyes up The Chronic, hoping to inaugurate some form of intelligent conversation. "So…" she begins, "you are from Team Argonaut."

"Uh, yea…" he replies, awkwardly.

"Sorry about the phone thing."

"It's fine. It's okay."

"So, uh," Anya crosses her legs, "you've been watching me ride. Any particular reason?"

Dezzy smiles. "Do you watch the Tour de France Anya?"

"Every year without fail," she interrupts.

"Um, okay," Sir Desmond answers, taken aback by her enthusiasm, "do you want to compete?"

Anya tries to nod appropriately, or with the same force of conduct as Desmond the Pleasant Dwarf's nodding. It becomes a nod-ethon. "Because," he continues, "you're pretty good on those hills, honey. I timed you."

"Thanks," she replies, uncrossing her legs.

"If you could get rid of those ugly fucking shoes, I'd be happy to take you on."

"Um…" Humour, as we have seen, is not her strong point, not that that was exceptional humour on Dezzy's behalf; the comedic equivalent of an 18th Century hurdy-gurdy: a crank-operated mechanized violin popularized by Haydn and Mozart, "what now?"

"Do you want," he spells out, "to ride for Team Argonaut?" after which he plays the employment card, "are you employed?"

"No."

"Then what are you waiting for?" he grins at her.

Anya crosses her legs, adding, "No thanks."

"You sure?" he says.

"Yea," she brushes him off, "I don't like drugs."

The Chronic stands up. He slides on his jacket, concluding, "Well I don't like losers…"

Turkis™ is one of those very general bicycle outlets. It was founded by Ukrainian poet Dymytro Ponomarenko, whose writing style was characterized by obscure metaphors, a broad melodic sense and controversial views on kitchenware, i.e. segregation: drawers organized into sections of Fulvous, Smaragdine and Sarcoline-coloured forks, for example. In his later age however, Ponomarenko became an avid pedaler, thus founding Turkis™. The one Anya visits is a little bit inland, near Sixth Principle Baptist Church. Parallel to the Islamic green desk in Turkis™, Larry le Manche examines Bruno, her bike. He runs his wiry hands up and down the seat tube. Then he straddles it, and looks down the forks. "They're torqued," he notes.

"I knew it!" she yells.

"All right," Larry laughs, "keep your hair on – not loads, but enough to make you crash. Especially if you're on rough road or it's raining or something."

He gets off the bike and parks it against his workbench. He folds his arms, positing, "I'm guessing you want to replace it?"

"Yea, could you do that?"

"Well," he begins, "the ideal thing would be to replace the forks. But it's connected to that whole sort of front chassis sitting in the headtube."

"Yea?"

"So," he goes on, carefully, "you'd basically have to get a

whole new front bit with brakes and everything. How much do you want to spend?"

"About a thousand," Anya says.

"Yea," he smiles, "that's not gonna cut it. You're better off just taking this round back and doing the deed." He laughs.

"What?"

"Sorry, it's just," Larry tries to explain, "my dad's got a dog he's thinking of putting down. So he's gonna do that. You know. Take it round back and – kill it."

"Your dad?"

"Yea, my dad," he smirks, "what, you know him?"

"Are you Piotr le Manche's son?"

"Christ. Small world. You know him?"

"I ride past his house. We have coffee sometimes."

"You have coffee with him? You guys aren't fuckin, are you?"

"Jesus, no," she scowls, "what's your deal?"

"Hey," he says, leaning on the front desk, "I'm just a guy who works in a bicycle shop, who hasn't seen his father in a while. He's not too well."

"He's got dementia."

"Yea, I know," he interrupts, "I don't need a newsflash about my dad, thank you." He stops for a moment, assessing what he's said. "Look, uh," he shakes his head, "sorry. Sorry about that…and thank you."

Anya casts her eyes over Bruno who looks a little sad reclining on that workbench there. Maybe Larry's right and he ought to be put down.

Larry clears his throat. "Uh, look, have a, have a new bike seat on me."

"No," she rejects him, "it's all right."

"No," Larry is serious, "I work here. So you're overruled,

and that's just how it is."

"Is it now?"

"Yea, it is. So have a new bike seat," he licks his lips, "but you probably know how to put it on, so here," he grabs an Erik Ormandy Bike Seat® off the shelf, "here you go."

She takes it. Larry walks Bruno to the door. Then she grabs her bike and walks out. Larry stares at her ass.

"Happy riding…"

◊

Zipping up her unwashed jersey, she fills her water bottle and slips it into her rucksack. Just as she's about to leave, she stares at the Ormandy bike seat on her kitchen table. Then she stares at Bruno. Then the bike seat, again—She unzips her rucksack, throws the bike seat in, and rides off. After an hour of pedaling down a barren country road, she spots a group of trees congregating on the roadside. It's almost like a miniature forest. She brakes and gets off her bike, observing the dense foliage. She looks up and down the road, hyperventilating. No one's coming anytime soon, so Anya drags herself and Bruno into the finite forest, and rests her bike on a trunk. Sticks and twigs snap underfoot. She pulls out the bike seat—an Easterly wind drags the trees to the left. There is creaking, yanking, and branches gripping other branches. She's safe in here; the wind outside the mini-greenwood. Anya removes her helmet and drenches her face in drinking water. She sits on the ground between two rocks and takes out the bike seat. The Ormandy seat is set against a nest of grass and other twiggy things. She slides down her bicycle shorts. The seat is slid past the labia majora, minora and under the vestibule into her opening. She gawks up at the trees. There are bits of white and blue and grey torn apart by branches. It feels good and weird to be doing this. She comes in the forest, and looks at Bruno.

◊

Doctor Fenway Ilyich takes Harmon through a series of fulvous hallways to the mess hall. Smaragdine chairs underpin a sestet of empty sarcoline tables. Ilyich picks one. They sit on the very end of it, eating pudding. To be accurate, Ilyich is the only one eating pudding. Harmon has barely touched his. Nor does it help that they're the only ones on the table. It's all a bit strange. The officers on the other tables, looking at them, can feel how strange it is. It's safe to say that there will be no officer joining Ilyich and Chikenyyt, making lewd conversation, and kindly buggering—when the sunken-cuboid dinner plate is polished—off. Harmon stares at his pudding. "It's weird."

"It's good pudding, man," Ilyich says.

"Even the uniforms are different," Harmon comments.

Fenway puts his cigarettes and lighter on the table, asking, "You don't remember any of this?"

"I don't lie," Harmon replies, "so, no – I don't."

Doctor Ilyich, an abuser of cacology with reference to insensitivity (hell, he's a doctor), takes his fork and penetrates his pudding at an angle of twenty-five degrees. Harmon observes the dark khaki substance being ripped apart, consumed.

"What's going on?" Harmon asks.

"Can I ask you something?" Ilyich mumbles.

"Sure," Harmon replies.

"The drug bust," Ilyich begins, "when you were dogging."

"What?"

"That's what we call it," the medical examiner explains, "you're a dogger."

"Jesus Christ."

"Just go with it for the time being. I'll—"

"Okay—"

"Fill in the blanks later," Ilyich gets back on topic, "so the drug bust you saw when you were dogging…"

"Yea."

"There're always a few people on a fair ride, for example, who've done the ride before. It's familiar to them. And you can tell because they behave differently," he looks Harmon dead in the eye, "was there anyone like that? Anyone who might've known more than you did," running his fork through his pudding, "it's crucial that you answer this as best you can."

"The dealers, maybe," the dogger suggests, "one of them did a runner."

"I assume none of your fellow officers acted that way?"

"What, ran away?"

"No," Ilyich corrects, "knew more than they were letting on."

Harmon shrugs. "Probably not."

"Well I know they didn't," the doctor says, "no Florin police officer is allowed to smoke," he cracks his knuckles, "apart from you, so I assume, then, since your orders are to locate Zachary Mullein, that it was the enemy agent Mullein in that hallucination who, as you say, 'did a runner'."

An atonal, contrapuntal idiom, as if we're in an Otto-Groß composition, or perhaps a triangular prism that refracts one beam of light into many spectral tints, fills the room. Truth is being levelled. The heartbeats of eight million men, women and children are being reorganized at the same thumping echelon. The arrogant advocate of psychedelic warfare nods, saying, "The memory of vapour, Harmon," he points at the dogger's pudding, "you gonna eat that?"

◊

Harmon Chikenyyt recalls what are maybe constituents of his childhood: Culpable happenings, requisite data for today's cock-ups…His father, apparently, worked in a leather jacket factory. The lens lulls down through lotion-white billows. Quail Chikenyyt, Q.C., (if you forgive the, uh…)—Pan to ground level: streets, the factory's employee's entrance. The crass worker statue smiles at its human counterparts who march along brick laid out by twenty-nine year old Russian imports. Q.C.'s buddy was a guy called Titus Almazan. The winters would strike his hands with metallic pink blotches, wetted by Quail's breath because he never fucking shut up: "One-hundred-and-twenty thousand a week, that's how much I make. My rent's about eighty thousand a week, so that's forty left. Great. Now I gotta feed my family and we're down now to ten thousand."

"You catch the bus?" Titus asks.

"That's another thing, then," Quail confirms, "and there you go. I got a thousand left. What do you call it, play money," he picks up his rucksack, signing out on the rota tablet, "in at four this morning."

"You come in earlier don't you? You put overtime on?"

Quail shakes his head.

"Why not?"

"You work and have no money," Quail explains, "you're unemployed and have no money. Ten minutes ain't gonna change that," after which he puts on his sunglasses.

They walk along the docks. The sun slides overhead and Almazan lights a cigarette. "Use the food-banks?"

"Nah," Quail says, pulling his shirt away from his chest,

"not that poor, getting there though."

"There she is," Titus announces, pointing to the other side of the harbour at the Captain Timmy Koolen Food Bank. Tomas G. Koolen, was a Scottish labour leader (and not actual captain) born to Dutch-Jewish parents in Belgravia, London. After moving to Scotland in 2063, he was the head of a cigarette-makers' union by the age of twenty-two. In 2086 he became the founder and first resident of the Scottish Partnership of Toil and Exchange. One of those ridiculous, always-male enthusiasts of nautical captain's hats, the fashion equivalent of kicking a child in the face, Captain Koolen opened this food bank himself, where three frog-like women now unload a truck filled with tinned food. Titus flicks his cigarette butt overboard. "If you need a few extra items like noodles or bread, it ain't too bad."

"I got a garden," Quail betters, "growing vegetables, carrots."

"Make a nice soup with those," Titus offers.

"Yea," Quail scoffs, "see if my son eats it."

And Harmon was an unwanted son—Four years prior, Quail and Camilla Chikenyyt had expected a daughter. She was born still in April. And when they'd mustered up the courage to, "try again," Harmon appeared nine months later, and a boy.

Camilla—by trade a player of *guslis*, a type of zither used by ballad singers as accompaniment, particularly in folk music—would tune her instrument for days at a time alone on the upper floors of their flat in Fergnan. When Harmon saw his Mother in the back garden, which usually indicated a good day on her part, she would look away, her quartz-coloured eyes suffering either from nystagmus or the eye-jitter of the recently cracked brain. Her senses had been dulled. Her attention was paid to weather. Harmon tried desperately to fit in. But in doing so, he became displaced, a lonely mucus-like creature dripping from others' noses. Or at least that's what he recalls, now, in front of Fenway.

◊

Ilyich—pudding completed, or, "uncompleted," as the Oba of Lagos Hermann Gläus-Pepple once said, returning home after a quite serious polo-cum-tapioca session with the boys—gets a phone call from Sergeant Copernicus Kapoor, even though he's probably in the same building. The force medical examiner takes it parallel to a vending machine. "Not the first time," Kapoor would say, here. Assuming a giant protractor arches over Fenway's head, he leans at an angle of 80° against the aforementioned machine. "Ilyich here," he says.

"Kapoor," the phone line gurgles, "he remember anything yet?"

"I mean, in terms of reality, he's completely baffled."

"You need to suss him out."

"I just did, I was thinking," narrowing his eyes, "if I could go dogging with him…"

"There's no way in hell—"

"Off the record, of course. Show him the ropes again. Maybe then he could be of some use."

"Well the board of governors are meeting Egelblöm about redundancies."

"You're joking, more cuts?"

"Ever since our favourite paedophile burnt down Florin prison they've been trying to shut us up, or shut us down."

"You think they'll shut the station?"

"The dogger program," Kapoor coughs on the other end,

"it's not exactly legal, is it, Fenway?"

The Force Medical Examiner's eyes slice open the vending machine's glass at a popular brand of Hungarian sweetbuns: Doctor Jack's Peppermint Fánks. The world is suddenly reduced to pointillism. Fenway's right eyelid twitches at this earth-shattering window of opportunity to pay, what is it? £5.25 – for an unusually delicious little bun with a dip in the middle; cartographical inconsistencies with reference to baked goods having always been immoderately more seductive than goods without cartographical inconsistencies. Arguably, then, the cinnamon bun is superior to the cookie; ring doughnuts more accomplished than Lo mai chi; the Fánk, indeed, trumps the muffin. And, oh gosh, darn it, doesn't he know it – that Fánk does look mighty fine with its powdered surface and captivating worktop dunk and whatnot. Doctor Fenway Ilyich is fat, however. Not the studmuffin he was before. Now on one of those don't-eat-anything-remotely-edible-type diets, he gapes, still, if only for Doctor Jack's Peppermint Fánks.

In a pianist's pocket of a secluded basement corner, Ilyich flips on a different type of vending machine – it looks like an upright piano. All the familiars are there: the soundboard, hitch pins, bass bridge, long bridge, single strings, bichords, trichords, dampers and wrest pins. Fenway tickles his stomach, saying, "This is a spliff machine."

Flicking the dichotonator (which has, "Dichotonator," written on it) along the base (or stylobate), the funnel drops ten tightly rolled D.E.R.P. cigarettes into a welcoming tray. Ilyich offers a light snigger, like, "Wasn't that fucking cool?" He glides the gamboge fags into a silver case and passes it to Harmon. "Your weapons," he comments, nodding, "don't smoke more than one in twenty-four hours. The dogger before you had four," then, with an ample slice of academic gravitas, "sufficed to say she didn't come back."

"Meaning?"

"She's in a coma," Ilyich explains, "has been for two months."

"Mullein's alive, then?"

"Of course he's alive."

"So," Harmon offers, "if I can meet Mullein when I'm – dogging – then I should be able to meet the dogger before me. Does that make sense?"

Fenway's face shrugs into the equivalent of a French Lay: a 13th Century form of poetry and music wherein the lyrics tended to be written in praise of a certain lady of utmost distinction, arranged flexibly in stanzas of six to sixteen lines with four to eight syllables per line, redolent of loss, inability, lethargy and failure. "Most things make sense," Fenway says, "she might as well be dead. Got about as much brain activity as a carrot," he points at the cigarette case, "so moderation, Mister Dogger sir."

Harmon asks what her name is.

"Classified," the medical examiner replies, "can't say."

Simultaneously, on the top floor of the Florin Police Station, Egelblöm congregates with the board o' governors in an isolated, inchworm-coloured room near the women's toilets. The three governors—Ulfred Riggan, Natasha Jlak and Kaat Moptin—sit opposite Egelblöm on a loblolly pine table. Riggan slides an ominous folder halfway across the channel. Egelblöm looks at it, saying, "Do you see the wheelchair?" The governor twitches and stands up. "Sorry," he says, handing her the folder, clarifying, "those are the, uh, proposed cuts for next year."

Jlak croaks at this duplicitous comment in a sort of, "just-tell-her-the-truth-you-goddamn-pussy," kind of way. Heeding this, Riggan continues, "Well, those are the cuts." Egelblöm parts the pages casually. This goes on for twenty seconds. She subsequently flops it on the table, complaining, "You can't be serious."

"We are," Jlak coughs.

"It was a rhetorical question," Egelblöm replies.

"No," Jlak continues, "it wasn't. It was a statement. You just accused us of not being serious and it's my job to tell you that we are just that."

"You can't lay off twenty officers," Egelblöm offers, "we have forty as it is."

"Moptin," Jlak turns to her colleague, "is there an echo in here?"

"Seems there is," Moptins concurs, tapping her fingers, "bit redundant, if you don't mind the pun."

"I don't," Riggan interjects, "I don't mind the pun. I think it's witty."

"Funny stuff," Jlak says.

Egelblöm rams the table with her wheelchair in a fit of disabled rage. The governors flinch. "Jesus Christ!"

"Are you crazy?"

"You could have killed us!"

Egelblöm reverses, tossing the folder further towards the tossers. "I know this is a complete exercise in P.R."

"Yes, it is," Jlak grants, "the Florin incident was a disaster. It would've cost the government the next election."

"If you three hadn't covered it up."

"Exactly, if we three hadn't covered it up. And with all due respect, despite your admirable record, we feel it would be beneficial to the country if we closed this particular chapter."

"Would things be easier for you if I were dead," the elder

policewoman suggests, "because I'm the only survivor? Is that what you're saying?"

"But since you are the only survivor," Moptin interjects, "wouldn't you like closure?"

Egelblöm frowns. "What do you think I've been doing here for the past four years?"

Governor Moptin folds her lips and looks at Governor Riggan. He, in turn, looks at Senior Governor Jlak, who is, apparently, an expert in rape. "Well," she starts, cleaning her glasses, "just because Mullein raped you during the riot preceding the fire does not give you an excuse to subject both suburbs and exurbia to some futile search for a man whom most have forgotten."

Moptin annexes her own contribution. "And there's the English factor."

"Mmm."

"Ahh."

"Florin," Moptin carries on, "sat directly on the border between Scotland and England, did it not? In terms of the legal jurisdiction of this investigation, it's a bit of nightmarish situation. There were both English and Scottish prisoners," she picks her cuticles, "unless of course you've heard otherwise?"

Outside the police station, the door to Fenway's jordy blue car swings open. "Get in," he says.

"We going to my place?" Harmon asks, "I assume I have a place?"

"Not safe," Ilyich justifies, "we're going to my place."

The doctor's phone rings. Egelblöm is on the other end. "Show him the ropes again," she vents, "and this time, when you send him in, send him in deep."

"I don't want him overdosing," Ilyich counters.

"That's not what I mean," she complains, "I want Mullein cornered. I want him fucked real good so we can find him out here and shoot the son of a bitch."

"Governors not go too well then…?"

He gets in the driver's side as Egelblöm continues to yell: "You're running out of time."

"We're both running out of time," Fenway argues, waving at Harmon, telling him to shut the door.

"Fenway I'll—what was that?"

"Car door," the doctor explains.

"I'll be dead soon," Egelblöm posits, "we can't let these bastards win. If they win then what the hell are we good for? What did all those people die for?"

"Uh," Ilyich keys the ignition, "nothing?"

"Correctamundo—" She hangs up as Fenway reverses out. The chassis vibrates over fallen hail. Harmon stares out of the window like a child visiting a train station he's never been to before. "What are we doing?"

"We," Fenway begins, peering in the back mirror, "are going to get high, my friend…"

Fenway's is a stereotypical doctor's apartment: used, unused oxygen cylinders, a loofa, cigarettes in an ashtray, Trippy's Peanut Butter™, matches, red salt packets, a lighter, Bosom Marmalade™, another lighter, a box of teabags, a yellow sponge, an unwashed tumbler, two handtowels (one grullo-coloured, the other mango tango) a crusty kettle, bottled water, two untouched tubs-worth of instant coffee, a basket full of this year's newspapers, a waste paper-basket, one potted welwitschia, a television, all twelve volumes of Doctor Norvin Tubaniña's magnum opus *Medicamenta Principis* (2073-78, Juggernaut Press; £935.00 on www.amazon.co.sb), two beige chairs, an inflatable mattress perpendicular to Fenway's Tubaniña volumes, a lava lamp (exterior white, the bubbling paraffin wax and carbon tetrachloride mixture a smokey topaz) and on the counter, most importantly and satisfactorily the morning after a night out, is a tub of Super-héros de la gynécologie (*"Pour lui…"*) facial cream, consisting of mineral oil, isohexadecane, lanolin oil, lime extract, microcrystalline wax, eucalyptus, medicago sativa seed powder, paraffin, tocopheryl succinate, niacin, beta-carotene, citric acid, aluminium distereate, octyldodecanol, magnesium stearate, panthenol, limonene, geraniol, citronellol, methylchloroisothiazolinone, methyl*isothiazolinone*, and Derpoloxin. Doctor Fenway Ilyich adjusts his speakers. They play late period Ulysses Lachnér: *the Viceroy-General Tapes*, to be precise. Fenway snaps open the cigarette case. "You like Lachnér?"

"I don't like any of this at all," Harmon replies.

"Look," Ilyich begins, fed up, "you were chosen because you had a creative mind. You're a psychedelic warrior, dude. So you can go outside in the rain and cry, or you can grow a pair of balls and go dogging with me. Which to be fair to me is a lot more appealing than it sounds."

Harmon snaps. "Give me the cigarette."

Fenway slaps his hands together, doing a little cha-cha and saying, "The truffle-hunter's back!"

"Why do you say that?" Harmon shoots back.

"I don't know," the doctor relaxes "first thing that came to mind. A bit like dogging."

Harmon lights the D.E.R.P. joint. He inhales and passes it to Fenway who takes a deep hit, highlighting, "Do it like I just did: big draws," he passes the spliff back to Harmon, "before I get my transfer."

The apprehensive dogger sucks in for what seems like three years. Then he passes the cigarette back to Fenway and stares at the ground. "…I'm gonna be sick."

"Well," Ilyich adjusts, "you need to get sickly involved with this girl I'm seeing."

What the hell? Harmon thinks. *Where did that come from?*

Harmon squints at his host. "W…what?"

"This girl," Fenway says, unsure, "well, let's say, 'woman,' *dude*. Great intel. Sees Mullein all the time. Know what I mean?" He turns to his twelve volumes of *Medicamenta Principis* and salutes them.

"I thought," Harmon does a massive burp, "sorry – I thought this was square one?"

"This is square one," Fenway agrees, "cuadrado número uno. Sex is the most efficient way to seek out, pursue and retrieve intelligence."

"I don't know how I feel about this," the dogger fades out, "Fenway – Fen – you still there—Hello?" Cannabis plays a significant role in Buddhist ceremonies. As claimed by Indian tradition and scrollings, Siddhartha Gautama, like, the *actual* Buddha, consumed nothing but hemp and hemp-seeds for six years prior to becoming *The* Buddha in the 5th Century A.D. Let us put to one side the state of his bowels, and the grave-turning of those bowels when Nepal had to impose harsh restrictions on cannabis in the 1970s as a result of an influx of Westerners in search of oblivion (as opposed to enlightenment), which led to increased cannabis cultivation, price inflation and a general sense of "Ah, *fuck*…"

"The gaseous composition of mainstream marijuana smoke viz. carbon monoxide (17.6 mg), carbon dioxide (57.3 mg), ammonia (0.3 mg), hydrogen cyanide (532.0 µg), cyanogen (19.0 µg), isoprene (83.0 µg), acetaldehyde (1,200.0 µg), acetone (443.0 µg), acrolein (92.0 µg), acetonitrile (132.0 µg), benzene (76.0 µg), toluene (112.0 µg), vinyl chloride (5.4 ng), dimethylnitrosamine (75.0 ng) and methylethylnitrosamine (27.0 ng) amounts to a potent THC-delivery system, and is perhaps the most important cultural activity ergo scientific area ever grasped by human fingers and research laboratories. Crucially, advances made in the field of Diethylamine and its by-product Derpoloxin—in coalescence with this cannabinoid chemical makeup—will permit a medicinal gate to the next, and the indulgence of reality 2.0. Just as politically manufactured enlightenment is still enlightenment, manufactured experience is still experience. It exists only in the mind, our sensory life being as much an abstraction as Marxism, or Buddhism. And when—the Derpoloxin exhausted in our bloodstream—we at last return to the realm of known experience, we will be more for it." (*Medicamenta Principis*, p. 2,955.)

◊

Dogger Harmon Chikenyyt stands maladjusted in a supermarket aisle. The fluorescent lighting renders every dirt-spec visible on the bone-white floor. The linoleum leads from Chikenyyt's feet, up the aisle, to the requisite inbuilt butchery: Fenway's Meats. Harmon, highly, walks down the aisle. The tins on the walls have his mother's face on them. Camilla. No gusli. The well situated grin of maternal grit. He reaches Fenway's Meats, observing the tenderloins for sale. They have those confectionary price tags that stick out like junkies' needles. The cut-quality is noteworthy. Harmon wishes he could take away the glass and touch them; the culinary solidarity of the primal cut. He touches his penis. "What am I doing," he says to himself, after which a moan bellows from behind the butcher's counter, "Fenway?"

He looks briefly to his left, for no reason in particular, and sees the manager marching towards him. *Shorticus Fatticus*, it could be said. He has a thick moustache of the Portuguese gardener persuasion, adept at shading obscenities. Then, an arching brow punctuates a militaristic, "Ah…one of the animals." Harmon mulls the utterance over, and sees himself on Foreman's Peak in the wastelands…

◊

Hydrogen car-raiders moss-camber like badgers. One of them opens a tin of sardines. Another scrubs her goggles. Vasilisa Rasputin, a little mentioned Russian mercenary operating in the S.B. during the Border Skirmish of 2065, lowers her binoculars, noting, "Lunchtime," she looks at Harmon, "who do you ride with?"

"Rezi," he replies, as though he's been doing this for ages.

"Where is he?"

"Takin a leak." Vasilisa shoves her tongue in her cheek. "Uh-huh," there's a bit of binocular-peeping, "there it is—"

"Who, Rezi?"

"No you idiot the package, let's go, Eury!"—Several metres away under a bush, Eury drops his sardines. "What?"

Vasilisa address everyone: "Let's hit the fuckin road!"

Raiders scramble onto their vehicles. Rasputin spanks her goggles on after downing two *Cimicoxib* capsules: a COX-2 inhibitor used to mitigate depression and schizophrenia. Harmon jumps on his bike. The erstwhile used-car salesman Rezi Dante scuttles up the hill, buckling up his pants. He stumbles over to the bike saying, "Can't a person get five minutes round here!" He hops on. Harmon grips his waist. Rezi revs the accelerator. "Poison ivy, man," he tightens his helmet, "goddamn joke." And here's all the motorbikes *roaring* downhill to the gravel road, the frigid air burning everyone's faces. Rezi laughs and says, "This hydrogen driver won't know what hit him!"

"What's he got!?" Harmon yells back.

"Hydrogen!"

"Yea, I got that far!"

"Routes too! Be there when his mates pass through! Easy pickins!"

Here's this cortège of motorbikes *vrooming* up to the bulletproof car. They all kick up the burnt umber S.B. dust. They try to run the car off the road. Inside the car, driver Allegra Beatty has other plans. She turns her radio on full blast: L.D.R.'s Grammy-winning (Best Pop Duo/Group Performance, 2061) single, *Lick My Chest Hair Baby* blows out of her speakers.

> Fuckin' on a Tuesday
> Grabbin' the Arapahoe
> Coffee at the Moose Inn
> Lickin' all the beta bits
> (*"Tres, dos, uno, ah!"*)

> Lick my chesthair baay-beee
> Lick my chesthair baay-beee

> Trippin' on a by-line
> Chokin' on a Wednesday
> Takin' all the takeaways
> Dealing with my mental health
> (*"Misogyny is rife, Tony—"*)

> Lick my chesthair baay-beee
> Lick my chesthair baay-beee

The Hydrogen-driver un-clicks her seatbelt, yelling, over the music, "You scroungers ain't gettin' shit!" Jamming her dagger in the dashboard computer, her database of routes is completely fried. Reaching up to a live grenade dangling from the mirror like an air-freshener, she rips it off and pulls the pin out. "Hakanakalakadeu!" she screams, it being Tonguetire (Hydrogen-driver language) for, "For the glory of the company!"

Outside, the car bursts like a lightbulb. The window frames are smoking. Harmon snaps his goggles off, shouting, "What was that!?"

"You watch!" Rezi says, "that gas ignites, shit goes up like roman cand—!"

The car explodes and a hubcap is sent twirling towards Eury. It takes his head clean off – bits of sardine fly out of his teeth and into the dust. The headless body falls off the bike, which is then catapulted into the air by his lifeless foot getting caught in the spokes. It lands a few hundred metres away with a depressing crunch. Rezi slows down. He rests his feet on the burnt umber S.B. dust. "You okay kid?" Harmon says he gonna be sick. "People get killed," Rezi replies, "no sermons here. Quick and quiet; you get schooled," he sucks his head in like a turtle, "I got this jacket real cheap…"

◊

Back in the hallucinatory supermarket, Harmon finds that he is still looking at *Shorticus Fatticus*. Bigode português. "Uh. No, man," the dogger explains, "I'm just – really high."

"No," Shorticus says, "you are the animals."

"Does, uh," Harmon is hazy, "I'm sorry," he looks at the

sign, "Fenway, work here?"

"Not for long," Shorticus replies, peering down over the counter, "this scumbag right here…"

Harmon leaps over the meat display-cum-counter and finds Fenway having sex with a woman called Grais Lugassi. Doctor Ilyich's erect penis sticks out of his butcher's coat like a plank on a pirate ship. Lugassi's cheeks are parted, and her perineum is exposed. The butcher plunges into her. The skin tightens around the anus ergo vulva. Fenway is rigid. The corpora cavernosa is flushed with blood, its prismatic form slipping in and out of Grais' cavity.

"I don't believe it when you say you'll go deeper," she exclaims à la PornHub, "but then you do! Oh God!" Perspiration rolls down the doctor's face. The manager looks at his watch, shaking his head. Lugassi's labias slosh about as Fenway wriggles himself even deeper. Then he pulls out and slaps her behind. She kneels beneath him, fondling her breasts. He ejaculates on her face, like, properly goes for it, and she swirls the semen around her mouth. It dribbles from chin to breasted cavity.

The manager points a girthéd index finger at Fenway and says, "You are *degenerate*!" Harmon supplants the postmodern from his brain, adding, "You're an animal, Fenway."

"See!" Shorticus says.

"Oh yea."

"Both of you! *Out!*"

"Sorry sir," Harmon persuades, "we're leaving right now; *aren't we* Fenway?"

Fenway nods, saying, "Don't worry Luciano or whatever your name is, I got what I needed to know." He buckles up and slaps Harmon on the shoulder. "Let's go," they jump over the meat counter and traipse back through the aisle of tinned food, "why is your Mother on the——?"

"How do you know——?"

"Yea," the medical examiner expounds, "don't try lying or anything because I have direct access to your mind, and vice versa. It's what dogging does to you," he laughs, "so the question really is, what now, Harmon Chikenyyt, if that *is* your real name?"

Harmon thinks for a moment. "Mullein's in the Alchemist's park."

"We ride on the winds of others," Fenway says, "*God* I'm lonely."

"What?"

"Doesn't matter."

"Outside," the grullo-coloured sky is dead. Grey by numbers; #A99AA86 to be precise, an airspace designed by committee.

Chikenyyt and Ilyich stroll down a provincial road. Then, a really kitsch high street with loads of shops. Total rubbish. Harmon's uncomfortable. He's not quite down with the whole, "high reality," thang. Harmon asks where everyone is. (Note: You can emulate the sound a squirrel makes by pressing your lower lip against your upper teeth and gyrating your tongue, therefore sucking and pushing air in and out really quickly. Ilyich makes this sound for no particular reason.)

"I'd say we're both pretty introverted," Fenway retorts, "your personality's always gonna affect your hallucination – you got any fetishes?"

"I don't think so."

"You may very well have fetishes. You'll see them here. But don't fret about it. Embrace it. In fact…" they stop in front of a large shop window full of neatly painted oil portraits. The artist has used an explicitly constrained palette of amaranth red (#D3212D), begonia (#FA6E79), brown sugar (#AF6E4D), dolphin grey (#828E84) and French wine (#AC1E44). The subjects of the portraits are a series of oversized hogs copulating with young hairless men. Their naked skin is like alabaster. Their cherubic faces are contorted in agony. "…You may even be repulsed," turning to Harmon, "there are no secrets in here. It's a kinder world."

"Are the pigs yours or mine?"

"They're mine," Fenway admits.

"How can that stuff cross your mind?"

"Scary," the doctor summarizes, "isn't it?"

Later, Fenway Ilyich acquires a cone of Caramel Balsamic Swirl ice cream from a shrouded proprietor in an unmarked ice cream van. The two doggers sit unbearably on a bench constructed from American hornbeam timber in the Alchemist's Park: 400 sq. ft. of unadulterated concrete and tarmac adorned by six and a half fledgling hydrangeas and a gun store—Dietrich and Daughter's Rifle Emporium—one hundred and four metres downstream. Harmon looks at the flowers, muttering, "I love hydrangeas," he sighs through his nose, "so when I was graduating before, that wasn't real?"

"Dogging," the doctor clarifies.

"But you were there," Harmon remembers, "so you must've been dogging at the same time I was."

"Nope," Ilyich clarifies, again, "that trip was *your* doing."

"What about Tara?"

Ilyich stops mid-lick. "Nuth Thara Thimmen?"

"Is she real?" Harmon says, rather baffled, "did she graduate at the same time I did? Like, in reality?"

"Thee, thorry," Ilyich swallows a chunk of ice cream, "she's your age. Same class, uh—Jesus," he realizes, "you *really* don't remember, do you?"

He's right. Harmon can't remember a damn thing. Ilyich clears his throat for the delivery of some bad news: "She, uh – she died in the first week."

This is an unrestrictedly strange and hurtful piece of information. Chikenyyt tries to imagine pillars existing under the already known sandman-made columns. But his eyes and ears are open now. All the oxygen has been jettisoned out of the spaceship. That reliance on blind chance is finished. The shackles are off, and liberation never felt so painful. Any offending truth is always felt best, or worst, in some park around 4.00 p.m. The kids are pissing off, and you're stuck with all that hailing halcyon soured by suburban wind. Harmon furrows his brow, mumbling an unsure, "What?"

"She was knifed," Fenway says, "one of those freak things. I mean, it shouldn't happen. But it does."

Harmon drops his head.

"Why? You like her?"

Harmon folds his arms, sighing. "I don't know."

"Wouldn't blame you," his fellow dogger assures, "good copper." He examines what remains of his cone. "We all got expiry dates," he chomps on it, "thome are juth earlier then otherth…"

On the other side of the Alchemist's Park, a figure hiding inside an oversized dark electric blue hoody is sitting on a bench. The figure's legs are glued together. He or she stares at the ground. "Hey," Harmon elbows Fenway, "you think that's Mullein?"

"He wouldn't wear a hood."

"Who is it then?"

"Someone else's dogging," Ilyich says, "that's all." He looks at his watch. Not like he had too. When you're dogging, a watch is about as useful as a bag of dicks. "Do you know why people get high?"

Harmon squints. "I always thought it was escapism."

"Escapism for you – or the drug? You ever think about that?" He studies the hooded figure. "You can feel it getting irritated. The D.E.R.P., I mean. Feel it messing with you. Like it's bored."

Harmon asks if he thinks the drug is intelligent.

"I'm not saying anything, Harmon," Fenway says, "what I say when I'm tripping out doesn't actually move my lips in the real world. So why should anyone care about it?"

"But seeing you in a photograph," Harmon suggests, "is another way of meeting you, even if that photograph is in your mind—wait, what?"

"It's hard," Ilyich admits, "it's spooky. I want to understand this stuff more than anything in the world. But at the same time, I don't think I can. And you know I'm telling the truth becau—Shit, there he is—!"

Mullein, a light-moustachioed male of Greenlandic Kalaallit descent, appears adjacent to the hooded person: He spots Harmon and Fenway, and sprints.

Harmon chases after Fenway as he takes off. They pass a department store selling 6-8 year-old children wearing leather jockstraps. "Jesus – FENWAY!"

Fenway turns briefly, saying, "We're crossing channels!"

"He up ahead?"

"Up front here!"

One Zachary Mullein—drug-dealing paedophile rapist— runs into Iverson's Health and Beauty: one of those pretentiously fancy organic supermarkets with products like 500mg turmeric capsules, 1000mg Omega 3 fish oil caplets, coconut almond butter, chia seeds, sea-salt hummus crisps, Doctor Tsukamoto's Powdered Organic Flaxseeds, yeast flakes, egg-free mayonnaise, and 125g packages of red split lentils. Here's Mullein sprinting down Iverson's chickpea-themed aisle. "Ropo, get me out; I want out!" He knocks over a display of 30g packets of Honey and Sesame-flavoured chickpeas.

Down the other end, Doctor Fenway flicks organic pear and apple spread and reduced-sugar three-fruit marmalade off the walls with a checkout stick; those plastic twigs used to split up groups of shopping, yelling, "You still fucking kids, Zachary?"

Mullein runs out of the aisle and through the gluten-free patisserie, two large swinging doors, and into a long hallway. There are bleach-ridden black and white tiles everywhere. The walls are an awful churning cream colour, the type seen in caravans and student-housing walls built from balsa-wood and air. Mullein is gasping for breath, begging, "Wake me up! Come on! Wake me up!"

An elderly woman of Northern Irish heritage called Gwendolyn Halliday taps him on the spine with her stick. "Why don't you get back to packing?"

Mullein turns in more ways than one. "What did you say, bitch?"

"Don't talk to your manager that way!" Halliday scolds, "you pack bags here, don't you?"

"When I was little, yea."

"Your mother called," she informs, "told me to tell you your father's dead."

"Oh," Mullein takes the piss, "thanks for that."

"That's what I said," Halliday corroborates, "all these snow-chinks having babies," and so begins her long shuffle to the patisserie.

Zachary Mullein cracks his neck, tacking on, "Hey Miss

Halliday," he arcs an eyebrow as she turns to face him, "fuck you."

Miss Halliday shakes her head, lumbering along unaffected and mumbling, "Yea, yea…" The two doggers burst on the scene and knock old Halliday over, "Ahhh—!'

They dart towards Mullein who yanks his AMT Hardballer pistol from his belt. Harmon skids to a halt, but Ilyich marches on, repeating the quotidian notion on p. 1,292 of *Medicamenta Principis*, "Weapons are—to the distress of the D.E.R.P. junkie and/or abuser—useless in hallucinations […]" over and over again in his head.

BANG! – a bullet nips through Harmon's harmonious heart. The dogger's torso twitches in the spurious light as he falls over, dead—And boy oh boy is Doctor Fenway Ilyich F.M.E. wrong about this one.

BANG! – a cartridge splits the doctor's chest open. He trips over and squeals along the black and white tiles leaving a murky paste on the black; a rufous stain on the white.

Having seen too much, being scared, alone in his thoughts and others', Zachary Mullein turns the gun on himself. He paints the wall behind him with his frontal lobe.

The dream goes silent. For the user, nothing is ever really gained.

◊

Back in the force medical examiner's apartment—in the bathroom adjacent to boxes of *Degarelix*: for the management of advanced prostate cancer; *Leflunomide*: for active rheumatoid arthritis; *Miglustat*: for non-neuropathic Gaucher's disease for whom enzyme replacement therapy with *Imiglucerase* isn't feasible; *Paliperidone*: for schizophrenia; *Valsartan*: for uncomplicated hypertension; *Zalepon*: for short-term treatment of insomnia, and *Zonisamide*: for adjunctive treatment of partial seizures in epileptic adults—Harmon waits his turn to throw up.

"Oohhagghhkkk!" Fenway grips the toilet bowl. "Fuck," he spits, "oh God…"

Harmon emits half a burp. "What happened?"

"What he did," Fenway grunts, "was impossi—Oohhagg-hhkkk!"

Harmon starts to consider the sink. Ilyich notices his colleague's wandering eyes, and says, "Mate, not the washba-sin…" Harmon just chunders everywhere in this guy's sink: A Sumptuous Glass Bowl Roughly Surfaced With A Bendy Ball-Tap, The Snood Expressively Pretzeled Ergo Optimized For Human Use (or at least that's what it said on the undamaged cardboard box in which it arrived last Tuesday; a rainy, windy, *raindy* day.)

A single tear runs down Fenway's cheek. "It's gonna take hours to clean that."

"I'm gonna die in this bathroom," Harmon groans.

Fenway nods, responding, "Maybe this *is* heaven…"

"Shut up," his colleague says, wiping the sick off the corners of his mouth, "but that was Mullein, wasn't it?"

"Yea," Fenway agrees, "that was him. We need to get back to the station asap."

"Why in God's name do we need to do that?"

"You got a drug bust to attend."

"Again?"

"Well," he explains, "since you've already experienced it you'll be the most qualified officer there,"

Harmon hurls over the ornate washbasin.

"Welcome back," Fenway says.

At the Ropo Adeyemi residence alias D.E.R.P.-central—in the back yard in front of his Beech hedging, Hostas, Lamb's Ear, Daylilies, Yarrows, Marigolds and Black-Eyed Susans—Mullein vomits obtrusively, forcefully and violently. Adeyemi stops eating his Granny Smith, commenting, "Zach? You good, man?"

"Hell no," Mullein replies, and the final upchuck slips out. He straightens his back, picking various bits out of his moustache. He waddles over to his Nigerian associate, who asks, "What happened to you?"

Mullein blows hot air out of his nose as he grinds his teeth. "I think we've got trouble," the sun touches his pale skin, "that rookie I saw when I was dogging."

"Yea?"

"I saw him again," he nods, "but this time he had a friend."

"You are being followed?"

"Yea," Mullein cuts his eyes, "they're in my head – shit I did years ago."

"Florin?"

"Long time ago," he thinks about lighting things on fire, "they're catching on with the channel-surfing," he thinks about Egelblöm, "they know where we are."

Ropo reengages the apple in his mouth, chewing sonorously. "We're jusht gonna have to get dem."

Mullein clears his throat and burbles up a roisterous cackle, a pallid residue running down the corners of his mouth…

In that spirit, a long time ago, Ropo Adeyemi used to be part of a crack team of cannabis traffickers. Departing Jordan with their Lebanese hashish, they would smuggle the stuff through the Negev and Sinai deserts into Egypt. As such, Israeli police vaults were full of the stuff. The Nigerian in question, having been, at that time, sober for one and a half years without attending Alcoholics Anonymous, decided to attend the Wednesday meeting of the Be'er Sheva chapter at 8.00 p.m.

Slanting out of a makeshift D.E.R.P. tent at 7:42 p.m., Adeyemi crunches honeydew-coloured sand under the Sha-ked, O-ren and Klil Ha-ro-resh trees, squinting in the night at their ge-za's and ornate tsa-me-rets. Deep-rooted sho-ra-shim, the good earth below. Edging through the back doors of Solomon Agassi Synagogue, a large man called Marshall ring-a-dings his little bell, thus bringing the meeting to psychological disorder for 45% of those in attendance, not including newcomers bereft of any idea of what the fuck actually goes on in these bookish rooms in Synagogues, Chapels and former fight club venues.

After an opening share delivered by thin-lipped British diplomat Arundhati, the floor is opened. Elad falls through it. "My name's Elad and I'm an Alcoholic—"

Everyone says, "Hi Elad," but some just say, "Elad!" expectantly.

The man has deep-set eyes and a small mouth. "Thank you Arundhati for the share," he begins, "Moshe for making tea, newcomers, everyone who's done service – I'm glad to be here, glad to be sober. It's like you say, from the moment I picked up a drink I stopped growing up, uh, and I met my wife when I was drinking. We've been together twenty-five years, and, uh, I remember when she said we should have a baby and I was like, a baby, yea, that's great, like genuinely, so we had a daughter and there's this euphoria when you hold your kid for the first time. There's nothing like it. But within about half an hour that'd worn off and I was thinking about where I was gonna get the next drink.

"And I remember I bought a nice bottle of vodka to celebrate, so my wife stayed at the hospital and I was up till six a.m. drinking this vodka so when I picked her up the next day I was still drunk, her and my daughter in the back seat. That's when I knew I had a problem.

"And I've only been sober for six months but this last weekend, I booked a guesthouse in Giv'atayim. I didn't tell her, so I called up and booked the place and they said do you want a bottle of wine on the bed for when you come and I said no, I was recovering.

"And so me and my wife went there and we had dinner in this nice restaurant, and she was just saying like, Elad, you've never done anything like this before but I like it," he chuckles, "and we've been together twenty-five years. So what I'm saying is, I am genuinely glad to be sober, because I was a boy in a man's body and quitting booze allowed me to develop and grow up, uh, so thank you everyone for being there, thank you."

Everyone says, "Thanks Elad," apart from a few silent members.

"Hi my name's Dalia," a member interjects, "and I'm an alcoholic."

Everyone says, "Hi Dalia," apart from a few who say, "Dalia!" expectantly.

"Thanks for your share Elad," she starts off, "and uh, the tea and biscuits. Service people. It's good to be here again, uh," she sighs, "I've been struggling and sometimes as Arundhati said it's the people around you that make the quitting difficult. I, um, I live with my son and I've been sober now for a good three months and had that veil lifted, finally. But my son he doesn't agree with what I'm doing. He thinks I'm a coward for not drinking. He says it's all in my head, which is hard because I know it's all in my head I mean I'm addicted, and there's nothing I can do about it apart from not drink, which is what I'm doing.

"But my son thinks I'm loopy. I'm not, I, it's just been really quite horrible not having a real home to return to I mean now it's just where I sleep because my son's there and I know that when I return on the bus from work—cuz he doesn't work you see he's twenty-seven—when I come back he's just going to be horrible to me.

"And so I go right to my room and just I pray for something not to do with drink because I know I can handle that. That's my job and I'm doing it, but for him…I pray for him I suppose. That he'll see my problem for what it is. It's a disease. And I'm suffering and he doesn't care or doesn't want to care," Adeyemi stares at her coldly, "I love Alcoholics Anonymous. I do. Because there's like decent people here and they can think soberly and eloquently about, about everything I suppose, so thank you. I'm happy to be sober."

Everyone says, "Thanks Dalia," apart from a few silent members. This is then followed by a tea break where many members go out for cigarettes.

A newcomer shivers at the end of a long biscuited table. Ropo Adeyemi leans over to non-smokers Elad and Arundhati and says, "How long has she been putting up with this?"

"Ever since she started coming in," Elad says.

"She always mentions the son," Arundhati tacks on.

"Twenty-seven?" Ropo says, dumbfounded.

"Yea," the dipolat continues, "and living with her. Treating her like that." Ropo slumps in his chair. He unwraps a Peppermint Fánk of the Doctor Jack variety. He bites into it, thinking about how he forgot to take his medication this morning: *Lanicemine* is a small molecule substance used for the treatment of depression.

Arundhati gets up to talk to the newcomer at the other end of the table. She puts her hand on his shoulder. Ropo watches, and then turns back to Elad. "Where does she live?"

Elad looks at him. "What?"

"Dalia," Ropo says, "where does she live?"

"There's an emphasis on the *anonymous*—"

"Come on man…" Ropo prods. Elad ignores him and picks up a nondescript biscuit; he stares at it for the rest of the break.

Ropo follows Dalia home after the meeting. She opens the door to this nasty little flat on Yeho'ash Street and disappears inside. Ropo waits for seven and a half minutes; the same amount of time waited out when an Israeli police officer comes along with a drug-sniffing deer. He walks up to Flat No. 45, and knocks: An emaciated lizard-lookin' dude opens the door. He has an Ölümsüz in the corner of his mouth, and a bottle of wine in his hand. "Who the hell are you?"

"Are you Dalia's son?" Ropo asks.

"Why am I talking to a porch monkey?"

"It's your porch," Adeyemi pulls an Astra A-60 pistol from his belt-line and shoots him point blank in his chest. A few seconds later, Dalia comes running to her son's corpse. She sobs uncontrollably, and screams for Yahweh to help her son. "Please, oh God, for the love of God! Somebody help him, please!"

Ropo Adeyemi, a first-time murderer, fled to the S.B.….

◊

Back at the Florin Police Station, up one flight of stairs and to the left of a dysfunctional water cooler installed by the cousin of now-deceased Constable Varsity Nertúny: one Dakasan "Legendado" Nertúny, wearing Honolulu-blue trousers on the day of installation/damage, Sergeant Copernicus Kapoor is preparing D.C.S. Anya Egelblöm for what feels like the ascension. "Feel free to use some emollient, sergeant."

Kapoor spits into his buffing rag, shining stars on his superior's diaphanous shoulders. It is sufficed to say, now, that Sophia Kravets is a police-issue sniper. In preparation for tonight's drug bust she jogs across the S.B. wastelands. She treks over small hills, brown grass and the occasional obstructing stream splatted by her boots. An M25 sniper rifle weighs her down. "Never thought a woman would have to carry this..." she mutters to herself.

Reaching her destination and commanding views of residential housing complexes on the edge of Florin City Centre, she unwraps and devours one of Профессор Михайлов Малина Зефир a.k.a. Professor Mikhailov's Rasberry Zefirs: a close competitor of Doctor Jack's Peppermint Fánks, battling it out year after year on two billboards in Kronstadt. Tossing the wrapper aside, she gets on the ground with her rifle, like a lover. Periscoping six hundred metres into the back-beech-hedging yard of a semi-detached house bedecked in Black-Eyed Susans, Marigolds, Yarrows, Daylilies, Lamb's Ear and embittered Hostas, she sees the following:

Adeyemi flicking a cigarette butt and walking inside to Mullein.

Kravets laughs. "Nigger and a chink, hoo-*wee* – lucky day," loading her magazine, "see if I can be on the receiving end of a bullet." The whooshing field flows beneath her. Rimless bottlenecked cartridges. Peering through her scope again, she slides her finger around the trigger. She thinks about the date she went on last night. "Filled him up at the buffet," she whispers to herself, "came home. We pulled us up a chair and sat there for three hours. Three hours watchin' the bug-zapper kill bugs. Watchin' the bug zapper on a date. Enjoyin' the night. Holdin' hands. Scooted over a little. Got me a kiss. Surprise too, he was chewin' liquorice. He swapped chews with me cuz I was chewin' liquorice too. Swapped his Finnish for my Bavarian...blew his fuckin mind, I did."

Egelblöm, meanwhile, pictures Sophia Kravets in her camouflage onesie, nodding as though she's just won the lottery. "Exemplary pongo," Egelblöm remarks. The wheelchair rolls on-board the raid tank. Inside, Harmon is pre-prepared in every sense but that of the microwave meal. Egelblöm watches him tightening his helmet. "How nice of you to join us Harmon."

"Pleasure's mine, ma'am," he replies.

"How was your refresher course?"

"Nothing like it, ma'am. Easy sailing. Mmm-*mmm*..." Egelblöm smiles and puts her brakes on. Copernicus ushers the officers in. They become part of the vehicle. Climbing inside the cockpit, Kapoor throws the dogger a glance. "You wanna sit up here Harmon? There's a bit more space."

"Nothing I haven't seen before."

"That's not the point," Kapoor interrupts, "make some space."

"Sorry, sir."

The dogger joins the overworked sergeant, and shuts his mouth. All the relevant bulkheads clam up. Depository gates open, and the raid tank slugs out to the wastelands. Kapoor is almost completely silent. He grunts like Maximilian Otto-Groß XI (2037-2079)—erstwhile Kassel postmaster and then second director of the Bettenhausen Music Conservatory in Kassel—would have done during recitals of his later, more successful work: The amorous and whimsical songs and piano pieces he wrote whilst engaged to his first inanimate husband, a four hundred pound rock called Liam. Kapoor doesn't have any rocks, currently. He's staring disinterestedly out the window. "You puke?"

"Why do you say that?" Harmon asks.

"I can smell it," the sergeant replies, "why'd you puke?"

"We had a – we had a bad dogging experience. Can I—"

"W-go ahead."

"Can you," Harmon gulps, "shoot someone? Like, kill someone when you're dogging?"

"No," Kapoor says, "that's not an option."

"Because that's what Mullein did. He killed us. In our own hallucination."

The brim of Florin is edging closer.

"I think," Kapoor dejectedly deciphers, "you two overdosed."

"That's the point, though," the dogger half-suggests, "did we go too deep? Can you go too deep?"

"Look, mate, why don't you ask your retarded predecessor if it's possible to go too deep," he turns red, "you idiot, Harmon. What do you think you're playing at?"

"Which hospital?"

"What?"

"I'll pay her a visit," Harmon says, "what hospital is she in?"

"I don't know, some bloody hospital…"

"You don't know?"

"I'm not an encyclopaedia Harmon."

"I don't believe that."

"What, me not being an encyclopaedia? What else are you on?"

"No, you not knowing which hospital she's in."

Kapoor's had enough: "Tread carefully, Harmon."

The raid tank halts. He continues: "I'm not gonna argue with a junior officer." He opens the door and waits for Egelblöm's finger.

"You have a sister," Harmon says, "what's her name?"

"Julia."

"Yea, but I knew that—"

"Don't fuck with me *Zarmon…*" He realizes—much like Sian Wagenknecht when she lost her first draft of *Flos Campi*: a suite for solo viola, choir and 25-piece orchestra with each movement prefaced by a quote from the biblical Book of Job, during a freak attack by a pigeon-flock upon her Newlyn home—that he's made a mistake. Maybe not on the level of losing your manuscript during an ornithological house-rape, but still pretty close.

Egelblöm suddenly points her finger towards the bulkhead. Sergeant Kapoor slams the door. Reverses—The raid tank trundy-bundling backwards towards Ropo Adeyemi's rather nice house. A chiming shot besmears Florin and the raid tank's windshield shatters. Kapoor jolts back with a hole in his forehead. All of a sudden he looks like a sack of eighty-nine potatoes, each with a cumbersome knitted brow…Outside, an impressive battalion of hookers bearing Ballester-Molinas, Beretta Nanos, FG PA-63s and Kimber Custom T.L.E.s are bounding into the back garden. They take aim at the dead, metallic meteorite headed their way. Inside the cockpit, Harmon shoves the sergeant off of the steering wheel. He pulls the handbrake and the vehicle elephants to a stop in the moist earth.

"Open the bulkhead!" Egelblöm screams.

Bullet-pricked yappings up and down the metal walls. Police officers run out of the raid tank, like ants, or Shaka, the Chief and founder of the Zulu nation who made a hasty departure from his elephantine command-base during *The Mfe-cane* ("the crushing") after one of his usually rock-solid plans backfired because he was playing chess with his cousin instead of chatting to his generals. The constabulary might of the Florin Police Force charge into this hookered territory. The jasper sun licks low. A heavy dose of overcast passing lasting shadow to the far reaches of Harmon's brow. He tosses a triggered grenade into the garden shed and *thwaakkkuumm*! The blackened smoke lilts in the summer sky along with a dose of hookers' arms and legs. A firefight ensues because everyone's pissed off and guns are involved. Round after round of .223 Remmington cartridges are police-pumped. Egelblöm, in her all-terrain Lucky Mark IV Travel Device, traverses eyeballs and grit. In response to the nihilistic situation facing the sober Ropo Adeyemi, the Nigerian Delirium (his A.A. nickname) plays at full volume the master Batá drum player Diekololaoluwa Oyekan, who sings:

> Gba ijoko rẹ nigbati ọkunrin funfun naa ba de
> Gbiyanju lati yọ ninu ewu
> Emi ni olori ti o pa awọn olori miiran
> Awọn olori miiran sọ eke
>
> Gold jẹ kere ju wura lọ
> Wọn yoo bẹru awọn ohun ija mi
> Awọn eekanna mi ti firanṣẹ nipasẹ ọlọrun
> Ọrun n ṣe ayẹyẹ

Ropo cocks his Walther P-22 and runs downstairs, only to join a collective spectating of prostitute Imogen Eilaüd's left breast getting blown off. Six hundred metres away Sophia Kravets says, "One down…" Adeyemi runs outside, firing at will. "Shoot my girls, heh?" He shoots an officer. "You want to take my shit? Fuck you!" He blasts another officer.

"Fuck you!" Another.

"Yea! Fuck you!"

Chikenyyt sprints sideways and jumps into the neighbour's yard. He waits, ruffling his hair. Praying. "Come on, Mullein," he says, "the money." *Has he come full circle?* Harmon thinks. *Can he see the future?* After which a green wad pickets over the fence and lands at Harmon's feet.

Harmon jumps up with his rifle. He aims at Mullein, who meets his tracker for the first time. He doesn't like it. The fire from an exploded grenade lights his face. His eyes are amber-coloured, and the pupils bleed into the colour. "Now," he smiles, and each tooth is too long, "which of us is gonna put down our gun?"

Harmon takes a dekko down his barrel, replying, "Put the gun down."

"Oh," Zach nods a negative, "and it was going so well…"

"I'll aim between your legs," Harmon says, "and you'll drop your weapon. That's how it goes."

"You gonna blow my dick off?"

"If I have to," the dogger says, "yes."

Zach moves a little closer. There are screams in the background. "That's what some of the jurors wanted," he says, "they wanted to fix me," he looks a little sad, "but I can still fuck in my head."

Harmon grips his rifle even tighter. "Put it down."

Zach shakes his head. "Nah, mate—" Harmon's neck is jettisoned over the grass by a Mullein-fired bullet, but the dogger subsequently unloads into the paedophile's torso, the bullets firecrackers decrepitating over his body.

The murkiness of a night misunderstood by both…

London/Belgium

The Right Honourable Walter Lupo MP, a Pinko and member of His Majesty's Opposition, reaches peak stress at 11:50 p.m. He masturbates in the Westminster tube station's unisex toilets: the third cubicle on the left, the one with the only functioning lock. As such, he comes and goes at the same time. Exiting the toilets he's greeted by England Today News on a too-big suspended television: *"The Belgian Prime Minister Clement Verlinden has declared a national state of emergency with The Archbishop of Mechelen-Brussels Dominique Van Hoof having formed her own government in the south."*

What a mouthful, Lupo thinks, examining the attractive an-chorwoman—*Again, what a mouthful*. His eyeballs slide up the oak-coloured cashier's arms at the Mucho Frijoles Coffee Bar. He sees her every night when he's heading home for the day. He wants to pull out his eyeballs and rub them on her skin. But they're attached. Life is less. *Her feet must be a mouthful – would be*, Lupo thinks.

He gets on the Circle line. Westminster. Embankment. Change. Then, the Northern line. Embankment. Charing Cross. Leicester Square. Tottenham Court Road. Then, off and up to the unemployed: the street. Lupo walks down Char-ing Cross road and turns right onto Manette Street. He turns left onto Greek Street, avoiding Bateman Street, as the inevi-table entrance to Soho appears. Club 1001, like Bucket's Club, is a cocktail bar inhabited by the wriggling of fingers up backs, the lowering of liquids in ornate glasses, and sweaty feet. In-side, Lupo stares at all the male and female toes perspiring, un-der- or over-pinned by music by *Trommel und Arsch*. The dance floor is catatonic. Light comes and goes like the public-toileting Lupo; leather squeaks; the sound of glasses landing on tables, the jingling of wallets, a zipper down in some Sherlock-Holmesian corner.

"Lupo!"

The MP's neck swerves. His eyes meet Novak Nekovar's—"Walter!" He grabs the MP's neck and pulls him in. "Miluj mě!"

"I don't want to!" Lupo says. They both laugh.

Novak Nekovar is a gay man of Bulgarian extraction. After the financial collapse of the Bulgarian Republic, the newly formed Bulgarian Domain of Social Democracy manufactured an electricity monopoly under the Federal Asset Fund: DFŸ b.r. was formed in the process, quickly becoming the leading electrical power producer and distributor in Bulgaria, accounting for over 60% of the Bulgarian market plus 72% of the European market. All that matters here, however, as a Balkan tongue is rammed into Walter's ear, is that Novak's Dad owns most of it.

Further out, bouncers are guarding the entrance. Even further out, Greek Street is lit like an A-level art installation. Four women exit Bateman Street. They turn right and tread softly down Greek Street, smiling. Miss 89 slides her headphones on. She consults her music library, selecting Basil Nathan's Greatest Hits. She selects *Baby, You've Been Testing Me*. As they approach Club 1001, their jackets fly open. Black Franchi LF-57 submachine guns. UB-157 black. They open fire at the bouncers and walk inside. The opening chords of *Baby, You've Been Testing Me* burglarize Miss 89's brain: the G minor, F major, C major and D minor chords rise like shovelled dirt, or mechanical wings folding over one another.

Dead.

There's another G minor, and Basil holds it.

Dead.

Basil Nathan lets his silly voice rip.

A bullet punches through Novak's cheek and the back of his head flies off.

The chord sequence parades through Miss 89's head again. Then, the pulsing of diodes fuzzing like plush walls, and the pre-chorus chords are D/B Dm, D/B, Dm x 3, if you got a guitar at hand, of course...

> *Baby, please!*

Walter runs.

> *Don't you test me aga-hain!*

Tables and people are pumped with cartridges.

> *I got this love, and-I-can break it again!*

Glass is sprayed. The bar snaps.

> *Take your heart, and me-held it to mine!*

The dance floor is empty. Patrons are shot in the face in corners. The game changer. D, F/A, B major, F, D/B.

> *I'll sell my lips and shoes...*

Walter Lupo always imagine Fernanda Li playing the drum lead-in to the chorus. F, G major, B, F major, G minor, B.

Ba-by don't yoo-hoo test me!

Whiskey tumblers are kicked across marble.

It's too-hoo late for a Mon-day night!

Walter hides in the toilets.

Ba-by don't yoo-hoo test me!

The Miss 89 starts crying. It's Basil Nathan. He's too much.

Tomorrow is a Tuesday like last Mon-day-yay-yay-yay-hay-hay…

The mercenaries run out of ammo. They leave the premises in a state of moaning smoke. A police siren buzzes over *Trommel und Arsch*; a puddle of sound at the entrance…

4:13 a.m. is part of that awful semi-night period. Not quite morning. Sleep needed. The Rubicon has, however, been crossed. And so, we stay up; awake. Detective Chief Inspector Gaszi Pasternak lights an Ölümsüz cigarette. He turns to his constable, saying, "Queer bar?"

The constable nods.

Pasternak starts quizzing Omar, the Club 1001 manager. "What did they look like?" the detective asks.

"W-women," Omar stutters, "f-*four* women."

Pasternak puffs on his cigarette. "You sure?"

"Yea."

"Lesbians?" Pasternak turns to no one, asking, "What street is this?"

"Greek Street, sir," the constable answers.

"Would be," Pasternak croaks, returning to the manager, "what's your name?"

"Omar."

"I want you to go inside, Omar. Pour yourself – you got scotch?"

"Uh-huh."

"What scotch you got?"

"Uh," Omar mumbles, "Oban…Laphroaig—?"

"Pour yourself a double-Laphroaig. Cut it with a table-spoon of water, and drink it. When you've done that," Pasternak finishes, "come find me – okay?"

Omar's teetotal. But he'll just have to nod for now. "Okay," he says. The manager steps over the many pricks of blood and vanishes.

Pasternak studies Walter Lupo MP, strangled in one of those foil blankets. He flicks his cigarette butt onto the road and kneels next to the MP. "Mister Lupo…?"

"How," Lupo looks at Pasternak, "do you—?"

"Good to see you're unscathed, sir – Nowicki…!"

The constable jogs over. "I want you to escort Mister Lupo home. Guard him. All right?"

"Yes, sir," Nowicki says.

One hundred yards away, Sergeant Marcus Hasegawa laughs on his phone. Pasternak stands up and spins towards him, saying, "Something funny, sergeant?"

Hasegawa coughs and walks inside.

Pasternak addresses Nowicki on the side. "Put him in bed," he says, "make sure he gets one hour's sleep, okay? After that, dress him and make sure he gets to parliament for nine a.m."

"And after that?"

"If you see the Turk," Pasternak explains, "tell him he's

welcome," and a pigeon shits on his left shoulder.

◊

The next morning, it's 10:14 a.m. The House of Commons is full. Reactionaries have bypassed the first reading of the Belgium Bill a.k.a.: *A Bill to provide temporary Commonwealth status to Northern Belgium, to provide aid and assistance, and to amend current spending relating to the National Debt and the Public Revenue, and to make further provision pertaining to such matters of finance.* Debate goes on for some time. The Speaker, Hekla Sigurdsson, recognizes the old-timing Pinko, Sharrah Saleem (Coventry North East): "I never thought I'd see the day," Saleem begins, loudly, "when a Prime Minister would bypass the first reading of a new Bill [*interruption*] evade the public [*interruption*] circumvent both houses, and still be worse off than she was before [*interruption*]. I ask the Prime Minister, can she please name the promoters of the proposed Bill?"

The speaker recognizes Nooda Shakra (Christchurch). "I thank the Prime Minister for giving way," Nooda begins, "as one of the sponsors for the Belgium Bill, I wish to speak in support of the motion, which is procedural and not about the Bill's merits. The promoters of the Bill, namely the Reactionary Party Chairman, The Rt. Hon Gentleman from Birkenhead, The Rt. Hon Lady from South Thanet, The Rt. Hon Gentleman from West Derbyshire, not to mention what one may call a cross-party coalition of promoters, have placed a statement in support of the motion in the Vote Office." She sits and Saleem is confused.

The speaker recognizes Eleanor Dunwoody (Crewe and Nantwich) "Thank you Mister Speaker," Dunwoody appeases, "will the honourable lady look at paragraph four of the promoter's statement in support of the motion, which asserts, 'The Bill has all Reactionary Party support.' Is she aware of the pacifist faction in her party? And is the honourable lady prepared to repeat the events that occurred in the Middle East at the turn of the last century, only this time in Belgium?"

Nooda stands up, saying, "I thank the honourable lady for her comments, though I think she's mistaken in suggesting this Bill constitutes an act of foreign policy. We seek to make Northern Belgium a temporary part of the Commonwealth [*interruption*] so that [*interruption: 'Permanently temporary!'*] so that we may provide the aid needed, quicker [*Government and Opposition: 'Hear, hear!'*]!" Nooda Shakra's peepers snap at El Greco, but, by his own admission, he's got this by the balls.

◊

Meanwhile, in Belfast, it is 10:22 a.m. On Lisburn Road, the Member of Parliament for Belfast West, Jake Duffy (D.U.P.), is throwing rocks at Slándáil Phoblachtach's office windows. At the turn of the century, Óglaigh na hÉireann (O.N.H.) was one of many Irish Republican Army splinter groups, none of which are active currently. But O.N.H.—ironically sharing its name with the actual Northern Ireland defence forces—decided to take a new direction. The private security firm *Slándáil Phoblachtach* a.k.a. *Republican Security* was formed in 2023. They started by farming out club bouncers in Northern Ireland, and then to the Irish Republic. As of yesterday, they have opened a second office in Morecambe. More importantly, however, they've been hired by El Greco to intimidate Northern Irish MPs.

"You like that!?" Jake Duffy screams. The window ricochets apart. "Am I invading your privacy yet!?"

An unusually large member of S.P. called Niall Gordon exits the building. He holds up his hands in that way that only a bouncer can do. "Sir," he says, calmly, "I'm gonna have to ask you to leave."

"I'm on the street!" Duffy protests.

"I know you're on the street, sir," Gordon explains, "but everyone's looking."

"Let them look, you prick!"

Inside the office, guns are being loaded.

"We wouldn't visit this on you," Gordon goes on, "but we'll let you off with a warning."

"You," Duffy hyperventilates, "fuckin…" He puts his hands on his hips. "You call my Grace one more time," he points at Niall Gordon, "and I'll do to you what I did to your daddy."

Gordon composes himself. "Thank you, sir."

"Catch yourself on, mate," Duffy says as he walks away down Lisburn road, "Don't you ever forget where you came from, and where you're going!'

◊

Back in Westminster, it is 10:31 a.m. The Speaker recognizes Fernanda Li by saying, "Prime Minister!" in a very loud and obnoxious way. Chamber flares up; a kind of prolonged oafish wailing complete with stomping feet and waving arms; the curvilinear warbling of brief notes.

"Cheeky *Nan*-dos!" the house chants, "Cheeky *Nan*-dos!"

The Syrian lobby look at each other. On the Opposition's side, Walter Lupo's head, having avoided being split open in a gay club, goes invisible. His eyelids stutter. He vomits a burp. It stings the back of his throat. Harley Tinker, the MP for Bury St Edmunds, is sat next to him. He opens his brief, "You all right,

Lupo?" and starts drawing a penis.

"No," Walter mutters.

"Could be worse," Tinker promises, "you could be Belgian."

"I disagree," Walter says.

"What, with being Belgian? Or that things could somehow be worse?"

"..."

"I reckon the whole fucking shit house is gonna go up. Here," he shows Lupo his drawing, "not bad, eh?"

The Reactionaries all nod collectively. Not at Tinker's penis sketch, but the whole situation. They're crossing arms and legs, compressing their bodies. They're going to burst like a line of pimples. Li stands over her brief and everything slows. She stares at the enemy: Robyn Brooke-Valentine, leader of His Majesty's Opposition. They both stand on the edge of something: a comeback, a comedown; some form, in each case, of national progress, repeating endlessly across official parliamentary reports authorized by Neil Kitchen.

Later, the Prime Minister will stand outside the Paddington Station Muchos Frijoles. She'll condemn the Club 1001 shooting as a June wind ruffles her fringe. At this moment, a lesbian will clap out of shot.

The Belgium Bill gets through the second reading unscathed. The committee stage is next: Scrutiny provided by external experts and interest groups. The Syrian lobby exit parliament individually— Nooda Shakra enters Westminster tube station at 11:55 p.m. She hops on the Jubilee line. Westminster. Green Park. Bond Street. She gets off, and jogs up the stairs to the street. Here she turns right down Davis Street, and crosses Brook Street. Grosvenor Street. She avoids Bourdon Street. She turns right onto Hill Street, heading up Hay's Mews and turning left on to Farm Street. Everywhere smells like lemon-scented candles. She stops at 5 Farm Street, London, X9H Y8F. It is 12:21 a.m. She rings the doorbell. The door opens. It may be Joram Falack's flat, but Sayid Chemtob lets her in. "Were you followed?" he asks.

Nooda shakes her head. She walks in, the door slamming after her. Sayid grips her chin, "We'll bring democracy to Europe," and snogs her.

Falack leans around the corner with a glass of red wine and says, "Do make yourself at home."

Nooda quits all this osculating, responding, "Is Maya here?"

"All the pieces," Joram says.

"People, Joram," Nooda corrects, "all the people."

"If something is scarce," the party chairman replies, "it's considered a product," sipping his wine, "I'd say good people are scarce these days, wouldn't you?"

Later, in the living room, Maya Terzi is kneeling on the sofa with a glass of red wine—She looks like an amputee. The other three gather around the cheeseboard, nibbling Roquefort, Cotija, Chèvre and Emmental cheese. Are they eating it because they like it, or only because they can afford it? And why Belgium? None of the Syrian lobby are L.G.B.T.Q.+.

Well, gay. None of them are gay.

Empathy then. The Merkel Tenor. Angela Merkel (1954-2042)—the erstwhile German Chancellor (2005-2020)—decided to open Germany's borders during the migrant crisis at the turn of the century. Germany didn't like this too much. But Merkel grew up in *Das Deutsche Demokratische Republik* or East Germany, pre-Soviet collapse. She experienced all the wonderful Marxist-Leninist aspects of living in a Communist country, like price-fixing and the oppressive Staatssicherheitsdienst, or *Stasi*: the state's secret police. The wall, subsequently, came down: Merkel free; Merkel euphoric, Maya Terzi can well imagine. And being an intelligent logical woman, she felt her contemporaries should be subject to similar freedoms. That's why she did what she did. Letting the migrants in. She wanted them to taste it. Real freedom. Or maybe she wanted to be that person who *gives* freedom. Maybe it was selfish. Either way, Germany hated her for it.

"Now," Falack begins as he smears Cotija onto a rice cracker, "first reading bypassed. Well done," nibbling and sipping, "second reading? Thoughts?"

"We need to let Fernanda talk," Sayid Chemtob says.

"Yea," Maya adds, "I was gonna say; that was a bit close today."

Nooda sighs. "But she's useless—"

"We know she's useless," Joram agrees, "but she's good at filibustering. Let her do that. Let the cogs work."

"Sander's good," Nooda interjects.

Sayid lights an Ölümsüz. "Worth every penny…"

"With Verlinden's approval now," the party chairman chairs, "looking forward to soldiers, what to do."

"If you want ground soldiers," Nooda says, "there're plenty of firms to choose from," the bobbing of nice haircuts; that Chèvre is starting to ooze, "we could definitely haggle with Argonaut, get mercenaries from them." Argonaut's a Bulgarian security firm, a subsidiary of DFŸ b. r.

Joram blinks a few times, thinking. "I'm not going to haggle with people who look at money like they want to fuck it," he decides, "let's pool our resources."

Maya Terzi says that most of this will come up at the committee stage.

"I hope not," Sayid says, stubbing out his cigarette, "but if we can convince the Bill committee that America—"

"No Americans," Nooda interrupts, "please."

"Britain for the British, Sayid," Joram adds, "if we can make it to the third reading intact, then we'll be fine. No more amendments. No nothing."

"What about El Greco's lot?" Terzi asks. "What is it? S.P.?"

"Republican Security," Falack says, "how many are they?"

Nooda replies that they have three hundred active members with fifty reserves. "If you want a taskforce," she concludes, "pongos in points, they'd be perfect."

"Save a pretty penny too," Chemtob chimes in.

"Cheaper than tuition fees?" Joram asks.

Nooda spreads an ample amount of Roquefort on a cracker, saying, "You bet…"

◊

The committee commences on Thursday, 7th June 2089 at 9:45 a.m. Unless parliament is hung, the government, in an effort to mirror parliament, always has more representatives in a committee than the Opposition. In addition, there must be a minimum of sixteen people on a committee. The chairman for the Belgium Committee is a total opportunist by the name of Jarod Thrussel: a Reactionary MP who sits at the bottom of a V-shaped table, the other members lining the two sides. To his left is another Reactionary MP called Aaron Lakin-Smithers. Jarod looks at him the same way his gardener looks at dirt. "What's the nature of our intervention?" Jarod asks, surreptitiously.

"It's difficult," Aaron says, fingering his cufflinks, "but what I would say is that given Belgium's in turmoil; politically, nationally, that is, our involvement would basically involve an intervention based on a premeditated judgement, you know, 'There's a line you don't cross.' It's foreign aid. We're telling Belgium, 'Hey, you can't take care of yourselves, here's some aid.' But you can't deny it's murky territory."

"We like murky," Thrussel smiles, "makes our job easier."

"With regards to what?"

Thrussel looks in his brief and says, "You're such a pug-faced little shit, Aaron."

Thrussel stares at Prime Minister Fernanda Li in the hot seat, then the other committee members. "First of all," he begins, "I'd like to welcome those committee virgins present, and welcome back the committee veterans. A pleasant experience I assure you it's going to be. Couple of announcements: coffee will be available in the end area from eleven-thirty onwards, and we'll be recessing at a quarter-to so that members can get to Prime Minister's questions. I'm sure the Prime Minister herself," pointing at her and smiling, "will be in favour of that motion."

Behind Fernanda Li is a viewing gallery. Sami Toller-Wallace, sent by Falack, watches the proceedings.

Thrussel lowers eyeglasses. "On that note," he continues, "I'd like to welcome the Prime Minister to her first committee questioning, since it was from her cabinet that the Belgium Bill arose, much in the same way that gas rises from a corpse," piercing a straw in a juice box, "and do have a sense of humour during these proceedings. It's not the end of the world."

"Sir," the Prime Minister says, "before we begin I'd like to say that the majority of my answers will be drawn from a prepared brief." She lifts a bunch of paper.

"Yes," Thrussel condones, "but just indicate to the stenographer that we do want it as it is in today's proceedings."

"I apologize in advance to Mister Grass," Li admits, "I'm afraid it'll be a bit tedious."

"Same as usual then," Thrussel remarks.

The Pinko committee members chortle. But the Reactionary members are breathing through their eye sockets. The violence of silence. The officialdom of violence. The rape of files; the rape of lock and key and chain, et cetera. And the fact that one might say *et cetera* at a time like this shows how violent it actually is. Professor H. Keighley-Jarvis wouldn't have had any of this passive stuff. Keighley-Jarvis (1971-2048) first came to London to sell roses. But after looking through a telescope he became inspired: He had an illustrious academic career at L.E.S. where he would eventually receive tenure. One day, as he's giving a lecture in the Zilberschlag lecture theatre, scribbling a whole load of differential equations—complex repeated roots concerning second derivatives—on the board, he stops to address his audience, "These are awesome," he says, resting his marker on a table, "some people ask me what these are good for, but they're idiots. If you go see the white cliffs of Dover, stand back and admire the beauty of it. And if anyone asks you what the cliffs are good for, kick him off the edge—"

It was then that Keighley-Jarvis kicked a chair halfway across the room. But when he did that, he wasn't thinking about linear homogenous calculations; rather, he was thinking about roses: the ignorance of beauty by blue-collar accountant-types. So here's a maths problem for you: given the working classes inhabit the real world but can't appreciate it; given the upper classes appreciate the real world but don't inhabit it; given the middle classes pretend they don't and/or can't appreciate the real world; assuming all that now, is Aaron Lakin-Smithers the reincarnation of Professor H. Keighley-Jarvis?

The Prime Minister has forty minutes of questioning left. Sami-Toller Wallace exits the viewing gallery. She walks past Walter Lupo, trailed by The Turk in the members' lobby, and goes outside to hail a cab. She gets in and says, "Twelve Downing Street," and off they go up Abingdon Street, around Parliament Square and Great George Street. Then up Parliament Street followed by a left up Downing Street. They almost run over Piers Meak. Sami takes a fifty-pound note out of her wallet and rips it in half, saying to the taxi driver, "You wait for me, you get the other half at Westminster Palace on the way back." The driver agrees and takes his half. Toller-Wallace enters 12 Downing Street and lunges up the stairs into El Greco's office. She walks in on Sayid Chemtob dictating policy (excuses, I-can't-recall's, untruths, and segues) to Nur Coombs who is frantically typing them up on her laptop. The printer farts a brief and Sayid pulls it out and passes it to Sami. "This is for Witherspoon," he says, "when's he on?" Chief of Defence Staff (C.D.S.) Air Chief Marshall Sir Pranav Witherspoon rolled out of bed this morning with a hooker called Imogen Eilaüd. He then found out he was attending the Belgium Bill committee from Imogen, since she often has very average sex with Jarod Thrussel.

"After Fernanda," Toller-Wallace replies.

"Take it," Chemtob says, "go."

"What about Bunny Driscoll?" Toller-Wallace asks. Being the C.E.O. of Stonewall, Bunny Driscoll woke up at 5:00 a.m. He had a full English breakfast with baked beans, fried eggs and bacon. He fed his goldfish and polished his boots. Then he hanged himself.

"We talked last night," Chemtob says, "he'll be good."

What neither Chemtob nor Toller-Wallace know, apart from Driscoll's suicide, is that Nur Coombs had a disastrous date with El Greco. Both regret the evening immensely; Coombs because she didn't run the preliminaries of dating a colleague through her head until she was standing at the bar; and Sander because he finally stopped lying to himself about wanting a partner. But those arguments against are always baked in small trays. He was terrified. Truly unnerved and agitated. Sander "El Greco" Papadimitriou finally encountered something he couldn't control.

Sami Toller-Wallace gets back in the cab with Witherspoon's brief. They drive back to Westminster, completing the fifty-pound note. She walks back through the members' lobby where Robyn Brooke-Valentine, Wiktoria Kozłowski (Shadow Defence Secretary) and Freya Cain (Shadow Home Secretary) stand around The Turk, speed-meditating on policy. The Reactionary advisor sprints back to the viewing gallery and sits next to Air Chief Marshall Witherspoon, who simply reeks of lovemaking. Marshall takes the brief and reads it: He hasn't read this fast since the Border Skirmish of 2065 when he was but a mere jingoistic tadpole. But there's so much paper to be seen at committees—on desks, in hands—that to suddenly argue that one piece of paper is in fact not just totally customary (seen by Philippe the cleaner Q.E.D.) but truly problematic, edging towards that big word, "corrupt," just ain't gonna happen. Parliamentary schedules are tighter than a crab's asshole.

Meanwhile, Li says her adieus and leaves. Witherspoon stumbles, hungover, from the viewing gallery and takes the Prime Minister's place in the hot seat. Jarod Thrussel parts an ass-kissing grin because he recommended Imogen to him.

"Sir Witherspoon," Thrussel says, "I'm honoured. But now, I must be shrewd."

The C.D.S. shrugs. He blinks one eye at a time, like a newt.

"Sir Witherspoon," the chairman continues, "if you could please turn to page seventeen of the Belgium Bill, I'd like your opinion on section four. Do you have it?"

"…"

"'The regulations under this part,' the part being concerned with Belgium's future as a temporary commonwealth territory, 'Regulations may not impose or increase taxation, confer a power to legislate, modify this act or repeal or revoke the Human Rights Act of 1998,'" he looks up at Witherspoon, "what do you think of that?"

Excuses.

I-can't-recall's.

Untruths.

Segues.

Witherspoon takes in a long breath and says, "I'm afraid they didn't teach much about exporting domestic affairs or exporting British legislation at the academy. It's beyond me, I'm afraid."

"No," Lakin-Smithers interjects, "but the fact that a military intervention in one's own commonwealth is going to be funded by a taxpayer who won't see the benefits of said intervention is problematic. This isn't like Iraq or Afghanistan, as I'm sure you understand."

"I can't ever recall," Witherspoon counters, "inferring that conclusion from what history has to offer us."

"Please excuse my honourable friend," Thrussel says, "he likes jumping to conclusions."

"There's a host of things we need to get through so if you could answer, Sir Witherspoon," Aaron interrupts, "is the enforced policing of a country, namely military intervention, not another way of changing that country's legislation?"

"There are many different angles to take into account,"

Witherspoon says, "but you need to fast-forward any situation to its logical endpoint, which, in this case, is the prevention of civil war—"

"But the deployment of soldiers," Pinko member Octavio Huxtable asks, "could be seen as a declaration of civil war, rather than a remedy for it, could it not?"

"Yea," Lakin-Smithers says, "what he said!"

"That's one way of looking at it," Witherspoon coughs, "but suppose for a moment, we turn our attention to Belgium itself. I think we're ignoring the real facts. Belgium's a country. It's not a Bill. It's not a piece of legislation."

"No, but technically it is," Lakin-Smithers argues, "since it has a constitution. You take away those things and gone are the borders, gone are the counties—"

"Yes," Thrussell says, "thank you, Aaron—"

"I'm not finished," his young colleague complains. "The chair recognizes Miss Esme Meal," Thrussel changes the topic, "Mister Lakin-Smithers gives way."

Esme Meal says, "Do you think you'll have enough money?"

"Miss Meal," Witherspoon slurs, almost falling off his chair, "racism…is a problem. Haemoglobia…is a problem, but moony? *Money*…" a few moments pass, "I'm in the military. I always get that sweet green."

"Sir Witherspoon," Aaron asserts, "I would like you to explain what you mean by that!"

"Well," Witherspoon slurs, "that's one way of looking at it, yes."

Aaron is asked to leave. He kicks a chair in the hallway. Much like H. Keighley-Jarvis, Lakin-Smithers' condemnation comes too late. And to students, or MPs, walking by, looks rather stupid. There's nothing clever about hitting things. Unless you have what the Syrian lobby has. Which is timing.

The committee terminates on Thursday, 14th June 2089. The final interviewee is Professor Elise Eikenboom who we last saw in the Zilberschlag lecture theatre. Given that she's a lesbian, Thrussel decides to have a gay man address her, which, realistically, is probably just about the worst thing he could do. Reactionary MP Mateo Martín (author of three gay graphic novels of various renown), therefore, does the talking. "Professor Eikenboom," he starts, "you're quite involved with the Stonewall International Organization and L.G.B.T.Q.+ rights in general."

"Yes," Eikenboom says, "Mister Driscoll was meant to attend, wasn't he?"

"Yes, he was," Martín returns, "I offer my condolences. But I've been told you have something you wish to ask us."

"That is correct," the professor answers.

Martín flops open his hand, saying, *"Please…"*

"What I'm asking is very simple," Eikenboom argues, "you are, as representatives, completely entitled to do as you wish, but I'm asking you to prevent the further passage of this Bill in parliament."

Martín, Thrussel and Talia Solomon look at each other. All the Pinko MPs (Niamh Barraclough, Cornelius White, Balthazar Khaskheli IV, et al.) exchange keeks. There is, for a moment, all but the sound of repositioning feet and nail-tappings on tables. Thrussel pretends to organize his brief, saying, "We've been told that this is a good Bill. And naturally we have to present an amended Bill back to parliament so that it may consider whether to take it forward or not."

"I understand that," Eikenboom replies, "are you in charge, here?"

"I'll be the one asking the questions from now on, professor," Thrussel says, tiredly, "may I belabour what I said to your colleague Doctor Jack Hearst: we're not able to go back ex post facto to deal with old problems. We must deal with problems currently presented to us. So what is your problem with the Bill, professor?"

"All of it."

"Not just some of it?" Balthazar Khaskheli IV asks.

"All of it," Eikenboom repeats.

Thrussel senses the Pinko MPs warming to her. "It is as I said," he claims, "out of our control as to whether or not any Bill passes—"

"I am talking about *this* Bill," Eikenboom interrupts.

"Let me finish," Thrussel says, "it is out of control—sorry, it is out of our control as to whether this bill will pass. It may very well not pass. And you have to understand that, this is — data collection, really."

Eikenboom hasn't even looked at her copy of the Bill. Not the one in front of her, that is.

But she did read it last night over a cup of hot chocolate, listening to Nazario Acquafredda's *Divertimento for Saxophones in A Minor* on Classic FM. Running the logistics of, yes, a Civil War in Belgium, and the possibility-cum-necessity of British military intervention through her head. But also her nickname at L.E.S., that being Dokter Neuken ("Doctor Fuck"), and how in light of an impending personal-cum-national crisis and an inveterate dislike for her nickname, given or attributed to her because of her chilly grey eyes, she should try to come off as more approachable in her department, yes, but also more generally in everyday life. Not that Thrussel cares about any of that.

"Is there anything specific in the Bill you'd like to scrutinize?" the committee chairman asks.

"No," she replies.

Thrussel clears his throat. "Do you have any further contributions to make?"

"No," Eikenboom says, disinterestedly, "I have a lecture I need to write."

"Well," Thrussel says, "that's wonderful. Thank you."

Mateo Martín, Esme Meal, Maryam Kromberg, Poppy Quinton, Talia Solomon, Tamar Warszawski, Ibrahim Spiller, Balthazar Khaskheli IV, Niamh Barraclough, Brooke Toomey, Octavio Huxtable, Cornelius White, and Carter Purd, mumble, collectively, "Th-thanks, thank you."

Eikenboom gets up, walks out, and slams the door behind her.

Thrussel decides, as such, to wrap things up in a bureaucratic bow. "The committee now stands adjourned," he says, "and we will report in due course."

The members stand up, declaring a state of hubbub of consummation, soon to be followed by the catching of taxis and trains. Jarod Thrussel fills his rucksack and he smiles at Niamh Barraclough. He then evacuates to the exterior corridors, marching to the closest toilet. He enters, ignoring the man at the urinal, and goes straight into a stall. He gets on his knees and gags over the toilet. He throws up, subsequently blowing sick out of his nose and spitting in the bowl. He hears the unmistakeable sound of a zipper going up: the man at the urinal moves closer to Thrussel's stall; standing in front of the door, he knocks.

"Who," Jarod spits, "who's that?"

"Who do you *think*?" the voice replies, and only one person in Westminster pronounces, "think," with an F.

Thrussel narrows his eyes, muttering, "Sander?"

"*I've cam do trink your blad*," he says as Thrussel looks at his vomit, panting.

"I'll die if I have to do that again," Jarod moans, "that was a one-off."

"Don't worry," El Greco replies, "I get premonitions," he sneezes, "I reckon you'll be Home Secretary by December."

"I...I can't..."

A series of happy footsteps fade out.

"Sander?"

The restroom ambience remains. The plumbing is angry and fluorescent lights are droning. Sander thinks you can hear the water, the still water, sitting in the toilet bowls, like it's thinking things over, swearing at itself like Thrussel.

"You there?" Thrussel asks again, almost begging.

As far as the committee is concerned, notes of any amendments and conclusions are typed up in a report. They get sent to the Commons to inform the third reading of the Bill.

Back in Coventry, Aaron Lakin-Smithers sits at home with his girlfriend. They watch television. Neither of them—since they both feel they work for Lucifer, whether in Parliament or the I.T.C.B. Bulkington branch—have anything to say to each other.

◊

A few days later, Piers Meak is unwrapping a Peppermint Fánk. "It was so cold today," he starts to say, "a Reactionary had his hands in his own pockets."

Seren Vogt, sat next to him, says, "Shut up, Piers."

The Commons is, once again, full. In the first row of the Government's benches, Fernanda Li sits with her hands in her lap. Her face is a mixture of national duty and corporeal fear.

Parallel to the Speaker, simultaneously, the Medical Advisor to the Speaker of the House, Doctor Jackson Carcass (O.B.E., F.R.C.P., M.R.C.S., B.O.b.s.t. and R.C.O.G.), inspects the Prime Minister. He notes her thighs. He notes her hips. He notes her breasts. Suffering from emphysema, the over-inflation of the alveoli, he keeps an oxygen tank with him at all times, administering the occasional whiff. If it can get him through heart surgery, it can get him through a parliamentary session. He notes her breasts again. "Less to," he wheezes to himself, "throw away."

The Speaker Hekla Sigurdsson has a dekko from her chair, saying, "What was that, Jackson?"

"I said," wheezing in clarification, "'it's good that some are gay.'"

"Fuckin A," the Speaker replies.

Subsequently, things get real easy for the Syrian lobby. It's impossible for either party to be against the Bill since both have reached the conclusion that the winning votes in 2091 will be from the L.G.B.T.Q.+ community. And a rejection of the Belgium Bill will result in public outcry. Not necessarily from the L.G.B.T.Q.+ community, but from the irritating low-IQ cousin of said community, *Raving Liberals*, whose numbers out-power the queer community by some margin. The Government is stuck, like the average alcoholic in a corner store at 11:00 a.m. In both cases, a metaphysical tummy-ache is parked in their brain. The metaphysics begin to wear off: any foresight is segued by some skin-deep adrenaline, and off they go like a toddler down an escalator.

First reading: The printing of the Bill for the Lords. Nothing is said.

Second reading: "Any concerns? Any specific areas needing amendment? Like, any?"

Blanchet Didier, the 46th Baron de Clifford stands up, announcing, "This is perhaps the most refined Bill ever brought before this noble house (*interruption: 'Hear, hear.'*)"

There are no mistakes. Proclivities collide. The Lord Atterberry of Hyde chairs the Lords committee. Members can discuss an issue for as long as they want. But not today. All the committee members, along with their colleagues in the House of Lords, have been invited to a Northern Belgian charity ball in Chelsea. King George VII is going. It would be, therefore, a mistake to not go. Not to mention, Quentin Squibb is whipping regardless nowadays, so Lord Atterberry—perspiring now with all the liquid of a 23-year-old chosen last minute to play for England in the 2091 World Rugby Classic—decides to adjourn the committee early.

There are no mistakes. Proclivities collide. The Bill is reprinted with the agreed amendments, which number zero.

The Lords's report stage starts fourteen days after the committee concludes business. But the report this time, typed up by one Mister Joseph Grass now hospitalized from exhaustion, is immediately delivered to the Lords.

The third reading by the Lords commences: Well, calling it that would be an insult to Lords-related third readings that actually commence. Blanchet Didier stands up, again, saying, "This bureaucracy makes my nipples hard."

Well, he doesn't actually say that – but he might as well! In fact, Quentin Squibb is sure that after this Didier will rush home, tear out the pages of Plato's *Republic*, or some other relevant text, and shove them up his ass. Yes. Why not celebrate? *Any threat of parliamentary ping-pong is kaput*, Squibb thinks.

Full-backing. Full-backing. Full-backing.

The Royal Assent, lastly, is more of a formality: The last time a monarch signed a Bill in person was in 1854. But this is 2089, and so King George VII appears in parliament. The Syrian lobby, as you can imagine, are nervous. The Royal Assent Act of 1967 enables the monarch to refuse the passage of a Bill on the advice of his or her ministers. This would be applicable if the last Reactionary government (2075-2084) didn't repeal the 1967 Act. So now, five years later, we're back where we should be: Little parliamentary rituals that mean absolutely nothing.

There are no mistakes. Proclivities collide.

And people, like countries, get what they deserve.

A commencement order is designed to bring a Bill into effect after the Royal Assent. This doesn't usually happen on the same day. But in extreme cases such as these, when blocking a Bill from passing is the equivalent of murdering the entire Royal family, commencement orders aren't needed. The Belgium Bill becomes an Act, and it comes into force on the day of Royal Assent, Thursday, 28th June 2089, at midnight.

Later that same night, it is 1:45 a.m. in Belgravia. Belgravia House is a mansion block. It has 24-hour concierge service, a residents' lobby with complimentary coffee and biscuits and a secure cycle storage space (S.C.S.S.). Each mansion spans seven hundred and twenty square feet with an en suite bedroom and galley kitchen. Flat No. 7 is no different—Sayid Chemtob pops a bottle of champagne and pours two glasses. Nooda Shakra sips from her glass, looking out the window. Sayid beetles up behind her and puts his hands on her breasts, squeezing them. He flicks her nipple and Nooda breathes.

In.

Out.

Sayid runs his hands down her thighs, rubbing closer –

and closer. But there's some supernatural barrier between her groin and his hands, implied and frustrating. And that would be fine if it didn't turn Sayid on. He pulls up her skirt, but she says, "No."

"What?"

"I," she stumbles over her words, "we need to," putting down her glass, "I need to think first."

"Think about this," her boyfriend says as he kneads her crotch, "you like that?"

"N—no..." She pulls away, knocking her glass off of the kitchen island.

Glass is tinkled across the floor, which makes Sayid angry. "Jesus Christ," he says.

"It's just," Nooda tries to explain, "not now."

"Come here," he says.

"I don't want—"

"I said come here damn it." He pushes her onto the couch, overlooking Belgravia.

The cars run through the orange lights. He rolls her over. The skirt and underwear are torn off. Sayid inserts himself and thrusts twenty times, after which he ejaculates, and thrusts three more times at half speed. He pulls her right breast out and crushes it with his right hand. In the expensive upholstery, dug deep in the high-density urethane foam, a voice. Not even a voice; rather, the lint of something vocal, mouthing a forgotten language, a terrified tongue banished by extraction, now rediscovered in a moment of abject fear.

"اي إهي...اي إهلي..."

Oh my God, she says, *oh my God.*

Sayid storms into the bathroom, locking the door behind him. Meanwhile, Nooda grips a pillow and the insides of her thighs. She sits up, then, dangling her head in her hands, a string of tears plummeting from the un-curled eyelashes. The tears land together like friends feeling in warm rooms, healing one another: an inarticulate, gargantuan fixing. She puts on what's left of her underwear and skirt. She begins to cry. Crying is represented with difficulty in our various cultures. And so even culture can be useless.

"*All of it,*" Eikenboom would say. "*I have a problem with all of it.*"

Harmon

Harmon, like Frasquita the ignominious wife of poet Naranja Sastré in the final act of *El Poeta Nicaragüense* (*The Nicaraguan Poet*, 2088), an opera by Wolf Quintana with text Rosa Molina-Guerra, based upon a short story by Luis Jasso: *El Poeta Escribe Tristemente* or *The Poet Writes Sadly*, sits bolt upright screaming. Falling off the asparagus-coloured couch and smashing a glass of water table-supported opposite, he becomes tangled in a woollen fandango-coloured blanket, resembling a gay amoeba running away from a band of homophobic amoebas.

Yolanda Polk, stood at the kitchen sink, turns around. She runs to comfort Harmon as he does a Technicolor yawn across the floor. She squeezes him, saying, "Calm down, baby. It's all right. You're safe. Don't worry."

Bloodshot dogging eyes force themselves open.

A glass table supports a bronze grail full of mail and paperclips. Next to that, a fulvous armchair frowns. There's another table, with a chessboard on top and a bust of Ulysses Lachnér boasting an apprehensive expression and a faux-Panama hat; an M.D.F. desk topped with a Requiem© (COAnàb subsidiary) Desktop Computer; the same twelve volumes of Doctor Norvin Tubaniña's *Medicamenta Principis*, amassed in fern-green mould and leaning against the desk at an 80° angle. On the other side of the room is a kitchenette with an open window, and breeze entering. Meanwhile, the radio plays *The Binning Men*, the operetta by Snell & Burst. Polk turns the radio off, returning with paper towels to soak up Harmon's vomit. She then lifts him back onto the couch. "You can relax," she says, "you're safe."

"I'm," he stutters, "s-s-so c-cold—"

"It's real," she comforts, "don't worry. It's real."

"I don't," moaning, grabbing his own face and charging full speed into the cushion, "I don't know."

Yolanda ruffles his hair like a dog's.

(The calm ≈ [scrunch + lift] Q.E.D. movement.)

"I got you out," Polk asserts, "you just relax, okay?" Harmon drags the blanket up to his nose, mumbling, *"Fánks,"* after which he closes his eyes.

Later, Harmon opens his eyes, again. This is getting to be a pretty daunting routine. Is he waking up from something? And if he is, who's doing the waking? Why that particular moment? No one ever gives a straight answer. He stares into Yolanda Polk's nostrils. "I need to tell you something," she says, although the actions of her nostrils say something rather different, "I was lying when I said this was real," her nostrils flare, "I'm sure you can understand."

If Chikenyyt knows anything, it's that it's impossible for him to reach the escape velocity required to punch through the gravitational field of dogging, allowing him to travel into something resembling space. The mind, surviving currently on a ration of pornographic experiences and velocity equations whose accelerations always points towards the center of curvature. Not that Y. Polk's an expert on velocity equations. "You were in bad *s*hape," Yolanda says, "but you're better now," running a finger across the lines on his hand, "I've crossed a lot of channels to get to you."

"Where's Mullein?" Harmon asks.

Yolanda smiles. "The only answers to that question are extremely complicated," she sniggers, "and kind of pointless."

Harmon grips her collar and says, "Try me."

"You spit on Egelblöm when you see her in the hallway?" she asks.

Harmon's temples fizz with blood. "…No?"

"Then let go of my collar," she warns.

He lets go, and she stands up, making her way to the window. "It's impossible to say where Mullein is," Polk expounds, aggressively.

Outside, the sounds of road-slides permeate the air.

"He knows what we're doing," she adds, turning to face Harmon, "he does – but more importantly, do you?"

"I can't answer that," he replies.

"If you think you do," she says, "you probably don't." She turns the radio back on and *The Binning Men* returns. "That's the conclusion I've reached," she folds her arms, "my two months." Yolanda's fishtail braids stream down her skull like water, blocking the sunlight entering the window. *The dams may burst,* Harmon thinks. *That would make this better.*

"Two months?" Harmon asks, after he blows his nose. "You're the one in the coma?"

"Jesus," Yolanda scoffs, "is that what they're calling it?"

"Sergeant Kapoor said you were like a…"

"…"

"A carrot."

"He's in here too," Polk tacks on as Harmon observes the Ölümsüz pack on the table.

He slides a cigarette out, asking, "There's a carrot in the apartment?"

"No you idiot," Yolanda corrects, "Kapoor. He's dogging."

"Oh," lighting the cigarette, "that last dogging trip, or," he leans back on the couch, "the one I woke up from. He got shot in the head."

"He'll be sick," she chuckles, "everyone thinks it's a way out, but it's not." Harmon stares into space, meditating, *"Sick in dreams…"*

"They're not dreams," Polk posits, "they're hallucinations."

"Difference being?"

"Have you ever died in a dream?"

Harmon thinks. "No," he says, "not that I recall."

"Your plane crashes," Yolanda narrates, "but you're the only survivor. Wild dogs hunt down your friends, but they never hunt you."

"What?"

"When you're dreaming, you get left alone. You're always bearing witness," she kneels down, resting her hands on Harmon's knees, "but you're the first to die when you're dogging. And when someone like Mullein lays you down, you die," her eyes freeze on his face, "and your fantasies die with you," she grips his knee caps, "it makes reality feel like heaven," smiling, "just about the only thing that does."

"Why go back?" Harmon asks.

"Cuz we have a job to do," Yolanda retorts.

Harmon stubs out his cigarette on the table, noting, "I don't smoke."

"Keep your words and actions separate," Polk observes, "I like it," she thinks, briefly, about having breakfast, "someone left them so you'd find me."

Then, out of nowhere, she lands a kosher snog on Harmon's lips. This is, for Harmon at least, stronger than any drug he has every taken.

After she finishes, Polk says, "He told me to kiss you because it'd freak you out," she nods, "my contact'll be happy."

"Uh," Harmon searches for one of his fillings, "uh – who's that?"

"Classified," she replies. "Can't say."

These opaque responses are reminiscent of the cosmological principle: the homogenous totality that no matter where in time and space you look from, you'll see the same stuff as anyone else, regardless of how big your telescope may be.

◊

Sergeant Copernicus Kapoor completes the upchucking of the 21st century. Egelblöm witnesses the event, rather irritated, nay furious that things haven't gone exactly to plan. The sergeant experiences that niggling irritation at the back of every man's skull that he might be useless at everything he will ever attempt in life. Kapoor suggests, apologetically, "There's an enemy agent."

"No there isn't, sergeant," she hisses at him, "everyone knows that Kravets is a full-blown D.E.R.P. junkie, for fuck sake."

"She was fired last week—"

"That doesn't mean she stopped doing it!" Egelblöm nuclear-bombs back. "If anything, she's upped her dosage of D.E.R.P., and bespokedly has a vendetta against the institution that terminated her service in the first place!"

◊

RGF-XXIV Criteria for Substance Dependence (Nicaraguan Psychiatric Association, 2076).

A maladaptive pattern of substance abuse leading to clinically significant impairment or distress, as manifested by three or more of the following, occurring at any time in the same 12-month period.

Tolerance, as defined by either of the following:

A need for a markedly increased amount of the substance to achieve intoxication, or desired effect.

A markedly diminished effect with continued use of the same amount of substance.

Withdrawal, as defined by either of the following:

The characteristic withdrawal syndrome for the substance.

The same [or a closely related] substance is taken to relieve or avoid withdrawal symptoms.

The substance is often taken in larger amounts, or over a longer period than was intended.

There is a continuous desire or futile efforts to cut down, or control one's substance use.

Large amounts of time spent in activities necessary to obtain the substance [e.g. visiting multiple doctors or driving long distances], use the substance [e.g. chain-smoking], or recover from its effects [sick days, societal withdrawal {*see below*}].

Important social, occupational or recreational activities are given up or reduced because of substance use.

The substance use is continued despite knowledge of having a persistent or recurrent physical or psychological problem that is likely to have been caused or amplified by the substance [e.g. continued cocaine use despite the user's acceptance of cocaine-induced depression, or continued drinking despite the user's recognition of alcohol-correlated psychosis].

Substance abuse with physiological dependence is diagnosed if there is evidence of tolerance or withdrawal. Substance abuse without physiological dependence is diagnosed if there is no evidence of tolerance or withdrawal.)

◊

Kapoor shakes his head, muttering, "She thinks we're hypocrites."

"Mu ckit, Kapoor," Egelblöm replies, "This is a fact."

"Good Tonguetire there—"

"Shut up," she says, "there's nothing wrong with being a hypocrite. All we have to do is ensure that there can be no bigger hypocrite than us," scooting around Kapoor in her wheelchair, "because that is when you lose the game."

The sergeant rubs his face with his sticky digits. "What do you want to do about Fenway?"

"You can leave people like Fenway," Egelblöm postulates, "to the chilly ways of the world." She cracks her neck.

"Let him do what he wants," she continues, "and if he gets too good, I'll send my boys and girls to put him out of his misery," exhaling, masking the unbalanced psyche strapped to her frontal lobe, "just so we don't have two Kravets on our hands."

Akin to Rastafarians, Egelblöm probably accepts a few bits of The Bible, but on the whole believes something completely different. For example, that Ethiopian Emperor Haile Selassie (1892-1975) was, effectively, a Black Jesus; the liturgical smoking of cannabis sanitizing body and soul in preparation for meditative prayer…

◊

The space between stars, the black stuff, is not empty. It's an interstellar matter, composed of particles; molecules of dust and gas. It has the ability to transmit red light, but it can only absorb blue light. This is why the furthest reaches of our galaxy appear in red clusters. There is nothing but everything.

Harmon and Yolanda are sitting in a booth in a hallucinatory coffee house, a cigarette dangling out of the former's mouth. "Tara," Harmon says, pinching the bridge of his nose, "I remember Tara."

Yolanda, mid-sip with her cortado: "Hmm?"

"Nothing."

"Tara Blimmen," she defines.

"I forgot," Harmon smiles, "Fenway told me she was dead."

"She's not dead."

"How do you know?"

"They keep the important ones alive."

"Who does?"

"The people in charge," Polk explains, placing her cup on its saucer, "you're alive, aren't you?"

Harmon stares into his coffee. "Can someone die and stay here? I mean, you're in a coma—"

"I'm not dead," she asserts, stirring sugar into her coffee, "I'm just doing my homework before I make my move."

Harmon exhales. "She's real."

"Who?"

"Tara."

"…Yea," Yolanda says, "she's real," she scoops the frothéd milk, slurping it off, "but don't go round like Fenway screwing everything that moves. We won't get on too well."

"This coffee sucks," Harmon says.

"It's not a real coffee house," she counters, "what do you expect?"

Harmon looks at his colleague. "What happened to you?" He decides to put it a different way. "What do you think happened to you?"

Yolanda cogitates. Mostly about how in Morocco *kif* a.k.a. cannabis is a means to soothe the existential crises among tribal groups living in those rather lonely Rif Mountains. Special rooms are dedicated to the rolling, lighting, lighting again, smoking, and lighting yet again of kif cigarettes amongst a melange of local culture: tall tales, gesticulations, ancient melodies passed onto younger generations in a haze of I-don't-give-a-fuck.

"Your brain gets used to it," Polk answers, finally, "it starts to think it's normal."

Harmon asks if it's addictive. Yolanda shrugs. "Some people have a problem. Some people don't. Do you?"

"I don't think so," Harmon says, "what about you?"

"Nah," she replies, bearing a toothy grin, "I'm just a workaholic." She laughs into her coffee.

Harmon, simultaneously, sees a body in his left eye, turning so his right can catch up. He recognizes 'The Kid,' alias Rufus Umbarglé.

◊

Prior to this, in reality, one of Sergeant Marcus Hasegawa's constables, Ingram, drives his car at full speed over the gravel highways of the Scotia Belt. The car is the length of one midget-quintet, arranged from head to toe. After he runs over a badger, he takes a sharp left, careering up a less-than-well-kept road. The car stops in front of a small cabin. He steps out, scratching his crotch and pulling his pants up. He then extracts a freighted pillbox from his left pocket like the pharmaceutical prognosticator he so happily is. After he pops a 500mg *Valerian Root* pill, the box disappears back into the pocket. Ingram chews dispersedly as he walks up to the cabin and goes inside. His colleague, Constable Appleby, practically jumps out of his seat and throws a lager tin at Ingram.

"Ow!" Ingram yells, "what the hell?"

"I thought you were——"

"Who did you think I was?"

"I don't know," Appleby concedes, "anyone."

Ingram brushes his sides. "Anyone?"

Appleby says, "Yea…" and slopes in his chair, ogling at the dewy ceiling-dangled light bulb. He asks if Ingram wants a beer, and his colleague shakes his head, saying, "Had two on the way," pacing around the room and rubbing his hands together, "cold tonight."

"You want me to turn the heater on?"

"We don't have a heater," Ingram reminds him.

"Oh, I swear to——"

"Hey," Ingram says, "wear a scarf, nigga." After he says that, he hunches up in front of the window. The cold light lingers on his features, lapping; his eyes are shining. "I don't like this," he punctuates.

Appleby stares at him. "Like what?"

"Gun," Ingram requests, and Appleby throws a Glock 17 towards him.

"Fuck," barely catching the gun, "you trying to kill me?"

"But you asked——"

"I tell you to get my car," Ingram demonstrates, "you gonna crash it in the porch?" He points the gun at Appleby, saying, "You daft?" and sits subsequently in a rocking chair. He looks at all the banknotes on the coffee table. "Why'd you get it wet?"

"I could hang them over the toaster," Appleby says, "dry them out a little bit. Probably the best way."

"Leave 'em," Ingram replies, scraping his scalp. His hairline is receding; his skin is white as milk. "It'll dry out where it's going."

"Meticula Hedge?"

"Yea," Ingram dangles the gun between his legs, licking his lips, "she called up yesterday."

"Meticula Hedge?"

"Yes, Meticula Hedge called me on my cell," Ingram explains. Appleby asks how she got that number. "That's what I want to know," Ingram says, after which he thinks about Super Kebab.

"So she calls me up," Ingram relays, "and tells me she's got a kid in her trunk…"

He recalls the phone conversation from memory:

"Hello?" Ingram says.

"Ingram," Meticula Hedge asks on the other end, "that's you, right?"

"I don't know. Who's this?"

"It's Meticula Hedge. We're meeting on Tuesday night. I'm picking up some money."

"Oh shit, yea. Cool. How'd you get this number?"

"Doesn't matter."

"It kind of does. This number isn't listed."

"Then how'd I get it?"

"…Uh. That's why I'm asking you."

"There are more pressing matters."

"Uh huh. Like what?"

"I got a kid in my trunk. Little boy. Feel like I'm gonna hurt him. You still there, Ongram—?"

"It's Ingram, yea, I'm here just, why? Who's kid?"

"You know Rufus Umbarglé?"

"Yea, I know Rufus Umbarglé. And you better not have Rufus Umbarglé's kid in your trunk."

"I don't."

"Oh good."

"But Rufus Umbarglé's got an associate called Hijira. From

London. I've got his kid."

"Christ almighty," Ingram exclaims, "Jean-Marc Maalouf's kid? That's even worse."

"I know, right."

"…So what does that have to do with me?"

"I figured I'd pick up the money you owe me, and then hold Maalouf to ransom for the same amount. Do the math. That's almost twice as much."

"No, fuck that. I don't want – look – I don't want Hijira's kid anywhere near me. Especially when it's in your trunk. Which is about to be filled with my money."

"No but for all intensive purposes it's my money."

"Intents and purposes. It's intents and purposes; forget it."

"Cool to pick up the money though, right?"

"Fine. But not with a kid in your trunk."

"Come on."

"NO means fucking NO."

"Fine. I'll be there at seven."

"Okay – don't bring that goddamn kid."

"I won't, I won't, calm down."

"AND DON'T TELL ME TO CALM DOWN!"

"Sorry."

"You don't know what you're messing with."

"…"

"Hello?"

At that time, eleven miles away, Meticula Hedge slammed the phone down. "Tell me what I can and can't do," she hisses as she walks out of the phone booth. She squints at the car's trunk and picks her nose. Meanwhile, The Kid alias Rufus Umbarglé is hanging his hand out of the passenger window, tapping his black-nailed fingers. "We good?" he asks.

Meticula Hedge meticulously adjusts her bra strap and

struts over to the car. She puts her hand on the roof and leans down to The Kid, saying, "Is seven okay?"

"Seven's fine," Rufus says, "I'm gonna miss P.P. O'Leary on TV. But if that's how it is…"

"There's a repeat on Wednesday," she interjects, "watch it then."

"I could," Rufus replies, folding his lips, "but all my friends are gonna be talking about it," he grabs her hand and squeezes it, "you'll listen to what they all have to say and you'll parrot it back to my goddamn face."

Meticula yanks her hand away.

Rufus shuts his eyes, whistling through his Ecstasy-addled nostrils. "You're just too fresh," he says, and sneezes, "get in the car. Let's go."

Within moments, Meticula Hedge is pulping that accelerator with her muddy boots, and the car barges down Hercules Road. Rufus blinks at everything like he hates it, and Meticula looks at him periodically. She asks if he's ever killed anyone. "Yea," Rufus replies, "it was okay."

"What?" asking for clarification, "who you killed, or the killing?"

And Rufus nods, saying, "Both."

◊

To be accurate in the same way that saying that a mirror is a highly polished boundary between two media, or that the instrinsic mass (M_0) total energy (E), and a momentum of the magnitude (p), where the constant (c) is the speed of light is indicative of any energy-momentum relation in Minkowski spacetime, it needs to be said, then, that Rufus Umbarglé's encounter with Constable Harmon Chikenyyt was not precipitat-

ed by any sort of child-smuggling or drug use, but for stealing
two Professor Mikhailov's Rasberry Zefirs from the Mason &
Beaney hardware store after a long day of purchasing plywood
for a hotbox in his mum's back yard, in which he could carry
out ample quantities of child-smuggling and drug use. As such,
maybe their meeting was brought about by drugs and stolen
children after all.

Recognizing Harmon from across the hallucinatory coffee house, The Kid walks over in that overly-confident-nay-
shit-scared way practiced by people under thirty. "Aren't you
a copper?" he says out of the blue. Harmon scans Umbarglé,
replying, "No."

"Mason & Beaney's," The Kid says, "you took those Fánks
off me."

"They were raspberry zefirs," Harmon resolves, ignoring
Rufus, "don't confuse the two."

"I didn't know you got high, officer."

"…"

"They put you up to this?"

"I'm in the middle of something," Harmon interrupts,
"so—"

"Are you undercover?"

Harmon drags Rufus into the booth, pressing his hand
against his groin and saying, "You feel that?"

Rufus squirms. "What the fu—"

"Keep your voice down," Harmon continues, "you feel
that? Answer me."

"Yea."

"You do?'

"Yea—"

"I don't sleep or eat," Harmon explains, "I think someone's
trying to screw me over, and I'm not in the mood. I am a police

officer. I'm also the meanest police officer," crushing The Kid's hand, "I guess you thought, what? Smoke some D.E.R.P.; try and get laid in your dreams cuz you can't in reality? Cuz guess what."

"You're hurting my hand—"

"I'm here too," Harmon says, "and I can kill your dogging in five seconds flat."

"It hurts!"

"I'm a psychedelic warrior," Harmon adds, tightening his grip, "so go have some fake coffee with your fake pussy—"

The Kid jumps out of the booth and walks, briskly, to the other side of the room. He stares, from a distance, at Harmon.

The dogger turns back, readjusted, to Yolanda. "You were a man in one of my trips."

"Probably my trip as much as yours," she says, smiling, "my parents always wanted a boy. But they got me instead."

"Your parents," Harmon pulling his coffee closer, "were they good people?"

"They glossed over the inadequacies of others," Yolanda simplifies, "so I joined the police."

Harmon knows that none of this is real. They're probably sitting in a cave, or something, in the real world. Whatever that is. The mission for the agent Harmon Chikenyyt is unclear. Does he work for the Florin Police Force? Egelblöm? Is he in this for himself? Maybe he's operating as an agent of an agent, whose job it is to know nothing, to be nowhere, to be static and waiting. Harmon stubs out the Ölümsüz. "Thanks for the coffee," he says as he stands up to leave.

As he walks away, Yolanda rotates in the booth, reminding, "Rendezvous at my place," and she blows a kiss after him, landing just above the ass-crack of Harmon Chikenyyt, Agent of Naught.

Exiting the coffee house, Harmon Chikenyyt walks down the street. It's cold. He shoves his hands in his pockets, hunching his shoulders as if it'll make a difference. Maybe he is outside, in a cave; a secretive toad beanbagging in its den. "Jesus," Harmon mumbles, telling himself, internally, to stop thinking about toads. He knows Jesus won't help him either—Christ is too busy hanging around in Dominique Van Hoof's command post. Harmon starts to bump into people walking the other way. None of them are real: the product of D.E.R.P. Suddenly, Patrik Brücke, a bisexual white supremacist, comes into Harmon's line of sight. "Good morning, constable," Patrik says. The streets are, without notice, completely empty. Now, it's only Harmon and Patrik. "What?" Brücke scoffs, "you never seen a racist before?" He chuckles. "I call myself a realist; not that that's much use in here."

"…"

"My ex-girlfriend," Brücke begins as the breeze blows his sleeves, "says you got a message."

"I'm sorry?"

"I'm the one that's sorry I gotta look at you," Brücke comments, moving closer, "I know who you are. Maybe you best listen," he squints, "I represent Mister Apple-Tennyson. He's taken an interest in this little journey you're on. In fact, I'd go as far to say that what I just said was an understatement."

"It's my fault, then?"

"Nobody's faults led to this," Brücke offers, "things have just gotten out of hand; my client's hand; and I'm here to tell you that Mister Apple-Tennyson is tightening his grip."

"…"

"Ask me a question," Brücke says.

"Do you know," Harmon asks, awkwardly, "where I can buy hydrangeas?"

"What," Brücke returns, "like, fuckin flowers?"

"Not like flowers," Harmon says, "they are flowers."

"Open your eyes," Brücke replies, "and look that way."

Brücke's tattooed arm points towards the Florin Police Station—And there it is, on the optic perimeters, like spilt mercury in a shag carpet.

Harmon cogitates, staring at the station. He turns back, saying, "Cheers, shipmate."

"I'll be," Patrik walks away, mumbling, "seeing you around Mister po-leece-man." Apple-Tennyson's agent laughs in that way that only a racist can do: the, "I-was-raised-on-beatings-and-readings," laugh, torn from two thousand corpses.

Belgium/London

The conversation went like this: "We have a new contract with the British government to police, patrol and/or engage on the Belgian border."

Lucas Heffernan, versed in Irish history and the kebab industry, replied, "I do gay clubs in Belfast. I don't do civil wars."

Shortly after that, Slándáil Phoblachtach a.k.a. Republican Security received a delivery of L85A2/SA80 selective fire gas-operated assault rifles with an optional grenade launcher that can blow a tyre eighty feet in the air, which, let's be honest, might be useful in a civil war type of situation.

On Friday 29th June at 6:00 a.m., three hundred Republican Security members are bussed from an undisclosed area in Downpatrick to George Best Belfast City Airport. They fill a fleet of six Boeing Chinook helicopters. Lifting off across Carryduff, Crossgar, and Killough, they float over the Irish Sea, Snowdonia, Birmingham, Coventry, Ipswich and finally Ghent and Brussels in Belgium. Descending into Wavre, three miles from the unofficial border, they touch down on the front line. Levitating down along Rue Sainte-Anne, her trees grown old and her grass rippled with summer-baked cities of tiny sentience, the Chinooks land. Slándáil Phoblachtach charge out of the machines with their weapons of mass destruction and they're ushered into a makeshift army base set up in the Ecole Internationale La Versau. Boots are clomping, ammunition snapping and the clips click. Humanisms are shouted in French, German and Dutch. The rooms are mushroom fields of berets and helmets. Republican Security is greeted with less gratitude than expected. Teeth are sucked. Lips are sneered.

The Defence Secretary Yana Verhoven swaggers through various troopers, followed by her Chief of Defence General Sem De Ridder. Niall Gordon, flanked by Lucas Heffernan and Aoife Mac Eoghain, greets the Belgians. Verhoven examines Gordon's mercenaries. "Is it true that more are coming?"

"Fifty reserve," Gordon replies, "they might get dropped in Liège tomorrow."

"Demandez au mick sur les armes,' De Ridder interjects with a sagged brow.

Niall flinches. "What did you just call me?"

"Sem," Verhoven scolds her general, "qu'est-ce qui ne va pas avec toi?"

"English," Mac Eoghain says, "please."

Yana Verhoven asks if they speak French.

"No," Gordon replies.

Yana tries again: "Dutch?"

"No."

"German?"

"No."

"Wuh," Yana can't believe her ears, "why can't you speak other languages?"

"Do you speak Ulster?" Gordon asks.

"Well," Verhoven stutters, "n-no—"

"You're a fuckin idiot, then, aren't you?" Gordon replies.

De Ridder, fired up by all of this, says, in broken English, "Manny, uh, Irish man," pretending to slice his throat with his finger, "dead Water-loo – that reference you get?"

Mac Eoghain pushes the general, shouting, "What's your problem?"

"J'ai travaillé avec les Irlandais en Syrie," De Ridder begins, addressing everyone in the room, "Ils sont tous les mêmes!"

Gordon asks Yana what he just said. "Okay," she replies,

changing the subject, "the south is coming through Rixen-sart—"

"What did he say?" Niall demands.

The jagged plink of broken glass backgrounds the argument. Just over Lucas Heffernan's shoulder, Mac Eoghain can see a Belgian serviceman with half his face missing. The soldier falls over, and bullets saturate the windows. Another serviceman runs through. "Ils sont sur l'autoroute!" he yells, "le e-quatre-onze!"

Republican Security members drop to the ground, shouting, "Where's that?"

"Is that outside?"

"English! We need English!"

"Jesus," Niall Gordon cocks his SA80, "Christ—"

He stands up and fires out the window for five seconds, the air filling with the rickety pumping of chambers.

A long silence follows.

Outside, in the distance, there are a few dull screams.

Niall reloads and faces his crew, ordering, "Let's move!"

Heffernan does the cross sign over his chest, singing, "Oh god-damn," to himself, "mother fuck-er!"

Loading the optional launcher, Heffernan spurts a live grenade out the window. Slándáil Phoblachtach, thereafter, beetle into the spooky wartime silence outside. Intermittent rat-tat-tats whistle by, along with jets of twig and dusty founts. The mercenaries begin to blow the piss out of the highway. They do more than that: they irrevocably dismantle the structure and all its components. Each support gives. The girders snap. Concrete crumbles and pillars shard apart. Patches of tarmac peel off and strokes of road paint splinter, after which twenty-three southern Belgians run from underneath the E411, screaming and shooting. Another British grenade lands to the right of the group, at which point two Belgians lose their limbs, landing twenty feet away, like one of those unfortunate exemplary tyres. Dozens of rimless tapered 5.56x45 mm cartridges (which, ironically, originated in Belgium) flare themselves across Belgian bodies. Abdomens are spewed and thighs peppered crimson. Shoulders are chunked off and fingers severed. Cheeks are drilled and ankles busticated. Somebody's head bursts; another's eye whites burst; another soldier's body literally snaps in half, his intestines foaming a yellow juice across the piping sounds of undergrowth – plagiarizing crickets and cicadas leaping through the buggy hamlets below human actions of vagabond cruelty.

◊

The intervention led by Niall Gordon & Co. is an ideological statement. But ideology is, often, not enough—One must become one's policies. Doctor Jackson Carcass's practice is located on 135 Harley Street, just off of Weymouth Street. The only noteworthy aspect of his practice is a nude calendar photographed and compiled with reference to ornithology that hangs on the wall of his operation theatre. Disregarding medical tradition completely, Carcass performs all of his surgeries solo.

Fernanda Li lies on the gurney at 8:00 a.m. on Saturday, 30th June 2089. Prior to all of this, in France, on Tuesday, 3rd September 1552, a Frenchman, bored during the latter part of the afternoon, writes the word, "Androgyne". Then, in Germany, in 1910, sexologist Magnus Hirschfield sits in his Charlottenburg practice doodling in his diary. Suddenly, his tea in all likelihood having been spiked by his housemaid, he coins the term, "Transvestite". More bored men will do similar things in the future. "Transexual" in 1949, "Transgender" in 1971, and "Trans" in 1996. Physically, Hirschfield led the way with his buddy Doctor Felix Abraham who performed a mastectomy on a trans man in 1926, a penectomy on Hirschfield's housemaid in 1930, and finally a full vaginoplasty on Einar Magnus Andreas Wegner in 1931. Over in the U.S.A. in 1952, George William Jorgensen Jr., former American G.I. and legitimate badass, returned from Denmark as Christine Jorgensen. Then Jorgensen's Danish psychiatrist Doctor Hamburger (real name) received letters from five hundred men and women, all of them explaining how they were unhappy with their gender. And considering how two hundred of those letters were probably taking the piss, that was still an impressive number. All hell broke loose: Hirschfield's protégé, Harry Benjamin, set up a clinic in New York where he trained a new generation of psychiatrists and psychotherapists, followed by another clinic in San Francisco. Back in the U.K., in 1999, an appeal court decision decided that the only treatment for transsexual individuals was hormone therapy and surgical reassignment. But it's not like that stigma went anywhere. It stayed. And even now, ninety years later, it's still screaming and growing and kicking. Just as Her Eminence The Archbishop Dominique Van Hoof embodies her views, so too must Fernanda Li. Technically they're Joram Falack's views, but let's at least pretend to act like this is Westminster—but there, that's the type of crass, self-evaluating bollocks that makes good Bills into bad Acts every week.

When it comes to relationships, bonds of love between Li and another person, her biggest fear isn't rejection, but the foreshadowing likelihood that when she gets a partner she'll mess it up. Not them, but her. Transplant that notion now to gender reassignment. Imagine a situation where the basis of your self-worth, body and soul, is intrinsically flawed to such an extent that normal life is not only not possible in the foreseeable future, but has also never been possible. An occasional subconscious flourish highlighted these feelings every other week, and maybe now you're faced with someone you really like, but you're entombed in a totally contradictory vessel, an innate double bluff. You reckon maybe if you get really drunk and pick up people that way it'll be all right, that those occasional subconscious parades of your spiritual void will stop, or change to something more intact or wholesome. But the opposite happens. Suddenly it's four in the morning and you're sleeping in a double bed, trying to feel an emotion that doesn't exist. That's awful. So awful that getting rid of your genitals becomes a release. And maybe it is—that's not for anyone to say—but if it means that some poor bastard or bitch isn't sprawled in his or her own vomit at four in the morning, trying to latch on to some attitudinal residue, then that's fine. Do what you have to do. Because *most people don't,* and any human being with a functioning brain should be hard pressed to call that "living".

Doctor Carcass pulls out a massive needle. "General," he wheezes, "anaesthetic, Prime Minister." Otherwise known as *Propofol* ($C_{12}H_{18}O$).

Li's veins begin to course with the stuff, and she is completely unconscious in twenty seconds, fading away to that place between the music in supermarkets and dreams.

"You're going to need it!" Doctor Carcass laughs, wheezing and coughing to himself. Arrogantly casting his oxygen aside, he picks up a scalpel to begin the surgery.

Oh.

Hold up.

He got a bit keen there.

The good doctor takes another thirty second suck of oxygen. Let's try that again…

Arrogantly casting his oxygen aside, Carcass picks up a scalpel to begin the surgery. First, he will perform a complete mastectomy, followed by a hysterectomy: the womb and ovaries are flopped in a medical bin. He closes her vagina with a needle and dissolvable stitches. Subsequently, the *antero-lateral thigh* (or A.L.T.) Flap Phalloplasty Operation is undertaken, being the most common method used to create a new phallus, or Neo-penis: this includes the requisite urethra duct, scrotum and nerve anastomosis, also, so there is a sense of feeling down there.

Doctor Carcass begins by slicing the skin needed for the Neo-penis off of the upper thigh. In cases involving overweight patients, skin is lifted from the forearm instead. The scalpel is inserted, carving the fatty tissue and blood seeping out. The grey-gloved fingers yank and drag off the now-dead skin. Jackson holds it up to the surgical lights, each vein throbbing off its own death. "Risks and complications," he explains to himself, "are as follows: bruising, bleeding, swelling," wringing the skin like a wet towel, "flap necrosis, infection, scarring and numbness." He flicks a vaginal component off his thumb.

"But I got twenty letters after my name," he concludes, "what do you say to that, Prime Minister?"

There is, obviously, no response.

Doctor Carcass sneezes, adding, "Ignore me."

The urethral meatus in women is lower than it is in men, so prior to phalloplasty, Doctor Carcass must lengthen, preferably towards the clitoris, the urethral orifice so that he can weld the Neo-urethra to the incoming Neo-penis. Using the "inner-labia-and-local-flap" technique where the mucosa surrounding the urethral orifice is used for the aforementioned lengthening (preferred since total phalloplasty and scrotoplasty can be performed at the same time) the scalpel is dragged in a Ω shape. Cuticles visible under the gloves jolt the flesh up, tugging and tweaking it. It's not a complete botch-job. Li's mega-prick, however, is literally spineless. "I hope you're ready for Miss Pneumatic," the medical adviser advises the unconscious man/woman.

The *Fibula Flap Operation* is quite simple—If you're Doctor Jackson Carcass, however, it's near impossible. The middle section of the fibula bone, known for its thinness and located on the lateral side of the tibia, is removed and placed within the Neo-penis for rigidity and structure.

"Here she is!" Carcass announces as he brings out the pneumatic autopsy saw.

It is, technically speaking, only *half* a saw, which spins at seventeen thousand cycles per minute. It practically chews through Fernanda's calf muscle; a retractor pulls the flesh apart—Spotting her fibula, he saws away and plucks the bone out with some forceps. The opening is sewn shut. He inserts the fibula into the Neo-penis, welds it together, and smiles. But Doctor Carcass, having filled and lighted his pipe in the meantime, puffs for a few pensive moments, and realizes that he has forgotten something. "Of course!" he splutters. Compiling a mass of tissue from the major labia, he designs and creates a ballsack. It is sewn over the liquidated vaginal cavity. The sex-change operation is complete. "That is without a doubt," Carcass concludes, coughing, "the ugliest man that I have ever seen."

◊

Meanwhile, in Propofol land: the bluebells in dreams – the dead light of a south-England winter past; suddenly, in the bellicose summer breeze blowing dog rose and lesser celandine. Twigs lay like snow, braided with green-bladed grass. And the amber effervescence of hay rolled in bales is churned across three Li-owned Edington fields under the North Slope of Salisbury. Beaming in the dew.

Inside the Li-clan's converted farmhouse, Fernanda runs on ancient flooring pattered always by two nannies at the kitchen island cooking Wu Gok and Char Siu Bao. Jingdezhen porcelain reproductions are washed. Their employers enjoy orange evenings: thin fingers hold glasses of wine, remembering themselves in their actions and drinking, the Guangdong cuisine they consume. The coriander leaves, black pepper and shards of ginger. Cheltenham Ladies' College takes Fernanda, ivy climbers of brick-fashioned shadows, wisteria wringing itself on the dangled afternoons and apriled lawns licking the soles of each expensive shoe. The Oxford application process is like a flood that drains away the week after, but in she gets.

Always getting in places, that Fernanda—Never getting out. "Out," is an ugly place; uglier than whatever is, "in". Fernanda Li: Weathervane in politics, weathervane in life; always on time, always prepared, re-elected, always. Stillness. Such stillness – the grimness subsides and blood is vacuumed up in dreams. Casting her eyes over the mighty Anglo-Saxon rod that now lives between her legs, Fernanda sees circles in her eyes. In her aqueous humour, electrolytes, amino acids and water, Fernanda is deprived of herself.

"Wake up!" Doctor Carcass shouts, slapping Mister Limousine with the back of his hand.

"Wake up, goddamn you!" He slaps her again.

Mister Limousine's eyes crack open. Doctor Carcass grins, bearing every filling he has ever had. "Mister Limousine arises!" Carcass laughs, "ho-ly," wheezing, "FUCK—" He suffers a heart attack, gripping his left arm.

"Ah—" He knocks over an oxygen tank, which bursts jetting O_2 everywhere.

He grabs hold of the operatory light, but the structure collapses on top of him, the light fixture smashing across the vital signs monitor. Sparks fill the operation theatre. An electrical fire starts as Doctor Jackson Carcass fades on the vinyl flooring. Flames engulf the curtains. The operation theatre starts to burn.

The fire alarm screams.

◊

On Union Street, SE1, the London Fire Brigade is notified of a fire on 135 Harley Street, Marylebone. Two fire engines are dispatched, screeching through the overcrowded streets and over Southwark Bridge. They turn left onto Upper Thames Street and zoom down the A3211. They shrill past King's College London, Aldwych Theatre, the New London Theatre, Dominion Theatre and the University of Westminster. They squeak to a halt in Marylebone where black and yellow bodies wearing buggy helmets scurry out of the trucks. Attaching hoses, valves are adjusted and gauges are observed. An axe, concurrently, goes through the white door of the Carcass practice. Firemen's boots fill the boiling hallways with muffled conversations carried out through oxygen masks. Each corridor is flooded with water, every room tackled with the same wet fury. Two firemen enter the operation theatre. Mister Limousine is gone and Doctor Carcass is not only on fire, but also dead.

Elsewhere, on Balcombe Street in the Marylebone district,

Sergeant Hasegawa sits in an unmarked police car. Sitting in the back seat are Constable Appelby and Constable Ingram. Being on the Reactionary Party payroll, they've been loitering here just in case anything goes wrong at Doctor Carcass's, which, evidently, it has. The sergeant's phone rings and he answers it. "Hasegawa."

"Get to Carcass's now," Joram Falack says.

"Why," Hasegawa replies, "what's happ—"

"Find the Prime Minister and just do as I say!" Falack hangs up.

Hasegawa, in some form of Hirschfieldian protest, shoves the phone between his legs, saying, "Class-A cunt – that one there."

The two constables "tee-hee" as their unmarked police car bolts off to 135 Harley Street.

"Give me more pressure!" the crew manager (C.M.) screams at his fellow firefighters. Water is battering the walls of the quickly melting practice. Having realized the building is going to collapse, firemen make for the front door. The crew manager warns, "Get out!" as an explosion erupts on the third floor, "Run!"

Hasegawa, Appleby and Ingram show up. They get out of the car and rush over to the crew manager. "Are you in charge?" Hasegawa asks.

"Yea," the crew manager replies with sweat rolling down his face, "and you are?"

"Police," the sergeant says, showing his identification card, "have you seen the patient?"

"Dave found a body in the operation theatre."

"..."

"But I don't know if—"

"Appleby," Hasegawa turns to his constables, "Ingram, search the area."

"Someone important?" the crew manager asks.

"It's an MP," Hasegawa answers.

The crew manager scoffs, adding, "Good."

The two constables wander around the black snow, swimming through the smoking atmosphere. Appleby finds himself in the alley behind Harley Street. He spots a male figure, willy and all, propped against a wall.

"Jesus," the constable covering his mouth so he can breathe, "Ingram!"

In no time the constables are pulling Mister Limousine out of the alleyway and wrapping him in police-issue jackets. They throw him in the back seat of their unmarked police car, after which Hasegawa's foot almost goes through the floor as the vehicle veers off. It careens around three blocks and pulls into King Edward VII's Hospital. Hasegawa turns to face the hallucinating, and quite generally messed up, Mister Limousine. "Take him in," the sergeant tells his constables, "I want a private, anonymous room. Repeat that back."

Collectively, Appleby and Ingram say, "Private eponymous room."

"I'll go park," Hasegawa says.

Ingram scoffs, affixing, "Yea, good luck with that—"

"Ingram get the fuck out of my car!"

On the fourth floor of King Edward VII's Hospital, Joram Falack and Nooda Shakra footslog their way down the hallway. Joram is wearing a dinner jacket cut by Kotori Nakamura. Nooda's wearing the usual Paulo Veronese blue skirt with a purple pizzazz faux fur coat. They reach a door labelled, 'Prime Minister,' and Falack rips the namecard off, bursting through the door. Doctor Maximilian "Raw" Leach, fiddling with a tablet, looks up, saying, "This is a private room, sir."

"This is a matter of national security," Joram replies.

"That may very well be the case," Leach purrs, "but we can't have people passing through willy-nilly."

"I'm Joram Falack, Reactionary Party Chairman. My associate here is Nooda Shakra, the Defence Secretary—"

"You could be King George VII for all I care," Leach offers, "now will you please leave!"

Sergeant Hasegawa, Appleby and Ingram walk into the room, ushering in an air of despondency, of corruption-cum-intimidation, which rattles all of Doctor Leach's bones.

The doctor stands his ground for four and a half seconds, until a quick session of controlled breathing and tablet-lowering precipitates an exit on Doctor Leach's informed—winner of the British Medical Association Book Award for *Phalloplasty And Other Words* (2088, Juggernaut Press)—behalf.

Over by the bed, the respirator pumps and the vitals beep. Nooda stares at Mister Limousine. "Joram," she says, slapping her hand over her mouth, "what have you done?"

The Party Chairman glances at her for a split second, until turning back to Mister Limousine. The patient raises his arm, beckoning Falack over to the bed. "Joram...?" a strained but familiar voice says. Falack blinks. Then he clicks his heels across the floor and sits on the bedside. All of this is done incredibly slowly. "...Joram?" the patient says again.

"Oh, my dear," Joram stutters, "man – my dear man..."

Nooda goes to leave the room. Joram nods at Ingram to go after her, which he does. Falack returns to the Prime Minister with some rather unrealistic empathy. "How are you?" he asks.

Mister Limousine parts his sticky lips, whispering, "I saw my Mother..."

Joram flicks his eyes to and fro, muttering, "Heh?"

"I dreamed," Limousine massages the interior of his mouth with his tongue, "there was a man in the kitchen, looking up…"

"But you've," Joram praises, "you've made it now."

"Yeesssss," the Prime Minister fades out. Joram leans over and hugs him, whispering to himself, "We're going to win," Hasegawa zipping up his fly in the background, "we're going to win…"

Zach

Doctor Byrony glares at your mouth, saying, "Not you too!" Turning on his heels, he adds, "Best if mum stays here."

You go into the man's office, newly furnished in *Umeclidinium*: a long-acting, once daily muscarinic antagonist taken during maintenance treatment for C.O.P.D. symptoms. He shuts the door. Miss Antoinette, staring at her laptop, taps the number pad. Her eyelids are twitching. I stand up and sit next to Byrony's door. Listening, again. The human ear can hear between twenty hertz and twenty kilohertz. There are two realms outside of that, two levels of backgrounding: *Infrasound*, which is really quiet, and *Ultrasound*, which is really loud. The vibrations are transmitted by the vestibulocochlear nerve to the brain, not unlike how most celestial bodies are highlighted by a star. Dark Nebulas are another matter, however: nebulae whose dust and gas quota is not immediately visible because of a nearby star. Instead, other celestial bodies, light years behind them, illuminate dark nebulae in the foreground, making them truly backlit; and so I hear an oxygen tank as Byrony hacks the morning off.

"Right," he says, "Say, 'Ahhh,' for me."

"Ahhh," you say, and there's no paedophile joke this time.

"Yes, that's it," Byrony comments.

"…"

"…"

"…Ah?" you ask.

"Yes," he replies, "keep, 'Ahhhing,' where's my, 'Ahhh'?"

"Ahhh," you go on as Byrony shoves a tongue depressor in your mouth.

"Very good," he notes, pulling the wood out, "if you could just take your shirt off…"

The fabric slides off of you. A stethoscope rattles around Byrony's thick neck, and the metal dish is planted on your chest. "Breathe in," he says, and you breathe in, "breathe out," and you breathe out, "Mmm – again, please," and you breathe in, "and out again," and you breathe out.

Byrony clears his throat, affixing, "Keep your shirt off for the moment." The stethoscope, having completed its task, lands on the desk: a galactic concentration of empirical tooling. Every implement used to bring bad news into the world is collected, it seems, and planted so that it can rust. "Do you smoke?" Byrony asks you.

"Yea," you say, and I know.

"How much?"

"Not that often."

"Do you smoke when you go out?"

"I don't do that."

"You don't smoke when you go out?"

"No, I don't go out."

"…"

"I've been trying to quit," you say, after which Byrony rolls up his sleeves. "Yes," the doctor highlights, "that would be a good idea."

Paedophiles are three times more likely to be ambidextrous or left-handed. They're also typically shorter than other convicted criminals. And considering that 10-12% of the adult population have sexual thoughts involving teenage children, it brings a whole new meaning to the term, "short man syndrome". But those thoughts, thrown to the far reaches of their limbic systems, are never acted upon – unless of course they're paedophiles.

Byrony presses two fingers on your jugular, asking, "Your son has the flu, doesn't he?"

"Yea," you say.

"Do you share cups, or cutlery?"

"Often."

"That's probably what you have then," spluttering for a moment, "his flu." He rolls his sleeves back down and sits at his desk.

"You can put your shirt back on," Byrony orders, "I'll give you the same drug but I'll up the dosage, naturally."

As a pen scribbles on a piece of paper, the material becomes irrevocable, like columns of calcium gas erupting from the Sun, propelled to an altitude where it re-condensates: comings and goings and retirements. When the pen clicks, Miss Antoinette squirts her neck out of the office, asking me, "Can I get you something to drink, or…?"

"No," I say, "I'm fine, thank you."

"You people are sick," she says.

"…Yea," I half-reply, "I'll have it next."

And the secretary's head is happy, floating back into its box. I look at the floor, listening. Inside Byrony's office, the chair cracks and wax paper rustles beneath you.

"Happens to families all the time," Bryony says, sucking for air, "a disease is passed from body to body, undetected," coughing, "everything collapses. All those little social occasions start disappearing. The nights are long and tiring. Then, a rebirth." He stops talking.

"You used to be a bobby," Byrony pries, "didn't you? This could be very important – speaking as your doctor, of course."

You breathe through your nose and say, "I was."

"What chapter?"

"Florin."

"That was shut recently, wasn't it? Madness," clicking his tongue, "what are you doing now?"

You tell him you're retired.

"Retired!?" Byrony gasps, "oh! Oh my!" he laughs, "I'll have spent all my lifetimes by the time I retire!"

He continues to splutter until he becomes serious again, saying, "You take the pill twice a day," clearing his throat, "side effects are nothing major."

He creaks out of his chair. I can hear the sweat sponging on his fingers. "Worst-case scenario is vomiting," he warns, "but I wouldn't worry if I were you. You seem healthy enough."

I read that the Comet Volkov will pass over the Florin exosphere tonight. It will return, in comet-time, to the plane of the Ecliptic. This is close to the orbits of several major planets, one of which is Jupiter. Twenty-four comets have their aphelion at the solar distance of its orbit. Tugged upon by Jupiter's gravitational pull, an outbreak of spots is visible on the planet's surface.

The red lake darkens.

◊

We drive home, ripping up the layers of water coating the tarmac. It becomes a sort of electricity. Water is arced over the windshield, regrouping and pooling where it lands. Inside, the heating is whispering over the doors. Our thighs pour sweat into the upholstery's invisible seams. Impossible seams. Static light delineates around you. You're like a star. But how do you measure the luminosity of a star? The absolute magnitude (M) may be derived from the apparent magnitude (m) and the parallax (π) by the formula: $M = m + 5 - 5 \log \pi$. Then again, I don't think you'd make a very good variable.

You lower the window. The air penetrates and sticks. It sounds like a helicopter. The highway is a toilet and driving a car is another way of seeing. Objects are removed. The eyes are focused on what's visible. Each car becomes special. Each car becomes unique. The car we're in now is a neutral tan, but Japanese neutral tan is two shades greener than American neutral tan. The American neutral tan looks too red to the Japanese to be considered neutral tan.

When Japanese people go home they park their car nose-out. Americans, contrastingly, park their car tail-out.

"I'll reverse in when we get home," I say.

"Yea?"

"Easier to leave," I explain.

For years, people used horses; it's no surprise, then, that we name our car and give them personalities, park them in garages for the night. Other cars fly by. Their headlights are whinnying.

"I might have someone over for dinner tomorrow," I suggest as you shut the window.

In response, you nip your nails and squint at me. "Carlos," I spell out, "that guy across the road."

"Him?"

"Yea," playing my cards right, "what do you think?"

"How do you know him?"

"He's on the other side."

"That's not why you invite people," you say.

"…Isn't it?"

"Do you talk to him?"

I ask, calmly, "Do you want a written confession, or—?" You turn your attention to the highway ahead of us, mumbling, "…The world's a toilet bowl."

Nature is our internal barometer. We have to follow it.

Chinese trucks have a lot of space between their windshields and lights. Western trucks on the other hand have very low windshields. Your barometer measures all these things. It keeps them safe, and secret. Unless you're an automotive engineer, in which case you export your insecurities in glass, metal and the mighty invisible seams of the future. A future is chosen from a list of many, and sewn shut.

Carlos Apple-Tennyson lives on the other side of the street. He gives us a call to tell us that his dog is in bad shape. He can't bring himself to kill it, though. I've seen his dog. It's got a lemon-sized, and not quite benign, tumour bulging under its right eye. It can't see anything. The tumour could either be *metaplasia*: a change of one differentiated cell type to another differentiated cell type, or *dysplasia*: an epithelial anomaly of growth. Either way, it's taking place under the skin, behind the eye, resting on the sphenoid bone.

You tell me Apple-Tennyson wants you to kill it. Jan sips a glass of milk and asks if he can come too. "No," I say, "you have to stay here."

You go into our bedroom and open a drawer. I hear the skin on the wood, and, as I walk in, you pull out a handgun.

"You have a gun?" I say. "You take that from work?"

You just look at me and say, "You never know – wanna hold it?"

"No."

"It's an AMT Hardballer," you go on, "standard police is-sue. Up here at least——"

"Is that meant to turn me on?"

"No just," you examine the gun as though you're seeing it for the first time, "call it what it is——" The stock snaps and you slump you shoulders.

I follow you outside, like we're on a drug bust. The afternoon light plays with our eyes. The sun is smudged. Across the street, Apple-Tennyson stands in his doorway with an arm outstretched. He shakes your hand, saying, "You're Zach, aren't you?"

"Depends," you respond.

Carlos laughs and says, "On what?"

"Nothing," you say, staring at him, "where's your pooch?"

"She's, uh," his eyelids lower, "just in here."

"It's a bitch?"

"Yea," Apple-Tennyson says, "it's a bitch."

We enter his quadrangled flat: square tables, stacks of newspapers (*The Financial Times*, mostly.); on the mustard brown kitchen island is a box of *PTI-801*: a painkiller able to reduce opioid tolerance, dependence or addiction brought on by repeated use of Oxycodone. There's also *Metamizole*: formerly marketed as Dimethone capsules, an injection, Protemp oral liquid and other drug products, and was associated with white cell destruction. It was withdrawn therefore in 1977, but re-introduced in a remodelled form in 2078. Some *Ohmefentanyl*, also: a very potent opioid analgesic drug that is 6,300 times more powerful than morphine.

Apple-Tennyson, in the fluorescent lighting, offers us tea. I think about the 10,000,000 colours my eyes can see, asking, "What's her name?"

"Martha," Carlos says.

Having two eyes means you can determine the depth and distance of an object. This is called *stereovision*. But sometimes when you're looking at an object, your eyes drift. These are called microsaccades.

You find Martha dribbling to death on her bed. You have

a brief microsaccade from her tumourous head to her mouth, even if you didn't realize it. All her lightness of breath is sliding out the occasional stream of saliva. The flesh is wheezing. Her good eye examines you and your sweat. The nervous liquid, self-conscious, like secretaries. You bend over, saying, "Hey, Martha," and pat her head, but you don't want to hurt her, so you rub her neck instead, "hey, girl," you look at Apple-Tennyson, "I never worked with police dogs."

"You work for the police?" Carlos enquires. And your fingers glide through Martha's hair when you say, "I used to," massaging the dog's neck, "ain't that right, girl?"

Smooth pursuit eye movements allow you to follow moving objects. Humans, like whales, are better at downward pursuits than upward pursuits. You need a target. "Do you have a back yard?"

Carlos, running his eyes across the floor, says, "Yea."

"Should we," you suggest, "pick her up and take her out back?"

"Yea…" Carlos clears his throat and picks up his dog.

The doors slide open.

The gun dangles below your wrist.

The owner burrows his face in her fur. "Bye, girl."

Martha licks the air, tasting the breeze. We all do that from time to time, like we're standing in the *Mare Cimmerium* on Mars: a long region parallel to the *Mare Tyrrhenum*, with several canals diverging from its northern end, such as *Cyclops, Cerberus II*, and the *Tritonis Sinus*. We've all been stood there at one point or another, sniffing, because it's too much to comprehend, a kind of half-blink punctuating the experience. Apple-Tennyson's feet thud back through the grass. You put your face into neutral and cock your gun. Then, you plant your feet and point. Twenty per cent of the Earth's vegetation is composed of six thousand different species of grass. You tense your arms and wrists. A one thousand eight hundred and seventy-five square foot lawn produces enough oxygen for a family of three. The dog coughs, lifting its head in pain. A six hundred and twenty-five square foot lawn produces enough oxygen for one person.

Bang.

In neolithic times, the scapula from a large animal would be used for shifting dirt. Then iron appeared, bringing with it the added benefit of leaving less evidence of you digging in the first place. Carlos Apple-Tennyson buries Martha next to the last one. He smooths the dirt over like shaving cream. The bald earth sits like hate. I'm the only one who can feel it.

◊

Growing up around here wasn't easy. We have to reach the conclusion, however, that it's not easy growing up anywhere. No one would ever admit that though. Best if all God's children are unhappy. We already share the oxygen. Still, growing up around here wasn't easy. My parents divorced when I was nine. I grew up with my dad, up here, where any warmth there is *stops* at the border.

There are two types of men: The first type is a group of men who aren't angry at anything. The second type is a group of men who are angry at everything. My father, even though he'd deny it, identified with the latter category. Clouds are collecting. God knows what goes on in people's heads. He was old when he died. He burnt himself out, I think. That's another thing people say too much. "He burnt himself out." I suppose there's some truth in that. Waiting for the rain. The leading cause of death in developed countries is biological aging, that is, the collapse of homoeostasis. A circling of leaves and trees roll in like bikers. The regulation of bodily fluids stagnates, after which your body temperature drops rapidly. Also, the pH of extracellular liquid may increase along with concentrations of calcium, sodium and potassium ions. The branches are waving. Cardiac arrest comes knocking with a loss of oxygen and nutrient supply, which causes irreversible damage to the brain and other tissues. I suppose you could call that, "burning out".

A long time ago, at a shack in a forest, I helped my dad take out his sliding glass doors. There was no porch. The doors hung above nothing, and so we pushed them out. There was, subsequently, a hole in our shack.

The clouds started to collect and the trees rolled in, like bikers. The branches started waving and the rain fell.

"Grab the sheet," my dad said, picking up his staple gun, "put it up," and a patch of black crinkled open like an asshole. We pinned it up and the four corners were blowing. "That's a big one," he commented on the storm outside. "Do you think it'll pass?" I asked.

"Most of them do," he replied, flicking his wrist and taking aim. *Schtup*. There was a gust than ran up the driveway. *Schtup*.

"This should hold out till tomorrow," he said. Meanwhile, the bushes were turning inside out. Bark was being stripped off the trees. The gravel tinkled by the garage and twigs sprinted through the undergrowth. *Schtup*. Branches were snapping. *Schtup*.

"Put the kettle on," my dad ordered, "we'll have a cup of tea," after which he stood back and sucked his teeth. You never met my Father. He wouldn't have liked you.

Slam.

Well, not so much a *slam* – more like the sound of a gun going off under a table in a room two hundred metres away, like a faint, *snapping* sound. The gate latch is broken. You're standing next to it looking sorry for yourself. Jan's parallel to the hydrangeas. I come out with a cup of tea. "What was that?" I ask.

You put your hands on your hips and say, "Gate latch."

"Did it break?"

"No," you say, "I – I slammed the gate. And it snapped."

I raise my eyebrows. "Why'd you slam the gate?"

"I stubbed my toe on the fence."

"You broke the gate because you stubbed your toe?"

"Well, I – I slammed it——"

"Yea," I say, "so it's broken." I look at a pile of mulch settling in the corner. "Jan," I warn, "ears."

Jan covers his ears. I look at you, saying, "You fucking pussy."

"Sorry."

"It's okay."

Jan, with his hands over his ears, yells, "Can I listen again?"

I send a nod. Then I walk over and kiss you.

Then we go to the bloody hardware store, so that we may amend your sins.

There are three categories of consumer experience, or psychology. The first is the *consumption of relief or expeditious glee*. For example: you finish a hard day's shop and you go to the checkout. By the checkout are some Peppermint Fánks, or Rasberry Zefirs, or a fridge full of sweet carbonated drinks, and so you suddenly think, "I've earned that drink." You may think you do, but you don't. You've actually been seduced and targeted during a period of exhaustion. It also becomes ironic since in this period of consumer-fatigue you end up buying more stuff.

The second category of consumer experience is the *consumption of poor memory*. For example—this one being particularly relevant in hardware stores like Mason & Beaney—you go to your local hardware store and buy material for a project. You buy what you need and drive home.

But, suddenly, you realize you've forgotten something. Hardware stores have a way of getting around this, and it's called *cross merchandising*. Let's say you want to buy a new toilet seat and you find the toilet seat section. But *next* to the toilet seats are different types of toilets. And next to the toilets are all the dangerous chemicals needed to clean your toilet. And, suddenly (again), you realize you're in a sort of self-contained bathroom section with sinks and faucets and piping and toilet brushes and long spidery pipe cleaners. And as you experience a sense of capitalistic euphoria your brain happily ignores the fact that it's been designed this way. As such, hardware stores are good at taking advantage of how dumb and forgetful people are in order to maximize their profits. The marketing Gods of Mason & Beaney slide their palms around your neck, bend you forward and shove that big capitalist dick up your ass.

Finally, the last type is *the consumption of sight, smell and touch.* This happened today, actually. We were walking along the garden section of the store and we came across a "model-in-use situation": a patch of astro-turf with a real gate, which had been set up to show how a particular—and because it was demonstrative, the best—latch worked. You lifted it open. "Don't break it," I said, after which you looked at me like you wanted to kill me. Anyway, we bought that latch because we could see, smell and touch it.

In summation, it would be inaccurate to say that all three consumption psychologies work all the time, but they are present.

Waiting in the undergrowth.

Then again, you might just go to the hardware store like we did, buy the new latch, pay for it without purchasing any Zefirs or Fánks, and go home. But even then, there, in my recollection and being, a dangerous denial is paired with rebuttals of fundamental certainties and non-memories coined in cold, squared-off parts of Mason & Beaney.

Loved ones present.

I need to send you back to the Zach Factory. I'm having some issues with the product. Insomnia. Jittering. The urge to slam gates.

The most common perpetrator of child neglect is the biological mother. By our standards, then, the most common perpetrator of child maltreatment is the mother. It's hard to define neglect. I think you always neglect your children, somehow. Having a job is a way of neglecting your child—Marriage at a young age prolongs the woman's fertile span, promoting offspring. One is quite enough for me. And having more than one child means you neglect at least one of them. Parents have favourites. They say they don't, but they do. Answer on a postcard.

Belgium/London

At 11:30 p.m., an unmarked helicopter, funded by The Baron Jake Fagan-Stout of Leicester C.B.E.—addled, currently, by early dementia and a fear of the phrase, "guest toilet"—flies the Shadow Secretary of State Ezra Withers, Shadow Foreign Secretary Caleb Langton-Bland and Shadow Defence Secretary Wiktoria Kozłowski from Westminster to the Church of Saint Loup in Namur, Belgium. Right now, Saint Loup is serving as the state building for the Provisional Government of the Democratic Republic of Southern Belgium. It is here, tonight, that the British Pinko delegation will meet Her Eminence The Displaced Archbishop of Mechelen-Brussels Dominique Van Hoof, along with her all-female cabinet.

Narrowly escaping shell bombardment, the Pinko delegation flies over the river Meuse and lands in the Sainte-Marie Community School courtyard. The helicopter's engine cuts out as a regiment of rag-tag mountaineering-types with rifles surround the chopper. The delegates climb down and meet the Minister of the Interior Lucrece Nijs. After shaking her hand, they are escorted by the freedom fighters (or terrorists) across Rue de Collège into Église Saint Loup. Eight and a half members of the Saint Loup children's choir, the half being a legless alto wounded yesterday by a rogue projectile, stand guard by the door. The breeze blurs their unwashed hair.

Inside the building, coats are taken as a contingent of second-rate ministers greet them, namely Secretary of State for Foreign Trade Liana De Winter, Minister of Pensions Isabel François, Minister of Mobility Ricky Michaux, and Secretary of State for Social Fraud and The North Sea Jeni Piron. They exchange simpers. Palms are slid across other palms. Broken English and nose blowing. The Belgians gesture towards a large wooden door and take their guests into the actual church. In this hijacked place of worship, baroque pillars support a yellow ceiling. White leads onto green and everything has been etched and sculpted within an inch of its life. The floor has been cleared of artefacts, that poor son of a bitch Jesus Christ notwithstanding. Tables are topped with ammunition and paper. But in the pulpit, dressed in full Bishop-prick regalia, is Her Eminence. Beneath her, her cabinet fills the floor, like they're expecting a photographer to mention a particular dairy product.

The Pinko delegates are silent. But you're always silent when you go in a church, which all in all, therefore, is a clever diplomatic tactic on Van Hoof's part. Everyone sits at a re-al-politick table with glasses of water and pads of paper, apart from Dominique Van Hoof who stays in her pulpit—Where you can get a good look at her.

"Vrienden, bezoekers, *welkom*," she preaches, "I trust your flight was safe?"

"Yea," Ezra respondes, sheepishly, "it was all right."

"Good," Her Eminence says, "now, I'm a busy woman—"

"Sie ist damit beschäftigt, Homosexuuelle zu töten!" Minister of Postal Services Pascaline Georges interrupts.

The cabinet chuckles as they study Van Hoof descending from the pulpit. "Meisjes, meisjes, *alsjeblieft*," she says, confronting the Pinko delegation, "Girls girls, *please*, now," getting right to business, "*Pinkos* – you are concerned about the next election. We, on the other hand, are concerned we might lose this war. But if we work together," smiling at the delegation, "I'm sure that both problems will fix themselves."

"You said you had damaging material on Fernanda Li,"

Langton-Bland says, "what is it, exactly?"

Van Hoof pulls a bemused look across her face. *"Fernanda Li?"*

In the meantime, Langton-Bland takes a serious dose of ecumenical silence.

"If I were in your position," Her Eminence explains, "I wouldn't worry about Fernanda Li. She's finished," her face turns red, "who you need to start worrying about is Mister Limousine." Van Hoof adjusts her robe and takes a seat at the table. "He's coming for you and your party," she goes on, "your way of life."

The Pinkos have clearly missed the memo. Ezra Withers looks around the room, asking, "Mister *Who?*"

Van Hoof leans her head back, emitting a mumblesome, *"Ohhhhhh,"* she looks at the other Pinko delegates, "you haven't heard, have you?"

Withers, Langton-Bland and Kozłowski stare into the "we've-been-fucked" abyss of self-flagellation.

Van Hoof turns to her cabinet, saying, "Ooops—!" cackling out, subsequently, the unmistakable laugh of a smoker.

◊

Select individuals suffer from *chronic anger*. Symptoms include high blood pressure, intracranial compression, irregular breathing, muscle spasms, and a decline in insulin, which results in a poor metabolism. Angry people die young—And yes, it has more to do with Glucose 6-phosphate than it does with that sense of umbrage experienced when England loses a rugby match against an obviously rubbish team. The Pinko Chief Party Whip, The Right Honourable Osman "The Turk" Küçük MP, is one of these select individuals. He's also ridiculously good-looking. If you don't find him attractive, the only recommended advice is to seek psychiatric help. This goes beyond gender. This is serious. Osman is unfathomably good-looking.

◊

Meanwhile, in Victoria Tower Gardens, El Greco is sitting on his favourite bench eating his lunch: an unpretentious, homemade, ham sandwich. He does this every day for six and a half minutes. On Abingdon Street, the Turk can see El Greco. He shuffles his medium-priced shoes through grass and dog shit, shouting, "You!"

El Greco peers up from his ham sandwich.

"Plato's gay sister!"

The Reactionary Whip sucks his teeth and decides to watch a pigeon. Shortly after this decision is made, the Turk is standing directly in front of him, complaining, "The Limousine program was our idea."

"What?"

"Don't look at the pigeon," the Turk says, "look at me."

"I don't know what you're talking about," El Greco segues, "I have one job; I do it well."

"Don't play stupid with me. All that lot, Verlinden——"

"What about Verlinden?"

"And Fiona Willems; the Belgians, you berk; she's with us, not you. She's a hard-line——forget the pigeon——she's a hard-line socialist."

"I'm perfectly aware what she is."

"You can't steal our policy, Sander."

"Well, you stole it from her, so it's fair game really."

"You have no right."

"Now that I agree with," El Greco understand, finally meeting eye-to-eye with the Turk, "but I'll tell you what I do have—"

The Thames gurgles past the regular dunking of Westminster.

"Timing," he says, "but let me get this straight: You're gonna go on FIRMtalk and admit that your party was so desperate for gay votes that it wanted its leader to have a sex-change…?"

Right now is an opportune moment to mention the Syrian lobby member and MP for South Thanet Maya Terzi who has been, largely, unexamined, precisely because she recently became the first of many full stops. We often base our characters upon others' personalities. We take things that other people do and work them into our routines. People like Maya, however, never quite manage to start themselves. They never find that external jumping-off point whereupon their own personality might begin. Maya was a porn addict hooked on the hole and the dark and the cold. Her diet consisted of rye bread and orange juice kept to the left of her desktop computer. This food was party daily to three videos that were standard viewing with reference to a breakfast/lunch/dinner porn-watching schedule:

The 46-minute *Tight Teen Rammed By A Big Black Cock*, the 23-minute *PAWG Ivana Beringer enjoys some big cock inside her*—with keen observation paid to 6:35 and 12:07—and the 3-minute, slightly more tender but not really *Drunk Sex at My Boyfriend's house.*

These were all followed by a masturbation session sat backwards on the toilet. But only recently, say, mid-June had Maya started to feel exhausted by these sessions. The masturbation sessions performed backwards on the toilet, that is.

And not physically exhausted, but mentally exhausted. She'd feel mentally exhausted by her sitting backwards on the toilet, masturbating. Combined with her life as an MP, in addition to being secretary of the House of Commons Commission, she'd become physically exhausted as well. And so she woke up physically and mentally exhausted on June 28th in her double bed, after which she stood up and touched her nose, except she couldn't feel her nose. She couldn't feel anything, actually. It was like something was missing between the touching and the feeling. Everything was numb as she walked forward. But it was like she wasn't walking forward. It was as though, in her half-woke state, she wasn't moving at all.

West Brompton, where she lived, was always loud at night, so she had earplugs in. But she forgot to take them out. And her brain decided to compensate for the silence. It took a song she knew and played it over and over again in her head. She couldn't stop it. And sometimes her brain would change the pitch, or the key in which the song was played. She didn't know where this music was coming from. Was someone playing music next door? Was she having a breakdown? Maybe she was only visiting her body. Maybe her soul had long since departed, remaining for ages at lampshade-level like the viscous smoke you get from birthday candles. That whitish colour that sticks around for just over the standard life span of smoke, allotted by whatever divine architect happens to be passing.

Maya didn't show up for work that day, or the day after that. In fact, she ceased completely in showing up for work altogether. And this, along with Maya's subsequent resignation, is on El Greco's mind when he finishes his rant.

"…You're gonna say that on live television? Really?"

The Turk punches El Greco, and his sandwich falls on the ground, unfinished. Destroyed.

The Reactionary whip, having never been punched, twitches in shock. "You," he stutters, "you killed my lunch!"

He hits the Turk back, who stumbles backwards colliding with a tree. He holds his jaw and hobbles onto the grass, beckoning El Greco to join him. Several moments later, the two Chief Whips are waving their fists at one another.

"You won't be so pretty after this," El Greco says, his nose dripping claret.

The Turk spits a red globule in his colleague's direction, saying, "All the halloumi in the world couldn't save you right now."

"Super Kebab called," El Greco says, "they want their chef back."

"Oh yea?" the Turk says, "w-what do you call a Greek with three hundred wives?"

El Greco can feel the sweat dripping down his back as the Turk says, "a shepherd."

El Greco's mitt flints across The Turk's jaw, but he doesn't budge.

"Phwe got Battersea," the Turk mumbles, "phwhat the phwuck did you get?"

The Reactionary whip adjusts his underwear, shaking his unclenched hand.

"In power," he says, after which he pulls back his right arm and flings it out into the Turk's forehead.

The Pinko's cranium darts backwards, experiencing a *coup* (a slap at the front of the skull) and a *countercoup* (a slap at the back of the skull).

It takes 3,200 Newtons to snap a brick, but the average punching force of an Olympic boxer is 3,427 Newtons. Unlike anabolic steroids, ham sandwiches are not performance-enhancing drugs.

The Turk's arms sink, nodding, as if to say, "Well done," and he falls face first into the grass. He laughs a series of muffled threats, "Greek git," meanwhile, El Greco wipes his nose, "...sheep," and tightens his tie.

The Reactionary Chief Whip staggers over to the insentient Turk, saying, "Marxism, innit?"

◊

It is 4:43 p.m. on Wednesday 3rd July 2089. *The Wall*, a Gay news outlet, does a live broadcast with trans anchor Arthur Rampersad: "...But more on thin bastards later; some breaking news for you now: footage of the Prime Minister at a Reactionary conference after-party has surfaced, and it's a bit controversial. Ava Yap in Westminster has this story."

The Wall cuts to a video taken on someone's phone: a fancy hotel room. There's a bed, palatinate-blue balloons and champagne bottles. Piers Meak is telling a joke. Ava Yap provides the requisite serious voiceover: *"This was filmed after the first Reactionary Party conference with Fernanda Li as leader. It looks like a standard evening for the Reactionaries, but then the unthinkable happens."*

The video's audio is boosted. An inebriated mumbling comes forward. "I fuckin hate trannies."

"Fernanda Li," Ava Yap continues, *"sprawled on a bed with a glass of champagne, starts rambling all too coherently."*

"I mean like," Fernanda slurs, "if you're a man-lady, where're you gonna take that dick? Up the ass, that's where. And that's not cool man. Not up the ass."

"In an unprecedented move," Ava Yap narrates, *"the Health Secretary Barnaby Pale tells her to shut up. But Li reacts violently."*

"The only thing worse than the niggers are the white people," Fernanda says, downing her champagne, "hands down.

They blew the fuck out of my …," she nudges Barnaby Pale, "listen you N.H.S. bastard; you ever heard of the Opium Wars? Let me tell you something—"

"You need to keep it down," the health secretary says, "you're drunk—"

"The English blew the fuck out of my ancestors," Fernanda continues, "yea, I'm drunk! Fuck does it have to do with you?" getting back on topic, "I may not have been there, but I'll never forget that."

"Everyone out," Barnaby Pale says.

"I didn't finish my joke," Piers Meak complains.

"It's not funny," Pale adds, "everyone out."

Ava Yap concludes her report by saying, *"The cameraperson leaves the room and moves into the hallway. We briefly see their face: a person with a moustache, wearing sunglasses. Who are they? Why are they filming? For the moment, no one can say. Ava Yap, Westminster."*

England Today News picks up the same story almost immediately. The anchor, Kasim Hamade, smirks into the camera, saying, "Now some rather damning footage of the Prime Minister at a party held after the Reactionary conference; her first as party leader," the camera angle changes, "Lesidi Govender sat down yesterday with Health Secretary Barnaby Pale, who can be seen in the video."

E.T. News cuts to an extreme close up of Barnaby Pale sweating under those awful studio lights. "No," he argues, "but it's clear that the Prime Minister says, 'trigger,' in the video."

"I'm sorry, minister," Lesidi Govender says, "but she doesn't. I don't see how you can argue—"

"N-let me finish," the health secretary continues, "I say this with complete conviction: The Prime Minister did not say the N-word. What she said, was, 'snigger'."

"But you just said that she said, 'trigger'."

Pale goes pale. "No I didn't."

After four executive meetings are held on the top floor of the C.C.B. building with lots of Irish coffee and burritos, C.C.B. News decides to cover the story. The anchor, Tulu Rahman, has an apologetic expression on his face as he looks just above the camera, saying, "While Fernanda Li clearly said, 'trigger,' instead of the other word, the events that unfolded at the Reactionary Party conference continue to confuse millions. An exclusive FIRMtalk at eight-thirty p.m. with Randy Vipond will investigate the matter further."

Half an hour later, Randy Vipond brushes his atrocious fringe to the left as the camera cranes in at a $30°$ angle into his atrocious fringe. "This," he announces, dramatically, "is FIRMtalk." His guest is the unusually relaxed and teal-suited Aaron Lakin-Smithers. He stares at Vipond's atrocious fringe, learning quickly the penalty for doing so. "Mister Lakin-Smithers," Vipond begins.

"Good to fringe—be here," Lakin-Smithers corrects himself, "good to be here."

"…"

"…"

"Have you ever seen a member of parliament pay off a police officer?" Randy Vipond asks.

"Oh yes," Aaron answers, "I was never an accomplice to it though."

"But you've seen it happen?" Vipond seeks to clarify.

"It happens all the time," Lakin-Smithers says.

"Jarod Thrussel," Vipond brings up half-heartedly, "what's he like to work with?"

"Jarod's not a civil servant so much as a corporate servant," Aaron explains, "you give him a job, and he'll do it."

Randy Vipond is rigid. "Are parliamentary jobs not like

other jobs?"

"Well, no," Aaron answers, "parliamentary jobs are more frames of minds than jobs. For lack of a better word, it's kind of a philosophical vocation."

"Yes," Vipond counters, "but, 'philosophy,' is quite broad. Freud, for example, was largely about making assertions that he couldn't back up."

"Yes, well," Lakin-Smithers says, "it was cleverness masquerading as wisdom."

"But is that what you do?"

"I think it's what most people do," Lakin-Smithers argues. "There's not much wisdom about these days."

"But given that your constituency voted you into a," Vipond sucks in some C.C.B. air, "philosophical vocation, can you, given what you've said, get away with more?"

"Yes," Lakin-Smithers says, "it's very easy to hide ideas. You just hide them behind other ideas."

In Camden, Dickeater, awaiting a cup of tea from his boyfriend-cum-L.E.S.-assistant-lecturer Doctor Jack Hearst, watches the exchanges between Randy Vipond and Aaron Lakin-Smithers with a diagnostic diligence oft-practiced by rappers when watching television. In those moments between the watching and the thinking, a song idea sprouts. Or maybe just a line, like, "I'm from Earl's Court, Jack's from Mayfair." The song becomes an architectural structure in which the rapper can walk. They, then, judge how long the song will be; a common question may be: "Given that any one of my proposed stanzas are fifty seconds long, when spoken, will be it possible to have three of those fifty-second blocks, considering what the song is about?" Questions like these are remedied by daytime television; and in Dickeater's case, his boyfriend's tea-making skills.

Three hours later at 11:44 p.m., an unmarked police car, sent by El Greco, will arrive at the Lakin-Smithers residence in Coventry. Sergeant Hasegawa and Aaron Lakin-Smithers will engage in a short conversation at the door, after which Hasegawa will get into his unmarked car and drive back to London.

Back in Camden, presently, Dickeater moves from the television set to his writing table, littered with Peppermint Fánk wrappers, whereupon he's possessed by the spirit of Belgian poet laureate Muhammad Albronda. The poet, recently killed by a mortar shell that struck his Tournai residence, subconsciously encourages Dickeater to remember one of his boss's songs: *Original Israeli*. Suddenly, words pour out of Dickeater in that blissful moment of self-exorcised creative bliss doubling as torment, doubling again as genuine happiness.

> London blocks where trannies'll
> Talk like Grace Blackstock
> And Ivor Seaby, education shit amaze me
> I'm from Earls Court, Jack's from Mayfair
> Rap legends, these tracks don't pretend to play fair
> Fuckin boys in the club, keep it secretive
> But now I fuck ten and that's considered
> Real lucrative, locked in on the sexy side of things
> Soho kings, paid for, no more, on door
> Gay guy kicks off as I'm about to grab cock
> 25-year-old and I'm gonna turn the lock
> *Whatchu doin, dem stalls ain't for screwin'*
> *Or blowin', if you wanna plant seed, do it with me!*

He slams his biro down on the table, deciding to sleep on it.

◊

Protestors begin to gather outside 10 Downing Street. They're upset because they feel they've been intimidated, like, politically. A line needs be drawn in crayon between those that are intimidated and those that do the intimidating.

Karl Marx (2023-2089), the Morecambe-born Chiptune artist and recipient of the Henry William Pickersgill Genius Grant, said, in response to the mass suicide committed in response to his album *Pandiculation* (Harari Records™, 2047), that the results of protest weren't important. What was important, rather, was the nature of the protest. The political prize of giving the middle finger to an entity or person (although it is possible for a person to represent an entity, but whatever), and, crucially, "whatever," is the great enemy of political thought. Saying, "whatever," means that anything can happen. Saying, "whatever," means that this whole cerebral construct you've created through hours of careful consideration of other ideologies is essentially hinging on one word. Well, three words, actually: "whatever," and, "et cetera". Linguistically, Lucifer never had it better. Especially for people like Filip Wronski and Santiago Paredes who take part in this protest because "whatever" happens, now, outside No. 10, they should expect riot police, people stomping heads, backs being beaten—

"Get back!"

"I said, get back!"

—a trio of lesbians tossing tampons over the gate, a man crying because his boyfriend is angry and he's never seen him this way, Harari Records™ negotiating a record deal with Dickeater, Tulu Rahman parroting C.C.B. truisms, et cetera.

Inside 10 Downing Street, Sami Toller-Wallace and Faisal Reddy type frantically on their respective laptops, crafting emotional notions that they hope will translate into policy. Sentence after sentence of well-oiled, soon-to-be-memorized polemic and/or praise (because we don't want to piss off Stonewall or Northern Ireland); a stick of dynamite wrapped in lace. Sayid Chemtob paces around with his hands in his pockets, spitting out one-liners, like, "'Usher in an age of tolerance with stateliness,' no, not that last one."

"Modesty?" Toller-Wallace suggests.

"No," Chemtob says, "stateliness as in, 'the majesty of the crown'."

"Dignity!" Faisal Reddy posits.

"Yea," Chemtob agrees, "that – put that in, 'age of tolerance with dignity'!"

Meanwhile, in New Scotland Yard, D.C.I. Gazsi Pasternak is preparing to supervise twenty riot police being delivered to Downing Street. He downs a plastic cup of water and throws it in the bin. Then he goes into the unisex toilets to take a leak in the middle urinal: an unusual decision given that another officer may walk in and choose either the urinal to the left of Pasternak, or the urinal to the right of Pasternak. Gazsi will, as a result of his urinal decision, subject himself to that strange sensation—the closest R-rated comparison being the infamous, "Duck Scene," in *The Lambing Men*, or any horror movie for that matter—of wanting to look away, but having to look, in the end, with reference to this urinal situation, at the dick. He'll just have to. Using an end stall, contrastingly, to avoid that situation is the policy of a coward.

Sergeant Hasegawa walks out of a stall and washes his hands. Pasternak turns from his center urinal, taking note of the recipient of the King's Police and Fire Services Medal, the Ezichi Rotimi Overseas Territories Police Medal re: service in Gibraltar, benefactor of the not-much-but-totally-crucial £600.00 per annum for the Relieve Hackney Children's Hunger Foundation, chairman of the Islington Chess Club, and 3-time winner of the London Marathon. "Where were you last night?" Gaszi asks, finishing.

"We got a call in from Earl's Court," Hasegawa answers, drying his hands.

Pasternak walks over to the sinks and says, "I can check you know."

"…I know," Hasegawa mumbles, "what is this?"

"What you been up to?"

The sergeant frowns. "What do you mean?"

"Just get your shit together," Pasternak says, "before I start thinking about presiding over an internal investigation. That wouldn't make any of us look good, would it?"

Hasegawa fills his trousers with his hands, saying, "Yea…" He turns away. Then he turns back, adding, "You know those mercenaries you were looking for?"

Pasternak remembers to zip up his fly, and answers, "What about them?"

"They're northern Belgians," Hasegawa says.

Pasternak replies with a long stare supported by paranoid vibrations going up and down his spine. "Okay," he finally responds, "we got names?"

"Photos," the sergeant offers, "and I feel like something's coming."

"Meaning?"

"I don't know," Hasegawa explains, "something doesn't feel right – I'll send them over anyway." He looks at his superior, having knowingly fabricated but also demonstrated that he is the King's-police-chess-playing-benefactor-cum-runner dude he claims to be; that there is, "good," in his bones. Duty. Intelligence. Hard graft. "You know what it's like, sir," the sergeant goes on, "you got a kid – you want a little extra money coming in," he nods, "just to fix things…" After saying that, he leaves Pasternak confused and irritated in the New Scotland Yard unisex toilets.

Back in 10 Downing Street: still recovering from his surgery, Mister Limousine intends to (or Sayid Chemtob, Sami Toller-Wallace and Faisal Reddy intend Mister Limousine to) address the protestors outside, as all hell has broken loose. Two hundred thousand protestors catch each other's heels as they march across Westminster Bridge. Transgender men and women, transsexuals, two-spirited shaman medicine men/women, lesbians, queers, questioning individuals, intersexual miracles of nature, gays, asexual supporters of E.T. News, allies of the movement (i.e. white people who use the word, "justice," at least twice a day), pansexuals, bisexuals, agenders, queer genders, bigenders, people who identify with other gender variants that are too complicated to go into here, pangender lovers of all genders, and a guy called Dave who came along for a bit of a laugh, slug down the A302. They move up Parliament Street past *The Cenotaph*. They pry open the black gates of Downing Street—D.C.I. Pasternak wriggles amongst his riot police like the filling of an egg custard. Batons are slammed. Helmets are bashed. Women are tripped in their high heels and men fall over. Trainers are soaked in blood and mud, and wife-beaters are sweated over. Cold laughter fills the air, overpowered by chanting: "Li! Li! Li! Out! Out! Out!"

Pasternak climbs over a Sixth Form field trip, shouting, "Call for backup!"

A four year old, brought along by his ally parents, is crushed beneath stilettos, espadrilles, pumps, chukkas, clogs, sandals, moccasins, loafers, wedge boots, oxfords, platforms and boats. The boy's body is scraped along the tarmac and over the curb. His head is, slowly, yanked off of his body, his shrieking ceasing in a strange radiophonic cut-off as his vocal chords *snap*—Elsewhere, his parents take a selfie with their, "gay friend". Westminster is ablaze with a buzzing hatred and bilious aftershocks. In Parliament Square Garden, sex-change operations are held in protest. Phalloplasties are conducted under the Winston Churchill statue.

"Li! Li! Li! Out! Out! Out!"

New penises are held up like Jesus Christ (or whatever holy sprog it is these people might endorse). Phallectomies are followed by vaginoplasties botched in shrubs. Knobs are pummeled into grass. Orchiectomies are performed in tulip beds, the testicles flung sky-high like cricket balls. Various experts on gender reassignment, such as Doctor Rohan Khatri F.R.C.S. (Edinburgh), M.R.C.O.t.h.p.h., Doctor Rudolf "Barking" Barrett B.D.S., F.D.S.R.C.S. and Doctor Renee Chen Zhou F.R.C.S. (Glasgow), F.R.C.A. bask in the summer sun smoking Ölümsüz cigarettes. Champagne bottles are popped and drinks are poured, and toasted, "To bringing democracy to Europe!"

"Li! Li! Li! Out! Out! Out!"

The grass is red.

Over on Downing Street, twenty riot police are guarding No. 10. Labias, penises and tomatoes are flung towards them.

"Li! Li! Li! Out! Out! Out!"

The door to No. 10 Downing Street opens, suddenly, and Mister Limousine appears as a bio-shock of protest stains the air until they recognize the face. The protestors note the nasal angle. The thin-lipped opening. The arch of the nape. It's Fernanda Li, except it's not, the trouser-bulge being sufficient evidence of that school of thought. He raises both his hands in the air and silence spreads through Downing Street, Parliament Street and Parliament Square Gardens, like malaria. A speech is delivered.

Debate in Westminster Palace, simultaneously, ceases. The Lords and Commons watch a master-stroke in diplomatic linguistics; a love letter to Machiavelli scribbled in Times New Roman, soaked in little European asides like, "After rain comes sunshine," and, "Everything has an end. Only the sausage has *two*."

Memorized and mesmerizing. A stick of dynamite wrapped in lace. It takes but a nanosecond for everyone to forget that stuff about, "trigger," or, "snigger," or, "the other word". Walter Lupo and Aaron Lakin-Smithers sit on their respective sides of the Commons, nodding appreciatively, almost at one another. Because, let's face it, they're the same. They're all the same. Outside, Mister Limousine finishes and all the protestors clap and go home satisfied. Except they're not. No one is—But, then again, how can you feel an emotion that doesn't exist? By way of example, let's suppose I'm told that a colleague of mine [X] fancies a female colleague [Y], and that they're messaging one another frequently with a means to secure a date, or the emotional cornucopia that is the one-night stand. The following day, I see them chatting over the printer. I sense the electricity. That weird can-do ecstasy that sparks the four-hour coffee-date. I ask X, "How Y is doing," hoping to get some delicious gossip.

But X replies, "Mate, we're not even a thing. She's just been telling me who she really fancies."

As you can imagine this blows my mind. "Who is it then?"

X looks around to make sure that no one's listening. Then he says, "Well," he tightens his tie, "it's actually Z. She's waiting for him to ask her out, but that's not gonna happen."

Now that's all great. But now this: Where did that electricity between X and Y come from? Did I make it up? Or did I simply see it because I wanted to see it? Yes. I wanted X to start something with someone because he's awfully lonely, drinks too much, etc. Let's apply this example to politics, however. If, suddenly, everyone's obsessed with race or gender and Tulu Rahman is spouting platitudes on C.C.B. News, it's because it's what all of us want to see. We want to feel like we belong to something—church, movement, some sort of crowd, the Islington Chess Club—until someone changes his or her opinion and everyone moves the other way. It's that artificial electricity we project from our eyes. It cloaks normal people in abnormal situations. Solutions, even. And for now, Mister Limousine is one of them.

Westminster is silent.

Back in Camden, Dickeater weighs up what he's just seen on TV. His boyfriend, Doctor Jack Hearst, is unimpressed. "Jesus," he says, "this can't be good." Dickeater's coupling grin twitches. It is as though, as a result of that reaction, he can no longer trust Jack. He can't trust him, like he used to, to be outwardly cool-cum-tolerant of the quote-unquote, "gay world," and all its facets. Turning now to his unfinished lyrics, he cleans under his thumb nail with a toothpick. He hears the traffic stopping. London in its entirety screeches, modestly, to a halt.

I take back what I said about Fernanda Li

I want this mad Mr. Limousine to fuck me
He took me upstairs, I held his knob
Not his hand—That was wrapped around my
Ballsack—Starin' at butter there was no
Going back…Tapped to be the best, I gotta
Make the most of my N.H.S.
Reactionary Party support, but I retort
Ain't nobody can last past the rubicon
Unscathed, London roads unpaved, man
Folk re-slaved, Parliament depraved
The man that made the Limousine burnt
In a castle, smoked a blunt in his asshole
Passed out, at his funeral called a rascal
I look on his work, got the ass, got the
Meek attitude—When he walks in the
Club, knock a bitch with the dick
But all the crackers thinkin' "My ass'll
Pop quick!" I almost fall backwards
When he look at me, I buy the tranny
A pint cuz all we want is equality

Zach

Innsbruck Latard pours himself a cup of coffee. In beyond, the cubicles are lined up, the keyboards clacking above le silence au bureau. I'm perfecting what my colleague Hisato Noguchi calls, "The Swan". Drawing the swan first didn't help. Let's suppose you have a square of white paper—Diagonalise that bitch. Then unfold it and bend the lower edges of the square into a centreline, like a kite. Next, you flip it over, double-folding both sides. Hisato peers over the divider, shaking his head. "I don't know about that one, Tara," he says, "the neck's gonna be all spindly, like an angered squid."

"Look," I say, "I appreciate you teaching me this stuff but I really can't focus when you're talking to me."

His eyes roll back to his desk. That is not an instruction.

Double-fold both sides and take the pointy bit of the paper. Fold that up—Then, take the point of that point and fold it downwards: This will be the head of your, "The Swan". Lastly, pull the neck away from the body, unfolding the entire structure. Follow these instructions to the nth degree and it should look exactly like my one – an angered squid.

There are two types of teachers: the *first* type instructs their student in such a manner that the student eventually becomes the teacher. The original teacher's function, in this case, is now null and void. The *second* type of teacher instructs their student in such a way that the teacher becomes integral to their students practicing whatever is being taught. The teacher becomes like money, or oxygen. It would appear that H. Noguchi resides in the latter category with his fucking, "The Swan".

Hours pass in pairs. Everything is one hundred and twenty

minutes long. At the reception desk, a tall man chats to Primrose "Primmy" Chakma. His beige shirt is tucked in and black trousers fall down his legs. His boots are unpolished. Zach has exactly the same pair at home. I tune my ears, hearing Primmy say, "So, you're a friend of a friend?"

"I worked with her husband in the police," the man says.

"Well, that's fine," Primmy replies, "but what do you want here?"

"I want to speak with her."

"Are you sure she's employed here?"

"Yes."

"What's her name?"

"Her name is Mullein. Tara Mullein," the man says, "Blimmen's her maiden name."

"Mmm hmm," she mumbles, typing away, "and your name is?"

"Copernicus," the man says as Chakma's eyes flick up and down his long torso, "Kapoor."

"So," she condenses, "C. Kapoor?"

"If you like," Kapoor grunts, "yes."

Primmy dials my extension as I watch her and Kapoor at the front desk. I pick up my phone: "Tara speaking."

"Hey, Tara," Primmy says on the other end, "I got a C. Kapoor here. He wants to speak to you."

"Uh…" Short-term memories become long-term memories through a process of consolidation: a semantic encoding of information that glues any meaningful associations and rehearsals together.

But I'm not you. And Copernicus Kapoor is not on the tip of my tongue. "What about?" I ask.

"He says he worked with your Zach," she says as I realize you know C. Kapoor: the squeak of his boots, the quiet sliding sound of each leg touching the other, that tiny squishy sound when he blinks. I bite my nails and ask if it's important.

"Seems like it," Primmy says.

"It is or it isn't," I explain.

"Yea," she goes on, "it's important, I guess – Mister Kapoor?"

Kapoor walks away, waving goodbye to me from across the office. At the same time, Chakma looks at me. I see her lips move and her voice comes out of my phone, saying, "He said he'll be downstairs."

"F—" stumbling over my words, "for how long?"

I look at her and she looks at me and I shrug a question and she shrugs an answer. Everyone's shrugging. I catch the lift down. My blocks of thought build themselves up, like young lawyers. The best fall, recuperate and are rebuilt on the side of time. They then atomize and disperse each other. Oblivion is always waiting. In the same way that writing is boxing for the physically unfit, the tall Mister Kapoor stands on the other end of the street. He beckons me over. There are no clouds. The sun is cold. It could fill a pinprick. You can blind yourself by staring at the sun. Too much ultraviolet light inundates the retina. This, "solar retinopathy," is rare because it's so painful.

I walk, quickly, up to Kapoor. He signals a counterpart who rolls up in a golden yellow car. The back door opens.

I'm like "no-thank you señor".

Kapoor highlights a bulge in his pocket, a gun, possibly. So I get in the car. The tall man is with me. I think he's with everybody. The door shuts, we drive and the counterpart in blue steers calmer than milk. We drive down four or five smaller streets – uninhabited streets. My host continues to stare at me. "You work there?" he asks, pulling his gun out and resting it in his lap, "I said – do you work there?"

The driver looks at me in the mirror as I reply, eventually, "What happens is I get there for nine each morning. I take a seat and start fingering myself."

The driver scoffs, but Kapoor is unamused. "Oh," he says, "really?"

"You wouldn't understand," I clarify.

"You're gonna waste my time?" he says, "I'll waste yours – pull over."

We pull up next to the back exit of a restaurant. Fire escapes. Dumpsters. There's a chef on her break, having a cigarette. The driver turns the engine off and leaves the key in the ignition. She looks out the window and Kapoor checks his watch, adding, "All it takes is one fuck-up for you to start pigeonholing people," he looks at me, "you're the pokey intelligent type, aren't you?"

I ask who he is.

"I worked with your husband in the police," he says.

"Are you still with the police?" I ask.

"No," Kapoor mutters through an unfortunate smile, "neither is she," pointing at the driver, "we're what you would call, 'private warners'."

It starts to rain. The chef throws the cigarette away and walks inside.

"We're just tying up loose ends," he continues, "make sure no one *un*ties them."

He checks his watch and looks at me. He starts off anew by saying, "I'm gonna tell you a very strange story…"

He tells me about D.E.R.P. He tells me about Harmon Chikenyyt. He tells me about Carlos Apple-Tennyson. "He lives across the street from me," I say.

Kapoor and the driver exchange grave facial expressions. The latter sneezes. "Did he say where he worked?" Kapoor asks.

I shake my head. I can't think straight. That's a lie. I'm thinking so straight it hurts.

"Don't go around asking questions," Kapoor advises, "you'll get hurt. All this—the D.E.R.P., the things going on in London—it's all connected. It's too much for one person to handle."

"What's gonna happen?" I ask, biting my nails.

"I don't know, Tara Blimmen," he says, removing his watch from his wrist, "I don't know."

Belgium/London

In 1817, a man called Henri-Gustave Delvigne joined the French Army, attaining the rank of Captain of The Royal Guard. After resigning from the army in 1830, he became an engineer. He designed a conical object, that when fired from a rifle would expand and the fit the rifling grooves. In turn, whoever was shot with the first bullet would agree that it was a game-changer.

Two hundred and fifty nine years later, it is Thursday 14th July 2089. In southern Belgium, in the municipality of Gembloux, an assault on the Château De Petit-Leez is launched by Slándáil Phoblachtach. Southerners are chopped from the knees down by a German 7.62x51mm MG-3 "general purpose" machine gun. The MG-3 isn't meant to be subtle; rather, it's meant to blow the fuck out of your target, which in this case are thirty-four Belgian kneecaps. And when you're engaging a group of British-funded insurgents, thirty-four fully functioning kneecaps is, ideally, what you want.

7.62x51mm cartridges are spat out and cartilage is displayed, blood ejaculating. The Northern Irish mercenaries advance over kneecaps and crimson feet as the MG-3 unloads into the château's windmill. Holes become cracks and chunks start to fall. Lucie Charpentier, a Southerner and mother of twin thirteen year old daughters, is decapitated by a piece of falling debris, dust covering the sunflower field opposite.

"Come on!" Lucas Heffernan says, ramming his fist into the air as fifty-three insurgents charge forward. Niall Gordon is blown up by a hand grenade, bits of him falling onto Heffernan and Mac Eoghain's shoulders. Boots kick up the fine soil, stained with blood. Dara Mcnerlin runs up to the château with a flamethrower.

"Il a un putain de lance-flammes," a Belgian rebel warns as his compatriots scatter across the gravel yard. "Courir!"

Mcnerlin pulls the trigger just as Ruben Claessens tumbles out of the château—the man screams, trying to scrub off the flames. Mac Eoghain shoots him in the head, sparing him the pain. The immolation is filmed on a phone by a Southern partisan; in an hour and a half, he'll post it online along with the others.

Later, King Nicolas of The Belgians is standing in the mirror room in the Palais Royal de Bruxelles. His phone dings. It's a video link from King George. Nicky follows the link. It's the video of a man crying because he's on fire—Nicky mutes the phone, and hides it in his pocket.

Back in London, a green Vauxhall car stops outside of Belgravia House. The driver, Victor Shakra, stares up at the building. In the passenger seat is a popular stand-up comedian called Hugh Mohadeb, known for his impressions. In the back seat are two men called Rifat Tawil and Nizar Haddad. They get out of the car and walk across the pavement. They enter the lobby and sample the complimentary coffee, after which they ride the lift to the seventh floor and step out into yet another lobby. This one is smaller and with a single door. Mister Shakra fingers the buzzer. A few moments pass. Sayid Chemtob, eventually, fizzles through the intercom. "Who is it?" he asks.

Victor nods at Hugh who leans over to the microphone and says, "It's Sander," which, it has to be said, sounds exactly like him.

"You got a cold?" Chemtob replies.

Nizar's eyes bulge, but Victor is cool as a cucumber. Hugh, his impression skills having been insulted, starts to improvise: "Yea," he goes on, "I got the flu from Nur," wincing afterwards, scarcely believing what he just said.

The intercom fizzles as a Sayid returns with, "Jesus..."

"Yea," Hugh interrupts, "uh – we need to talk," there's a long pause on the other end, "...you there?"

"Y-yea," Sayid says, "what do you want?"

"The usual," Hugh says.

"What does that mean?"

And Hugh shoots back with, "Open the door and find out?"

Rifat cracks his knuckles as Nizar stands back. Hugh refines his El Greco voice, adding, "Sayid?" But they can hear this shuffling on the other side, at which point Nizar bolts at the door and it cracks. He backs up and bolts again, the whole door splitting open.

"Oh, shit!" Sayid shouts as Nizar, Rifat and Hugh storm the flat.

They pull Sayid away from the phone, but Mister Shakra bounces over them, ordering, "Don't hurt him! Don't you fucking touch him!"

Everyone goes still and Chemtob stares at the chilly man. Those ears. That nose. Those stunning green eyes focus on Chemtob's—It's Nooda's father.

"I want to look into his eyes," Victor says as his friends hold onto the MP.

Mister Shakra leans over and sniffs Sayid, a vein pulsating on the side of his forehead, after which he points at his daughter's rapist and says, "She can do better..."

Sayid Chemtob is never to be seen again.

It is Tuesday 16th July 2089. Two hundred and forty thousand vendors, protestors and hedonists stretch from the Jewish Museum to the Royal Free Hospital. One-point-nine miles frolicked in honour of this new age of 'Tolerance With Dignity.' Constables roam like dogs. The summer rays sweat out pangender flag-twirlers known as Flaggots, an inexcusable stench secreting from spandexed groins and spasticated armpits. It fills the atmosphere and then some. The Brummagem double-decker rolls up Camden High Street, and surrounding the vehicle is a purple banner that says, "We refuse to be invisible!" Allies and their children clap like idiots. Below them, an army of bi-curious teenagers light Ölümsüz cigarettes and drink bottled Belgian Oorlog Lager. Seven quatrains of black cabs drive up the High Street, each cab supporting a single word and forming, together:

"Our pride is unlimited."
"Our pride is unlimited."
"Our pride is unlimited."
"Our pride is unlimited."
"Our pride is unlimited."
"Our pride is unlimited."

Eggs are beaten as salt is stirred into a mixture of flour, yeast, butter and milk. The smell of it spreads like Ebola. "Mister Limousine doughnuts," the vendor shouts, "get your Mister Limousine doughnuts!" Clouds of powdered sugar disperse from vendors' tents. Various brigades of fat tourists straddle the streets. They carry their doughnuts, spotting cocks and fannies. "Don't like your doughnut hole?" the vendor announces, "no problem! Fill it up! Get your Mister Limousine doughnuts today!"

A gaggle of Rabbis march up Chalk Farm Road with a banner that reads:

Lesbian and Gay Immigration Corporation:
Supporting LGBTQ+ Asylum Seekers and Refugees

"How many Zionists does it take to change a light bulb?" Piers Meak says to Mister Limousine, "well," answering his own question, "one to stay at home and convince the others to do it, a second to donate the bulb, a third to screw it in and a fourth to proclaim that the entire Jewish people stands behind their actions."

"Heh!" Mister Limousine laughs, "that's a good one, Piers!"

Meak looks ahead, mumbling, "Yikes…"

Meanwhile, Pasternak and Constable Nowicki sit in a police car on Harmood Street. The D.C.I. adjusts his yarmulke in the rear-view mirror, studying the police officers stalking the alleyway behind. Nowicki clears his throat, asking, "What's that stuff with Hasegawa?"

Pasternak yanks an Ölümsüz from behind his ear, replying, "Circumstances," lighting the cigarette, "why do you think you're with me?"

"…You trust me?"

"If I could have eight million people answering their own questions like you just did," Pasternak adds, "I'd be out of a job," billowing smoke from his nostrils, "do me a favour…"

On Chalk Farm Road another battalion of Flaggots joins the Rabbis: the First Flaggot's Devon Regiment, which, as far as regiments go, is kind of a non-threat. Their actions are supported by legions of hype-men with balloons that spell out,

"Love Wins!" in Nadeshiko-pink lettering.

"Gay curry," another vendor shouts, "get your gay curry!"

For the record, there's nothing even remotely homosexual about The Gay Rogan Josh—But that line of lesbians around the block isn't for the service.

"You like curry?" the vendor continues, basking in his glory, "this is gay curry, so, better than other curries!" A lesbian has an identity crisis.

Elsewhere, Mister Limousine traverses crowds of advocates and allies with the Culture Secretary Piers Meak. Limousine is subjected to a parade of grins, little flags, handshakes, party-poppers, eyeliner and offensive haircuts and chanting. A transgender woman screams, "Take it off!" as Meak tells another Jewish joke: "So the census taker comes to the Greenberg house and he says, 'Does Louis Greenberg live here?' Greenberg says, 'No,' so the census taker says, 'Well, what's your name, then, sir?' And Greenberg says, 'Louis Greenberg.' So the census taker's confused, and he's like, 'But you said Louis Greenberg didn't live here.' And Greenberg laughs and points at his house and says, 'You call *this* living?'"

The transgender woman screams, "Take it off!" again.

Mister Limousine, taking notice this time, points at himself, like, "Moi?"

"Yea!"

The Prime Minister looks at Piers Meak. "Hey," Meak advises, "fuck it."

Not so far away, on a raised platform, The Frog Allen Band churns out a series of tunes from their back catalogue. To the layman, they are a group of asexual musicians dressed as frogs playing freeform rock. The Frog Allen Band is watched by thousands of people playing drums in a multi-shebang collage of colour.

> The toads are coming!
> *(Guitar riff)*
> Yes! The toads are coming!
> *(Guitar riff)*
> If I touch the lilly
> I won't feel silly
> If I touch the lilly
> I won't feel silly
>
> *(Serious guitar strumming)*
>
> The toads are coming!
> *(Clarinet riff)*
> I've told you Piers
> The toads are coming!
> *(Clarinet riff)*
> If I take a leap
> The parking's cheap
> If I take a leap
> The parking's cheap

Slightly adjacent to The Frog Allen Band and their amphibian followers is a shaggy flock of students and academics. "If you're going to argue," Professor Elise Eikenboom begins, "as Joram Falack does, that Mister Limousine is totally committed to what he's doing, ergo is a complete individual, then by logical necessity you require a camp that, crucially, is not that. By that I mean a camp that denounces Mister Limousine as a charlatan, a liar, a hypocrite, a sort of political creation. Reactionary policy made flesh—"

"Here's a question," a University of Westminster student replies, "was Mister Limousine's sex change outlined in the Reactionary Party manifesto?"

"No," Eikenboom and her followers reply in unison.

"We can reach the conclusion, then," the student continues, "that Mister Limousine is a kind of supra-political occurrence, therefore—"

"I disagree," an L.E.S. student interjects, "you can't reduce a human being to an occurrence—"

"Therefore," the Westminster student finishes, "it's safe to say that the decision was made by Li herself and that the proposed polemic camp is redundant."

"Are you reducing a human being to an occurrence?" the L.E.S. student asks again.

"Napoléon était une occurrence," an Imperial College student posits, "Hitler et Staline étaient les deux occurences parce qu'ils ont fait d'autres, 'happenings,' se produire."

The L.E.S. student, being fluent in French, responds: "But happenings begin with people. People are not happenings in and of themselves. They don't leave some baby-making factory with a sticker on their forehead explaining what it is they'll do. If that were the case, we could have avoided Stalin altogether. He would've been confined to the 'chaise vilaine', the 'naughty chair', immediately."

"I don't not believe it is right to compare Mister Limousine to Stalin," Professor Eikenboom concludes, "first of all, Stalin had thoughts, whereas…" As she says this, a dart of excitement fills a crowd parallel to her posse. They all look to see what the matter is. Mister Limousine, bar a stolen top hat, is standing there stark naked and parting the crowds with his massive penis. Eikenboom sucks her teeth, saying, "I rest my case…"

◊

Last night, El Greco contacted Miss 89's Northern Belgian mercenaries via Sergeant Marcus Hasegawa. The mercenaries provided three important pieces of information. Firstly, they explained that they have a private backer based in southern Belgium. The backer is neither Domenqiue Van Hoof, nor any other member of the Provisional Government of the Democratic Republic of Southern Belgium; Secondly, they explained that their original mission was to carry out a series of attacks on L.G.B.T.Q.+ areas in London. This was meant to shatter any ties between Northern Belgium and the United Kingdom; Lastly, they explained that they were working on subcontract, and were only accepting direct payment to an I.T.C.B. bank account in the name of Norvin Tubaniña. El Greco subsequently offered the mercenaries double what their backer was offering. Miss 89 and her team agreed, and voted forward the following plan: Instead of an attack on the Pride Festival, the mercenaries would create a disturbance. Sergeant Marcus Hasegawa would then apprehend the mercenaries and put them on the first plane back to Belgium. Naturally, the public wouldn't know about the mercenaries leaving the country, and would celebrate instead the government for foiling the terrorists, i.e. another victory for the age of 'Tolerance With Dignity'

In turn, a private bank account was opened in the name of Carlos Apple-Tennyson with account descriptions pertaining to "mirror manufacture". The requisite €2,500,000 was deposited at 1:31 a.m., and transferred to the Norvin Tubaniña bank account. But then something that was not meant to happen, happened—An hour after the money was transferred, Miss 89 was contacted by Dominique Van Hoof. Weary after one and

a half months of civil war—an amateur, clearly—she made
three crucial points: Firstly, that the implementation of foreign currency controls had resulted in the rapid conversion of
Southern Belgian Coppers [♀] to US Dollars [$] by citizens.
Inflation had, as a result, skyrocketed by 995.8%; secondly,
that because supplies had been exhausted a reliance on imports had arisen. Southern Belgium's G.D.P. was now a mea-
gre ♀263,000,000,000 (roughly €24,000,000,000); lastly, that
Van Hoof and her cabinet had decided that a, "final stand,"
should be taken. The British Prime Minister, the architect of
their woes, had to be killed. To this the mercenaries agreed to
ignore El Greco's orders and to carry out the assassination of
Mister Limousine for Van Hoof.

◊

Pasternak stares again into his rear-view mirror at the
police officers pooling in the alleyway, resting their arms on
MP5SFA3 semi-automatic carbines. They all, occasionally, ad-
just their hats. Bulletproof vests are tightened. Feet planted on
cobbles. To Pasternak they look relaxed – too relaxed. Pasternak looks back at Nowicki who scratches his neck. There's a
call on the radio from the station, or The Factory. Gaszi picks
up the call, answering, "Pasternak-actual, over."

"Received your last transmission loud and clear," The Factory replies, "four female IC1s," police code for White People,
"have been identified as Northern Belgian Mercenaries. Moving north west up Chalk Farm Road."

Pasternak looks at the opening of Harmood Street as a
few Flaggots skip by. "Do not engage," The Factory goes on,
"Repeat. Do not engage, over."

"Roger, Pasternak-actual," Paternak says, "clarify position

of four female IC1s please, over."

"Roger," The Factory answers, "position is passing Hawley Street on Chalk Farm Road. Do not engage, over."

Pasternak turns to Nowicki and says, "That's one street over from us—Roger," he says, ending the call, "wilco, out."

"So…" Nowicki exerting a rookie kind of nervousness, "we're not gonna engage?"

"Yea," Pasternak replies, undoing his seatbelt, "and I'm actually a woman."

The inspector jumps out of his car, greeting the idle constables behind the car. "Hey," trying to get their attention, "excuse me…"

The officers perform an aggregate turning towards Pasternak.

"Okay," Gaszi begins, "four IC1s are a street over from us. That's them, so we're gonna engage."

They all stare at him blankly. Constable Dwayne Church steps forward, saying, "We've been told not to engage."

"I know," Pasternak interrupts, "but I'm telling you to engage."

"I don't think that's—"

"Don't talk back to me, constable," the inspector snaps back.

"It's not the Reactionary way, sir," Church returns.

Pasternak can't believe what he's hearing. "We should do," the constable says, "as the factory tells us."

Pasternak can hear the sounds of guns clicking, fingers moving closer to triggers. The inspector smiles, lightly, returning to the interior of his car. Doing up his seatbelt, he keys the ignition. Nowicki looks in his mirror, asking, "What are they doing?"

Pasternak hands his yarmulke to Nowicki, saying, "It's

gone to fuck," after which he shifts into reverse and jams his foot on the accelerator. Bodies move out of the way.

"Oh shit!" several officers say as their guns go off.

The car is shifted into fourth gear and drives out onto the road.

"Hey, man," Flaggots are sprinting out of the way, "what the hell?"

The car stalls. Pasternak and Nowicki climb out and point their Glock 17s at the ground. They decide to run south tripping over tampons, penknives, dildos, forks, fleshlights, inflatable bananas, anal beads, vuvuzelas, vibrators and issues of Cock-A-Doodle magazine.

Time slows.

Pasternak slides his yarmulke back on as he watches Miss 89 ordering a Gay Curry—She looks at Pasternak, after which her three accomplices join her, all staring dimly at Gaszi. Miss 89, suddenly, flips a Franchi LF-57 from her trench coat and unloads in the general direction of Pasternak and Nowicki. They duck and the bullets meant for them punch through a pair of intersexual men, a lesbian wearing a grey tunic and a pangender arsonist called Tim wearing a parrot-costume. Feathers fly everywhere and pricks of blood mark the street. Hundreds of celebrators scatter like ants, screaming. The Hasegawa delegation limps out of Harmood Street, firing at random, it seems. Two of Miss 89's colleagues flip out their Franchae, picking off the men. The injured policemen's bodies jerk like puppets and their bodies start to fill Chalk Farm Road. But then, Constable Church, suffering also from chronic anger, runs at the Gay Curry stall, using his carbine as a flashlight. One mercenary's breast is blown clean off and she falls backwards onto the ground. Another mercenary's cheek is split open and she collapses into a pile of pre-prepared poppadoms.

Miss 89 and the last remaining accomplice sprint south: the latter takes a right towards Gilbey's Yard followed by Nowicki. Miss 89 takes a left up Hartland Road followed by Pasternak.

The mercenary trailed by Nowicki hotfoots it down a backstreet. She turns and fires back. Then she climbs a fence and jumps onto the railway track. Lunging over the rails, she fires back again and again. Then she climbs another fence and falls into the Morrison's car park. She runs across the tarmac, sprinting, evading trolleys. She twirls around to fire back but a bullet rips through her left shoulder. She yelps, stumbling around. She thinks about her name. Anaïs Ryskamp. Nowicki aims, thinking about his twelve year old cousin—He shoots Ryskamp in the chest and her body sucks back and thuds on the tarmac. She's dead.

Meanwhile, Miss 89 is running like an animal, blasting the occasional bystander and darting around corners as gaily aromatic as candle shops. Pasternak tries to keep up, but the summer sun is boiling him alive. Windows slam shut as he trips on a Pride flag and she gets away—*Where is she going?* Mister Limousine's giving a speech in an hour. She's probably going there. She might go down Farrier Street to Kentish Town Road. *No*, Pasternak thinks, *she wouldn't do that. She'd cut onto Camden Street.* "Shit," he grunts, standing up and adjusting his underwear. He radios his constable, asking, "Nowicki, you all right?" There's a pause. He doesn't register the residents staring at him, although, he has realized that he is sporting an erection. "Nowicki?"

"Yea," Nowicki answers on the other end, "are you?"

"I lost her," Pasternak replies, smiling, "you lost yours?"

"No – I got her."

"She go for you?"

"You could say that, yea."

"Meet me on Buck Street off High Street," Pasternak says, "you copy?"

"Wilco," the constable finishes, "over and out."

Two days earlier

El Greco is pacing up and down his office in No. 12 Downing Street. Faith Midgley is flicking through a pile of documents. Nur Coombs, having recovered from her date with El Greco, is calling someone on her phone. Erin Jernigan is scrolling through the Reactionary party database. And Baron Quentin of Berkeley alias Quentin Squibb is scratching his crotch, like, a lot. In front of them all, projected onto the wall, is footage from the Reactionary party conference, frozen on the image of a man with a moustache. El Greco turns to Sami Toller-Wallace and Faisal Reddy, saying, "So you say he was at L.E.S. when Tuckey gave his address?"

"I remember a guy with a moustache," Sami says.

"I want you to look at the wall," Sander orders, "is that him; yes or no?"

Faisal comes to the rescue, saying, "It's him—"

"Shut up," El Greco says, "is that him?"

"That's him," Sami answers.

"Thank God we cleared that up," Sander exclaims, "Erin…"

Jernigan continues scrolling through the database on her tablet.

"Erin!" Sander shouts as she jumps awake and looks at the Chief Whip, "possible candidates? Any of them?"

"I got Hasegawa on the line," Nur interjects, "he might have a lead."

"One at a time," El Greco says, "Erin – candidates?"

"None so far," Erin replies, "he might've—"

"He had a pass," El Greco interrupts, "I saw it. Check the guest-list for the conference."

"Hasegawa's got a match," Nur interrupts, again.

"Jesus," Quentin mutters.

"Who is it?" El Greco asks, "what's the name?"

Nur squints herself through a substantial pause, sucking her teeth. "Anyone got another phone?" she announces to a now-reverential silence permeating the room. Sander's head is, literally, about to burst. "What's wrong?"

"I ran out of money on my phone," Nur explains.

Everyone feels their pockets. Pens fall on the floor. Business cards are tossed away. Watches jingle. Faisal Reddy reaches his phone out to Nur. She dials Hasegawa.

Elsewhere, opposite Club 1001, Sergeant Hasegawa's unmarked police car is parked on the curb. Appleby and Ingram are sitting in the back, the former picking his nose. "Would you shag a bird who used to be a bloke?"

Ingram thinks for a moment, then saying, "I don't know mate. Maybe if I was pissed."

Hasegawa looks at them in his rear-view mirror, shaking his head.

Then Appleby shakes *his* head, advising, "You need to think about that, mate."

"Think about what?" Ingram replies.

"Your lifestyle," Appleby says. Ingram is unconvinced. "What's wrong with getting pissed and shagging?"

"No way to live, mate. If you love someone, you don't need no fuckin lager."

Ingram shakes his head. "Do I love this bird who used to be a bloke I'm meant to be shagging?"

"You might mate," Appleby says, "you don't know."

"You didn't make that clear in your hypothesis," Ingram explains as Appleby starts singing, in a mock-Indian accent,

"Take me back to-San—Fran—cisco…"

The phone rings and Hasegawa answers it. "You back?" addressing Nur, "what happened? Jesus. All right, yea – the name is Carlos Apple-Tennyson. You got that? Yea, real name. Arrested for drunk and disorderly behaviour three nights ago. Got off with a Belgian woman—"

Appleby and Ingram high-five in the back, saying, "Da pussay!"

"Shut up!" Hasegawa cuts in, "the Belgian woman's under investigation for terrorism – where is – he or she? Where is *he*? Well, we can't find him. He might be dead for all we know— my advice – my advice, entertain the possibility that she was the one who leaked the footage, which means she pinched his phone, which means he's – yea – *she's* a mercenary. Not the only one either. Someone's paying her. But this is getting into MI6 territory. I don't think there's any domestic funding in this. This is big…" Hasegawa pinches the bridge of his nose, answering, "Yea – bigger than *England Today*…"

After that phone call, El Greco's office became a third-cousin-Mark-Christmas-lunch situation, that is to say, when after several hours of awkward Yuletide discourse, your third cousin Mark finally has something to say, what Mark mutters is so meaningless that it goes unregistered by everyone around the table. And this is, by way of example, what happens when Nur Coombs says, "Carlos Apple-Tennyson," in front of her whipping colleagues.

Erin stops scrolling and looks at Faith. Faith looks at Quentin who is eating his way through a chocolate orange. Quentin looks at El Greco, who starts to sweat. El Greco looks at Nur who doesn't really want to be there. And Nur nods at Erin, who types the name, "Carlos Apple-Tennyson," into the Reactionary Party database—"Uh," she mumbles, apologetically, "there's *two*."

"What do you mean," Sander asks, "there's *two*?"

"There are two distinct Carlos Apple-Tennysons," Erin explains, "what do you want me to do?"

Sander erupts: "I want you to kill me some Carlos Apple-Tennysons!"

◊

Carlos Apple-Tennyson *A.* is a Reactionary party donor and the current C.E.O. of the Flonflynn Corporation, recognized as a world leader in the manufacture of auto-dimming mirrors for the automobile industry, hence the Flonflynn Automotive Products Group. The group itself sells mirrors to automobile manufacturers worldwide accounting for 91.4% of Flonflynn's sales. With an excellent earnings record, a vigorous balance sheet and a dominating market share in the automobile industry, Flonflynn is expected to enjoy substantial growth. This is why, having relocated their head offices from Michigan (U.S.A.) to Winchester (U.K.), Apple-Tennyson has become an important party donor and lobbying force. According to the database and eyewitness accounts, his hobbies include fishing and models. His last donation to the Reactionary party was £200,000.

Carlos Apple-Tennyson *B.* is also a Reactionary Party donor, in addition to being the Chairman of the Combined Risk Committee, a member of the Monetary System Jeopardy Committee and an independent, non-executive Director for I.T.C.B. Holdings plc. In 1995, I.T.C.B. announced that it had signed a one million-year lease for a 3,500,425 square feet headquarters in Belgravia, London. Coinciding with this,

I.T.C.B. decreed that all subsidiaries would be unified under the name I.T.C.B. Holdings plc. These subsidiaries included the Colonial Bank of Rabat, Kuala Lumpur Bank Malaysia, Aquatic Holdings plc and the flagship InternationalT-Corp-Bank itself. The combined forces of the I.T.C.B. empire have been regulated since 2076 by Carlos Apple-Tennyson *B.* who is a shareholder in Harari Records™. Again, according to the database and eyewitness accounts, his additional hobbies include golf, meta-elegiac economic philosophy and Dim sum. His last donation to the Reactionary Party was £1,240,000.

El Greco, by the time Erin wraps up her C.A.T. presentation, is rubbing his temples. "Yea," he mutters, coolly, "but which one's got the moustache?"

"Oh," Erin replies, "the second one."

"Carlos Apple-Tennyson B.?"

"Yea."

"Black book the first one, then."

Erin is confused. "What?"

"Black book Carlos Apple-Tennyson A.," Sander says, "we can deal with mirrors," he explains, "we can't deal with I.T.C.B."

Everyone acts like they didn't hear that.

London

There is a capitalist intersection of roads that consists of Greenland Road, Parkway, Kentish Town Road, the A503 and Camden High Street. It is here that Mister Limousine will address the multitude of festivalgoers pounding the tarmac with L.G.B.T.Q.+ brutality. Uphill from that, next to Trinity United Reformed Church, is Buck Street: home of Saskatoon Richard's Tattoo Parlour, a sex shop called Poisson, and a used pets emporium. Outside of the emporium, D.C.I. Gaszi Pasternak is a plate of glass and one Ölümsüz away from a shaky Alsatian Shepalute. It stares at him with confidence, intelligence, obedience, curiosity, courage and whatever else is in the temperament description in the window. At the end of the street, Nowicki appears with twenty-one policemen. They march towards the used pets emporium and greet Pasternak.

"What the *hell* is going on?" Sergeant Natalee Tollemache asks, removing her cap in frustration.

Pasternak explains that Hasegawa is working for the government.

"But," Tollemache begins, "that's what we——"

"Not like that," the inspector interrupts, "we don't work like he works. I want four officers on each entrance point to the square. No one gets close to the Prime Minister."

"You heard him," Tollemache says, "let's go."

Suddenly, the Hasegawa faction appears at the other end of Buck Street. Sergeant Hasegawa waves at the other group of policemen.

"There's been a serious misunderstanding," Hasegawa says.

There are now forty-four officers on Buck Street, flanked

on each side by tides of festivalgoers marching towards the intersection.

Pasternak flicks his cigarette towards Hasegawa. "Sergeant…"

"We're needed on Chalk Farm Road," Hasegawa tells them all, "there's been an—"

"Altercation?" Pasternak cuts in, "yea, that was me," raising his hands up, comically, "you got me, Marcus!"

There is an awkward hush as the inspector lowers his arms. His grin disappears as he lays out his vision for the future: "Here's the deal, folks," he addresses the Hasegawa delegation, "either I can arrest all of you, right now, and have you putting out traffic cones for the rest of your lives – or you can follow my orders. It's that simple."

The constables reposition themselves. Constable Vodenicharov, one of Tollemache's officers, pulls his Glock out. "What are you doing?" he shouts over his gun.

"Calm down, constable," Hasegawa says.

"No, look!" Constable Böttcher chimes in, "they're girdling us!" He and Constables Bonney, Sherazi, Spitznogle, Jeong-Yi and Ahmed remove their Glocks from their holsters.

"Put the guns down!" Hasegawa orders as his eyes flick from Leblanc to Woodward; then from Spurling to Pickle. "You need to calm down," he warns again.

"You calm down!" Constable Ruggles says.

"Put the guns down," Grzeskiewicz advises.

"What's going on," Zima asks.

"You deal with these, I'll flank the High Street."

"We're on the same side, we need to—"

"If they're aiming at us," Levitt says, "we're not on the same side!"

"What happens if I shoot a policeman?"

"No policemen are gonna get shot!"

"Don't push me, Tollemache!"

"Who's pushing who?"

"There's a terrorist out there, we should neut—!"

"Fuck the terrorist, this is bigger than terrorism!"

"Speak for yourself, arsehole!"

"Stop arguing, that's what they want!"

"PUT YOUR FUCKING GUNS DOWN!" Pasternak screams.

"YELLING'S NOT HELPING!" Spitznogle replies.

"Are you aiding and abetting terrorists?"

"Ask questions later, act now!"

"What's with the Sweeney shit?"

"Shut the fuck up, Chris!"

"Not helping!"

"Jesus Christ, oh shit!"

"Ah, *fuck this*—!"

"We need backup on Buck Street," Constable Vodenich-arov radios, "asap, Hasegaw—"

There's a *zipping* sound and he falls over, dead.

Constable Jeong-Yi cuts his eyes at the murdering officer of the other side. "You FUCK!" He shoots him in the leg and the bone snaps.

A firefight ensues. Due to the close proximity of the two factions given the size of the street, the officers exhaust their clips over and under people's heads and elbows, missing for the most part. Ruggles and Woodward throw their fists at Appleby, but they miss and hit Sherazi instead. Leblanc starts to throttle Dwayne Church. Ingram picks a fight with Tollemache and she beats the living shit out of him—A fistfight ensues.

"Get off me!"

Groin and boot connect. Legs trip over one another.

"Piece of—!"

Hands slide over necks and vests are ripped off and bare chests are rubbed.

"Let go of my leg!"

Dumpsters gong. Backs and knees couple and bodies slam onto one another. Pasternak, through Hasegawa's legs, sees Miss 89 gliding through the Kentish Town Road crowd. Miss 89 locks eyes with the inspector for two and a half seconds, after which she disappears behind the multi-coloured thighs, calves, dicks and pussies, shoulders, abdomens, arms, necks and chests and stupid grins directed at Mister Limousine who is holding court at the intersection. Pasternak legs it over this constabulary heap and into that latitudinarian cortège, loping downwind to destiny…

D.C.I. Gaszi Pasternak is obscured by neckline perspiration, shoulders and folded arms. There are sweaty genitals, man-breasts, hard pectorals, bee-stings, boobs, bellies, tight vaginas, loose vaginas, long and short dicks and heavy-set thighs jiggling in the daytime dark. There are fat asses, thigh gaps, hair, vacuums of hair, feet, flips-flops and penny loafers. There's a Pride flag of black, brown, red, orange, yellow, green, blue and purple stretched over peoples' heads. Miss 89 shimmies through the crowd and sunlight catches her eyes and glistens. Footpaths are purpled. Agender adolescents blue friends. Time is yellowed. Men are greening women. Women are reddening men.

Pasternak pulls out his Glock 17 in the multi-coloured shadows. He sees Miss 89 but he can't get to her—He squeezes past three bigender academics, Filip Wronski and Santiago Paredes and Dave who came along with the other two for a bit of a laugh. Miss 89 butts and jolts in Technicolor hues of yesterday's faggotry, smelling her way towards Mister Limousine: Eau de Toilette, Obsession, En Passant, Organza, Cool Water and the heavy scent of willy.

"In these changing times," Mister Limousine is saying in his speech, "we march forward, willingly into the dark, our heads held high with Pride, tolerance and dignity—"

On Chalk Farm Road, a breast-less mercenary struggles down the pavement, stumbling onto Camden High Street and holding her melting chest. As she listens to the Prime Minister's speech, she remembers that she has a job to do – to *finish*.

"The war in Belgium will end soon," Limousine states as the audience applauds, "those who are in the wrong will have wronged themselves to starvation, and those who are in the right will have won because it is simply in their nature to do so—"

Pasternak battles through five queer golfers, a lesbian and her wife and a gay man wearing a Viking helmet – the inspector's yarmulke is slapped off by a tall antisemetic man-child called Igor. Miss 89 turns briefly, glimpsing the soggy inspector squeezing past a pangender bridge club marching with matching pinstripe suits. Meanwhile, more mastectomies, phalloplasties and vaginoplasties are performed on the street. Newborn clits and dicks are tickled. Faces redden. Onlookers are chanting blue. Entrails in the gutter begin to green. Doctors with purple faces are dancing in an almost-yellow daylight. Mister Limousine, gesturing with his top hat, asks the crowd, "How can a man profess to be a man when he came first from woman? All citizens are all genders because all genders are all citizens. We are, all of us, innate double-bluffs—"

The dying mercenary takes the detonation phone from her right pocket as everything begins to spin around her.

"But two double bluffs make a truth, and oh," Mister Limousine says, "I see so much *truth* today! And Belgium, soon, will as well."

Miss 89 yanks a semi-automatic Berretta Nano from her bra, pointing it over a fat man's shoulder. Pasternak points his Glock over a thin woman's shoulder and he pulls the trigger and the back of Miss 89's head flies off. Mister Limousine pauses. "Was that a gun?" he asks.

The last mercenary dials the number, whispering to herself, *"Sommerzeit…"*

Tricalcium silicate ($3CaO \cdot SiO_2$), dicalcium silicate ($2CaO \cdot SiO_2$), tricalcium aluminate ($3CaO \cdot Al_2O_3$) and a tetra-calcium aluminoferrite ($4CaO \cdot Al_2O_3Fe_2O_3$) together with lime, alkalies and magnesia embed themselves in peoples' faces. Blood is a tissue and a fluid. Its composition is regulated by circulation through the lungs, kidneys and gastrointestinal tracts, all of which lay strewn about Camden in masses of piles of organ-coloured coagulations. Dirt. Cement. Blood desecrates, perverts, delineates, sketches over, paints and violates the Camden intersection. Miki's Muesli Factory has been gored. The Hummus Warehouse has been levelled. Coffee-Cum-Arcadia has been shattered. (A Normal Sandwich Shop is relatively undamaged.) Tolstoy's Toffees has been blown to bits. Bonds between restaurants like Die Beste Scheiße (winner of the *2089 Restaurant Dérision* plus the prestigious *Pas L'étoile Michelin Award*) and Sexy Beef (a runner-up in the *2089 London restaurant guide inclusion prize*) have been disintegrated. Their foundations have been split from pavement to roof. Roof panels slope off onto blasted bodies on the ground. Dead on Greenland Road. Dead on Parkway. Dead on the A503. There is nothing left but rubble.

There seems to this recurrent acceptance of, or tolerance for politicians fucking up. We inject this idea into children via prancing through cloud nine every time something political happens on C.C.B., E.T. or The Wall. But the kids aren't stupid. Well, some of them are—but most are highly receptive of what adults do because they're so much bigger. And as any erstwhile inmate of any British correctional facility will tell you, you pay attention to things that are bigger than you—In jail, in politics, and in life...

Meanwhile, survivors are swearing in pain. Lungs are hacked up. Eyes are rubbed. Ribs are snapping mid-turn. Tears drip onto blood and dust. Floating down through particles of dead powder, you can see the shape of Mister Limousine. He and his massive penis are covered in the ash of the people. There are jabs of smoke everywhere and various cinders are propelled through the air and tiny swirlings by fingers. The truth in admiring a politician that is a nothing: Mister Limousine is deceased. But not, evidently, forgotten.

"Anna!" Two gay Fathers search for their daughter. "Anna! Where are you?"

Elsewhere, through the smoke, her little feet trip over the rubble as she runs over to Mister Limousine's body. She stops and stares in that totally unaffected youthful way. Her eyes scan the ground opposite the Prime Minister. His top hat covers a heap of bits of dead things.

Anna points at the hat, and says, "Hey!"

Her Fathers perk up their ears. They can't see anything. There's too much debris and smoke and they can hear ambulances in the distance. "Anna?"

Their daughter, "yoo-hoos," from somewhere, still pointing and saying, finally, "Look, Mister Limousine lost her hat...!"

Harmon

The goldenrod sun limericks the corners of Harmon's eyes. Squinting he steps into the hallucinatory Florin Police Station. Customer service lingers in the air. The dogger mitigates this unreality by resting his arms on the particleboard reception counter and saying, "A-*hem*." The woman behind the reception desk looks up. It's Tara. Tara Blimmen. T. Blimmen. T.B. Tuberculosis—Part of the disease and only a product of the hallucination: a facsimile. She clicks the pen in her fingers as Harmon stares at her, commenting, "Tara?"

"Can I help you?" she says.

Harmon purses his lips. "I was told you have hydrangeas." Her face goes all woody. This fiendish little operation planned out in Harmon's head is about to go bust. "Could I buy some?" he asks, politely, "like, from you?"

Blimmen emasculates a bureaucratic nod, replying, "May I ask *whom* the hydrangeas are for?"

"I, uh," the dogger drifts, "I don't remember."

"Do try," Tara interjects. Harmon does an extreme inhale, sucking in all the available information in the room to answer the question. Air-conditioned air-conditioning. A thoroughly illiberal pastiness stains the room. Pasteurized and artless as pneumonia, or tuberculosis, that is. Harmon sighs. Leaning harder on reception, he croons, "I think I'll remember when I see those hydrangeas."

Tara lends an alluring smile, cooing, "I believe you," and she walks through a door behind reception, parading through various offices. Just as she's passing through a room, a voice says, "Tara…" She stops to address the speaker.

Copernicus Kapoor is sitting on his desk. He's wearing a slim-fit suit pre-fabricated from lawn-green flannel with single-breasted buttons, notched lapels, four-buttoned sleeves and the requisite vent flapping on his sizeable gluteus maximus. "Who's out front?" he asks.

"Harmon," Tara replies, "I'm getting him hydrangeas."

Kapoor's nostrils flare. It's time to set Chikenyyt on the straight and narrow path, preferably on a planet with no oxygen, like Mars; a path not unlike a dead canal; again, like the Martian Gehon canal running northwards from the western fork of Furca, forming the western frontier of Moab.

Two can play it this game, Kapoor thinks. "Harmon's out front?"

Tara says, "Yep."

"Well," Kapoor suggests, "you better get those hydrangeas, then."

Tara continues on to the back garden. Kapoor, meanwhile, tightens his cosmic latte-coloured tie. "I don't get paid enough for this shit," he says to himself as he briefly crosses channels with Grais Lugassi…

◊

Grais Lugassi is doing a PhD in Mathematics at L.E.S. The course is driven largely by independent study and research. But Lugassi only recently recognized that she was becoming impassive with reference to anomalies in her work. During that indifference, she decided to visit her cousin, Clemmie Sadik, in Blukleim.

Lugassi arrives at the train station with a camera in her rucksack. Her body, much like Clemmie's, has been squeezed by two holy fingers: she has wide hips and her chest is slim.

She also has a toothy smile that sells comfort to passers-by and weather. "Sorry I'm late," Grais says as the train begins to depart.

"They're always late," her cousin replies, "let's go, I'm freezing."

"Whole day gonna be like this?" Grais half-complains.

"Like what?" Clemmie replies, walking down the stairs to the parking lot.

"You complaining," Grais illustrating, "and me changing my day to fit yours. What do you think this is?"

Clemmie smirks, replying, "Get in the bloody car."

Their breaths sponge the windshield. The Clemster buckles up. She tightens her metallic seaweed-coloured scarf and Grais looks at her. "How's Evan?"

"Not with him anymore," Clemmie says.

"...Sorry to hear."

"You get faced with options," Clemmie goes on, "you can only take one."

A luminous oratorio of sunlit soloists fills the car with light. It illuminates the little hairs on Clemmie's face – those invisible hairs that can only be seen with the cold light of a dead sun.

Later, they're in Clemmie's flat. They throw their coats on the couch. Clemmie drops her keys in "the stuff pot": those little containers in all the houses where everything goes: keys, paperclips, pens, pen drives, etc. Clemmie's container has the keys, yes, but also her medications: *Isometheptene*: a sympathomimetic drug that accelerates vacoconstriction in order to subdue migraines and tension headaches; *Clotam*: another name for Tolfenamic acid, a nonsteroidal anti-inflammatory agent used for migraine treatment; *Thiamylal*: a barbiturate administered intravenously for brief, but *complete* anesthesia, almost a kind of hypnotic state, and *Butalbital*: a barbiturate that is often combined with other drugs such as aspirin or Acetaminophen for the treatment of pain and headaches. Clemmie Sadik (obviously with no headache at all) goes into the kitchen to boil the kettle. "Do you want tea?"

"Yes, please," Grais replies, disappearing into the spare room, "I'm just getting something!"

The kettle comes to boil and Clemmie fills the mugs. *"God help us…"*

Grais returns with a video camera and a little tripod. She sets it up, observing the viewing screen. There's enough room for two people. Perfecto. Clemmie bangs around the kitchen, saying, "You back?" leaning into her cousin's view, "you want sugar?—is that a camera?"

Grais confirms that it is a camera.

"What are we filming?"

"Just wait," Lugassi says, "it'll make you feel better, like, when you watch yourself in a video it boosts your confidence."

"That's weird," Clemmie says.

"No sugar," Grais adds, after which Clemmie rewires her brain to complete the tea sans sugar.

She hands the relevant mug to her cousin and they sip, together, thoughtfully, as though a storm has forced them inside, allowing them the spoils of self-medication: Hot cocoa, whiskey, hugs and smiles.

"Good tea," Grais comments, awkwardly.

"Yea, I—"

"What, do you not think you're attractive?" Lugassi asks.

"That's not – for me to say," Clemmie stumbles around, "Um – no – not particularly…"

"You are."

"Uhm," she mumbles, perturbed, "…thanks?"

Meanwhile, Grais checks the camera and she takes her shirt off. "It's meant to be fun——"

"G-Grais," Clemmie enquires as though she's adopted the mantle of psychiatrist with reference to her cousin, "what the fuck are you doing?"

"I'm getting naked," Grais replies, "see, watch!" She flashes her nipple. "Bloop," she says. Then she takes her bra off. Clemmie wants to laugh, but she's not terribly sure why.

"Why?" Clemmie asks.

"It's fun!"

"No, it's not – this is *weird*."

Grais tells her cousin that she's just jealous.

Clemmie scoffs. "Of what?"

"That I'm cool with being naked," Lugassi explains, "and you're not."

This upsets her cousin, but she doesn't show it. Lugassi yanks her jeans off and she slides down her underwear. Suddenly, she's completely naked. "Come here."

Clemmie backs away, declaring, "I am not getting naked, Grais."

Grais wears this enlightened look on her face as she clarifies that this is not about sex.

"Oh," Clemmie mumbles, "great."

"It's about loving how you look," her cousin adds, although Clemmie, still, is unconvinced—She feels as though she hasn't touched her tea in years. "Uh huh…?"

"And I'm naked and you're not," Grais goes on, "I'm not going back, you know."

By now Clemmie is shaking.

"There's no backtracking in this," Grais says.

Clemmie excretes a hacking laugh from out of her twisted gut as a look of surrender fills her face. It's the same expression men have on their faces when another man convinces them to climb something with a sign that says, "Do Not Climb".

"Fine," she asserts, pulling off her jumper, "turn the heat up in here."

"You cold?"

"I will be at this rate," Clemmie says.

On the other side of the room, Grais adjusts the thermostat.

"Hey Clem," Grais gets her cousin's attention.

"What?" And Grais clenches one butt-cheek at a time, asking, "Can you do this?"

"I'm thinking no," Clemmie comments as her bra falls off, followed by her trousers and underwear. "There," she says, turning to Grais for acceptance, "you happy?"

"Are you?" Lugassi replies.

Clemmie nods, adding, "…I'm all right," watching her cousin pressing her legs together, "what now?"

"Over here," Grais directs, motioning towards the camera set-up, "now just, sort of, lean on the table, like—"

"Like this?"

"Yea," Grais says, "like that." Grais separates her legs and lets her butt hang open naturally. "You have to show it to the camera."

They both do this for a few moments. Then her cousin seals herself back up, insisting, "That's enough," and she turns off the camera.

But it's not like Clemmie puts her clothes back on. She goes in the kitchen and finds her pack of Ölümsüzes. She pours two glasses of merlot, handing one to Grais, and sits at the dining table. Grais, meanwhile, sits in an armchair. They both smoke and drink their wine. They talk without talking. But some things must be said. "We'll watch it later," Lugassi expounds.

"Yea," Clemmie mutters, swirling her wine and counting the freckles on her arms.

She counts them again. "Evan," she says, "I should've told you…"

"Told me what?" Grais says.

"He died about – two months ago," Clemmie clarifies.

Her cousin's body is almost absorbed by the armchair as she says, "Oh…"

Clemmie Sadik nods and clears her throat. "He had a heart thing," she goes on to say, "some crappy valves or something. They were gonna do a heart transplant. Everything was set up," sipping her wine, "but then he asked who the donor was."

Grais is thunderstruck.

"Whose was it?"

"…It was an eighteen-year-old girl," her cousin explains, "she'd died in a car crash, like, a week prior. And the doctors were looking for hearts and hers came up. There was nothing wrong with it. It was just," sighing, "Evan didn't want anything to do with it, you know," scratching her breast, "actually – I think maybe what he thought he was doing was giving the family closure – but to me, he was just killing himself."

She looks at Grais, ash falling between her legs. "And he did."

◊

Harmon stood at the reception. He looks behind him. There's a man reading *The Florin Guardian*. The dogger does one of those maladroit grins worn by white people when they talk about colonialism, saying, "Anything new in Florin?"

"Get your own fucking paper," the man says.

"And a good day to you too, sir!" Harmon replies, turning back to the counter and looking over the edge. There is a gainsboro-coloured pen-pot containing two pencils, one guppie green, the other laser lemon, three mustard pens each with dark blue ink, a collection of paperclips buried under rubbers and pen-chamber lids, a male rowing calendar with twelve significantly different photos with reference to nudity and a telephone of the, "pick up and put down," variety. There is also a child's drawing – with a triangle on a stick and the young artist's signature:

He sees Tara's calves jiggling back to reception and looks up. She carries with her a mass of cyan-coloured tissue paper. She puts it on the counter and pushes it towards him. "Here you go," she says. Behind her, standing in the doorway, is Copernicus Kapoor. He has this way about him. It's hard to describe.

During the great Greenlandic Resettling (2071-2084) led by Herman Bjorn Aakulu, much of the S.B. land disputes, wherein Greenlandic peoples were prosecuted by Scottish folk, were settled by one Douglas Maccruhim. Maccruhim was a Presbyterian minister and attorney known for his fiery temper both in and out of church and court. During one heated exchange with H.B. Aakalu on Foreman's peak, around mid-August when all seemed lost for the Greenlandic refugees, Maccruhim resembled, as Aakalu would write later in his memoirs, *The Suburban Edge*, 2088: "A man who resembled, as my Father would've said, 'a wanker'." That's it: Kapoor resembles a wanker.

Harmon points at the tissue paper, saying, "Flowers?" suggestively. Tara nods. The dogger rips apart the elaborate package and finds a Colt AR-15 rifle. "Uh," staring at it, "thank you – they're – they're beautiful." Kapoor tells him to pick it up. "What?" Harmon says.

"You're not partial," Kapoor adds, "to handling flowers, are you Harmon?"

"No," the dogger replies, smugly, "I'm not." He picks the rifle up and pretends to stifle one of those gratitudinal giggles. "My God," he says, "it's like Christmas."

"I'm glad you like them," Tara chimes in.

"You know, Copernicus," Harmon begins, his head tilted, theatrically, "I can call you Copernicus?"

"Get to the point, jackass."

"I'm what you'd call an amateur botanist," Harmon continues, sliding his finger around the trigger and turning his attention to Tara, "you wouldn't have an AMT Hardballer would you? I love the feel of them. The grills by the safety notch and the stock, well – it's perfect." He emits a polite laugh. "Intelligent design, if I ever saw it."

"If you want some of those," Blimmen begins, "you'll have

to go to Truff—"

"Why don't you take the rest of the day off, Tara?" the sergeant interrupts, "get all that bad energy out of you."

Harmon turns to the man reading the newspaper shoots him twice: Newspaper flies everywhere, soaked in blood from Agent Eli Reggol's chest. He dies on the tacky polymer floor. Harmon points the rifle at Kapoor, shouting, "How many agents you got in here?"

"That's classified!" his superior exclaims. "You know that!"

"Not good enough!" Harmon replies, blasting a hole through Tara's sternum—She flies back onto the printer. "I'll go through this whole building!" Harmon screams.

Kapoor backs away from him, saying, "What the hell's wrong with you?"

The printer is filled with bullets, falling apart with bits pinging through the air. Kapoor asks, "What did the printer do you?"

"I've been going around in circles," Harmon says.

"You've been going down a straight line," Kapoor replies, "you're just too doped up to realize it!"

"That argument," the dogger responds, "isn't valid in here!"

"All right," Kapoor says, "then you're just too stupid to realize it!"

"Move," Harmon barks at him.

"As your commanding officer," the sergeant says, "I'm ordering you to—" Harmon cracks his rifle butt in Kapoor's nose. "Ow! Fuck!"

The dogger is a man of his word: He marches through the building shooting anything that moves. Weather patterns of walnut timber fill the offices as Harmon blows everything apart. Elsewhere, Kapoor grips his bleeding nose and sounds the fire alarm. The rictus scream fills the hallucination. Sprinklers are triggered. Everything gets wet. Harmon enters the mess hall-cum-swimming pool where he sees Fenway's informant, Grais Lugassi, eating pudding on a table on the far side of the room. Inelegantly hopping out from under the table, she sprints for the exit. Harmon fires and the bullets rip across the walls—they catch her shadow and, *zip*, she's hit—and, *zip*, she's hit, again. Sporting a dichotomy of fatal slits in her back, she falls through the swinging doors leading out of the mess hall and lands with a *splat* on the wet polymer floor. She wanted it just this way. She rolls herself over for the last time, the sprinklers dampening her face. The whites of her eyes fill each socket and, *zap*, back she goes to the real world – if there is one; a land of occupational hazard where someone is pushing her to the edge.

◊

In reality, it is a quiet afternoon in Florin. With each twenty-storey building, I.T.C.B., Lubban Inc., C.B.T.G. and COAnàb, the concrete glistens deadly in the chilly sun. A pixie-powder-coloured, Malaysian-manufactured Honda Civic Type Z GT 2086 with tinted, 70% light transmission, windows, undercar neon lights of the mystic maroon variety and Solar Blue 4x4 suburban tyres with aquaplaning protection drives up an unbusy street.

Grais Lugassi falls past the double-glazed windows of an unfinished building.

The car's dashboard is filled with *Benzocaine*: a surface anaesthetic that prevents the transmission of nerve-fibre and nerve-ending impulses; *Lidocaine*: a local anaesthetic and cardiac depressant used as an antiarrhythmia agent, and *Menthol*: a waxy, crystalline substance that can be made synthetically or obtained from peppermint or other mint oils with local anaesthetic and counterirritant qualities.

Paedophile-cum-drug dealer Harmon Chikenyyt is looking for a prostitute of his called Grais Lugassi – one of his girls. He thinks she might be an informant, a snake in the grass. Presently, Chikenyyt sees a police car further up the road. *"Shit,"* he mutters to no one, sucking his teeth—Lugassi's body falls on his roof and the car collapses as though it's made of tin foil. Harmon's head strikes the wheel and the car trundles onto a snow bank. In the police car, simultaneously, Constable Erin Dąbrowski drops her coffee, and sputters, *"Fuck…"* She flips on her siren.

◊

Harmon squeaks over to where Grais Lugassi was sitting, studying the unfinished pudding. Next to the pudding is a Pacific blue-coloured napkin. On top of the Pacific blue napkin is a pack of Ölümsüz cigarettes, surreptitiously placed by Doctor Fenway Ilyich F.M.E. Harmon has been going backwards this whole time. He needs to go to the beginning—He needs to go to Truffle Hunters. Kapoor, suddenly, finds himself in a raid tank. "What happened?" he says, turning to his left and facing none other than Harmon.

"What do you mean what happened?" the dogger asks.

"Yolanda's been teaching you tricks?" Kapoor asks as Harmon points outside, responding: "We're here."

Outside is a huge diner with pink neon sign that says, "Truffle Hunters". It starts to rain and thuds fill the roof.

Kapoor's profile smoudlers in the pink diner-light as Harmon points at the lowbrow, apparently busy, restaurant. "What's in there?" he asks.

"The future," Kapoor replies, "…they're gonna kill me – I'm out of date. Even you know that."

Harmon looks at him, asking, "Who wants to kill you?"

The good sergeant blinks in the pink light. "I thought I could," he says, folding his arms, "manage it – the dogger program – but all those cuts."

"Can you tell me something?"

"Yea," Kapoor sighs, "you'll figure it out anyway."

"Where's my body?"

Kapoor says, "You're somewhere—"

"WHERE AM I?" Harmon demands to know. Above them, the rain's petite feet are skipping across the roof.

Kapoor's eyes wiggle with intensity. "You're in London," he says, "Half Moon Lane," breathing, "it's near a kebab shop."

"You're lying," Harmon says.

"I'm not lying."

"You can't lie in here," the dogger threatens him, "you know that." But as he's saying this, Kapoor pulls out his Hardballer, saying, "Fuck this…"

"No—!"

The sergeant pulls the trigger and his parietal lobe slaps the head of the chair.

Then his body falls forward, blood pouring out of his mouth, his eyes sealed as though he fell asleep on a windy August afternoon with a semi-present acoustic cover of *Schnipple My Dipple* by L.D.R. reverberating over the wilting cress salad.

◊

Near Harmon Chikenyyt's depressed car, Detective Inspector Ropo Adeyemi steps out of a police rover accompanied by three other officers: Constables Peter Van Den Berg, Kamar Ghazali and Giulia Fiorentino. Highly pretentious police tape sections off Maccruhim Street. Constable Erin Dąbrowski and her officers, Constable Olaf Wiśniewski and Rainer Conti, patrol the area. Adeyemi scratches his crown of thinning black hair. He flips the collars up on his Guyabano trench coat, watching his breath float towards Harmon Chikenyyt's car—Lugassi's body is still nestled on top. Adeyemi turns, an arrogant modesty displayed, towards Ghazali, asking, "How many onlookers over there?"

"Six," Ghazali replies, studying the distance, "seven, maybe."

"Yea," Adeyemi adds, "tell them to fuck off." Ghazali carries out the order.

"Dąbrowski," the detective demands, "get over here."

Erin walks over, rubbing her hands to keep warm. "Sir?"

"What have we got here?" he asks, "homicide?"

"Don't know, sir," Dąbrowski replies. "Anyone recognize the body?" Adeyemi coughs, "she familiar?"

"We checked out her fingerprints," Dąbrowski says, "she's from Blukleim. Got a few instances of petty theft."

"Any, uh, serious convictions?"

"Fines, mostly," Dąbrowski replies.

"Has she done any time?"

"No, sir," Dąbrowski says, "she's uh," observing Lugassi's noodly broken ankles flopped over the sides as though it were the edge of a ramen bowl, "she's unemployed."

"I got that far," Adeyemi scoffs, "is she a nobody or somebody?"

"I'd say she's nobody, sir."

"Homicide then," Adeyemi concludes. He takes a deep breath and buttons up his coat. He and Erin walk towards the car. "You know we're getting shut down today?" he comments.

"They can't do that, surely?"

"Yes, they can," Adeyemi assures, "the board of governors has had enough," running his tongue along the inside of his cheek, "no one gives a damn about Florin – not with all this D.E.R.P. hooey." Dąbrowski says she doesn't know what he's talking about. They stop in front of the dead Honda Civic. The detective shuts his eyes and leans forward, opening his mouth. "There are a lot of things that are going to come out," he tries to explain, "in the open, where the blogs can get a good whiff of it."

Dąbrowski puts her hands in her jacket pockets, offering, "Do you want me to deny anything?"

Adyemi shakes his head. "I don't want you to deny anything. Just be yourself. You seem to be good at that, as things are."

Dąbrowski nods and thinks about her career prospects. Adeyemi looks at the sky as a plane flies overhead. "Bit late for us oldies though," he tacks on, "don't you think?"

Erin kneels down, running her gloved hand over the wheel. "I wouldn't say that, sir," she replies, looking up at him, "you want us to continue here, or…?"

"If you like," Adeyemi hurls back, "it all goes on the pile. The homicide pile."

Erin nods and stands up. "Who the hell was she?"

"Informant," the detective says.

"I've always said we have too many," Dąbrowski complains, "if everyone knows what's going on, what's the point?"

"You might as well burn the whole city down," Adeyemi says.

"It'd get rid of that homicide pile," Dąbrowski makes clear.

"You bet your white ass it would," Adeyemi replies as a chill runs down his spine. He rubs his hands together, breathing in. "I'm going home," he says, looking at her for the first time, "good work, constable."

◊

Harmon opens the bulkhead and walks out of the raid tank. He lurches towards Truffle Hunters with its neon sign. The rain is horizontal. The weight of a fake world sits upon Harmon's shoulders. He surveys the ground. Each footstep is less confident than the last. But he keeps going; a man within visions, within other peoples' visions. Is he early, late, on time? He opens the door and steps inside Truffle Hunters. People are sitting smoking Ölümsüz cigarettes and drinking coffee. There are bowls brimming with the soup of the day—squash & basil. Glasses hold orange soda. Plates support the lettuce and tomato removed from burgers. There is chitchat. Harmon makes his way across the Harvard crimson-coloured tiling to the counter where a waitress, shortly, saunters over. "Hey," she greets, "what can I get you?' The dogger doesn't say anything. Instead, he takes out the pack of cigarettes, pushing it towards her. In turn, she clicks her tongue and turns towards the kitchen window. There he is—Fenway Ilyich, flipping burgers.

The waitress raises her eyebrows, asking, "Friend of yours?"

The F.M.E. sniffs the air, looking at Harmon. "Nope."

"He's got your cigarettes, Fen," the waitress continues, "awful nice of him to bring 'em."

"I gotta burn the British first," Fenway says.

"You making orders up now?"

"Hey," Fenway cuts her off, "I like English muffins, okay?"

Later, Harmon and Fenway are sitting in a Kenyan copper-coloured booth. Harmon stares at his coffee. Fenway is waiting for his English muffin to cool down before he takes a bite. Harmon says that the coffee sucks.

"It's not a real diner," Ilyich replies, "what do you expect — if you don't like it, then get out—"

"Fenway—"

"It's over. We lost, Harmon," Fenway says inspecting the muffin's temperature, "we're out of time."

"What do you mean?"

"It means we're out of time," Fenway scoffs, "you think we just stay on the same case forever? We got other shit to do — not that that applies to us."

"…"

"We're getting shut down," Ilyich explains, "Egelblöm told *me* to tell *you* that you're getting transferred to Lachlan. On the coast."

"What," Harmon counters, frowning, "so we're just gonna forget about all this?"

Thunder outside and all the patrons look, briefly, out of the window. They then return to their conversations. Fenway gives Harmon a bureaucratic look, explaining, "The board of governors, in due time, will slip a confidentiality agreement towards you," sliding an imaginary piece of paper across the table, "you keep your mouth shut? You keep your job. You don't wanna do that? Take an early retirement. You don't wanna do that? Go fuck yourself."

"Those are all pretty dire choices," Harmon replies.

"We're not made of money, Harmon," Ilyich interjects, "we joined the police to pay the bills." He picks up his English muffin and chomps down on it.

Harmon says, "But—"

"It's a job."

"What do we do?"

Fenway's mouth is full of egg: "Whoat? *Naow?*"

"Yea, now."

Ilyich swallows, painfully, answering, "I don't know about you, but I'm enjoying this English muffin."

His colleague stares at him blankly.

"They'll wake us up with smelling salts," the medical examiner corrects himself, "we're safe, if that's what you're wondering…" exhaling hot air through his nostrils and asking, "Where's Kapoor?"

Harmon sips his cortado and says, "He killed himself."

Fenway bites the muffin again and chews. "Guy needsh to shtop doin' at."

"He said," the dogger interrupts, "he said that someone was trying to kill him."

The erstwhile fry cook laughs, ham and egg flying everywhere. He slams the table, guffawing and demanding, "Who the hell wants to kill Copernicus?"

"I was hoping you could tell me."

Fenway replies with a guttural snigger and puts the muffin down, adding, "He was pulling your leg."

"We pull our own," Harmon says.

"What?"

"Never mind."

"It doesn't sound like him," Ilyich assures, folding his arms and leaning over the table, "it takes a lot of energy to frighten Sergeant Kapoor," smiling, "and it takes a lot of skill."

Harmon, on the other side, thinks before he says, "What are you gonna do?"

"Me?" Fenway says, "I'll take the transfer. Easier for a force medical examiner than an officer," laughing, "can't afford to retire…"

"You married?"

"Yea, so?"

Harmon looks out the window, asking, "Kids?"

"Two girls," Fenway says, un-phased, "what about you?"

Harmon steers his head back to the table with a tactful nod, tacking on, "And you don't think you owe it to your daughters to catch a paedophile?"

"No, I do not," Ilyich replies, "you know why?"

"No, Fenway, I don—"

"Because that assumes I'm gonna let the son of a bitch come near enough in the first place."

"So, you think you're adequate protection?"

"Yea," Fenway says, "I do."

"Well I think you're wrong."

The medical examiner smacks his plate off the table and it smashes on the ground, bits of egg and muffin jetting everywhere. The restaurant goes silent. Then it returns to normal as if nothing happened.

"I," Ilyich begins, rubbing his face in frustration, "I know what I am," looking at Harmon, "and I have to live with that – no one else. That's the trick."

Harmon pushes his coffee away, saying, "What is?"

"You," Fenway explains, wiping the crumbs off the sides of his mouth, "we're looking for you."

"Who's looking for me?"

"Everyone," Ilyich goes on, "the Dogger Program. It's part of the game. Performance. You can call it undercover work but it's more like *under*-undercover work."

Chikenyyt may have totally lost the plot, but his colleague carries on with, "You become the wanted individual: think like them, trace them – by doing so you try to catch the real one," biting his upper lip, "the person you're *pretending* to be."

The dogger sits back in his seat, starting to breathe more heavily and saying, "I don't know what the *fuck* you're talking about."

Fenway bends his mouth, nodding his head from left to right. "Yea, you do" he replies, "...*Zach*..."

"...*Zach*...?"

Fenway finishes Harmon's cortado and leaves the booth. Zooming past the waitress, he mentions, "I quit..." throwing his apron over the counter. He walks outside into the rain where he begins to wave at the sky. The downpour soaks his face and shirt. It's like the biggest window in the world has shattered and glass is falling everywhere.

"Egelblöm!" he shouts at the sky, *"we've made a terrific discovery!"*

The ground is totally soaked and his nipples are visible through his shirt. The rain darkens his trouser legs. *"He finally knows who he is!"* he continues, waving at the sky.

He slips in the mud and gets back up. *"I'm ready for my transfer!"* he shouts as puddles turn into ponds and ponds into lakes. *"We're ready for you you bastards....!"*

London

It is Thursday 7th August 2089. A by-election is being held for Nooda Shakra's Christchurch constituency. Three days earlier, at No. 7 Beaconsfield Road, Nooda woke up in her bed. She stumbled down the stairs, feeling the walls with her hands. She would do this half-conscious sensory experiment every morning to make sure the day was not completely different from the one before or the one to come. The day before, she had resigned as the MP for Christchurch as a result of her father and other things. Meanwhile, the search had begun for Sayid Chemtob. The Metropolitan Police and his mother Lenore Brigham-Teel—Brigham-Teel is also the former head coach of the women's England National Rugby Union team and the I.T.C.B.-funded Clarity For Chemtob (C.F.C.) Foundation, a think-tank-cum-pressure-group dedicated to the probably deceased MP for West Derbyshire—had joined forces, injecting the occasional inflammatory statement for local media.

Back at home, Nooda agitated granules of coffee into a mug and poured boiling water over it. She stirred it, put the spoon in the sink and sat on her couch. In the middle of the couch, she was, overthinking things.

Ivar Olofsdotter, Professor of Philosophy at L.E.S., was faced with a similar predicament in 2073. He decided to dedicate his first undergraduate lecture to an exam. He held up a pen and said, "Prove this biro doesn't exist." Everyone started scribbling. Some students wrote up to twenty pages of theory.

But one student finished in ten seconds flat and delivered her paper to the professor, after which the student walked out of the lecture theatre. Olofsdotter examined her paper that said, simply, "What biro?" The professor smiled, but, arguably, there was neither a pen nor an answer. They were both wrong. The thing about Whitehall is that there is no thing, that is, whatever it is is not real. The buildings may be real, but nothing else is – it's all forgery and no different from the good professor's pen, witnessed by one pragmatic student who disagreed with its existence, thinking it libellous and wanton: a hard-earned mirror of herself, perhaps.

◊

Now, however, it is 6:25 a.m. Joram Falack gets on the Jubilee Line, travelling through Bond Street and Green Park. He gets off at Westminster and hears E.T. News blaring through the tube station: "With an unconditional surrender offered by the Democratic Republic of Southern Belgium, and impending enquiries into legalities facing the government's Belgium Bill, where exactly does the Reactionary party stand?" The Party Chairman's trench coat seems heavier today. There is an overbearingly high, "oh-shit," quotient in all of this. He struggles up the stairs to face, ultimately, the awful non-intensity of a London daybreak. The breeze clings, commuters rush by and children yell at their parents who are not listening. Joram Falack whistles into Westminster Palace. Here he is, later, sat in a red armchair in No. 12 Downing Street. Sander "El Greco" Papadimitriou and Sami Toller-Wallace are present. They are all watching C.C.B. News: "Condolences from around the world have been sent to honour the death of the Prime Minister Mister Limousine, known previously as Fernanda Li, until having a well-received sex-change last June. His assassination has been condemned by the United States as an act of terrorism, and President Mao offered the following statement: 'This is bad, like, real bad. This is as bad, if not worse, than the last assassination.'" El Greco turns the TV off and throws the clicker onto the couch, after which a bank of sighs follows from everyone except Joram. Sami sits with her head in her hands as El Greco's eyes stare into the dead television. "So what do we do?" the Chief Whip asks.

Joram clears his throat, rubbing his face, answering, "We need to call a snap election."

"Why?"

"The Opposition is having a field day," Joram says, "how can we get anything done?"

"We have a majority," El Greco says.

"I am quite aware we have a majority, Sander," Falack replies, "but we have lost three MPs, not to mention the Prime Minister. If that doesn't constitute a reason to call a snap election, then I don't know what does."

"I'll find some fuckers," El Greco replies.

"Shut your filthy mouth Sander," Joram interrupts, "just be quiet…I need to think."

"It's my office," the Chief Whip says, "if you want to think then get out."

"Please stop…" Sami interjects.

"Tread carefully," Joram says to Sander.

"Stop it," Sami shouts.

"Why are you shouting?" Joram asks, "Republican Security are returning, everything is going to be fine—"

"But there!" Sami says, "you're doing it again!"

"What am I doing?"

"You just—!"

"What, *precisely*, am I doing?"

"You don't listen!"

Joram jumps up, shouting, "What do you want me to do?"

The room goes silent.

"What would you suggest that I do?" He starts pacing the room. "You build a foundation and someone removes it. You propose a bill and someone says it's dangerous. You employ women and someone feels the need to touch them—"

"You know twelve have written to the C.C.B.," El Greco says.

Joram cuts in: "I'm not interested in *that*."

"But you knew," Sami says.

"Don't try to guilt-trip me," Falack warns, "is that what you're doing? You're smarter than that."

"So you did know!"

"I did not know!" Joram screams, "I did not!" He goes quiet for a moment, saying, eventually, "Do you know what I do? *I work*. I'm the first to leave the cocktail party. I'm the one who gets up at four a.m. I'm the one who does all the hard work because no one else will – what, you think Li? You think Tuckey made these bills? *I made these bills!* I am the Reactionary Party Chairman. It's my job. It's my life. I risked everything for this. *Everything.* My sanity. My colleagues. My friends!"

"You don't have any friends!" Sami screeches at him.

Joram Falack, suddenly, becomes middle-aged, looking at Toller-Wallace with those piercing hazel eyes of his. Then he looks at the ground, and finally turns to the window in silence.

"We should've seen this coming…" El Greco says, shaking his head.

Joram continues to look out of the window at nothing.

"Chemtob's fucked," Sander goes on, "he's so fucked…"

Joram walks out of the room—He walks into parliament,

sitting in on a debate concerning fox hunting.

None of them get what it is we're dealing with here, Joram thinks. *This is it. Parliament, Whitehall, whatever—THIS IS IT. What's not to like about something that never changes?*

◊

We are in Gallery Four of the I.T.C.B. Postmodern Museum.

"So, this teacher decides to," there's an awkward, expectant laughter from the audience, "this teacher decides to let her students go, but only if they can say which people said which famous quotes. So she's like, 'Right, who said, 'I think, therefore I am?' And little Euphoria says, 'René Descartes'. So the teacher says she can go, which pisses off little Johnny because he hates quote-attribution exercises.

"Then the teacher says, 'Right, who said, 'Whereof one cannot speak, thereof one must be silent?' And little Johnny goes to put his hand up, but little Petunia answers first and says, 'Ludwig Wittgenstein'. So the teacher's like, 'Correct, you can go Petunia, whoever named you that,'" polite laughter spreading through the audience, "and this is a small class, so little Johnny's the only one left.

"And he says, 'Christ, I wish these dumb fucking bitches would shut up.' The teacher turns around. She's shocked. She says, *'Who said that?'* And Little Johnny says, 'Sayid Chemtob'. And the teacher's like, 'Well done! You can go!'"

The sound of ice clinking in glasses punctuates the post-joke silence. Throats are cleared. There are a few sneezes. Joram Falack stands up, raising his glass of champagne. "And with that, or in that spirit," he announces, "I'd like to congratulate Piers Meak on his leadership victory. The Reactionary

Party has never been stronger. To the next—"

"Disraeli eat your heart out!" Meak says.

"Yes, thank you," Joram interrupts, "to the next Reactionary Prime Minister of the United Kingdom!"

Raucous applause with plenty of stomping and cheering fills the room. Tables are flipped and drinks are spilt. People are pulling their hair out. Piers Meak? Piers *fucking* Meak? Everyone will get drunk tonight – very drunk, indeed.

A week later, Aaron Lakin-Smithers is sitting in a select committee room. He is chairing the *Belgium Intervention Enquiry*, so-named to disassociate itself from the Bill. A few members of the Belgium Bill Committee are present, however. The Right Honourable Members of Parliament introduce themselves: Octavio Huxtable, Talia Solomon, Ibrahim Spiller and Carter Purd, in addition to five new MPs and a special advisor: "My name is Elise Eikenboom. I'm professor of political science at L.E.S."

"Thank you for your introductions," Aaron Lakin-Smithers begins, "welcome to you all this afternoon. We are first talking about the delivery of Belgium Bill priorities. Mister Thrussel, you chaired the Belgium Bill Committee did you not?"

Jarod Thrussel is sitting in the hot chair. His bum is sweating – quite a lot. "That is correct," he squeezes out.

"Would you agree," Lakin-Smithers says, "that one priority of the Belgium Bill was for it to be made into an Act – to be passed?"

"I think priorities and passage are," Thrussel pauses, "I'll focus – I'll focus on the first—"

"Could you target on the second part," Aaron replies, "because we will be dealing directly with military potential and human rights in a minute with some other questions?"

"Of course," Thrussel says, "I apologize."

"Can you apologize to a landmass," Lakin-Smithers interrupts, "Mister Thrussel?"

The former committee chairman's mouth is hanging open. He looks just above his questioner's head.

"If that were the case," Aaron continues, "I would seek in vain to find any reason why this enquiry should exist. But given that that is *not* the case, I would like to proceed accordingly with the question, and further questions I shall raise – is that *understood?*"

Thrussel swallows an imaginary boulder.

◊

Meanwhile, newly promoted Sergeant Antoni Nowicki skims constabulary tabletops on the third floor of New Scotland Yard. He walks with the type of confidence usually reserved for the best man at Prestonian weddings. Prestonian weddings are invariably held in £4-a-pint watering holes staffed by students from local universities. The best man always drinks the most, and will continually tell the bar staff to, "put it on the tab," even though he doesn't have a tab. It is the untabbed aplomb, the tabless poise, the cool-headed lack of tab therein that Sergeant Nowicki channels. Newly promoted Inspector Natalee Tollemache waves at him from her desk, lit by the early-evening overcast outside. Nowicki nods back, preparing himself to address the matter of Sergeant Marcus Hasegawa's desk—the sergeant's palm slides from lamp to nameplate, the latter thudding in the bin. 'Sgt. Marcus Hasegawa' no longer exists. The remaining colleagues work away on their respective cases. Above them all, hanging on the wall, is a portrait of the now-deceased Detective Inspector Gaszi

Pasternak, an alumnus of L.E.S. with a 2:1 in Forensic Science BSc Hons (Class of 2063).

Alav Ha-shalom.

◊

In a bar called 'Cuz I'm A Juggernaut', Sander "El Greco" Papadimitriou reaches for his wallet. Not being able to feel anything, he realizes he must've left it at home. "Shit…" He needs to pay for these plates of Thai Spiced Stone Bass with Green Papaya Salad and Red Chilli, King Crab sautéed in Bone Marrow, Truffles and Shallots and Honey and Shichimi Duck Breast. He flings a crab leg across the bar. The Chef de Salle, i.e. head waiter, looks at the Chief Whip, saying, "Why?"

"I don't know," Sander says.

"Can you," the head waiter says, "like, not?"

"I'm sorry," Sander replies, "I didn't know I couldn't do that."

The Chef de Salle looks deeper into the Greek's eyes, asking, "Don't I know you from somewhere?"

"You don't want to know me," Sander replies as a junior waiter drops a plate on the far side of the room, "I don't have my wallet; but I'll leave my pass with you so when I come back, I'll pick it up and pay the bill – all right?"

"Whatever," The Chef de Salle says, examining the pass, "aren't you – aren't you *El Greco?*"

Papadimitriou looks at him blankly, saying, sheepishly, "Don't call me that," after which he walks out of the restaurant.

Later, back in No. 12, Sander is looking for his wallet. He pulls the pillows off the couch. He looks under the microwave. He looks in the teabag tin. He looks in the fridge, the cheese drawer and the freezer. Then he goes in the bathroom. He looks in his shaving kit and finds it. Searching for the relevant credit cards, he walks into his living room. He hears something – something that should not be in his house. Dara Mcnerlin comes out from behind the dresser as Lucas Heffernan lays out a black sheet in the kitchen doorway. Aoife Mac Eoghain stands with a Glock 17 wearing a silencer. She guides Sander towards the kitchen. "Right there," she directs, "stop."

Sander shoves his tongue in his cheek, saying, "I've got money," biting his upper lip, "I came back for my wallet."

"We don't want money," Mac Eoghain explains.

Sander scoffs, saying, "That's bullsh—"

Mac Eoghain shoots him in the back of the head and blood jets out of his nose. He falls face first onto the black sheet. Mcnerlin and Heffernan produce their own pistols, also with silencers. They shoot Sander's lifeless body for several moments. Mac Eoghain punctuates these actions with a sneeze, after which she wipes her nose.

"Wrap him up," she says, "let's go."

The mercenaries' brown Volkswagen van darts across Lambeth Bridge, Albert Embankment, Harleyford Road, Brixton Road, Loughborough Road and Milkwood Road. It then drives over some trainrails onto Half Moon Lane and stops in front of a takeaway called Super Kebab. The door to the restaurant opens and a Lebanese cross-dresser called Jean-Marc "Hijira" Maalouf struts into the sunlight. He gestures at the van. "You cannot park here, my friend," Maalouf says, "unless you are mentally disabled."

After he says this, the van's back doors burst open and Lucas Heffernan jumps out. "Hey, Hijira," Heffernan says.

"De poison dwarf," Maalouf replies, "I thought I left you

where I found you."

"We got meat," Heffernan offers, "you interested?"

Hijira is suspicious. "Oh…?" he mumbles, pointing at the van, "let me see it, then—" At this moment, a young man runs out of Super Kebab. "Daddy!" he shouts as Heffernan backs away, awkwardly.

"Daddy!" the young man continues, "there's a new movie! A new movie by Pet'ka Dvorak! I'm going to see it tonight with Leonid!"

"That's great, Marty!" Maalouf says, turning to face his son, "very good, now—"

"But Daddy!"

"Now, Marty," his father explains, "your Daddy is doing business with nice little man. You go back inside. I will come inside in a minute and we will play Xbox."

"Okay," Marty agrees.

"We will play Xbox," Hijira announces, "like champions!"

"Yes!" Marty says, "yaaaayyyy!" running back into Super Kebab.

Heffernan, confused, scrunches his brow and looks at Maalouf. "Who's the idiot?" Heffernan asks.

"Fuck you," Jean-Marc mumbles, "I love him."

A few moments later, Hijira examines the body of Sander "El Greco" Papadimitriou. He looks at all the holes in him. Then he blows his nose, grunting approval. "Another one, eh?" he remarks, suggestively, as Heffernan looks at his watch, "how much you want?"

"Let's talk inside," the mercenary says.

Hijira laughs, waving the mercenary on. "Come around back my friend," Hijira narrates, walking towards the alleyway behind Super Kebab, "that is de money!"

The van subsequently parks in the alleyway and Jean-

Marc "Hijira" Maalouf purchases the Chief Whip's body for £45.00. Afterwards, the clothes are torn off and burnt. A Quattro MG32SS meat mincer dissolves the body. The flesh is churned with an added ten kilograms of salt. After this, it is racked and cooked. In a few hours, it will be ready to eat for any suspecting drunkard who wanders into Super Kebab...

The following day, it is 9:46 a.m. The blue sky outside fills the green drawing room in Buckingham Palace with natural light. George, meanwhile, sits on an encrusted sofa. Close by is a baby grand, tuned every month by Maurice Parent, Master of The Household to The Sovereign. Master of sight and sound. The King thinks about his upbringing, bearing thoughts of dreams to himself. Latinate bastard-words and bastard thoughts – what makes a person? We are made of pieces of people, bits of other things.

"Sire—?" The King jumps out of his dream and looks at Maurice Parent.

"Are you all right, sire?" Maurice asks.

George juts out his lower lip. "Seventy-six years," he notes, chewing the inside of his mouth, "I've been in and out of things."

Maurice looks at the baby grand, and then back at George, who says, "Out of things..." The King pulls a toy black cab from between the cushions and runs his fingers over the tiny hood. "What are you doing there?" George asks, smiling, slightly.

"I think," Maurice replies, putting his hands in his pockets, "the Pinkos are going to win, sire."

"Hmm? Yes," George mutters, inspecting the cab, "I like what's her name – Brooke-Valentine? Strange choice in hats, I find…" George slumps deeper into the couch. "Nicky's refusing to speak to me," he tacks on, "his own cousin. I've achieved a damn sight more than he has. But there's this…" He thinks to himself for a minute. "I never fit in," George explains, "never. I was incompatible," chuckling briefly, "and mother wanted grandchildren. I think she was very angry with me when she died." He looks out the window when, suddenly, the look on his face is thunderous. "It's," clearing his throat, "it's not fair – why did I have to wait for everyone to die before I could fit in? What type of – just so I could – I could make my own—"

"Life?" Maurice suggests.

"My stupid little life," George agrees, "yes…"

George and Maurice try not to look at each other.

"I'm too old to be going around in circles like this," George says, "I feel so ghastly. It's like I'm trying to speak a bloody foreign language. I can barely speak German," shutting his eyes and sighing, "if – two men – love each other, then surely nothing should stop their partnering."

Maurice Parent nods, replying, "I must agree with that, sire—"

"And stop bloody calling me, sire, all the time," George interrupts, "you old fool."

Maurice, modestly, smiles and puts his hand on George's shoulder.

Zach

Constable and Chief Dogger Zachary Thomas Mullein, aged thirty-two and with a slightly inward-turning right foot, nystagmus and a case of sinusitis slides off of a gurney with an intravenous needle yanking on his wrist. The four policemen wearing riot gear and guarding him catch and flop him back onto the platform. In the corner, Egelblöm, sitting in her Lucky Mark IV Travel Device, is fumbling her heliotrope key chain with added pocket watch. To the side, Sergeant Copernicus Kapoor vegetates in a foil blanket, two policemen are holding him back, watching the other gurney joggling. Doctor Fenway Ilyich F.M.E. is starting to wake up, thanks to Doctor Patrik Brücke F.M.E.'s magical Ammonium carbonate. All the officers in the room clap as the doggers return to reality. But one, on the third gurney, doesn't make it. Yolanda Polk's lifeless body pales in comparison to Zachary's and Fenway's. Various negative glares are directed at Egelblöm and Kapoor, punctuated by comments, like, "lunatic," and, "fuckin disgrace".

Governor Kaat Moptin appears in the doorway, followed by a crowd of journalists and bloggers; academically qualified but childishly untested flesh. One of them, Saanvi Nowak of the Blukleim Guardian, will start her article on the train back home. It will be an anti-government article with many words like "justice". Her editor, however, will refuse to publish the piece. Not because it isn't good, but because of the subsequent government embargo on any story concerning D.E.R.P., Doctor Norvin Tubaniña, or the Scotia Belt police force. This is because in an effort to control the media, the S.B. government, in collusion with Brooke-Valentine's Pinko government in England, will saturate the media with a manufactured terrorist threat. The first step taken towards this collective state of paranoia will be a dramatization of said terrorist threat commissioned by the C.C.B. Drama Series Department. It will be approximately ninety-three minutes long and star Oksana Fuego as *Colonel Rujim*, and Markus Tapered as *Amos Dempkin...*

Script Extract

A scene from *I Was Having a Pleasant Day Until Terrorism.* dir. Pet'ka Dvorak, 2089:

EXT. BUILDING ROOFTOP – DAYTIME.

COLONEL RUJIM COAXES A BOMB SQUAD RUNNING OUT FROM A HELICOPTER.

COLONEL RUJIM
Move, move, move!

A **TROOPER** KNEELS AND DRILLS A HOLE THROUGH THE ROOF-HATCH LOCK. RUJIM LOOKS AT ULIK.

COLONEL RUJIM
Tell Dempkin to get out of the server room
and back on communications!

A TERRORIST CALLED **RHONDA** BURSTS OUT OF AN ACCESS HATCH. RUJIM'S MEN TAKE AIM AT HER.

RHONDA
I'm not a terrorist! Don't shoot!

ULIK
Get on the ground!

RHONDA
Don't kill me!

RHONDA IS SOBBING UNCONTROLLABLY, NOT BE-
CAUSE SHE IS A WOMAN BUT BECAUSE SHE IS A
PERSON WHO IS A TERRORIST.

ULIK
Get on the ground! Get on the ground!

RHONDA
But I'm not a terrorist!

ULIK
Get on the flipping ground!

RHONDA
Oh my goodness!

THE TROOPERS FIRE AT HER. BULLETS RIP THROUGH
HER BODY. HER ENTIRE FRAME IS REDUCED TO
SHREDS OF FLESH. THE SHREDS OF FLESH ARE THEN
REDUCED TO ASHES BY A TROOPER WITH A FLAME-
THROWER. ALL THE TROOPERS PUT DOWN THEIR
WEAPONS AND CLAP. RUJIM LOOKS AT ULIK.

COLONEL RUJIM
Any response?

ULIK
No ma'am.

COLONEL RUJIM
He'll be fine. DEMPKIN always gets his person!

EXT. FIELD – MORNING.

THE S.B. FLAG IS BLOWING IN THE WIND. A LOOP OF
THE S.B. NATIONAL ANTHEM, "FUIRICH AIR FALBH
BHO DHAOINE LE CNAPAN MÒRA", OR "STAY AWAY
FROM PEOPLE WITH BIG LUMPS" PLAYS OVER THE
SHOT FOR 21 MINUTES.

Zach

Cameras are flashing and tablets waved. Questions are shouted at the erstwhile members of the Dogger Program. Egelblöm pounds her fist on her armrest, shouting, "Get these snakes out of here!" The officers squeeze them out like the attenuated final squirt from any toothpaste pocket. "Get them out!" Egelblöm repeats.

Governor Moptin brushes her shoulders. She leans down to Egelblöm, saying, "I don't know how they got past security—"

"Yes, you do," Egelblöm interrupts, "out, please – thank you!"

Mullein opens his eyes and stares across at Fenway. Then he sees Doctor Brücke standing over Yolanda Polk, taking a reading with his phone. The medical examiner shakes his head and scoots a surly expression at Egelblöm and Moptin. "We fucked up," Kapoor mutters, tightening the foil around his shoulders, "we fucked up…"

◊

Lyrids is a meteor shower that occurs every April 22nd. It tends to last for about eight hours. It has a radiant bordering Lyra and Hercules, 8° west of Vega, and can be traced back two thousand five hundred years. As he stands on the hospital roof, Zachary Mullein feels the exact same age. He sucks on an Ölümsüz cigarette as the cold air blows between his legs, the raw sienna-coloured hospital frock floating an inch above his skin. He watches the gibbous moon. Next to him, Constable

Kamar Ghazali does the same. "We'll have to go back to the station in twenty minutes or so," she says.

A line of smoke comes out of Zach's mouth when he asks, "Why?"

"Debriefing, sir."

"Debriefing?"

"Yes, sir," Ghazali affirms as Zach folds in his lips.

He stops his frock from flying away, adding, "Then what?"

The constable rests her hands on her belt, answering, "Then you're finished."

"This isn't real," Zach asks, "is it?" Ghazali cuts her eyes at the ex-dogger. "The moon," Zach goes on, pointing at it with his cigarette, "it's all wrong."

"It looks moony to me," the constable argues.

"What's your name constable?" Zach changes the subject, "I assume you're a constable?"

"Ghazali, sir."

Zach nods, dragging on his cigarette. "Have you ever," he starts again, "have you ever thought about being a boy?"

Ghazali coughs. "I beg your pardon?"

"That's a negative then," Mullein expects, "is that right?" The constable looks at him and cracks her neck. "So," Zach tries again, "your name's Ghazali?"

"Yes," she says.

"My name's Chikenyyt," Zach explains to her, "Harmon Chikenyyt."

The constable's face, upon hearing this, drops a little. An awkward silence fills the night air, after which she sniffs the air, tacking on, "You'll feel better after the debrief."

Zach throws away his cigarette, shaking his head. "Just shoot me."

"Okaaayyy," Ghazali says, "we should be going now."

The ex-dogger moves closer to her, holding his hands up. "Listen to me," he says, "I want you to shoot me in the head."

His escort pulls out her police-issue AMT Hardballer. She aims at his head, echoing, "This is what you want?"

"Yea," Zach confirms, "that's perfect."

Ghazali smiles back, saying, "Okay fine – but first we have to go to the station."

Zach, staring at the gun, asks, "Is that a Hardballer?"

"Zach," she interrupts, "we're going to the—"

He jumps off the roof.

◊

Mullein wakes up in the Florin Police Station medical bay. Another day. Another gurney. Scattered around the room are boxes of bandages. There are also drugs, like *Bupivacaine*: a small molecule and widely used anesthetizing agent used for local or regional anaesthesia or surgical analgesia, oral surgery procedures, diagnostic, therapeutic and obstetric procedures. *Prilocaine*: a local anaesthetic that is pharmacologically similar to Lidocaine and used primarily for dental infiltration anaesthesia. *Lidocaine*: a local anaesthetic and cardiac depressant whose effects are more prolonged than those of Procaine, but shorter in terms of action-duration than Bupivacaine or Prilocaine.

One of the reasons, it must be said, as to why Sergeant Kapoor's behaviour is so erratic in the quote-unquote, "dogging realm," is because he is, in fact, suffering from withdrawal symptoms from Lidocaine. On an average day, Kapoor will numb whole parts of his body before he goes on patrol. In turn, if some jackass takes a swing at him, he won't feel a thing. Lidocaine is highly addictive, however. In fact, Doctor Norvin Tubaniña noted the dangerous side effects of Derpoloxin consumption in combination with the most common medicinal drugs in his *Medicamenta Principis* (2073-78, pp. 989-1078). Moreover, Kapoor is not alone in this. Most of the Florin Police Department is addicted to at least one drug—Apart from D.E.R.P., that is. For example, Egelblöm has chosen *Morphine* to be her bedside partner: the principal alkaloid in opium and the prototype opiate analgesic and narcotic with pervading effects on the central nervous system and smooth muscle. It was approved one hundred and eighty years ago for the treatment of chronic pain. Egelblöm uses it to treat her *spinal stenosis*: an abnormal narrowing of the spinal canal or neural foramen, triggering pressure on the spinal cord and nerve. Doctor Patrik Brücke F.M.E. uses *Butorphanol* on a daily basis: a synthetic morphinan analgesic designed, much like Derpoloxin, to block pain impulses at specific sites in the brain and spinal cord. Constable Karam Ghazali, even, orally administers *Levomethadyl Acetate* to herself every other day: a far more toxic and/or lethal alternative to Morphine, which is used almost entirely for narcotic dependence and extreme, like, really extreme, pain in terminal patients. Doctor Fenway Ilyich F.M.E., on the other hand, is but a mere cannabis user, besmirching the Florin Police Department with the occasional heavy-duty but, may I add, institutionally instigated smoking of D.E.R.P. But now, as Fenway stands over the recovering Mullein, he does regret it a little. "Wake up you lunatic," he says.

Zach jerks awake, splitting his eyes open. "Fenway?"

And boy, does Fenway look like shit. Red eyes. Elasmobranch skin. That said, he smiles, saying, "You're fucking lucky."

Zach emits a few gurgles from his throat and asks, "Why

am I lucky?"

"Why did you jump in a tree?" Fenway counters.

Zach's body aches as he whispers back, "I thought I was still dogging."

"So," Ilyich attempts to clarify, "a tree presented itself and you thought that jumping in it would clear things up?"

Zach raises his eyebrows as though it was the sanest thing he ever did. "I had to be sure," he says.

The F.M.E. sniggers, replying, "You weren't."

"I can see that."

"Don't do that again," Fenway advises, "that was silly." He pulls the blanket up to Zach's neck.

The ex-dogger then tries to sit up and feels every vertebra sliding by its neighbour. "Oowwww…"

Fenway frowns, highlighting, "You see my point?"

Zach asks if he's hurt.

"Somehow," Fenway replies, "you managed to get away with minor concussion, uh," pulling a pill case out of his pocket, "they wanted to give you some – what was it…" reading the label, "*Betaprodine* – but I, uh, chucked them down the drain." He looks back at Zach and nods. "Enjoy the headache while it lasts," he says.

Zach forms a grin, which quickly turns into an expression of the pain he's in. "How long was I out?"

"A day," Fenway answers, throwing the pill case in the bin.

"She was—"

"What?"

"She was there," Zach says, "wasn't she?"

"Who? Egelblöm?"

"No," the ex-dogger mumbles, "Yolanda."

Fenway scratches his chin and looks at the floor. "She, uh," he says, rather morosely, "she didn't pull through…"

◊

Sotto voce in the raid tank depository: today, it serves as a debriefing room. There are rows and columns of plastic chairs, six by six, and all the ex-doggers start filing in. New faces. Old faces. All dressed in blue jumpsuits. The 'clomps' of boots on concrete charges the space. Gurgling stomachs ill from Derpoloxin fart the room to death as chairs are scraped across the floor. At the front of the room, damning files are passed between the board of governors and Police Commissioner Eric J. McKinley. His eyes lick page after page of data, stats, estimations and outputs of desirability with a secretarial intensity. His audience, the ex-doggers, become an orchestra of incidental coughing as officers from the Blukleim Police Station line the perimeter. They guard today's event with a type of teetotal zeal, watching the ex-doggers smoking cigarettes, their fingers shaking as ash falls on concrete like snow. Others lean back and fold their arms. Others, still, observe the commissioner with an unconfident discontent. Mullein and Ilyich, simultaneously, are sat in the back row. Zach sucks his teeth every now and then and Fenway drums in his lap. They recognize a few people, but on the whole, the room is one that is full of angry unfamiliars: known agents are the worst agents. This is why spy novels are bullshit. Governor Kaat Moptin stands and *claps* her hands three times, settling the room. "The Commissioner," she begins, "has come all the way from Utton to speak with you men and women today." An ex-dogger on the second row shouts, "Shit!" after which a Blukleim officer cracks her in the head with the butt of his pistol. In the deafening silence, she holds her bleeding forehead. The Commissioner stands up, sliding his hands into his pockets. He moves to the front of the improvised auditorium. "Now," he starts, checking his watch, "let's talk about something important. Let's talk about you. You men and women will be suffering from withdrawal for the next few weeks but, thankfully, because of the D.E.R.P.'s chemical and biological makeup, your withdrawal will be more psychological than physical. What do I mean by that? Well, that is to say your habit is your community and your community is your habit. For these reasons, you must disconnect from one another if you wish to kick it.

"Now I know some of you will be asking why it is that we're not helping, to which I reply that this is a public police station funded by the taxpayer. We did not, nor do we advocate drug use among our officers. To me; to the board of governors; to the officers from Blukleim here today, this here right now constitutes a criminal investigation. Suffice to say then that our purposes for being here are to find out how the D.E.R.P. came into your hands. But it is not our job to get it out of your hands. You must do this yourselves. This will be difficult. But I see it this way.

"Let's suppose a man catches the bus every day and that he dresses in a flamboyant fashion. When he gets on the bus, as he does every day, everyone looks at him. But one day the dynamics change. That same man, dressed as he usually does, steps onto the bus. But this time, nobody looks at him. Everyone is, instead, looking at their phone.

"And so, from now on, this happens every day. Man gets on bus. Nobody looks at him. Let's assess this situation, then. What happens now? Well, if the only reason the man dresses that way is because he craves attention, his dress will change and he will, hopefully, re-assimilate into society. That is to say, his little social experiment has failed and therefore, things return to normal. If, on the other hand, he dresses flamboyantly because he actually thinks he looks good, or because it's comfy, or it's a matter of taste, he'll keep wearing what he wears regardless of what anyone thinks of him.

"Let's say that you men and women here today are in the former category. You've been told—I know you've been told—to perform in a particular way. But if people ignore you, or if you allow people to ignore you and each other then you will find yourself on the road to recovery and, shall we say, successive success in whatever trade you take up. Whether it's carpentry, accountancy or begging. You'll be good at whatever you do because you'll be yourself.

"Now, I'm sure some of you are thinking I'm doing the opposite. I'm ordering you to be yourself. To go with any societal flow you find yourself struggling against, day after day. I'm also sure that some of you, in light of your recent experiences, would like very much to raise hell. To those people I say this: people like Harmon Chikenyyt raise hell. People like your former Detective Chief Superintendent raise hell. And look now where it's gotten you. And hell isn't other people. What matters here is that hell *affects* other people. So, you may ask, what's to gain in being the person who raises it? The answer is *nothing*. So be yourself in the same way that others try to be themselves every day with varying results, *just* away from one another.

"Go home now to your partners if you have one, do some gardening – just whatever you decide to do, stay out of it," he finishes, looking directly at Mullein in the back row. The commissioner turns to Moptin, saying, "Miss Moptin?" The governor does a smug smile and takes over. Commissioner McKinley sits down, adjusting his watch as though he's jerking off The Invisible Man.

"The commissioner," Moptin says, "raised some good points there—"

McKinley flinches and says, "What do you mean, *some?*"

Moptin lifts her tablet and scrolls to an appropriate point. "Uh," she continues, the, *ahem*, commissioner has raised *a lot* of good points. So for that, I thank him," staring into the audience, "I think there will be people who will not understand the experiences you men and women have endured. But that is not their fault. With regards to your early retirement from the force," now staring at her tablet, "you will receive a retirement package of three year's salary," scrolling through, "in addition, you will receive the same pension as those officers who retire at the standard age…"

◊

Later, ex-dogger Zachary Mullein sits in a toilet cubicle with his rucksack. He masturbates for two minutes. He comes. Then, he wipes the batwing between his thumb and his index finger. All the evidence is flushed. Outside of the stall, now, he stands in front of an oxblood-coloured sink and washes his hands, making sure to use sufficient soap. Doing the same, a few sinks down, is the ex-dogger Garthman Lewbâdak, who is the type of guy who takes advantage of the erotic tension in restrooms. As he's scrubbing his pink lace-coloured nails, he looks up at Zach, and says, "Are you all right?"

Mullein glares at the mole on Lewbâdak's upper lip, which moves when he says, "That early retirement sure is some bullshit."

Zach splashes water on his face. He hangs his head over the sink to let it drip and says, "Oh yea?"

"You watch," Garthman says, "they'll get us in traffic division putting out traffic cones. They can kiss my ass, man."

"A lot of us are saying we're up for it," Zach replies.

"Then we're full of shit," Garthman says.

Mullein laughs to himself, saying, "Agreed."

Lewbâdak scoffs and puffs away as he continues to clean his nails. Then he says, "I don't remember your face."

"Different dreams," Zach says, indifferently, "different faces."

"Told us we'd reel in the big one," Lewbâdak complains as he washes his face, "matter of national pride – fucked us good, didn't they?"

Mullein picks his nose and washes his hands, saying, "It would appear so…"

The two men continue their washing and rinsing for longer than necessary. Garthman dries his hands on his jumpsuit. "Hey," he says, scanning the cubicles for eavesdropping feet, "me and some guys are gonna numb up and do some boxing. You're more than welcome."

Mullein dries the moisture off his face with a tissue. It shreds in his fingers and he throws it in the bin. After this, he looks at Lewbâdak with a sort of half-formed grin and says, "Nah, it's cool. Thanks though."

"You sure?" Garthman checks, "cuz we're gonna have to make these winter nights fly by. Might as well do it together."

"I'll find something," Mullein replies, nodding, "maybe another time."

"Hey whatever," Lewbâdak says, "it's your neck…"

Zach slings his rucksack over his shoulder, replying, "Yea, ain't that the truth – take it easy mate…"

He leaves Garthman stood over the sink, staring at himself in the mirror.

Mullein steps out of the restroom. His boots cheep across the corridor's polymer flooring as he walks up to a Blukleim officer called Constable Olaf Wiśniewski. "Excuse me?" Mullein says.

"Yea?" Wiśniewski replies, suspiciously, as though he's working in an insane asylum as opposed to a police station.

"Yea, hi," Mullein opens, "there's an ex-dogger in the toilets talking a whole lot of garbage about you Blukleim guys."

"Oh, lovely," Wiśniewski taunts.

"Not just garbage," Zach explains, "like, proper mean stuff, I mean—"

"Take your time—"

"I mean, thanks, uh," the ex-dogger collecting himself, "I think he wants to kill you. Like, all of you. He means it. So I'm thinking about your safety, obviously, but also the city's – I mean, this could be a total revolt."

Wiśniewski looks at him with a concerned expression on his face. "Jesus," he says, "thanks, mate."

"No problem," Zach assures, after which Wiśniewski leans around Mullein and shouts, "Hey Rainer!"

Constable Rainer Conti, another Blukleim officer, marches down the hallway, joining his colleague and the ex-dogger.

Conti, a distant cousin of Doctor Brücke, looks up and down Mullein's body, saying, "This darkie giving you trouble? …Just joking mate, what's up?"

Mullein is thoroughly confused by the overt and ironic-but-not-really racism. Wiśniewski, in turn, clears his throat, explaining, "This guy says there's an ex-dogger in the toilet. Means to commit G.B.H."

"What?" Conti's face doesn't move, "like he's gonna commit G.B.H.? Or he's got the means to commit G.B.H.? Does he have a gun?" then turning to Mullein with a mean look in his eyes, "are you lying to us?"

"I'm not lying," Mullein assures, "when I was in there he

was properly having a go at the Blukleim officers – you, especially."

Conti's face moves, finally. *"Me?"*

"He called you a dago," Zach says, "he said he was sick of seeing officers with greasy hair."

Conti flares up like a sunspot, remarking, "Little prick," turning to Wiśniewski and adding, "well?"

"You sure you want to engage?" his colleague asks.

"Yea," Conti says, "I don't want another T.P.A.C."

"Me neither," Wiśniewski says. Conti and his colleague share a moment of silence.

"All right," Conti says, clicking his heels, "let's do this—" They march towards the restrooms and Conti turns, briefly, to say, "Thanks for the tip, kid."

"I'm thirty-two," Zach says.

"Yea whatever," Conti mutters as he and Wiśniewski disappear into the toilets.

They find Garthman Lewbâdak stood over the sink. The ex-dogger looks at them with a mixture of confusion and a total comprehension of imminent pain.

Conti extracts his baton, saying, "Call me a dago you fucking—" He cracks his baton on Lewbâdak's skull. It starts to open and Conti *strikes* again, shouting, "Fuckin junkie!"

They slam his head against the oxblood-coloured sink and down he goes. "You want to suck my dick?" Wiśniewski asks, cracking his baton on Lewbâdak's back.

"No," Conti says, "he's too good for that," after which he unzips his trousers.

"Bullshit," Wiśniewski says. They kick Lewbâdak over and pull his trousers down. Conti strokes his penis and shoves himself deep and raw in the ex-dogger. "You want that good dick?"

Wiśniewski kicks Garthman in the head, saying, "We don't

want him waking up, now, do we?" Conti thrusts again and again, short of breath.

"*Oohhhh…*" he lets out.

Wiśniewski asks if he's okay.

"Oh yea," his colleague explains, "I'm gonna come," he pulls out and dangles his penis over Lewbâdak's face, "*Aaaahh-hhhhh,*" he moans, ejaculating, "*Uggghhhh…*"

Wiśniewski laughs, scratches his groin and smells his armpit.

Endings

Zachary Mullein plods down a gravel road with his rucksack. The afternooning sunshine is making him sleepy. Clouds are slowing; smells are climbing up his nostrils. The moss is cold, and the leaves are rotting on rocks. Pheasant droppings fill the streams. In the distance the sheep are fornicating. Closer the beetles are fornicating. Everything smells and now the fog is rolling in. Mullein puts his hands in his pockets where cuticles are picked. Traffic, in the distance, is whispering—everything is a thousand miles away. Zach drops to his knees and dissolves into tears.

◊

Additionally, the Reactionary advisor Faisal Reddy (2056-2094) became Joram Falack's bodyguard when the ex-Party Chairman retired to Locher. Falack was assassinated in 2093. The following year, Faisal went to Brussels on business. Being as good a bodyguard as he was a husband, he received a phone call from his third estranged wife in Florin—she told him he needed to catch a plane and fly over immediately. Arriving, subsequently, in Florin, he walked out of the airport and his wife shot and killed him.

Antarctica

It is Thursday, 15th September 2089. It is a brittle day and the time is 10:02 a.m. A Mi-26 helicopter, capable of holding eighty-two fully armed soldiers and twenty tons of cargo, lands at the *Amundsen-Scott South Pole Station*: an American research facility located on the high plateau of Antarctica, 9,301 feet above sea level. In front of the station five women, members of the research team dressed in Tea-rose pink parkas, are waiting for their visitor to leave the chopper. The blades slow and the engine cools. The back doors below the tail boom open like a missile silo and a ramp lowers—Eighteen men dressed in Persian-rose-coloured parkas, neck gaiters and safety-orange goggles march toward the station's entrance. The leader of this atrociously coloured brigade, striding out of the chopper, stops in front of the scientists, saying nothing. "Mister Apple-Tennyson," one of the scientists says, eventually, "we're glad you arrived in one piece."

Apple-Tennyson, removing his goggles and dangling them beneath his finely coifed moustache, explains, "I'm not from Flonflynn, you know."

There is a pause. The scientist nods an affirmative, replying, "I know who you are."

The I.T.C.B. regulator squints his eyes, looking up at the honeycombed research dome. Then he shrugs, adding, "I didn't come all the way here to soak up this climate change." With that, Apple-Tennyson's men invade the Amundsen-Scott geodesic dome.

Inside, sitting in the middle of the vast space, is a kind of Yuletide village with trailers and cardboard boxes full of non-perishables, like Professor Mikhailov's Rasberry Zefirs and Doctor Jack's Peppermint Fánks. There is no sunlight. They light the dome themselves. Apple-Tennyson's chaperones cloak the area and two guard the five scientists next to the only rubbish bin in Antarctica. Its contents consist of a Karl Marx album: *Pandiculation* (Harari Records™, 2047) and a used condom. The shorter of the two guards focuses on the condom and shakes his head in disgust as though it represents the end of western civilization. Apple-Tennyson, meanwhile, ruffles his parka. He stares at the canteen trailer, quite aware that it is now 10:23 a.m. No one should be eating anything. But Carlos knows, for sure, that one person is.

After a knock, the flimsy M.D.F. door swings open and Doctor Norvin "Wristy" Tubaniña appears with four Dabby Doughs in his right hand and a black coffee in his left. Additionally he is chewing an apple pie slice, the pastry jutting out of the corners of his mouth, when he looks up at Carlos Apple-Tennyson and freezes.

The fan of meta-elegiac economic philosophy examines the good doctor, pulling off his gloves and almost sings, "Hiya Norvin!" The sound of the wind outside colliding with the dome fills the Yuletide village. Apple-Tennyson steps forward, smiling. "What," he scoffs, "you didn't think I'd come?" Doctor Tubaniña drops his coffee and a seal-brown stain swells through the white ground. His boss relaxes his shoulders and flattens his facial expression. "Where is she?" he asks.

Doctor Tubaniña unfreezes his jaw and says, in Spanish, "¿Puedo terminar mi desayuno?"

"Where is she?" Apple-Tennyson interrupts, crunching forward.

The door to Norvin's trailer squeaks open. Inside, there is

a fully furnished genetic laboratory with beakers, retorts, glass rods, funnels, Bunsen burners, tripods, gauze mats and flasks, clamp stands holding burettes full of God-knows-what, pipettes and droppers, petri dishes, crucibles, evaporating dishes and a series of compound light microscopes – one of which helps to embellish the D.E.R.P. corner in Doctor Tubaniña's laboratory.

Carlos, eyeballing the cannabis, says, "That Florin police station's been quarantined. We're pulling the plug on your little experiment."

"The second-hand smoke," the pharmacologist replies, "it's too late—"

"Occupational hazard," Carlos says whilst turning to Norvin. "I pay you to look after her."

"But she is everywhere now!"

"The bacteria found in the body," Apple-Tennyson interrupts, "enters a state of dormancy when faced with extreme conditions. When her environment resumes stability, probably in the far reaches of space, the bacteria reanimates. She looks after herself; that's what you said!"

"Señor Apple-Tennyson," Norvin says, "it is only with analogies and metaphors that I'm able to explain the bacteria's functions."

"Is that so?" Apple-Tennyson replies cautiously, the humming of the lab's generators filling the background.

"…"

"Go on," Carlos says, "show me what I came here for."

Norvin, sporting a bemused and slighty frightened expression on his face, walks over to a quick-silver-coloured wall. On the wall is a palm-sized shape on it:

Slapping his hands upon the shape, it flashes, having activated a lock mechanism. Panels begin to squeal across the floor as the entire wall rotates, revealing a large aquarium-glass tube. Much like the dome itself, it is unwelcoming and frosted with metallic rims. Invariably, gaseous squirts of Benzotriazole, Alkylphenol and the pH buffer Triethanolamine de-ice the vessel, breaking up the silence within the laboratory. Inside the tube, a female form begins to take shape. The body is roughly five-foot-three tall with Van-Dyke-coloured skin. She is well built with black hair and explicit lips and collarbones. The hips and legs and feet and everything else represent, as far as Apple-Tennyson is concerned, the perfect woman. Her eyes are shut, and the faint life-supporting thrum fills the foreground of her chilly corner of the laboratory. Doctor Tubaniña backs away as Apple-Tennyson walks in front of the tube, hanging his head over the glass.

The glowing inside irradiates his eyelashes that twinkle when he blinks. *"My lovely Martha,"* he murmurs to himself.

Doctor Tubaniña seals the wall behind him. And the final squeak of the wall against the floor alerts Apple-Tennyson to the fact that now he, a pharmacologist and an alien body brimming with bacteria are trapped in a room with no other exits. He turns, slowly, to face his employee. Norvin is holding a loaded pistol, and says, "I'm sorry."

"…Now, Norvin," Carlos says, "I'm assuming from the gun that you want my men to bury you alive when we get out of here."

"My team have dealt with your men," Norvin explains, calmly, "their instructions are to evacuate the dome and to make their way to our sister-station twenty miles north of here."

"Then why aren't you going with them?" Apple-Tennyson replies slyly.

"Because someone has to detonate the explosives," Doctor Tubaniña says.

"Th-The explosives?"

"Or did you think buildings leveled themselves?" There is a moment of silence shared by the two men. *Martha is listening,* Norvin thinks; he asks, "Do you know why I left Boundaries™?"

Carlos Apple-Tennyson looks at Norvin in the same way that Martha is looking at them.

"I was tired of killing good people," Doctor Tubaniña's left hand flicks two switches on an operating board adjacent to Martha's tube, "and so now, after all this time, I get to kill *you*," a small triangular panel flips open, presenting an ignition and key. Norvin's fingers grip the key delicately. "Goodbye, Mister Apple-Tennyson."

"Are you gonna shoot me?"

Norvin, sarcastically, says, "No…" after which he twists the key. An electronic voice announces, "Pod door open. Quarantine now in effect. Quarantine now in effect," as Apple-Tennyson's eyes bulge underneath a sea of nervous sweat. The combined clouds of Benzotriazole, Alkylphenol and Triethanolamine flood out of the tube as Martha's bacteria-ridden body is exposed to the laboratory's air. Her Van-Dyke-coloured skin decomposes at an accelerated rate as both Norvin and Carlos grip their respective collars, gasping for air. Just as Norvin removes the detonator from his left pocket, however, his entire neck collapses in upon itself and he falls onto the waterproof vinyl flooring in a marsh of his own excrement. The now-zombified Martha steps out of her tube in front of the suffocating Carlos Apple-Tennyson. She picks up the detonator with all the serenity of a dental hygienist, and then turns to Carlos. As his neck, too, collapses upon itself, Martha lifts her right index finger to her mouth, and whispers, *"…Ssshhh…"* as she applies pressure to the detonator's sole button. Martha, for a brief moment, cannot remember anything as the entire dome erupts into flames, lighting up the already illuminated sky over Antarctica.

Morecambe, 2018

Author Bio

Walker Zupp is a Bermudian writer who specializes in Speculative Fiction. He was educated in Bermuda and in the UK. Martha is his debut novel.

Printed in Great Britain
by Amazon